Praise for Philippe Boulle's Victorian Age Trilogy:

"There is a palpable sense of dread and anticipation throughout… Definitely a book to devour…."
—Chris Madsen, *Culture Dose*

"Lush, sensual, and ultimately terrifying…. A spooky Gothic treat for a cold winter's night."
—J. L. Comeau, *Creature Feature*

"A good vampire story is as good as it gets [and] Philippe Boulle has a good one here—extremely compelling."
—Jim Brock, *Baryon Magazine*

"Boulle [does] an exquisite job of writing a period story without falling into the clichés and stereotypes that so often occur in vampire fiction…. I heartedly recommend this book."
—Ralph Dula, *RPG.net*

"A rare gem…"
—John Margaritsanakis, *RPG.net*

"Anyone who likes their vampires 'classic' will probably get a kick out of this series."
—Michael M. Jones, *Green Man Review*

Vampire: The Masquerade Fiction from White Wolf
The Clan Novel Saga

A comprehensive, chronological collection of the fourteen-volume best-selling Clan Novel Series. Includes all-new material.

Volume 1: The Fall of Atlanta — foreword by Stewart Wieck; new material by Philippe Boulle

Volume 2: The Eye of Gehenna — foreword by Eric Griffin; new material by Stefan Petrucha

Volume 3: Bloody September — foreword by Anna Branscome; new material by Lucien Soulban (forthcoming)

Volume 4: End Game — foreword by Gherbod Fleming; new material by Janet Trautvetter (forthcoming)

The Clan Tremere Trilogy

Widow's Walk by Eric Griffin
Widow's Weeds by Eric Griffin
Widow's Might by Eric Griffin

The Clan Lasombra Trilogy

Shards by Bruce Baugh
Shadows by Bruce Baugh
Sacrifices by Bruce Baugh

The Clan Brujah Trilogy

Slave Ring by Tim Dedopulos
The Overseer by Tim Dedopulos
The Puppet-Masters by Time Dedopulos (forthcoming)

The Dark Ages Clan Novel Series

Dark Ages: Nosferatu by Gherbod Fleming
Dark Ages: Assamite by Stefan Petrucha
Dark Ages: Cappadocian by Andrew Bates
Dark Ages: Setite by Kathleen Ryan
Dark Ages: Lasombra by David Niall Wilson
Dark Ages: Ravnos by Sarah Roark
Dark Ages: Malkavian by Ellen Porter Kiley
Dark Ages: Brujah by Myranda Kalis (forthcoming)
Dark Ages: Toreador by Janet Trautvetter (forthcoming)

Also by Philippe Boulle

A Morbid Initiation (Victorian Age Trilogy, Part 1)
The Madness of Priests (Victorian Age Trilogy, Part 2)
"Red Talons" in **Tribe Novel: Red Talons & Fianna**
Demon: Lucifer's Shadow (editor)
Orpheus: Haunting the Dead (editor)
For all these titles and more, visit **www.white-wolf.com/fiction**

The Wounded King ™

Philippe Boulle

Third Volume in the Victorian Age Trilogy

1554 Litton Dr
Stone Mountain, GA
30083
USA

Cover art by Christopher Shy. Book design by Chris McDonough and Mike Chaney. Jacket design by Chris McDonough. Art direction by Richard Thomas. Copyedited by Diane Piron-Gelman and Jonathan Laden.

The text quoted in Chapter Eleven from the *East London Advertiser* of October 6, 1888, was drawn from Ryder, Stephen P. (Ed.). "Casebook: Jack the Ripper - East London Advertiser - 6 October 1888." Casebook: Jack the Ripper. Accessed: 25 July 2003. <http://www.casebook.org>

ISBN 1-58846-858-5
First Edition: October 2003
Printed in Canada

White Wolf Publishing
1554 Litton Drive
Stone Mountain, GA 30083
www.white-wolf.com/fiction

Authority forgets a dying king,
Laid widow'd of the power in his eye
That bow'd the will.
—Alfred Lord Tennyson, Morte d'Arthur

What Has Come Before

After the suspicious death of her mother, Regina Blake is unable to abide by her father's unwillingness to question his wife's demise. With the help of the seductive Victoria Ash—who claims to have been a friend of her mother's—Regina begins to peel back the secrets of Lady Emma Blake's birth family, the Ducheski brood. Suspecting that Lady Blake's death has been faked and following faint leads in London, Regina lifts the veil on a nocturnal secret society of lords and ladies. Before the end of the social season, Regina has discovered the awful truth: this is a society of the undead and her mother, and Victoria, are among their number.

When Lady Blake and the vampire who remade her—a blood-sorcerer named Anton Wellig—flee to the Continent, Regina cannot let her go and returns to the company of Victoria Ash, who has become her protector and lover among the undead. Together, they follow Lady Blake's trail to Paris, but are waylaid by old obligations dating from the time Victoria was a newly made vampire in the City of Lights. There, they suffer the twisted instruction of Father Anatole, a mad vampire who preaches a perverse religion.

Meanwhile, Regina's father Lord Blake and her fiancé Malcolm Seward pursue leads of their own, intent on finding the wayward girl. They discover fragments of the truth and fall in with the ragtag Society of Leopold, a secret organization of latter-day witch-hunters. Seward travels to Paris where he and the witch-hunters help free Regina and Victoria from Father Anatole's clutches. In a bitter reunion, Regina reveals to Malcolm that he too has come under the sway of the undead, under the guise of the Taurine Brotherhood—a soldier's order that has taken him under its blood-stained wing.

Leaving Malcolm behind, Regina and Victoria finally learn that Wellig and Lady Blake were traveling to Vienna. (Little do they know that Lord Blake has followed his own leads there.) Aboard the Orient Express, Victoria confronts Regina with the reality that, knowing the truth of the undead, she must either be enslaved or be remade as one of their number. Owing her escape from Paris to Regina, Victoria cannot abide by enslaving her protégée and so curses her to undeath….

Prologue:
Parsa, Achaemenid Persia,
Fourth Century B.C.

*In which two fallen gods find comfort in
one another, for a time.*

Kemintiri Set's Daughter came to Parsa with the last tributary processions in the seventeenth year of the reign of the Emperor Artaxerxes III. The spring capital sat in the Zargos Mountains, north from the great road that ran all the way from Sagartian Bampur to Babylon, along the Euphrates into Syria and then south along the coast to the Nile Delta. From all those provinces and many others, the tributes came: Arian and Arachosian leathers, Sogdian horses and swords, Indian gold, Syrian urns and chariots, Ethiopian ivories, Armenian and Arabian textiles. From everywhere came taxes paid in silver talents, along with the finest slaves and the correspondence of satraps and less haughty officials, all expressing worship for the emperor.

Two years before, Artaxerxes' forces had sailed down the three mouths of the Nile, destroyed the walls of Pharaoh Nectanebo II's cities and made of Lower Egypt an especially wealthy Persian satrapy. The emperor himself had slaughtered the Apis bull in Memphis, destroying Egypt's religious power along with its independence.

Kemintiri came to Parsa neither to protest the conquest nor as part of the new province's tribute. The aging Artaxerxes was not who she had come for. Traveling in a carriage of some splendor, with a full complement of slaves and soldiers of her own, she had come to this mountain city to see a god. For Parsa was not only the spring capital of the largest empire ever to grace the face of the earth, but also the home of that favored creation of Ahura Mazda, the god of warriors and oaths.

Under the great palace was the lair of Mithras.

It was nearing midnight when she made her way up the eastern stairs of the palace toward the vast apadana, the columned audience hall built for Darius the Great two centuries earlier. Torches and braziers bathed the whole palace complex with a yellow and red flickering of light. Two guards—the reportedly immortal soldiers of the empire whom the Greeks called *Athanatoi*—stood at the top of the stairs and she had little doubt they were strengthened with the blood of the god.

When she reached the top step, the two soldiers crossed their long spears with a loud rap, blocking her way. Neither man said a word.

"Let me pass," she said, her voice soft as a gentle desert breeze. The spears parted and she walked on.

Three dozen columns, each the height of ten men, held aloft a soaring timber roof framed by yet more colonnades. The stone floor resounded with the slap of her sandals as she walked between the stone pillars. She headed for the south of the audience hall, toward the imperial quarters. She stopped when she sensed a heavy but diffuse presence, like an oncoming storm.

"Those guards will commit suicide for their failing, once they realize it." The voice was calm and cool, allowing room for neither doubt nor fear. It was the voice of a god.

"Suicide seems a paltry thing for deathless soldiers," she said. "Like the ocean surrendering a wave, or the desert, sand."

"Only the corps itself is deathless. Each soldier can still perish, and be replaced by another."

"I see." She searched the night for the perfect form that must accompany these words, but the shadows of the apadana hid him even from her gold-hued eyes. "A somewhat paltry immortality compared to that you could offer them."

A slight laugh, like fine gravel escaping a hidden chute, reached her ears. From the south, she thought. She proceeded through the leftmost of the two doors in that direction and found a tight series of passages. Another *Athanatos* stood at one juncture, his spear slanted southward to suggest she should proceed in that direction. Would he too die for his god? She supposed they all would, eventually.

The passage opened onto a smaller courtyard, providing a view of the southern part of the sprawling palace city. To her right stood the winter palace built to house the same Darius in whose honor the columned hall she'd just left had risen. Ahead, however, was the more impressive—and more recent—structure of Xerxes, a successor of Darius's to the throne of Persia. The woman smiled to see the influence of Egypt in the designs. One did not conquer the Nile lest one be conquered by it.

She crossed the courtyard and entered the first great hall, heading for the reception hall that must wait further in. Piles of tribute, arrived throughout the spring, were already stacked along the walls, silent representatives of the tendrils of empire. She paid it no heed.

"The riches of Persia do not interest you," the voice said. Still she could not quite find its source.

"Reminders of the obvious do not warrant attention." She entered the receiving chamber beyond the great hall's southern wall.

A silhouetted form sat atop the towering throne. "And what does, stranger?"

"The presence of an equal," she said.

***

Mithras Bull of Persia and Kemintiri Set's Daughter kept a compact for seventeen summers. An eyeblink to a creature who had walked the earth for centuries, this time was nevertheless holy to the god of soldiers and victory, for only Kemintiri understood him. Just as he had once been a mortal man, so had she once been a mortal woman, until they had been remade into gods who walked the earth but feared the sun.

Through long winter nights, Mithras regaled Kemintiri with stories of those long-ago times when he had walked under the flaming disc now worshiped in his name. "I was a general," he told her, "fighting a war against a savage enemy backed by sorcerers and the gods themselves, or so it seemed. For every league we advanced, I lost a hundred men, but for every man I lost, the enemy lost two. Finally, we reached their stronghold. Their witches brought fire from the heavens, but we did not falter. We lined the pass with pikes mounted with our enemies' heads.

"Their chieftain eluded us, however," he continued. "We made camp to pillage their goods and use their women, and waited. I knew he would return to face me. When he did, he did not come with wrath but with garlands. 'I am Vedartha,' he said, 'and you have survived where none other have. For this I give you eternity.' And he remade me into a god."

Kemintiri told a story much the same, about having been once a priestess, then chosen to enter the being of her own god. She had set forth to claim her own domain and after long wanderings come to Mithras' side. No King of Victory should be without a queen, she said, and he agreed.

A child was born in Parsa the very night of Kemintiri's arrival there. Both gods took this to be propitious and made of the boy a project, naming him Noushad, meaning the happily born. Neither had yet remade others as their sires had remade them, and they saw in Noushad the perfect candidate. He would grow to manhood in the palace city, under the watchful eyes of his immortal parents and be remade into the next member of their pantheon. All Persia would one day bow for Noushad, son of Mithras.

Raised in the cult of his erstwhile father, Noushad rose in the ranks starting in his eleventh year. He wore the mask of a raven, then the gown of a bridegroom, as was traditional for the worshipers of Mithras. By his fifteenth year, he had become first a soldier and then a lion in the cult, showing the feline mask to his inhuman parents with pride. Mithras and Kemintiri watched him, well satisfied. They would soon raise the boy to eternal divinity.

In that year, however, he was also first visited by a beauty named Daeva. Pale-skinned and nimble, Daeva bore the name of terrible demons but spoke of the redemption of the soul. She said she kept her name as a reminder of the debased witch she had once been, before she learned to follow the higher word of the prophet Zoroaster, also called Zarathustra. Noushad of course knew of the prophet and his teachings, for the kings and emperors of mighty Persia claimed to follow those same teachings, and so he accepted this newcomer's friendship.

Over the following years, the boy—now a man—made of Daeva his lover and the girl stood at his side as he became the most influential man in Parsa. She was a faithful companion, pleasing her man at night and leaving him to manly affairs by day. But Noushad knew a sadness lay upon her. "What is the matter, darling?" he asked again and again, but for many months she did not answer.

Finally, as they lay in bed late one evening, Noushad asked again and Daeva finally answered. "It is your father," she said. "I cannot trust him."

The prince was shocked. "How can you say that? He is Mithras, favored creation of Ahura Mazda, the King of Oaths, the Great General, the Lord of the Sun. Mithras is all."

"My eyes tell me so, but my heart does not," she answered. "When I am at prayer, I see other things."

"What do you see, my love?" Noushad asked.

"The prophet teaches of the great conflict between good and evil, my love, between Ahura Mazda and Ahriman. Gods and deities are but reflections and instances of this great battle between the Creator and Adversary."

"But Mithras is the general of Ahura Mazda," Noushad exclaimed. "He leads the struggle of good against evil!"

"I wish I could believe that," she answered, "but I fear your father stands on the other side of the battlefield." The prince tried to object, but she continued. "The prophet teaches us to avoid the presence of dead flesh, but your father's skin is as cold as the grave. He teaches us to avoid the fast unless to purify ourselves, but your father—who should be the purest of all—avoids all food and drink. Mithras is the King of the Sun but you only see your father at night."

Noushad spouted the explanations he had long ago learned. His father only appeared at night, for in the day he traveled from east to west across the sky. His flesh was cold for he rested from shining during the day. He would feed from the bounty of sky and the offerings of his followers' sacrificial blood, but from nothing else. Yet spoken to the troubled face of the woman he found he loved, Noushad's words sounded hollow even to his own ears.

In the end, they prayed together that night and for several nights to come. When he was ready, the prince approached the emperor of all Persia.

Thus it was one night not long after that when Mithras

rose from his holy of holies to find flames licking the sky, while soldiers and priests crowded the court yard. The emperor, the weak-willed Arses, was there and he called on the "false god" to flee. Mithras allowed himself to laugh and prepared to lay this presumptuous potentate low, when he spotted his son nearby. Noushad was dressed simply, having shed all the ritual finery he'd earned over eighteen years.

"Leave now," the once-prince bellowed. "In the name of all that is good and light, I cast you from this place, creature of darkness. Begone false god! False father!"

Mithras had dreamed of an eternity with his son at his side and the shock of that happy hope crumbling was like a hammer-blow. Rage welled in his cold heart, however, at the thought of his empire stolen from him. He could smell the blood of his own priests put to the sword and he made a step forward to have vengeance on those who would reject him.

That step was agony. Noushad pointed and yelled "Begone. In the name of Ahura Mazda and the prophet Zoroaster, begone!"

The force that came with those words was like flames pushed through brush, hot and unyielding. Mithras turned his back on his son forever. Before he left Parsa altogether, however, he was determined to have his vengeance on the woman who had planted the poison seed in his beloved son's ear: Daeva.

He found her standing by the road, as if waiting for him.

"You!" he raged. "I will destroy you!"

He grabbed her by her slender throat and raised her off the ground. He was about to throw her onto the cobblestones of the road when an amazement occurred. Daeva's features shifted and she revealed her true form. Kemintiri smiled at her lover of the last decades.

Mithras fled into the night.

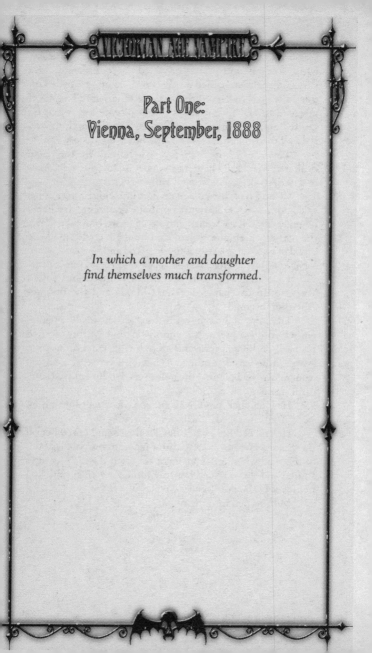

Part One:
Vienna, September, 1888

*In which a mother and daughter
find themselves much transformed.*

Chapter One

The woman's distress rose in a crescendo of rage. Her mouth, once delicate and sophisticated, became a maw of terrible fangs and spat invectives. Those soon gave way to incoherent screams. Her hands tore at her clothing and skin, and swiped at imagined enemies. She darted to and fro like a wild beast and God save the damned soul who got in her way as she circled and cantered in search of prey. She leaped forward, turned suddenly, and scurried back almost the way she had come.

Not three paces from the point at which the madwoman had turned, stood two men who displayed none of the fear or even revulsion others might in such a situation. These gentlemen remained entirely confident in the ability of the thin line of carefully mixed salts to cage this wild-woman. Unlike many dabblers in mysticism and theosophy, they had found their occult arts altogether reliable.

That was all for the good, since both men had surrendered their lives to gain insight into them.

The first man, the taller of the two, went by the name of Ardan Lane. Dressed simply in woolen trousers and a starched white shirt with no collar, his clipped auburn hair and mild face gave him the look of a middle-class man caught in the midst of dressing for the evening. His companion, shorter, rounder and dressed somewhat more formally, was Dr. Edward Bainbridge, visiting from London (as was, in fact, the incoherent woman in the warding circle). An observer who might somehow have gained access to this underground chamber in the vaults below the private Viennese library and college known as Fortschritt—one who might be convinced to ignore the screaming harpy, the occult pattern of salt, and the seven candles (each held in a severed and mummified human left hand)—would have guessed Bainbridge to be the superior of the two. His clothes, his posture, even his language spoke of greater education, standing and refinement.

That theoretical observer would have been wrong.

"I feel I must apologize again for the behavior of my companion's childe, Mr. Lane."

"Do not over-dramatize just yet, Herr Doctor," Lane answered, his English only the slightest bit accented. "It would be a great shame indeed if Fortschritt could not contain one childe temporarily lost to the beastly urges of our blood. This house is the very core of our order, after all."

"You are too kind, sir," Bainbridge said. "I am more accustomed to the rather limited resources we have available in London."

The woman in the binding circle let loose another ululation and frantically turned in tighter and tighter circles. The men watched, seemingly unfazed, and continued their conversation.

"Yes," Lane said, "I imagine that practicing thaumaturgy in your great city has not been easy these last few years. Your Prince Mithras has never been very welcoming to our sort, not even in long-ago nights."

"London itself is fertile soil, actually, if only because of the laudable interests among the breathing for all things arcane and occult. Secret brotherhoods and theosophist circles abound, some of them doing very credible research into arts parallel with our own."

"So I gather, but I think more of the situation among our kindred."

Bainbridge bowed slightly, conceding a point. "The prince and his proximates do not hide their disdain for us, I'll admit. We certainly enjoyed a far better position under Mithras' regent, Lord Valerius. Nevertheless, with a modicum of discretion, we can practice our arts."

"Your companion Herr Wellig seems dissatisfied with that arrangement."

Bainbridge smiled. "Quite. As I'm sure he has been explaining to the worthies at council here, matters would be easier if Prince Mithras were to return to whatever distant land he visited for much of the century."

"Councils and tribunals are conservative beasts, Doctor. No matter how desirable the result, they are unlikely to endorse bold acts that have yet to prove themselves wholly successful."

"Tell me, Herr Wellig, just when were you expecting to inform the Fatherhouse about your experiments?" Claas Drescher, magus pontifex in House Tremere, asked his question with a glee that belied his dour Germanic appearance. He drummed his gloved fingers on the oak council table, his thumbs making oddly dull *thuds* on the wood. Anton Wellig was certain that Drescher was playing to the other two sorcerers sitting in judgment on him more than conducting a serious inquiry.

The council chamber was, Wellig thought, a good fit with the building that housed it. Fortschritt, the head chantry of House Tremere, stood just beyond Vienna's great ring road and overlooked the site where a mad Hungarian had stabbed Emperor Franz-Josef in the neck thirty years ago. It was a grand, baroque structure. There had been talk of building a church on this site, but that had not come to pass. Instead, this brooding structure had risen. Popular wisdom held that it was a private library sponsored by the Hapsburgs, a story that was half-right. The sorcerous scholars of House Tremere had been collecting lore for longer than the Hapsburgs had been a family and the huge library that took up three levels of the Fatherhouse hid works of such a heretical and blasphemous nature that few even among the damned souls cursed to wander the night between life and death dared consult them.

That, Wellig thought, *is the key difference between the Tremere and the rest of the blood-drinkers in the world. Where others fear, the Tremere dare.*

Still, such daring coexisted with a vexing structural rigidity. Those who had spat in the eyes of death herself in the darkest nights of the Middle Ages had little tolerance for their juniors straying. The pyramid was a powerful symbol of power and wisdom, but it was also a heavy burden around the neck of those on its bottom levels. Anton Wellig had been the regent of the Lions Green Chantry in County Durham since the Wars of the Roses and thus had done a goodly job of isolating himself from the bite of his superiors. His last visit to Vienna, some twenty-five years ago, had been distinctly friendlier, he felt.

"Mister Wellig?" The speaker was a blond-haired scarecrow of a man who'd introduced himself as Anastasz, apprentice and assistant to the much more powerful magus Claas Drescher. This little Slovene was no threat, but his master was not a warlock to be trifled with. "Might you answer Master Drescher's question?"

"Yes, of course. I have never made any secret of my work with selective breeding. It was, I believe, those same predilections that led to my initiation into this house."

Not this house, exactly, he commented to himself. In the faraway nights when he had been a living heretic, the order had still looked to the mountains of Hungary as its center. Despite the quaking fears of youngsters like Anastasz, Vienna was a newcomer to the Tremere.

"We'd thank you for not boring us with platitudes, Regent Wellig," said the black-haired beauty who sat to Drescher's left. "There is a difference of some proportion between the cross-breeding of your pets and the results you claim to have accomplished in this childe."

"Quite so," said the sycophantic Anastasz. He seemingly spent his nights blindly agreeing with whichever magus he felt ranked highest.

Unfortunately, at this particular instant he'd chosen appropriately. The beautiful woman with the pointed comment was, after all, a nearly peerless magus. She was also the witchwoman who had founded Lions Green during the reign of King Richard and several centuries later ushered Anton Wellig into the mysteries of the blood.

"I respectfully disagree, Lady Meerlinda," he said, causing a satisfyingly audible gasp in the Slovene child. "I would rather say that little Emiliana is the culmination of my work with the Ducheski line over these last several centuries. I have worked to create a perfect receptacle for the blood and in Emiliana I have done so."

"And how," Drescher asked with further finger-rapping, "does this relate to the current condition of the Prince of London?"

"Surely I don't have to tell you that Mithras bears ill

will toward our order?" Wellig knew both Drescher and Meerlinda had spent time in England. They would know the pains of the prince's biases.

"No," said Lady Meerlinda, "we are familiar with the prevailing situation."

"Then you will also understand why I felt it necessary to act," Wellig said. "Mithras is a creature of very ancient blood and to bring him low required a unique instrument. Emiliana was that instrument."

He paused for dramatic effect and felt Drescher and his sycophants leaning forward in their seats slightly. Meerlinda gave a slight, almost imperceptible nod, and he continued. "Through the use of a concoction of the prince's own blood and the preparation of Emiliana as a vessel, I made her both irresistible and poisonous to that ancient despot."

"You speak as if the obtaining of blood from an ancient such as Mithras were easy," said Drescher. "How did you accomplish such a feat?"

"Through the application of the lessons of our order, sir: perseverance, daring and judicious research. Just because a task is difficult does not put it out of the grasp of a true magus."

Drescher bristled at the rebuke and visibly choked back a response. Once his façade of superior calm was restored, the German sorcerer and magus pontifex of the order continued. "Thus, were Mithras to drain this childe of yours…"

"He would assure his own destruction," Wellig said with some pride. "And the hunger for her blood would be irresistible."

Drescher smiled. "Mithras is destroyed then?"

"He shall be."

"There is a great distance between 'shall be' and 'is,' Herr Wellig. Is your rite so slow to act?"

It was Wellig's turn to rise to the bait. "No! My ritual was perfect. Had Mithras drunk his fill he would be ash right now."

"But he did not drink his fill." Meerlinda's voice was laced with icy disappointment.

Drescher, in contrast, was quite pleased. "What happened to prevent the fulfillment of your rite, Regent Wellig?"

"Interference from one of the locals. Mithras weakens by the night, however. He will soon be dust."

"So you say," said Drescher. "We shall see."

***

The Grand Express d'Orient arrived at Vienna's Westbahnof at 11:17 on the evening of Wednesday, September 19, 1888, two minutes behind schedule. The delay was caused by an unfortunate rainstorm near the Bavarian border that had forced a reduction of speed that afternoon. The conductor, Monsieur Henri Boisfranc, had increased the speed through the night to make up some of the lost time, and was happy to know that they could afford a full ten minute stop at the Westbahnof, then circle the city at a leisurely pace to be prepared for their scheduled departure from the Hapsburg capital's more southerly station, the Staatsbahnhof, at precisely one minute past midnight on the 20th. Mr. Nagelmakers, the Belgian founder of the Grand Express, had built his reputation on an unparalleled combination of luxury and punctuality and Boisfranc felt he was living up to that tradition. He paid little attention to the fact that the storm clouds that evening had been an especially sickly shade of green. Such phenomena were not uncommon in Europe this year, and many believed them to be a result of the cataclysmic eruption of the Krakatoa volcano, which although it occurred five years before and a half-world away, had spewed so much ash into the atmosphere it still tinted the skies.

The Grand Express derived its cachet from being a direct train from Paris to Constantinople (although the final leg from Varna was still by ship for the time being), but many of the passengers did not make the whole journey. Indeed, the luxurious accommodations of Mr. Nagelmakers' famous sleeper cars attracted well-appointed travelers going between points on the line. Thus a goodly number of passengers embarked and disembarked at the major stops, such as Vienna.

One man who remained aboard at Vienna, however, was Jacob Israel Horowitz. Mr. Horowitz had joined the Express in Munich, where he had a successful business as a jeweler and watchmaker. He purchased a ticket as far as

Budapest, where his third cousin Abraham was to marry one Sarah Weinstein at the beginning of next month. Jacob hoped also to convince Abraham, at long last, to go into business with him and open up a shop in Pest.

Horowitz was, like many men in his profession, well-traveled and cosmopolitan. His business was built on trust as well as craftsmanship, and he made it his practice to befriend fellow travelers when abroad. As a seller of jewels, he knew also that a woman's eye was the more refined and that in the majority of cases it was she, and not her husband or lover, who made the ultimate decision as to what was purchased. Jacob noted this fact because he was, as well as a shrewd businessman, a genuine appreciator of women. He had been married once, but his lovely wife Rebecca had died in childbirth and taken their son with her. In his most private heart, he still grieved for them, but in general he had found he quite liked the life of a successful, handsome widower. Blessed with a fine frame and dark, brooding eyes, he had never been at a loss for female companionship.

Thus, when he left his compartment in the second sleeper car soon after sunset on the 19th, intent on heading forward to the dining car for a late-night drink, he was delighted to see the door to the last compartment open to reveal the hint of a female form. Unashamed, he peeked his head around the door to find not one, but two ladies playing cards. They both smiled, and he soon joined them for several hands of speculation, a game popular in England, from which the ladies hailed. Jacob's English was accented but only slightly broken, and he felt his natural charms and willingness to let the ladies win most tricks stood him in good stead. Their quick smiles and light, happy laughs seemed to prove him right. They kept score on a small pad of paper so helpfully provided by the Grand Express.

Although the women shared a certain similitude in fashion and bearing, even before sitting down he'd decided they were not related by blood. The eldest of the two, who was surely no older than Jacob's youngest brother, was named Miss Ash and was a beauty indeed, her hair a fiery red and her eyes the deepest green Jacob had seen away from an actual emerald. She introduced her companion as Lady Regina, her ward. This girl was even more to Jacob's liking: hair and eyes a similarly rich shade of hazel, a slight frame that spoke of womanhood still blossoming, and above all a gaze of the most amazing intensity.

When he learned they were to disembark in Vienna, Jacob resigned himself to enjoying their company for a few hours, but the encounter not graduating to what men of his sort would call an adventure. Perhaps, if he could extricate young Regina from her protector, something more than cards and laughter would be possible, but that seemed unlikely. *Still*, he thought, *the company of two such creatures is far better than a cup of dessert wine alone in the dining car.*

As it turned out, he needn't have worried. A half hour after the train pulled out of the Austrian town of Amstetten, they switched to a game of piquet. Normally a two-player game, Jacob and Lady Regina ended up cooperating against Miss Ash, who sat on the opposite bench from them. Leaning together conspiringly to share their hand of twelve cards, Jacob and Regina were pressed together very pleasantly indeed. Just before entering the station at Saint-Pölten, Jacob experimented with placing a hand on Lady Regina's lap, feeling her thigh through the petticoats and gown. She reacted by caressing the wool of his own trousers.

The train pulled out of Saint-Pölten after a stop of just under a minute and gave a start when it did. Lady Regina's hand shot along Jacob's thigh then and he must have given something away in his expression, because as the train accelerated along the Danube, Miss Ash put down her cards and made to stand up. Jacob was caught between simple disappointment and actual mortification—it was one thing to be a man of the world, it was another to be confronted with having taken liberties with a young aristocrat. When, instead of scolding him, Miss Ash extinguished the compartment's lamp, folded the train-table away, and slipped onto the bench beside Jacob so that he was caught between these two delightful creatures, he thought he had been granted access to some heretofore unguessed heaven. When Lady Regina's surprisingly cool lips brushed against his neck, and Miss Ash's gloved hand traveled up his chest, that impression was confirmed.

Jacob Israel Horowitz awoke in his own compartment, before dawn the next morning. His tie was undone, along with several buttons of his shirt, and what roused him from slumber was the shrill voice of a portly Hungarian countess explaining to him, in no uncertain terms, that she had the ticket for this compartment and that he must disembark within the next few minutes, lest she call the conductor. They had, it seemed, arrived in Budapest.

He pushed past the countess and out the door, weak at the knees and half-convinced his nocturnal encounter had been a feverish dream brought on by too much wine. He could not resist, however, sticking his head into the next compartment. It was empty, save for a pad of Grand Express paper, lying on one bench and showing the score for several hands of speculation. Although he was late for his cousin's wedding, was thought to be suffering from some anemic condition by his relatives, and failed to expand his business into Budapest, Jacob would forevermore remember that trip and a glorious adventure.

"English women," he would say in later years, among men who had known the world, "are the finest of them all."

***

"How many others?" Regina Blake's question broke a twenty-minute span of silence, during which time the carriage she was riding in had made its way along Mariahilfer Strasse from the western suburbs of Vienna, heading toward the city's heart. The question was directed at the striking, red-haired woman sitting opposite her in the carriage.

"Pardon?" Victoria Ash, the redhead, glanced at her traveling companion, but kept her attention focused on the street scene passing them by. It was past midnight but the streets were hardly empty—they were heading into the theater district and the factory workers and other laborers were giving way to well-heeled gentlemen and their less reputable female companions. If anything, Viennese nightlife was more populated than that in Paris or London.

"Have you made," Regina completed. "How many others have you remade?" Her hand traveled to her neck, unmarked despite the fact that the other woman's sharp teeth had pieced a major artery there.

Victoria's attention returned to Regina. "Only one, and he is no longer with us."

"I find that hard to believe."

"That my Ethan met his end years ago, or that I would have the self-control not to bring others across as I have you?"

"Ethan. Tell me about him."

Victoria's green eyes held Regina in their gaze for several long moments before she spoke again. "He was a musician, the son of a planter in the Georgia colony, in the years King George was making a mess of North America. He fancied himself a patriot, in fact."

"An American."

"Yes, quite. His brother attended their Continental Congress, unless I'm mistaken. By that time, Ethan was no longer the man his family knew."

Regina tried her best to return Victoria's cold gaze. "He was undead."

"Yes. Remade by my blood as I have remade you."

Regina swallowed and fought to keep the nausea of memory from overwhelming her. Remade was such a cold descriptor for the metamorphosis she'd undergone on the train from Paris. Could such a simple word encompass the horror and pleasure of having one's blood drained by a creature risen from the grave? Of feeling the darkness of death fall only to discover a fiery hunger that rips at the heart and draws the body from the reaper's grip? Of a hunger for warm and living blood?

"My dear girl," Victoria said, piercing the gauze of recollection over Regina's senses, "you haven't yet had time to recover." The redhead reached over to stroke Regina's cheek with her gloved hand. Her thumb traced the line of the girl's lips, gently pressing the soft flesh against the hardness of a dagger-sharp canine that had sprouted from tender gums.

"Oh," Regina said, raising her own hand to feel at these pointed newcomers that felt so natural in her mouth. Her tongue seemed to dance around them, allowing for unimpeded speech.

"They will withdraw when you relax, my dear." Victoria smiled, revealing teeth only slightly sharper than normal. "Like a cat's claws."

Regina tried to keep her lips from drawing up, but did not grow quiet. "What happened to Ethan?"

"What happens to so many of us. The years crept by and he saw all that he had known transformed. His affection for a newborn nation had a cheering effect on him certainly, but Georgia is not England and Savannah was most certainly not London." Victoria looked out the window of the carriage at the façade of a large baroque church, where a lone woman was kneeling before the closed doors, seemingly in prayer to the Virgin Mary depicted over the entrance. "There was no crowd in which to become lost, no anonymity of the great capitals. He avoided close contacts, and traveled to Richmond and the North at times, but he could not help but keep a close eye on those he'd left behind in the daylit world."

"But surely the proximity of family was a comfort to him?"

"At first, yes, and he certainly took pride in their prosperity. It wasn't so long, however, before a reversal of fortune occurred. In a single winter, he saw two nephews die in duels over the fate of the plantation he'd helped secure, and watched his youngest sister—whom he had known as a baby—succumb to the infirmity of old age."

"How long had it been?"

"For his sister, a lifetime. For him, not nearly long enough. It was that spring that he greeted the dawn."

"Suicide," Regina said, her voice chilled.

Victoria answered with a patina of callousness over a core of melancholy. "Such acts do not seem so sinful, once you've tasted lifeblood and played with devils. Not so sinful at all."

Regina thought of the sweet tang of Jacob Horowitz's blood and held her tongue.

The carriage, which they'd hired out of the Westbahnof, carried on for another quarter-hour, finally pulling up into the great Ringstrasse, or ring road. Anxious for a distraction from thoughts of her condition, Regina looked down the broad avenue which, according to what she had read, encircled the historic heart of the Hapsburg capital. Really a connection of several grand streets, the Ringstrasse was framed by baroque buildings and fine parks and was the pride of the Austrian city. In Paris, Regina had seen the straight lines of the *grands boulevards* of the Second Empire, and the rising framework of Mr. Eiffel's tower. In London, she'd walked among the architectural wonders of the Great Exhibition, the Embankment and imposing public places of Victoria's metropolis. Judging by her view from the carriage as it turned onto the ring road proper, the Ringstrasse surpassed them all. This was an architectural vision fully realized, an urban showcase designed to display the wealth and wonder of a grand capital. From the soaring spires of churches to the great opera house and the palace of Emperor Franz-Josef, the ring virtually vibrated with a beauty that bordered on marvel. It was no great leap to imagine the music of Beethoven, Mozart, Strauss, Haydn and other masters of the past and present wafting on the pleasant autumn breeze that caught Regina's upturned face.

The carriage finally came a halt in front of the opera house itself, a Neo-Renaissance marvel that soared above the avenue. Climbing several stories, the façade was set back from the street, letting Regina see its full splendor as she descended from the cab. Victoria handed several coins to the driver and headed toward the great hall. Two fountains gurgled in the center of fine, grassy squares flanking the opera house proper, which was made of ecru sandstone with a green copper roof. Intricate moldings and statuary made of a building contemporary with the giant steel-and-glass constructs of modernity, a rich, classical temple to music and drama. In fact, statues depicting drama and other operatic qualities stood guard over the main entrance, and Regina had the distinct impression she was entering sacrosanct ground. Gas and electric lights filled the echoing entrance hall with a light golden to the point that it seemed the staircase might lead to the throne of a new Midas rather than the foyer of the great concert hall.

This temple was not without its parishioners, either. The sustained murmuring din of a large crowd surrendered to a thousand polite whispers floating through the air. Men in the finest evening attire and women in gowns of silk and brocade overflowed from the upstairs foyers, and more than a few in the hall turned to take in the two women entering during what was obviously an intermission.

"Are we looking for anyone in particular?" Regina scanned the crowd on the off chance of finding a familiar face. They had come to Vienna in search of her mother, and she'd never forgive herself if they did not find her.

"No," answered Victoria, who seemed to pay little heed to the attentions of the crowd. "We are here to be seen. Those to whom we need to speak will find us. I hope."

Regina did not care for the lack of certainty in that last comment.

*　*　*

"Your presence tonight poses certain problems, Miss Ash, Miss Blake." The minister's accent, although clearly Germanic, was not at all heavy. He had the pleasant, worldly tone of a diplomat, and looked the women in the eyes when addressing them. He only glanced once at two ivory-colored visiting cards bearing the women's names in crisp script.

Victoria raised an eyebrow. "Lady Regina and I have no desire to cause any disturbances, Herr Mikel. We only thought it best to see to tradition and present ourselves to the archduke."

Regina gazed at the minister and had a difficult time believing that he, like herself, was anything other than a breathing mortal. And his archduke was no child of Emperor Franz-Josef, but another vampire potentate like those she had encountered in London and Paris. *I have crossed fully into this doppelganger world,* she thought.

"Yes, of course," Mikel said, "and that diligence is appreciated, but I must make clear that visitors from Paris are not entirely welcome in these times."

"As I'm sure you've detected, sir," Regina put in, "we are English, not French."

Herr Mikel gave her a smile. "Nevertheless. We are preparing for the ball season, and Archduke Leopold is concerned about matters of population. We wouldn't want to see the city overrun with the wrong element."

"Are you informing us that Vienna will not extend us her welcome?" Victoria shifted slightly on the divan. "Where is the hospitality the archduke has become so famous for? I am, I must say, shocked."

The Austrian minister lifted his gloved hand in a calming gesture. "Please, Miss Ash, you read scandalous rudeness out of simple caution. The walls around Vienna were torn down decades ago and we make an especial effort to welcome guests from across the civilized world. I shall carry your cards to His Highness."

"Thank you, Herr Mikel." Victoria bowed her head ever so slightly when she said it.

Regina followed suit a split-second later, bowing deeper to compensate for the delay. "You are most generous."

"Come," he said, getting up, "the second act is about to begin and I think I shall regain my seat for it."

Just as he left the small tearoom they'd retired to for their discussion, the minister turned to give one last comment. "Do remember, ladies, that the mark of a civilized guest is not overstaying her welcome." He closed the paneled door behind him, cutting off the rising music of Beethoven's *Leonore Overture No. 3*.

"I imagine Herr Mikel would apologize very politely before fitting one for the gallows pole," Regina said, after a few moments had passed.

"More likely," Victoria answered, "he would assure us he was busy reviewing the injustice of our case before sending word to the hangman to speed us along."

"We came here not so much to be granted leave but to be seen, then."

Victoria smiled, a flicker of delight piercing her mask of poise. "Quite. Vienna welcomes many visitors among our kindred and for the archduke's minister to reject one out of hand would be unseemly. We can be sure that our welcome here will be short-lived, however."

"Then we had best be about our business. Have you any sense of where Mother might be found?"

Victoria smiled again, this time tinged with melancholy. "Your zeal does you credit, my dear, but we have a few matters to attend to first. Most importantly, it is well on toward dawn and we still do not have shelter in this city."

Regina turned and strolled to the tall, broad window of the tearoom, which looked out over the elegant boulevard outside. They were on one of the upper levels and it was easy to see across Opernring, over the facing buildings, and to look at the starlit sky. In as little as four hours, she realized, that sky would turn from black, through purples, reds and pinks, to blue. The thought of the sun—whose warmth on a summer day she'd once so treasured—now sent a chill deep into her bones that caused her to shiver.

Victoria approached and laid a hand on Regina's collared neck. "There, there, my dear."

***

They did, ultimately, find shelter for that first day in Vienna. The opera-goers dispersed relatively quickly after the final curtain of the late-night, preseason performance of *Fidelio*. Regina moved through the crowd of gowned ladies and top-hatted gentlemen, while Victoria scanned the assemblage. "There," she whispered eventually, pointing to a rakish man, one who seemed without female companionship. He was exchanging pleasantries with a couple and another lone man, and although he was too far away and the din of the crowd too loud for her to overhear, Regina was quite certain he was wishing them goodnight.

By the time the two women had descended the broad, red-carpeted stairway to the main lobby, the man was already slipping out the front doors onto Opernring. Regina lost track of her companion for a moment when she slipped by a heavyset woman in an exquisite robe who exuded a subtle perfume of jasmine. The scent triggered a stunningly powerful memory in Regina, of sitting in the drawing room of the family's Cairene house as a young girl. Her mother had worn that same scent, obtained from who knew what perfumer in Cairo or London. For just a second, Regina became convinced that her lost mother was in the crowd and turned to find her, to no avail. She picked up her pace to catch up with Victoria, who was heading for the door.

What is it about smell, of all the senses, she wondered, *that triggers such memories?* She could still see, in her mind's eye, the light coming through the muslin drapes of that sitting room, small motes of dust dancing in the sunbeam. It filled her with melancholy.

"Come quickly, our host is getting away." Victoria slipped out the door and onto the busy square that fronted the opera house. Regina was now right behind her. "Focus," Victoria said. "We must catch him."

Regina scanned the crowd as best she could, looking for the man Victoria had pointed out. As in England, almost all the men wore the same basic attire of black eveningwear, although scarves of white and red silk were more common as flourishes here. Queen Victoria's penchant for mourning attire had obviously not percolated to Hapsburg society. The women were in extravagant and colorful gowns and it was difficult to pick one man from another, especially as Regina had seen this gentleman only in passing.

Damnation, Regina thought, an unfamiliar pang of hungry frustration in the pit of her stomach. A long line of carriages was waiting on Opernring, footmen and valets moving to and fro to guide their aristocratic masters to the right transport. A couple who must have been Hapsburg royalty—the man walking slightly behind the woman, an indication that she was the highest born—was the center of attention and none dared make for their transports before these did. Their carriage was as well-appointed as they, featuring a team of four white horses and elaborate fixtures in silver and brass. The boulevard proper was a snarl of carriages and wagons waiting for the royals to depart.

Regina wondered whether she was seeing the exit of some mortal archduchess or one of the undead masters of Vienna's own night society.

Not all the crowd seemed content to wait their turn in the snarl of horse and buggy. Others were filtering out around the back of the waiting passengers and taking their chances on foot. Regina imagined there were hotels, cafés and clubs within easy walking distance and certainly there would be other places at which to hail a hansom cab (or the Viennese equivalent thereof). She scanned the dispersing crowd, looking for the man. He'd been wearing... what? She searched her memory and surprised herself by coming up with details: A red scarf and cravat flourished with bands of gold. Yes, and a cane of some sort. Ivory.

There. He was heading around to the eastern side of the Opera House, walking at a leisurely pace. She tapped Victoria gently at the elbow and the other woman gave a slight smile. They made to follow.

He skirted the grassy square that sat at the southeastern corner of the Opera House, taking the time to look up at the fountain in its center and the carved figure of a bare-breasted beauty sitting on a rocky pedestal that formed its top. He comically tipped his hat to that stony siren and headed north up Kärntner Strasse, along the theater's eastern façade.

He was hardly the only one to take this route, but neither was the sidewalk choked with people. This made it easy for Victoria and Regina to follow, keeping enough distance to not be obvious without losing him in the crowd. At the corner after the Opera House, Philharmonikerstrasse, he seemed to hesitate. The two women got closer and Regina had to admit that although he was not quite of the stalwart military type that had always appealed to her, he was a tasty morsel indeed.

Seeming to have made up his mind, he headed across Philharmonikerstrasse, angling west so that he quickly disappeared behind the Opera House. Regina felt a little tickle of panic and picked up her pace. Victoria laid a hand on her arm.

"Give him a little distance, my dear," she said. "Our rabbit won't get away so easily."

The comment brought Regina up short. She realized she'd been treating the man as an object to be had, as prey. The pursuit—the *hunt*—sent a tingling thrill through her, quickly followed by a backwash of nausea. She felt as if she were on the deck of a ship, gripped by motion sickness. Suddenly chilled, she followed Victoria.

When they got to the corner, they could see him entering an establishment facing the back of the Opera House. The whole block was taken up by the façades of five-story buildings that might well be apartments for the well-to-do. The central façade featured on its ground floor larger windows on either side of the central door and from these, the light and chatter of a restaurant or café in full swing was emanating. On the balcony two stories above the central door—through which their "rabbit" was entering—twin signs declared the establishment to be the Hotel Sacher.

They crossed Philharmonikerstrasse and entered the Sacher's front door not a minute after the man they pursued. The ground-floor café occupied two rooms on either side of the entrance, while heading forward brought the women into the hotel lobby. A red-clad doorman nodded at them as they entered. The man in the red and gold cravat was heading deeper into the hotel, presumably toward his room or another salon.

"This way, little rabbit." Victoria's voice was barely a whisper, although one full of forbidden pleasures.

Victoria's blood had remade Regina into one of the undead, and even before then, the two women had shared blood several times. Although the iron bonds of loyalty that experience had imposed had been loosened by the traumas of their visit to Paris, Regina still felt very much connected to the vampire who had Embraced her. Thus, even though Victoria's invitation was directed to the man they'd been following, Regina felt much of its eldritch nature. A cool chill rose up her spine and a heat spread across her throat and chest. She had been looking at the man, but now it seemed foolish not to gaze at this siren beside her.

She was still looking when she heard a man's voice say, *"Entschuldigen Sie, Fräulein? Bin ich… kann ich… "* The man they'd been chasing was standing there, awkwardness and desire clear in his face.

Victoria spoke easily. *"Sprechen Sie Englisch, mein Herr?"*

"Ja," he said. "Yes. A little. I am Baron Matthias Grünwald." He bowed awkwardly. "Do we know one another?" His distraction was delicious.

Victoria smiled and indicated Regina. "My companion, Lady Regina Blake."

"A pleasure," he said. When he looked at Regina it was as if he had not yet noticed her. He smiled and blushed slightly, clearly pleased at the discovery.

"And I am Miss Ash. I was wondering if you might show us to our rooms, Herr Grünwald."

A momentary confusion played itself over Grünwald's features, quickly replaced by a wave of nervous pleasure. "Of... Of course. Please follow me."

They headed for the stairs, and Regina barely noticed that her nausea was completely gone.

Chapter Two

Gareth Ducheski had never been handsome. He had been a gangly, awkward child and he grew into a rail-thin man of too-great height. His face was pinched and his nose overlong, giving him the aspect of a serpent or vulture. His skin also had not formed in quite the standard fashion, fusing certain parts of his anatomy. Both his small toes were joined to the adjacent digits, and there was too much flesh under his left arm, meaning he could not raise that limb higher than shoulder height. His gonads, largely absent during childhood, painfully revealed themselves to be imbedded in his right thigh as he entered manhood. Not a handsome man.

None of this had been either a surprise or the subject of much concern among Gareth's relatives. The Ducheski clan was the home of many and varied physical abnormalities, after all. Eleanor, the great-aunt who most directly supervised Gareth's upbringing, taught him that the pains in his loins were simply part of the price their family paid for their special destiny. It was the same with the profusion of large moles, like firm black nipples that occasionally lactated pus, that dotted Eleanor's own torso and back. It was the same with the albinism that had afflicted Eleanor's brother Michael and the hydrocephaly of Michael's daughter Maria. Michael and Maria were Gareth's parents, which technically made Eleanor both his aunt and his great-aunt, but such complex relations were also common among their kin.

Certainly the pain of rejection and mockery as a student first in Manchester and then in London had been difficult at times. The longing for the female flesh forever placed beyond his reach by his twisted genitalia was a hardship as well. Eleanor's instructions in the secret gifts of their family— the dark, potent humor granted them by the masters—did much to offset this. With the blessings of his blood-more-than-blood, Gareth could make himself strong, could heal wounds to his flesh. He also learned to refine his sense of smell, always acute, into an instrument that would make the finest foxhound jealous.

Whereas other men longed for the slick wetness of female flesh, he craved the heady scent of its wantonness. He could inhale that rich musk just by being near them as they coupled, or even by scenting their skin or clothing in the aftermath of coitus. When, at the age of sixteen, Sarah Pincourt found him smelling her bed sheets, he discovered that the odors of fear were even better than those of sex. No one ever found Sarah Pincourt's body and until his current troubles began, Gareth had kept a tanned strip of her skin (still bearing a hint of her scent) as a reminder of that transforming moment.

So, being a physically attractive man had long since stopped being a concern for Gareth Ducheski. Nevertheless, even he would admit that recent months had witnessed a precipitous decline in his already imperfect visage and physique.

That decline had begun in the last nights of the previous year, some nine months ago, when a treasonous cousin of his, one Thomas Ducheski, had attempted to incinerate him with greenish balefire. The Ducheski line, as well as being marred by malformation and the eldritch blood that built up in their veins, also had a proclivity for dark arts. Gareth's sense of smell was his most potent such gift, but others had uncovered more varied arts. Aunt Eleanor could shatter the will of weak men, for example, and Cousin Thomas could summon up the occasional gout of verdant fire from the bowels of hell itself. When, last Christmastide, Thomas decided to gallantly defend their half-cousin Regina from Gareth, he'd paid for it with his miserable life, but not before setting the very air around Gareth alight.

Gareth had survived thanks only to the healing gifts of the familial blood, but his skin, once simply odd, had become truly horrific. Half-healed tissue glistened across a third of his body and angry scars covered the rest. His hair was entirely gone and every instant involved pain, but worst of all, the flames scorched his nasal passages, deadening his sense of smell.

He had spent the winter and spring healing as best he could, and the summer stalking his half-cousin. He'd also distracted himself with the murder of several convenient London street-women, but that did not lead to any further degradations. In August, however, he moved to murder the relatives and loved ones of his little cousin. He managed to slay one John Claremont, but the man's wife stabbed Gareth and then the damnable Lord James Blake (little half-cousin Regina's father) and the equally damnable Malcolm Seward (her fiancé) beat him into unconsciousness. They then abused his body with blows, blades and what tools they had available in an effort to extract information about Regina's whereabouts. When they hit upon the idea of dousing his skin with lamp-oil and setting it alight, something inside Gareth broke and he told them where to go.

That they arrived too late was a credit to his resiliency, but ultimately did him little good. Indeed, Lord Blake decided to keep Gareth under lock and key and continue the interrogation. The viscount had the inspired idea of leaving Gareth dangling from a meat hook in the underground larder of Monroe House, the Blake family's London residence. Gareth hung there, with the hook entering under the shoulder blade and exiting between rib and collarbone, for several weeks, receiving repeated beatings, branding and burnings from Lord Blake.

This did nothing to improve Gareth's appearance. The various beatings left only superficial scars—and what were they on skin already burned and puckered?—but the hook left its mark. Gareth's flesh had healed around the damnable thing, leaving an ugly shunt through his shoulder. This unnatural wound had the aspect of a bellybutton several inches wide. It was also bottomless, since it went completely through to join its twin on his back. When he had lifted himself off the hook to escape his imprisonment, he'd thought his body's preternatural healing a blessing.

Now he barely thought at all, generally responding only to yanks on the rusted chain that ran through the hole in his shoulder. He was a madman on a leash.

Gareth had experienced madness before. The painful healing of his burned skin last winter had chased away any rationality and when he'd emerged to discover his precious olfactory gifts gone, he'd journeyed through the halls of lunacy a while longer. In the spring he had traveled to

London to rejoin Aunt Eleanor and had recovered some of his wits. The sideways glances and outright jeers he received on the streets and—most painfully—within the Inns of Court where he had served as a solicitor, were enough to erode his will a little further. He found joy in the torture of women, certainly, but never enough to recover fully.

That had only come when hanging on the hook under Monroe House. It was then that the rich, dark blood that ran through his familial line had finally worked its blessings on his scorched nasal passages and returned his sense of smell to him. Then, with the hook no longer painful, and Lord Blake's desperation a clear scent reminiscent of urine and rotting fruit, his mind had returned to its full faculties. His confidence in his own superiority was once again confirmed.

Until the damnable stranger.

Gareth had had Blake at his mercy. He'd tied the idiotic aristocrat up and was berating him with his own failings. The man had, after all, managed to alienate his son, and lose both wife and daughter to the worlds of the undead. Worse, he *pitied* his women for their supposed damnation. Blake had no idea of the glory of unlife, a glory Gareth longed for himself. The sour realization that he had failed in every way that counted gave a delicious tang to Blake's fear.

Then the stranger appeared. Long-haired and roughly dressed, he smelled of undeath. Unlike the unliving masters who guided the Ducheski family, however, this one smelled of grave dirt and hog-leather. The thing had smiled a fanged smile and gutted Gareth with a swipe of animalistic claws.

The wounds were terrible and were taking a damnable slow time to heal—Gareth had linen straps wrapped around his torso to keep his innards from slopping out like so much sausage—but it was the timing that drove him mad. The intruder left as soon as he arrived and intimated that he'd arrived largely by coincidence. *Coincidence!* That one word was irrefutable proof that there was indeed a God in Heaven and that He despised Gareth Ducheski just as men despised rats. Gareth's sense of superiority vanished in that instant, and with it, his mind.

It was much easier to be a beast on a chain. Sitting in

the coach, his chain partially concealed by a dark riding cloak, he gave no thought to the consequences of his actions. His new master—the man whose gloved right hand had the end of the rusted chain wrapped around it—gave him directions and he responded. He paid no heed to the glories of Hapsburg Vienna passing by the window, despite the desire he'd once had to be here.

Lord Blake wanted to find Fortschritt and that was all that counted. Lord Blake had the chain.

***

"Go on," Blake said and rapped on the underside of the coach's roof with his cane. "To St. Joseph's."

The coachman, a fat Austrian with an extravagant mustache, leaned down and over from the driver's seat, his face peering awkwardly through the window. "*Was? Zum Josefsplatz?*"

"No, the church! On Karmeliterplatz." The coachman was deaf in at least one ear, but at least he seemed to understand English as much as he did anything else. Soon enough they were circling around and up Universitätsstrasse, away from the fortress that held his beloved Emma.

Fortschritt may have called itself a library and private college, but he knew it to be the home of unliving monstrosities who had kidnapped and perverted his wife, and possibly his daughter. If the cur facing him was to be believed, and that was far from certain despite the impetus of the old chain running through his shoulder, then this was a fortress of deviltry most vile.

Even putting aside Blake's suspicion that his wife was forever lost to him and to God, he could not simply rap on the door and demand she be returned into his loving hands. He needed allies.

He put down his cane and reached into the pocket of his coat to thumb the hard leather of the Bible he now carried with him at all times. God would provide.

They headed down Maria-Theresien Strasse to the Danube Canal and traveled along its quay for much of the breadth of the old city. Lord Blake's knowledge of Viennese geography was sketchy at best, but it was relatively easy to get the basics: The great Ringstrasse, a series of broad boulevards fronted by grand public buildings, formed a rough U shape around the old city—the Innere Stadt, if he'd understood the coachman—with the top of the ring closed by the banks of the Danube Canal. Blake was old enough to remember some of the shocks of 1848, when uprisings and revolutions of the most radical sort had seized many of the capitals of Europe and some had even feared the scourge would spread to England's own shores. Back then, Vienna's heavy medieval walls had stood in the place of the ring, and although the colonel in Blake could understand that they had done their work in staving off Turks and other invaders, they must have made quelling an uprising difficult indeed. No surprise then, that the Austrian Emperor had decided, once order returned to his capital, to tear down the massive walls and replace them with open boulevards. The architecture was certainly impressive, but Blake couldn't help but see how easily cavalry could move between monuments and opera houses.

He was somewhat disappointed then, when the coach made a left turn onto a bridge across the canal and headed into the district of Leopoldstadt. Would they keep heading north and cross the Danube proper and head into the deeper suburbs? No, after only a few turns, the coach came to a stop in a small square clearly marked as Karmeliterplatz. Across the way was the three-tiered, off-white façade of St. Joseph's Church, a large wooden door in its very center. Built in a style Blake recognized as popular among Catholics, the church's front featured small alcoves that sheltered statues of saints and martyrs. Further saints stood atop the decorative swirls that capped the façade's first tier. The church seemed to draw inspiration from the classical architecture Blake's daughter Regina loved so much, but used flat planes instead of colonnades.

"*Danke,*" he said in his accented German as he disembarked. He yanked on the length of chain in his hand, forcing the Ducheski cur to follow with a grunt. The coachman noticed the action of the chain and frowned, but a few additional kronen quelled his curiosity.

"Where now, milord?" Ducheski's voice retained a tone of mocking subservience, one seemingly made especially to drive Blake mad. "Shall you drag me before Roman priests in chains?"

"Quiet."

It was a good question, of course. Blake fished the hard leather Bible from his coat pocket and opened the inside front cover. This was not the Bible of his youth. Not only was the text the Catholic Vulgate—in damnably opaque Latin—but there was a great deal more text between these covers. This Bible had as its preface a text that claimed to be the history of the Society of Leopold, which called itself the successor of the immodestly titled Holy Inquisition Against Demons and Other Agents of the Devil on Earth. The inside covers unfolded to display a series of spaces reserved for seals and signatures of lodges or chapter houses visited by the society member who carried this text. This particular Bible, given to Lord Blake last month by a nun with a history perhaps even more terrible than his own, listed among others *Leopoldhaus, gegenüber Josefskirche, Karmeliterplatz, Wien*. How does one recognize then, the home of a society that must, by dint of the evils of its opposition, shroud itself in secrecy?

Blake turned on his heels and took in the entirety of the small square. The church was clearly dominant, but there were also several private homes nearby. One featured a large image of a stag over the front door and Blake thought this peculiar enough to cross the square to get a closer look. He was contemplating knocking when he felt Ducheski moving, the tension on the length of chain that tied them together shifting slightly. He looked up to see an elderly man standing near the fiend, looking up at the stag figure.

The old man said something in German, obviously expecting Blake to understand. He wore a long coat of gray wool and his flyaway hair was of the same color, although of a significantly lighter shade. It danced in the light afternoon wind and a light shone in his eyes which Blake took to be senility.

"*Bitte*," Blake began, hesitantly. "I do not speak German."

"Ach," the man said, becoming if anything more jovial, "you are British, *ja*? Or American, perhaps."

"English," Blake said, trying his best to keep any

defensiveness out of his voice. He'd known several Americans well worth trusting, but he was not used to being mistaken for one. "From London."

"*Ja, ja.* My apologies, *mein Herr.* I meant not to offend." The man's English was a touch broken, certainly, but easy to follow. "Ach, I remember when I was traveling in your country as a young man—I became so very angry once when a man called me a Prussian. Foolish, the pride of nation and youth."

"Um, yes, perhaps."

"*Entschuldigung,* I was saying the amazement of so much great music coming from a house like this. Have you heard the Strauss Kapelle yet? It is to play beginning at the end of the month, I believe."

"Pardon me? I'm sorry, but I'm not sure I understand, Mister…"

"Oh, forgive me, gentlemen. I am Herr Johann Kohler."

"James Blake," he said, and after a pause, "My companion, Mr. Gareth Ducheski."

"A pleasure…" Kohler's voice trailed off as he got a good look at Ducheski's wreck of a face. Although his long cloak, high collar and tall hat did much to cover his flesh, the glistening scar tissue of his face was still visible. The left side especially seemed more akin to melted wax than actual human flesh. Ducheski grunted his only response.

"Forgive him, sir," Blake put in. "He was the victim of a train accident." The journey from London had given Blake plenty of practice in developing a credible story to explain Ducheski's appearance. The chain was because of occasional fits.

"Not at all, Herr Blake." Kohler turned back to the house. "Yes, I was discussing the amazement of this house. My own mother, God keep her, gave me my Christian name in honor of the elder Johann Strauss, so I have lived with the family's music. I come often to this house, where the family once lived. It humbles me."

"Ah, I see," Blake said, trying to cover the snicker coming from Ducheski. "No, I must admit I was not aware of the musical pedigree of the house. I, um, was more interested in the church."

"Ah, the Karmeliterkirche! *Ja*, dedicated to St. Joseph and built by the Carmelite order some two hundred years ago." Kohler seemed overcome by the joy of speaking of such things. "The façade is a tribute to the Gésu in Rome, although less of a direct copy than the Dominikanerkirche across the canal. If you like religious architecture, Herr Blake, you have come to the right city. I think you will find our city's churches the equal of any outside Rome itself. Why Stephansdom alone—"

"Yes, yes. St. Stephen's. I haven't had a chance to visit it yet—"

"Ah, but you have!" Kohler said, returning the interruption in his enthusiasm. You can see its spire from here. The Stiffl is the central axis of the city itself."

Blake turned slightly and did indeed note the needle-shape of the great cathedral's tower reaching up above the roofs of the inner city. He'd glanced at it a few times in the coach but hadn't quite grasped its significance. "It is beautiful, sir. Truly."

"To the glory of the Blessed Father, as it should be."

"Yes, quite," Blake said uncomfortably, eliciting another snigger from Ducheski. Hoping against hope to steer the conversation in a more useful direction, he reached back to his conversation with Sister Mary-Elizabeth back in England. The nun had gifted him with the Bible that had guided him here and told him a phrase to be recognized, a way to invoke what must be the patron saint of this erstwhile Inquisition. "In fact, I'm interested in a few specific churches. I'm attempting to retrace the steps of St. Leopold."

The old man chewed at his lip for a second. "Klosterneuburg is where you wish to be then, Herr Blake. Just up the river from the city itself. St. Leopold founded the monastery there and the Leopoldskapelle—the chapel—has several of his relics. I do not know if the monks will allow you to visit, but a true pilgrim perhaps might convince them."

"Yes, that is…"

"*Ja*, I understand, you think that this is Leopoldstadt and thus must be the city of the saint, but that is a confusion. This community gained this name from Emperor Leopold, who expelled the Jews from this district. That edict did not stand what you English call the test of time, but the name remains."

Blake could feel a headache blooming behind his ears. Damnable Catholics and their endless multiplicity of saints! Viscount he might be, but he preferred the simplicity of the low church over the endless variations of ritual. Would he have to trace every church in Austria before this was over?

"Thank you, sir. I suppose I will make that trip tomorrow."

"Yes, yes, of course," Kohler said, suddenly fishing in the pockets of his coat. "I have, yes… *irgendwo*… the name of a guide in Klosterneuburg…"

"That's quite all right…"

"No, I insist," the old man said. With a frustrated jerk he tried to extricate his hand from the folds of his garment. It caught in one pocket or another and the movement pitched him off balance. "Oh!"

Blake, although retired, still had the reflexes of a cavalryman, and he moved smoothly to catch the old man before he collapsed on the cobblestones. The man was making the fool's mistake of thrashing his trapped limbs instead of moving into a tumble and his elbow went directly into Blake's gut. The pain of the blow, the awkwardness of having a chain wrapped tightly around his forearm, and the fact that Kohler seemed to be made entirely of boney joints, all conspired to make Blake's aid less than graceful. In the end both men were on their knees and the Austrian was panting heavily.

"Oh, *danke*, Herr Blake." Pant. Pant. "What a fool I am."

"It's quite all right, sir," Blake lied, setting the man aright again and standing up. "But my companion and I must be going."

"Yes, of course." The man bowed slightly and tipped a hat he seemed only to note too late wasn't there. "*Guten Tag, mein Herr.*"

"Yes, to you as well, sir." Blake turned and left, doing his best to ignore Ducheski's throaty laughter.

Only three hours later, after they had taken a suite at a discreet hotel outside the Ring and Lord Blake had secured

Ducheski to one of the heavy sconces in the room's wall, did he find the object Kohler had slipped into his pocket. It was a lead or pewter token, stamped with a Maltese cross on one side and on the other an inscription in Latin: *Oculi Dei*.

Blake's Latin was poor, but he could still manage a translation: The eyes of God.

Chapter Three

Regina Blake did not wake, precisely, on the third night of her new existence caught between breathing life and final death. To have woken, she would have had to sleep, and the slumber that had overtaken her the previous morning had not been mere sleep. It had been something akin to death. When, a half hour after the autumnal sun had dipped under the horizon beyond the Danube, awareness returned to her, it did so unlike any waking of her eighteen years.

First there was simple awareness, devoid of any and all physical sensation, and even somewhere on the far side of thought. The philosopher Descartes' *cognito ergo sum* was reversed in that eternal moment—first came Regina's awareness that she existed as a material thing, and only then did thinking emerge from the wooly mass of her brain. With that thought, it became possible to understand, or at least categorize, the sensations slowly dawning on her. They were not pleasant.

The single strongest sensation was weight. Not the simple press of Sir Isaac's laws on her body, but an all-encompassing sensation of mass. That sense gradually resolved itself into a vague impression of her own body, or at least some parts of it. Her chest—lungs, heart, stomach—felt as if it were forged of lead, like an immovable thing. Or, the thought struck her, as if a great weight were pressing down upon it, preventing breath or escape. It was as if she were drowning under a mountain of sand.

That image, stark and vivid, sparked something deep within, the beginnings of some hot, hungry force. Her eyes sprung open, flooding her mind's eye with blurred shadows and milky shapes. She was aware of her eyes now, and could feel how parched and scratched the orbs were. One lid was stuck to the flesh, further distorting her view of a world she couldn't quite make sense of.

Something moved among those blurs and that brought the idea of movement to her mind. Wedded to the still-growing panic of the crushing weight of her own flesh, that idea translated itself into an imperative: she must move. The small, hot spark in her grew a touch stronger and she latched onto it, hoping to find the means to escape whatever constriction bound her. She clenched hard teeth she'd just now realized existed around a tongue made of cotton draped in cracked leather and willed herself forward.

Up and down resolved themselves from the ether as her head and chest swung up from a partial recline, past upright and into a face-first crash into a vertical surface—a wall. The sudden pain of a sharp tooth piercing the dry flesh of her own tongue fueled that inner fire enough for Regina to call upon her right arm in an attempt to push herself away from the offending wall. The next sensation was somewhat familiar, a memory from true, deep sleep in which the circulation to a limb is cut off so that upon waking it is a dead, insensate weight. This time, however, the limb was not like rubber (as it had been on bygone mornings) but akin to creaking wood. Her joints, forced into movement, complained with audible creaks and the uncomfortable sensations of bone rubbing on bone and tendons stretching to their breaking-points. Her wrist and forearm slammed into the same wall her faced rested upon, while her hand remained folded back at an awkward angle.

Still, she managed to push back slightly to a position that approximated sitting upright. The idea struck her to stand, or at least to ascertain the condition of her legs, for she had by this point come to understand that she had such things as legs. This proved a difficult proposition for they were clearly folded under her and as soon as she tried to move them, she pitched to the right.

Instinct took over and her inner drive grew stronger. Her left arm shot out palm first to arrest her fall before she could collapse. She ended up with that hand tight against another wall, and the right pressed flat on the ground. This gave her the leverage to slip first one and then another leg out from under herself. She was starting to get a sense of herself again and that buoyed her spirits.

Until she realized that she had yet to take a breath.

Panic bloomed hot and strong and sudden. What had been a spark became a blaze and then an inferno, overwhelming any conscious decisions and spreading like a web of molten iron through her body. Movement became not only possible, but unavoidable, and she thrashed to get to her feet and opened her mouth to let in air. When that didn't help, she madly probed her lips with her fingers, finding long sharp teeth and a swollen tongue. She pushed at the offending organ, trying to free her airway. Somehow she managed to push it aside, or to will it back into its proper place in her mouth, and she pushed out her chest, letting in a gulp of air.

She'd expected the overwhelming refreshment of water from a cold spring taken after a long, arid walk. Instead, it felt like tepid, even fetid, well-water, and she gave a shallow cough to expel the offending miasma. With that cough, however, the panic passed, and her senses resolved themselves. Her vision sharpened, and although it was indeed gloomy in whatever small space she occupied, some light crept in and she could recognize the silhouette of Victoria Ash.

Hearing brought Victoria's voice, soothing and calm: "Move slowly, my dear. It is natural to be confused. Remain calm and everything will resolve itself…."

And underneath it all, from that hot core that had drawn her back from death, Regina Blake felt a hunger deep enough to consume the world.

"Wha—?" she croaked. Air slipped into her lungs, but not nearly enough to power her voice. Her throat felt raspy and dry, as if her vocal chords were made of rusted steel wire.

Victoria placed the fingers of her right hand over Regina's lips, not clamping down, but merely touching to indicate silence. "Slowly, my darling," she said, "don't try to speak just yet."

Regina obeyed. She closed her eyes and tried to simply concentrate on the silence that now enveloped her. It was something much like the heavy, enveloping silence she'd experienced when plunging her head underwater at the sea. Not quite the same, however. The rhythmic swishing of circulation, that wave-like sound one hears when all other sound is gone, was now a raw staccato, a series of starts and stops. She concentrated on that ugly sound and tried, in a way she couldn't have explained, to have it conform to her peaceful memories. Slowly, very slowly, the irregular sounds gave way to a semblance of back-and-forth flow, and with it other pains were relieved: the parched sensation in her eyes, throat and mouth receded; the pain in her tongue faded; her joints grew limber again. By the time she opened her eyes again and registered the relief on Victoria's beautiful face, Regina could almost ignore the gaping stillness where her heartbeat had once been.

***

They had been at the Café Landtmann since an hour past dusk, the two women. Intellectuals, artists and many who considered themselves such had filled the time with endless chitchat, countless cigarettes and coffees. Emma Blake was sitting quietly at the back of the room, nursing the same Türkirscher and pastry she'd ordered upon her arrival, accompanied by her aunt Eleanor. The Landtmann, like most other Viennese *Kaffeehäuser*, built part of its reputation on an admirable allowance for customers who ordered little and stayed long. For every such poet, it seemed, there was an expansive aristocrat or other tagalong who would buy plentiful drinks to bribe himself into whatever cohort had made the café its home. Herr Landtmann's establishment attracted a clientele drawn from the middle classes, including scientists, students and politicians. The famous coffee-maker would probably be surprised to know, Emma thought, that it was also the haunt of not a few sorcerers and vampires.

Located a short walk from Fortschritt itself, the attendants and novices of House Tremere gathered here. Emma, whose senses had sharpened to an unheard-of degree in the last nine months, had noted customers who had a distinctly pale appearance and a less-than-usual enthusiasm for eating the foods they ordered or taking regular breaths.

Dr. Bainbridge had first brought her to the coffee house, soon after his arrival from London in August. The preeminent member of House Tremere in the English capital,

Bainbridge was also, she'd discovered, something of an aberration among the undead. Unlike her or the vampire who had remade her in his image, Dr. Bainbridge could ingest food and drink with ease. She'd once tried to do so, to deaden the craving for blood, and vomited violently. She'd watched in amazement as Bainbridge consumed pastry after pastry, filling his unliving gullet with jam-filled Buchteln buns and washing it all down with a Kaisermelange—dark black coffee served with brandy and a raw egg yolk. She had very little doubt that Bainbridge enjoyed the discomfort such displays of intestinal fortitude created in others of his ilk, and in her.

The unpleasantness of the portly vampire's consumptions—for it could not truly be called feeding, since only blood could feed the unliving—was a price Emma was almost happy to pay to be granted leave from Fortschritt. Mr. Wellig and his cronies had kept her under close observation in the first week of her stay and that they now allowed her to visit the city was a great relief to her.

She was never alone, of course. Dr. Bainbridge accompanied her some nights, her sire Mr. Wellig on some others. When both were in council, then Aunt Eleanor would serve as a guardian. Eleanor Ducheski had been the matriarch of her family for Emma's entire life, and although not a vampire herself, she nevertheless had a way of intimidating the stoutest man. A wizened crone and witch, she seemed even more terrifying now than she had been when Emma was a little girl in County Durham.

"Still," Eleanor said in her croaking frog-voice. "Still you think of fleeing. Pfah!" The old woman had the foam from her coffee caught on her bloodless lips and the porcelain cup she clutched rattled with the shaking of age.

"What could I possibly hope to escape, Aunt Eleanor? The very blood of my veins? The attentions of Dr. Bainbridge, Lady Meerlinda and the others? How could I even hope for such a thing?"

"Bah, you mock your betters with the truth disguised as lies." She pointed a bony finger at her unliving niece. "Your blood *is* what you want to escape. The Ducheski blood that gave you life."

"That," she said, suddenly keenly aware of the faint pulse in Eleanor's neck and the lack thereof in her own, "is no longer my concern."

"It is! You think that you stop being Ducheski when your are chosen? That it is not Ducheski blood in your veins and heart? You are a fool!"

"Perhaps," Emma said, thinking of the young violinist she had fed from two nights ago. He was no Ducheski and it was his blood in her veins now.

"You know nothing of your family. You are ignorant."

Emma had heard this refrain many times before, both as a child unversed in the full truths of her birthright and as a woman trying in vain to escape it. She had little patience left.

"Yes, yes, Aunt Eleanor. The Ducheski were scholars and kings before the Magyars and the Germans came to our lands, before the Slavs and the Greeks. Mr. Wellig delivered us from the east and brought us to County Durham and Lion's Green, where we have rebuilt ourselves. He and the Tremere order are the saviors of our line." She said the last with an especial lack of enthusiasm. "I have heard it all before."

"You hear nothing," the old woman spat. "You say the words but don't understand. You don't know what we have given up, what price your mothers and fathers paid. All for you."

"Were it up to me, they need not have done a thing."

The old woman spat a string of syllables Emma could not follow. Lady Blake had been raised largely in English and spoke little of the old language of her family. She recognized a curse when she heard it, however, and understood that in a family that served blood sorcerers, such things were not said lightly.

"Come," Eleanor said, returning to accented English as she struggled to rise from the bench of the small booth they occupied. "I will *show* you what you would throw away. Come."

They proceeded down the aisle of the long coffee house, past intellectuals and sorcerers and out onto the street, facing the north wing of the newly redesigned Burgtheater. Emma had practiced her German by reading the local press and much was made of the completion of this grand theater in the style of the Italian Renaissance. Work had been ongoing for almost fifteen years and artistic and aristocratic circles were especially excited about the grand opening to occur this October, Emperor Franz-Josef in attendance. Work on the exterior had been complete for some time, but Emma could well understand the excitement of the city's elite. It was a spectacular building, with façades that incorporated pillars and colonnades, with classical statuary peeking down from the balustrade that ran around the edifice. If the reports in the press were to be believed, the interior, lushly adorned with frescos and featuring grand staircases leading to five different levels of seating, would put all other theaters to shame.

Eleanor caught Emma gazing at the façade and made a scoffing exhalation. "Beauty is for the weak and foolish, girl. Come with me."

They boarded a cabriolet on the section of the great Ringstrasse that ran between the Burgtheater site and Rathauspark, the green esplanade that stretched out before Vienna's Gothic city hall and its three-hundred-foot central tower. This space—across which the two grand buildings faced one another, each built in the last two decades, each clashing with the other while trying to outdo it in opulence—said a great deal about Vienna, Emma thought.

Neither woman noticed the long-haired man in red-tinted spectacles who came out of the Café Landtmann shortly after them, just in time to see them go.

***

Regina and Victoria took a barouche from the Hotel Sacher southeast along Kärntner Strasse, toward Karlsplatz and past the huge baroque Karlskirche. Regina was struck once more by the beauty and ostentation of Hapsburg architecture. She had spent much of her youth dreaming of the vanished glories of Mycenae and Rome, and she found some of her sensibilities echoed here. While London and Paris seemed to be forging the stamp of modernity in steel and glass, Vienna favored marble, granite and copper. The front stairs of the church may have been flanked by cross-bearing angels, but they rose to a façade taken from the temples of pagan Greece and Rome. The two great columns that were the church's most striking features sported winding bas-reliefs styled after Trajan's Column. Regina did admit, however, that with their rounded tips and small balconies, the columns reminded her most of the minarets of the Mohammedan mosques of Cairo. Surely not the designers' intention, that.

"You are gaping again, my dear."

Victoria's comment sounded more like teasing than a serious reprimand, but it struck a chord in Regina. She turned to face Victoria and was all too aware of how far she'd twisted her spine to look out and up past the carriage's folded-back top to admire the church. She *had* been gaping.

"It is beautiful," she said. "There's nothing like it in London. Westminster Cathedral is a marvel of course, but it has very little of this city's flair."

"You have an admirable taste for things architectural," Victoria said. "But remember that we are here with a purpose, not to admire the glories of Franz-Josef's city."

Regina felt a spark of anger growing in her. How dare Victoria insinuate that she was forgetting why they were here? But her own thoughts of a moment ago argued against her. Staring up at the finely sculpted columns of the Karlskirche, she'd forgotten entirely about her mother. "I'm, that is…" Words failed her.

Victoria's features warmed and she laid a hand on Regina's. "I understand, darling. It is one of the compensations of our nature, this refinement of the senses, but it can be overwhelming. One can get lost in the very richness of the sensation."

"Yes, of course," Regina said after a moment, in an effort to stifle the denial forming in her mind. It had nothing to do with beauty. It was about memory. Looking at the façade of that glorious church, she'd forgotten not only about Mother, but about herself. She'd forgotten that her heart no longer beat, that her skin was cold as death and that she existed now as a ghoulish intruder among the living.

She closed her eyes lest she jump from the carriage and race back to gaze up at the Karlskirche and recapture that blissful moment of ignorance.

***

They left the carriage soon after it turned off Rennweg and onto Jacquingasse, both of which framed the famous gardens of the Belvedere Palace. They'd passed before the darkened façade of the Lower Belvedere and its stables, but the greater Upper Belvedere Palace remained hidden behind its smaller cousin. Victoria signaled the driver to stop at the gates on Jacquingasse of what turned out to be the Imperial Botanical Gardens.

"I assume we are not here to admire the Hapsburgs' taste in flowers," Regina said as they walked toward the iron gates. "Whom are we meeting here?"

"'Hoping to meet' would be a more accurate phrasing, actually." Victoria reached the gates and gave them a slight push, but they refused to budge. She looked into the gloom of the gardens beyond. "Come here, please, Regina."

Regina was already by her side when she spoke. "Yes?"

"Can you see that path there? To the left?"

Very little light penetrated into the gardens. There were streetlights along Jacquingasse, but not a huge number of them, nor were they much use against the walls of the gardens or the thick branches of the trees. It was autumn, but very few trees had shed their leaves. Regina could just make out the gray-on-gray outline of a gravel path heading deeper into the enclosure. "Yes, I see it."

"And upon it?"

Regina suppressed the twin urges to blurt out that she saw nothing and to berate Miss Ash for quizzing her like a child in lessons about something she obviously knew the answer to. Instead she did her best to peer into the shadows, like a myopic devoid of spectacles. She blinked a few times, more out of simple irritation than any need to relieve her eyes.

And her vision cleared.

It was something like her experience had been when studying with Ibn Saleh, her tutor in Cairo. Poring over a text in Latin had, at first, been a frustrating experience, each word a battle and actual sentences and thoughts beyond her. Even after she'd learned some basic syntax and vocabulary, the first reading of a passage was often a jumble of fragmentary meaning.

There was one moment, however, on an especially hot spring morning, when the sentences had suddenly resolved themselves. She had stopped translating and started to understand.

The same thing occurred now, staring through the iron gates of the Botanischer Garten. The night remained as dark as before, but the occluded shapes and shades resolved themselves into recognizable forms. What had been, at best, gradations of gray, whispered colors to her so that she could almost imagine the beauty of the scene under full sunlight. The path, its pebbles more beige than slate-gray, she now saw, curved up and to the right. Green grasses climbed the hillocks to either side. And at the top of the path, looking straight at her, was a midget.

He wore formal evening wear—a black silk suit with a shirt so white, Regina was astonished she hadn't seen it before, and a comically tall top hat. He bowed ever so slightly in her direction and then raised his gloved hand, which held a small cane.

"A man," Regina said. "A tiny man. He is pointing off to the left, I think."

"There's another entrance further along, I believe." Victoria started to stroll down the street and it was a moment before Regina could pull herself away from the newly revealed panorama of the shadowed gardens. The midget was indeed heading off the way he had indicated, however, so she turned to follow.

When she did, the street positively blazed with light.

"Wha—" The streetlamps, which had cast a wan glow over the midnight street, were now each haloed by a bright circlet and much of the scene seemed washed out in white. Regina blinked back and held out a hand, her eyes stinging. "The light."

"Remain calm," Victoria said. She was little more than a silhouette before Regina. "Close your eyes, my dear."

"But—"

"Please, darling. Trust me." Miss Ash's voice was like a cool compress on a fevered brow and Regina complied. "There, dear girl. Take a moment."

"I don't understand."

THE WOUNDED KING

"Our condition affects every part of us, but can have an especial effect on the senses." Victoria's words were whispered, but Regina understood readily, so close were they. "You'll find that in time you can see a great deal more than you once did, darling, but it can take some time to adjust."

Regina reached out to hold onto her protector and hazarded to open her eyes again. She was looking down and used her free hand to shield herself from the expected glare of lamplight. She found only a mild scene, clear, but hardly blinding.

"There," Victoria said and squeezed her protégée's hand. "Are you well?"

"I believe so." She glanced down the street back the way they had come and found she could see clearly all the way to Rennweg, well enough even to read bills posted on the walls where street-cleaners hadn't had the chance to take them down. "Is it always like this?"

"It can be," Victoria said. "Come, we can't keep Herr Schiller waiting at the gate."

They headed up the street to the next break in the wall around the garden, to find the small, tuxedoed man holding the iron gate open for them.

"*Guten Abend*," he said in a lilting, girlish voice. It was then that Regina realized this was not a midget, but a boy.

"Good evening, Herr Schiller," Victoria said, slipping a visiting card from her small handbag. "We are acquaintances of Lady Merritt, from London."

The boy looked at the offered card and smiled. "Please, Miss Ash, do come in." His English was excellent.

"Herr Schiller, may I present my ward, the Lady Regina Blake."

"Charmed," he answered glancing up at Regina with a cherubic smile. "After you, milady."

Regina had to force herself to move. "Thank you, sir."

They headed in and Herr Schiller closed the gate with a minimum of struggle. Its weight did not seem to bother him overmuch, but the iron lock into which he fit a large key was placed well over his eye-level and he had to lift himself onto his tiptoes to get the bolt into place. That accomplished he headed up the path, signaling for the Englishwomen to follow.

Regina did her best not to stare, but failed. Herr Schiller was clearly less than four feet tall and a thin-boned thing. Not the stocky, plump shape of a midget or dwarf but the proportioned, still-growing frame of a child barely into short pants.

"I received your letter last month, Miss Ash," Schiller said, as they followed him along the paths and past a variety of plants and trees, "but I was not under the impression that you had plans to visit."

"Our travels took us to Paris first," Victoria said, "but our business has brought us here, at last."

Regina thought back to the slew of letters Victoria had sent out from Calais in the hopes of finding information about Emma, Lady Blake—Regina's mother. It seemed an eternity ago. Could it really have only been a month?

Schiller turned and gave Victoria a small smile. "Well, all the better, then."

Twenty minutes later, the three of them were sitting in a well-appointed parlor situated on the second floor of one of the small manors near the Upper Belvedere Palace. Drawings of flora decorated much of the space, with fresh blooms resting in several water bowls tastefully placed about the room. Regina sat near Victoria on a large divan, while Schiller occupied a fine chair custom-built for one of his stature.

He was going on about the setting. "It was the Empress Maria Theresa who first commissioned these gardens, for the growing of medicinal plants. Old Doctor van Swieten was a proponent of their healing abilities, you see."

"Are you a botanist, Herr Schiller?" Regina did her very best to ask the question as she would to a full-grown man, since that was the demeanor Schiller adopted.

"It is my passion, Lady Regina." He rose from his diminutive chair and pointed toward an especially beautiful bloom pictured in one of the framed watercolors on the wall. "This is the blue lotus. Such beauty, it blooms—"

"On the banks of the Nile," Regina completed.

He turned to face her, joy on his face. "You have studied botany?"

"Not formally. I spent my youth in Egypt, however, and

can remember my mother picking just such a bloom during a trip to see Mr. Petrie's dig at Naukartis."

Schiller's smile was full of longing, speaking of years well beyond those of the child he appeared to be. "To see, to touch, to smell the bloom itself, in its natural habitat. Marvelous. We speak so flippantly of the curse of our blood, but it is in these small things eternally taken from us that I feel its weight most acutely."

"Pardon?"

"Forgive my floridness, Lady Regina," he answered. "I content myself with night-blooming varieties and the observation of closed blooms, of course, but I could curse my short years in the sun for not having appreciated the beauty around me. I sometimes think I would face the tortures of the sun itself to catch but a whiff of a rose in full bloom."

"We all have regrets, Mr. Schiller," Victoria said, "the question is to what point we can accept the loss."

Schiller smiled more broadly now. "How true, Miss Ash, and I'm afraid I'm painting a very melancholy picture of myself. What would my long-dead mother think of her little Karl as master of the imperial gardens and still not satisfied? A scolding would be in order, I believe."

"Were you close to your mother, Mr. Schiller?" Regina asked. "That is, I do not wish to offend, but—"

"It's quite alright, Lady Regina. Yes, I suppose I did cling to my mother's bosom more than was healthy, even for a boy my age. The plague took care of that, taking her to a pauper's grave and sending me out to be found by my overwrought sire. I once attempted to script an operetta about those sad events, but I found my tragedy was far too mundane."

"I'm searching for my mother still, Mr. Schiller. She was taken from me, and made into, that is, she is undead…"

Schiller made a little *tsk* sound and Regina felt a knot of caution well up in her. After the traumas they had suffered in the bowels of the Santé prison in Paris, the eldritch bond between Miss Ash and Regina had weakened some. Nevertheless, Regina felt sure her caution was tied to an unspoken warning from Victoria.

"Perhaps it is a matter of translation," Schiller said, "but your choice of terminology speaks of base origins and uncouth manners, Lady Regina. In Vienna, we are kindred."

"Yes, of course, my apologies Mr. Schiller. I meant no offense."

He turned his attention to Victoria. "She is very young, *ja*? Your letter last month was very vague about your traveling companions. I do believe you have taken liberties on the road, Miss Ash."

"Lady Regina has been presented to your archduke in accordance with tradition, Herr Schiller." Victoria's voice was cold and hard. "I fail to see how other matters of our relations are any of your concern."

"And does the sire stand culpable for the childe's actions as is also our tradition?" His voice remained tinged with childish amusement.

"Of course."

"And tell me this, Lady Regina," he continued, shifting attention again. "Has Miss Ash explained the seriousness of such considerations? Flouting the codes by which we exist can have dire consequences."

"I know of your—of *our* iron law of secrecy," she said, "and as Miss Ash has plainly said, we have given our regards to the archduke. Do you fancy yourself a magistrate in such matters, Mr. Schiller? Has this parlor become a court of assize?"

For a long moment, the unliving boy said nothing and Regina felt her knot of dread grow. Why had she goaded him? For all she knew he *was* a magistrate of sorts.

"Ha!" he said, a broad smile spreading across his pudgy child's face. "Well said. I admire your spirit, Lady Regina. No, to answer your question, I am no sheriff or scourge. I am but one of the too-plentiful kindred in this city of artists and warlocks. Now, tell me about your mother."

Regina did just that, up to a point. She told Schilling how Emma, Lady Blake had been remade into one of the kindred against her will during Christmastide last. How Regina, determined to uncover the truth had gained the assistance of Miss Ash and entered, somewhat blindly, into the night society of London's kindred. How they had tracked

Emma to the Continent, first to Paris and then to Vienna. She skirted the elements of her own fall into undeath—something she could hardly bring herself to speak of—but had the uncomfortable feeling that Schiller was filling in the blanks with ease.

"And just who remade Lady Blake into one of our kindred?"

"A Mister Anton Wellig. I believe he is a member of the Tremere fraternity."

"I see." Schilling raised himself out of his diminutive chair and walked to the window of the parlor. A sideboard of sorts—or a low chest, Regina could not tell which—served him as a platform to gain enough elevation to gaze out at the gardens and palace beyond. "This complicates matters. Has Miss Ash explained the position of House Tremere in our fair burg?"

"I'm afraid I am in no position to explain very much on that subject," Victoria said. "Dr. Bainbridge mentioned that a college of sorts had been built here, I believe."

"The Tremere generally prefer the term 'chantry,' actually. Bainbridge is your countryman, yes?"

"He is, I believe, the preeminent member of House Tremere in London," Victoria said. "At least he has been the most socially active since the return of our prince, Mithras."

"Be that as it may," Schilling said, "it seems he has a gift for understatement." He turned to face the two women, leaning on the window sill. "The chantry here is the most important in Europe. For all intents and purposes, Vienna is the center of the entire Tremere brotherhood."

Regina felt a chill flow down he spine, and got the distinct impression that Schilling was pleased by his words' effect.

"It wasn't always such," he continued. "Until our Emperor Franz-Josef tore down the walls of the city to build the Ringstrasse thirty years ago, Vienna was constrained and claustrophobic. The number of our kindred here was quite small."

"You have been here far longer than that though, Herr Schilling," Victoria said.

"True, true. And I suppose many of the older set have been as well, but the inside of the city walls were largely off-limits and we received few visitors. With the rise of the Ringstrasse, however, the city has come to preeminence in the worlds of art, music and even sorcery."

"How so?"

"The Tremere have maintained a chantry here for centuries, but it always remained a small thing, home to a cabal of warlocks at most. With the plans for the Ringstrasse, it became possible for them to build a far grander house. The kine think of it as a private library and college, but Fortschritt has become the heart of their arcane society. In the last twenty-five years, Tremere initiates and elders from across Europe and the colonies have come through our city to study at the new chantry and to consult its stacks, or so I have observed."

"A library is one thing," Regina said, "the center of a society is another."

"True, but the Tremere are scholars—of black arts, perhaps, but scholars nonetheless. And it is my understanding that the eldest of their house now reside somewhere in Fortschritt. The pyramid is the preeminent symbol of their house and that fine chantry just off Schottenring is its very tip."

"And the archduke allowed this?" Victoria asked. She meant, Regina understood, the kindred potentate whose emissary they'd met at the Opera House.

"His Highness serves at the warlocks' pleasure, as I understand it. The true power in the city lies inside Fortschritt."

"Where Mister Wellig and my mother surely are," said Regina.

"Precisely. You see then why I must regretfully admit that there is no further assistance I can provide in this matter."

"But, surely…" Regina said, struggling to keep a plaintive tone out of her voice.

"Crossing the warlocks can be quite costly," he said.

"Then perhaps there is some way we could offset that cost," Victoria said. "Some service we could provide in exchange."

"Yes," Regina added, "and you could of course count on our absolute discretion in this matter. We would never presume to put you in an uncomfortable position."

"That is quite kind of you to say, Lady Regina." He paced the room slowly, whispering his thoughts to himself. "I don't quite see... no, wait..." He turned to face Regina. "You will be returning to London in the aftermath of whatever foolishness you have planned?"

"Yes, yes, of course." She hoped she was not lying.

"Then, perhaps. There is the matter of Herr Wim Hendriksen."

"Who?" It was Victoria who spoke, although the name was equally unknown to Regina.

"A Dutchman," Schilling said, not taking his gaze from Regina. "A merchant and antiquarian I have done business with, and who cheated me. Kine, but one who has made a living dealing with members of our nighttime society."

"This man is in London?" Regina asked.

"Yes. I believe he maintains a shop on Exeter Street. It would be of great relief to me were Herr Hendriksen to no longer be a concern. I find he weighs on my soul and I long for that weight to be lifted." He smiled. "Permanently so."

Regina swallowed and felt tingles of tension building in her shoulders and neck. Was this little boy truly asking her to participate in a murder? Starring deep into his brown eyes, she noted flecks of amber there, and wanted nothing more than to take back the last months of inquest and horror. But having come so far, she found the prospect of leaving empty-handed the most frightening of all.

Victoria filled the pregnant silence. "I will see to it, Herr Schiller," she said.

Regina felt a wash of relief trickle over here until she glanced again at the unliving boy who was their host.

"You'll forgive me, Fraulein Ash," he said, "but given that I am endeavoring on Lady Regina's behalf, I fear that I can only accept her own assurances. Were you and she to have some sort of falling out before your return to London, then I could well be left exposed."

He turned his eyes back to Regina and she felt a cold,

vermilion pleasure waft off him like an ill wind. He was, she realized, like a drowned man reaching up to pull her down into the murk, seeking company in the stygian depths. She should refuse—this was murder he was asking of her—but what choice did she have? She swallowed needlessly and tasted the coppery flavor of Jacob Horowitz's and Matthias Grünwald's blood.

"Yes," Regina said. "I agree to it."

"You understand," Schiller said, "that I take you at your word, Lady Regina. Were you to lie to me—"

"Whether or not you believe me, sir, is your choice," Regina snapped. "I would appreciate it, however, if you were not to ask me a service and then openly question my willingness to carry it out. Would you rather I decline to pay your price?"

His smile widened. "I believe you, my dear. And that being the case, there is an introduction I shall arrange that may, I believe, assist you in your search for your departed *mater familias*."

"Thank you."

"Please meet me at the Café Landtmann on Saturday evening. I will expect you at eleven o'clock precisely."

Regina broke eye contact with the boy-man and looked up at Victoria whose expression was just shy of polite neutrality. The bond of the last several months allowed Regina to glimpse—she thought—some melancholy there, however.

Chapter Four

The doors to the town church in Josefsdorf were closed for the night. The temperature in late September had a hint of winter in it, but it was a good deal warmer than London or certainly County Durham at the same time of year. Emma, Lady Blake, watched as her withered great aunt trotted from the carriage that had brought them through the Vienna Wood to this village north of the city, and up toward the façade of the baroque Church of St. Joseph.

"This was the place," the old woman said. "Come child, you must see."

Emma followed reluctantly. There was a gnawing at her spine, some tingle she couldn't quite define that spoke of danger in this quaint, night-draped square. Perhaps it was being away from Mr. Wellig and the other warlocks who had been so keen to examine her in the last month. Could she truly miss the endless questions and examinations? The gruesome artifacts that put the lie to their learned pretense, like the withered and waxen "hand of glory," a candle made from the severed hand of a condemned man? It revealed truth, Herr Drescher had said when he talked to her last.

It was ludicrous to long for the proximity of such macabre company, but she did. She was undead and fed on the blood of the living. She had bid her husband goodbye and hoped against hope her daughter had been left behind as well.

"They built this church to keep the truth locked away," the old woman said as she led the way around the small house of worship. "They hoped the sign of their crucified god, their shallow sacraments and weak worship would all work to keep our gods in the ground." She stopped, overcome by fatigue or memory, and wheezed several long breathes in the silence. "Ha! They were too late, as they always had been. Just as the Turks were."

"Our ancestors fought the Turks?" Emma knew the Ottomans had once posed a grave threat to all of Europe.

"Those who stayed in the old country and fought were

slaughtered," Eleanor said, "by the Sultan's men, or by the old ones, or the churchmen. But not before they allowed us to escape, with the relic."

"I'm not sure I understand."

The bent crone didn't answer until they had both made it around the back of the church into the small, crowded graveyard there. Then Eleanor turned around and hissed, "Look!"

Using the cane that supported her slight form, Eleanor pointed to the backside of the church. Emma's gaze followed, but at first she saw little. The night was dark here, away from even the pale streetlamps of the Ring and the Innere Stadt. The woods came in close and the sky was covered by clouds so that even the moon- and starlight were absent. Still, Emma's unliving senses were adapted to the dark and slowly the relief on the church's back wall came into focus.

"They told the story," Eleanor croaked, "so their children would not forget."

The carving was intricate and gothic, made up of crowds of leering and distorted figures—some human, others distinctly devilish. Thick horizontal lines separated the portrayal into three large panels, the whole scene framed by other stonework. It was, Emma thought, something like a stained-glass window petrified.

"The old country," Emma said, pointing to the topmost panel. "Where the family comes from."

"Yes," Eleanor said, her frog's voice brightening with a touch of pride. "Before all our troubles, before the betrayals and the lies. When the gods were with us."

"I'm not sure I understand. What gods?"

"Feh," Eleanor spat. "The memory is in your blood and still you ignore it. Do you think all this, our family, the masters, these dark woods even, exist for the love of the god of the Jews? Or thanks to the death of a measly carpenter's son?"

Emma swallowed thinking of the prayers she'd offered up with her husband by her side. The psalms they had read together. The vows of love, obedience and honor. The bonds of marriage before reverend and God. But then, there were

THE WOUNDED KING

the other times—the dalliance with Lady Ophelia Merritt so many years ago and the honeyed words of Anwar al-Beshi in Cairo. When had she felt the presence of God more? "I, that is—"

"You see the truth," Eleanor exclaimed. "You know because your blood knows. Ducheski blood."

Emma looked up at the top panel and its lurid portrayal of paganism. The carved figures—little men and women displaying the warped proportions of medieval woodcut or stained glass—worshiping at the feet of goat-headed devils and twisting, winged serpents. "These were your, our gods?"

"Byelobog the White King," Emma said, indicating a crown and two leering eyes in the very background of the panel with a rap of her cane, "the Coiled Dragon"—rap—"Shaagra the Queen of Beasts, and Orik the Prince of Skin." Rap, rap. "These were the gods of the woods, the hills and the blood of our veins and we honored them."

Emma looked at the next panel. The naked men and women, their screeching devil-gods at their sides, were hemmed in by cassocked priests on one side and turbaned riders on the other. "Until the Gospel came," she said, "and the Turks."

"Bah, the gods would have torn them to bloody chunks and spat them back to their pretty churches and across the hills. They would have—"

"But they didn't," Emma said. "Your gods abandoned you."

The zeal left the old woman's voice and she looked away, her gaze falling, Emma noted, on the carved figures of priests, bearing the cross forward into pagan lands. "No, not before we abandoned them."

Emma glanced at the carvings. "I don't see…"

"No, the priests and masons who made this knew nothing of the treachery of the last priest of our blood, Ehovar Krevcheski."

Emma had heard the name Krevcheski before. In the twisted, terrifying world of Ducheski lineage, it was one of the oldest matrilineal names, but one rarely used.

"He was the priest of the blood, Ehovar was, and the

wise women respected him. But there had been omens, stories that he was jealous of the secrets reserved for the women of the blood. He led the sacrifices, but only they could listen to the whispers of the flesh and wind. He spoke to the gods—but the old women *listened*.

"So when the harlot came from the south, he was welcoming. Her skin was perfect and her breasts full and firm, that one." Eleanor advanced on her niece. "Like you and your daughter. Beautiful and poisonous."

"Who was she?"

"None know. A whore of the Nailed Christ, perhaps. She came and whispered to Ehovar that he could have the god's powers all his own. That he could rise and take their place. That he and his sons could slaughter the wise women and wear their holy ears on necklaces of bone and gut-twine. The land would run red with god-blood and the sons of Ehovar would reign." Eleanor coughed. "She promised it and the fool priest believed."

"What happened?"

"What do you think? Ehovar's sons listened to their father and made into the camps of the wise women. They raped the daughters and killed the mothers. They gutted their very sisters like goats for Shaagra. And all the while, Ehovar performed his last, greatest rite. He called the gods and spat the blood of their daughters at them. He burned the altars and pissed his spite in the intricate circles of hatred. He rejected the bonds of his very blood and abjured the gods, hoping to swallow their own might into his heart. He would become the god of the mountains and woods, he said."

The image of this pagan rite of rites grew in Emma Blake's mind until it resonated with some deep part of herself. The calling of gods whispered of the secrets of Cairo to her, of the rituals Anwar al-Beshi had cast to raise the Sleeping Lord. She thought of the Tremere's examinations of her and knew the black sorcery—always powered by blood—existed here in Austria and in England too. And for all her revulsion at the thought, part of her thrilled to the idea of these bloody and savage rites.

Eleanor continued, seemingly unaware of the effect her

words were having. "And so, feeling that the gods were coming to him, their treasonous high priest, Ehovar turned to his concubine, to the harlot who had told him the secret of god killing. And she smiled, and wrapped her cloak over his nakedness, and turned away. She left him and the gods arrived and his rituals could not save him." A dark glee entered Eleanor's cloudy eyes. "Shaagra's wolves ate his manhood and ripped out his liver. Byelobog's frost shattered his eyes and filled his lungs. The dragon-children bored into his heart. And Orik forged a dagger from Ehovar's own leg-bone the better to slice the wayward priest's raw, bloody flesh."

"So, he failed." Would she end up like that, consumed by the black sorcery her unlife had become?

"To become a god? Of course. But the damage was done. The priesthood fell to lesser lines. Our raped women birthed twisted children who showed Orik's displeasure. The land rejected us as we had rejected it. All the remaining sons of Ehovar were eaten by Shaagra's wolves over the course of a single year and what women were left had to mate with foreigners and degenerates. Our family, which had been the chosen of the gods, became weak, small and hated by them."

"And the Christians? The Turks?"

"When they came, there were only weak priests and deaf women to lead the people. The country was planted with crosses and crescents. The other families blamed us— and rightly perhaps—and chased us from the land. To here and to the warlocks called Tremere."

"The masters," Emma said by rote.

"For now." Eleanor spat on the ground and uttered a phrase in some long-forgotten language. "For now."

* * *

"You will forgive my little deception, I hope, Herr Blake." In the two days since their meeting on Karmeliterplatz, Herr Kohler had apparently not had any more success in taming his gray, flyaway mane. "Precautions are necessary for those who follow our calling, *stimmt's?*"

He was sitting in one of the chairs in the rooms Blake had taken at the Hotel Herzog. Blake was in the other chair of the suite, Kohler's small pistol pointed at his chest. Retired soldier that he was, Lord Blake weighed his chances of disarming the old Austrian before he could discharge that weapon. Slim, he concluded, given that the hammer was already cocked. He might be able to dive to the side, or push the gun aside before it fired, but *might* was a great deal less than *certainly would*. He'd resort to that only if there were no other choice.

There was, of course, the matter of the other two men in the room. One was a burly sort Blake would have taken for a stevedore had he been lurking along the nearby canal. He had just finished securing Gareth Ducheski to the bed with heavy ropes to supplement the chain Blake used. The other man was reed-thin and seemed less dangerous. He was busy removing items from a traveling bag, each wrapped in cloth, and laying them on a table placed along one side of the room. He wore the collar of a priest.

"Why did you send me to that bloody monastery?" Blake asked. He'd spent all of the previous day traipsing around the village of Klosterneuburg, negotiating access to its monastery and the Chapel of St. Leopold therein. The monks had been less than welcoming.

"To observe you, Herr Blake. Friends of ours watched your progress and reported back. We wished to see how you would react to being stymied."

Blake bit back an answer. He'd reacted by coming back to Vienna and, in the relative privacy of these rooms, taking out his frustration with a belt on Ducheski's damnable flesh. He'd collapsed out of sheer exhaustion late that night and woken to find these men in his rooms.

"Now tell me," Kohler went on. "How did you come to search for the Society of Leopold?"

"My wife and daughter have been taken from me."

The priest muttered something in Latin and Kohler said, "Amen. But as sad as that is, it does not explain how you came to be on Karmeliterplatz looking for soldiers of Christ."

"In my overcoat. The left side pocket."

The larger man brought the coat forward and fished out Blake's Bible from the pocket he'd indicated. He handed the leather-bound book to Kohler, who took it in his left hand and kept his pistol trained with his right. He flipped open the book on his lap, glancing down.

"*Verflucht!* I thought these had all been destroyed."

"Pardon? That was given to me by a nun in England."

"With the best intentions, I'm sure," the Austrian said. "And if you are being truthful, it is all for the best, but I'm sure you understand that such a record of chapter houses is a serious risk for us. The agents of the Devil are everywhere."

As much as he would like to deny it, Blake had to agree. They were.

"Will you accept baptism, Herr Blake?"

The seeming change of subject was jarring and he took a moment to answer. "Excuse me?"

"We face the evils of Satan armed with the love of Christ and His church," Kohler said. "The evil cannot stand against that. If you are an enemy of ours, neither will you."

"I have already been baptized, sir."

"You are Catholic, Herr Blake?"

"Anglican, sir."

"Only baptism in the true church can protect the soul, Herr Blake."

"Now listen here, I will not sit here and have my faith—"

"Herr Blake!" Kohler punctuated his exclamation with an emphatic pointing of his pistol toward Blake's chest. "This is not a time for debate. Will you accept to be baptized?"

"You are holding the gun, sir. I don't suppose that I have much choice."

"Do you fear death so much, Herr Blake?"

He had an urge to throttle the old fool, pistol or no. That would end this whole mad business one way or the other. Instead, he said, "Either call your priest or shoot me, sir, but let us get on with it."

A half-hour later, James Blake had rejected Satan along with his works and pomps, and had been baptized in the name of the Father, Son and Holy Ghost by a priest who spoke to him entirely in Latin, Herr Kohler acting as translator. He was wiping the oil and water from his brow and head, when the priest headed toward the bed.

"*Und er?*" the priest asked.

"*Warten Sie,*" Kohler answered, then turned to face Blake. He'd put away his pistol when the baptismal ceremony was complete, but his hand reached in to that pocket now. "I am very happy you have joined us in the Church, Herr Blake, but I must now ask you about your choice of companions."

"He is a cur," Blake said, wiping the last ablutions from his head, "but a useful one."

"The scarring and wounds," Kohler said, "they are inhuman."

"His flesh heals more quickly than I have ever seen. Wounds that have cost many good soldiers their lives are mended in days or weeks. Some in minutes. But they always leave terrible scars."

The Austrian withdrew his hand—sans pistol—to stroke at his goatee. "*Ja, ja*. I have read about such things. One text in particular speaks of wild men from the Black Forest, pagan infernalists who worshiped a wolf-idol and had such unholy resilience. That was centuries ago."

"This man was no wild barbarian. He was a solicitor in London until last Christmas, and all the while cavorting with the undead things who stole my wife and child."

"A lawyer? An educated man, then. Fascinating."

At that moment the priest exclaimed and pointed at Ducheski. "*Mein Gott*," he said, "*Das Wasser. Sehen Sie*." In the cleric's outstretched hand was a silver flask—the very one he'd used to pour holy water three times over Blake's head.

"*Vater!*," Kohler exclaimed, rising out of his chair, "*Ich hatte Sie doch gebeten zu warten!*"

Blake and Kohler made it to the bed at almost the same moment and saw the strange effect that had caused the priest to exclaim. He'd evidently poured a small quantity of the blessed water onto Gareth Ducheski's scarred and raw cheek. Blisters were growing there at a prodigious rate and the man began to thrash against his bonds as the effect intensified. Before the very eyes of the four men—for even the stalwart guard left his post at the suite's door to come see what was happening—the small quantity of water dug a visible furrow in Ducheski's right cheek. It was not so much a wound opening up as a channel eroding, like rainwater through mud.

"Bloody fools," Blake spat and reached for a nearby

linen. He daubed at the water and blisters until the effect stopped. "I need this man if I'm to save my family! He knows too much."

"Does he know where these creatures are keeping them?"

"Of course," Blake snapped, "it's not far from here."

"In Vienna proper?" Kohler seemed shocked.

"Near the university. Fortschritt, he called it."

Kohler didn't move for almost a full minute, simply staring like a mute. Blake wasn't quite sure how to react when the old man flung his arms around him and then promptly took to hooting and dancing around the room like a castaway who spots a ship on the horizon.

Chapter Five

Sunset on the night of Saturday the 22nd came just before 8:00 p.m., leaving Victoria and Regina several hours before their scheduled encounter with Herr Schiller at the Café Landtmann. Baron Grünwald, the man they had followed from the Opera upon their early arrival, seemed largely incapable of resisting the charms of his two English guests and granted them full access to the suites he maintained at the Hotel Sacher. That these charming ladies requested that the inner suite be inviolate during the day seemed to him an endearing eccentricity rather than any real imposition. In any case his days were spent with wife and child, and the Widow Sacher, who ran the hotel, had made it her policy to indulge the requests of well-heeled patrons like the baron.

Lady Regina woke less traumatically that night than the last. The day had again passed in insensate slumber, uninterrupted by dreams of any kind, but her return to consciousness was sudden and complete this time. Her limbs returned to full mobility with a thought and she felt the rush of too-cold blood in her veins within moments.

"Much better," she said, mostly to herself. "I feel more prepared to deal with this whole affair tonight."

"Confidence is a valuable tool," Victoria said, from her place at the large vanity across the room, "but do not become foolhardy. We are still in a very precarious position."

"Of course, but surely with the assistance of your friend Mr. Schiller—"

"Herr Schiller is no friend of mine, Regina."

"He was reluctant to endanger himself, I admit, but he did welcome us into his home. I thought the two of you were acquainted previously."

"He is a correspondent of Lady Merritt's, not mine." Victoria looked at Regina through the reflection of the mirror, pausing from her application of rouge to do so. "I mentioned her name in my letter to him and again when we arrived at the gardens, so in deference to her he heard us out. It is a long journey from politeness to friendship."

Regina approached. Still freshly woken, she wore only her light nightdress and the weave of the Persian carpet dug itself into the tender underside of her bare feet. "How old is Herr Schiller?"

"Such questions are rarely raised in polite company, you understand," Victoria raised one hand to her own shoulder, to receive Regina's. The girl, now standing behind her, gave it with ease. "But it is my impression he was born sometime during the War of Spanish Succession. I imagine he was remade by some fool no more than six years later."

"That boy is then…"

"Approaching two centuries of age, yes. All of it spent in the awkward, pique-prone shape of a man-child."

A wave of something not unrelated to nausea swept through Regina, threatening to collapse her legs under her. Matters of age seemed to be a hidden code among the kindred of the night society, much like rank and precedence in the best London dinner parties—a social force so clearly understood by all it need never be discussed or advertised. In Paris, before she herself had been remade, Regina had determined that Miss Ash was herself a creature aged more than two centuries. They had both then come under the sway of a mad priest among the undead, a certain Father Anatole, whom Regina felt must be older still. Nevertheless, the thought of the cherubic Schiller having last drawn breath before a Hanover sat on the English throne was a far heavier blow to her sense of equilibrium. She too would be frozen in this physical moment, in the shape of a young woman while all those whom she loved aged and perished. She could never be another's mother, sister or child, for the course of years would inevitably destroy those heavenly ordained relations. Even a babe born this very night would slip withered and aged into his grave long before even the merest hint of age played across Regina's features.

"In God's name," she said at last in a voice breaking with emotion, "what have you done to me?"

Victoria turned to face her charge. "What I thought best."

Regina backed up on wobbling legs. "What have you done?"

"Would you rather I have imprisoned you in chains of blood? Made you drink from my veins until you were a willing slave, thus ensuring your silence? That was the other option. That, or I could have simply ended your life altogether."

"You *have* killed me," Regina said. "My Lord and Savior, please…"

"This not an easy existence, but it was the least odious of horrible choices." Victoria extended her hand. "I will help you carry the burden as best I can, darling."

Regina Blake had received what was an exceptional education for one of her gender. Not so much in the quality of learning—although that was impressive in itself—but in the liberties of thought and action her guardians had allowed her. Her father had treated her with respect and tolerated boyish escapades that would have scandalized his more traditional peers in London. Nevertheless, physical violence was not part of Regina's education. The idea of lifting a fist against another person, most especially another woman, was simply not part of Lady Regina's spectrum of action. At least not in any circumstances approaching normalcy.

Thus, she did not immediately recognize the compulsion boiling up from within her. She barely noted the tunneling of her vision, so that only Miss Ash's beseeching, hypocritical face filled her eyes. She felt the hot tension of blood charging through her muscles without noting it as odd. When she opened her mouth she honestly expected to spit an invective or berate her erstwhile sponsor. Instead all that emerged was a hateful hiss shot from between long, pointed canines.

Her last coherent thought was, *How dare she offer me help now!* Then the ball of rage and hate that had once resembled Regina Blake exploded in a mad leap headlong toward her prey, teeth gnashing and hands extended and hooked as if simple nails were deadly talons.

Victoria's seat was empty before Regina reached it, so the girl took out an iota of her bottomless rage on the offending piece of furniture. Her delicate hands smashed and tore the chair to scraps and tinder with little effort, but she could not spare the thoughts to find that odd. Instead she turned on her heels, searching the posh suite for the murderess who'd escaped once, but surely not again.

There! Standing still, but balanced on the balls of her slippered feet like the coward she was. Regina leaped again, and again was too slow. The phantasm that had been her prey dissolved into a blur of motion, like a train at full steam or a horse at full gallop—nothing but a streak of color. Regina slammed into the wall behind where Victoria had been, and tore at the paper, plaster and wood. She was dimly aware of a prickle in her digits, but did not let it distract her. She turned again—

The slap was swift and powerful, resounding like a whip-crack and turning Regina's face away. A hot stinging radiated from her cheek. She spotted Victoria, but she was across the room. Regina made to lunge at her—

Slap! This second blow made the first seem like child's tap. It struck her opposite cheek and she had one clear instant of perception in which she saw Victoria, mid-movement, bringing her open palm to bear. A terrible cracking sound reverberated through Regina's skull and she collapsed onto her hands and knees.

For what seemed like an eternity she just stayed like that, looking through blurred vision as several teeth tumbled in a mess from her mouth. She wondered why she could not seem to close her mouth, and noted with some dismay that the fingers on both hands were torn and bloody. There seemed to be a carpenter's nail stuck crookedly in the fleshy webbing between her right-hand index and middle fingers, in fact.

Slowly, sound returned to Regina's world. She heard Victoria saying, "Stay calm, darling, everything will be all right soon." Then came an awareness of terrible, wild pain, and right after that, darkness and the dull thud of her face on the wet carpet.

***

Four of them walked down the main hall on the third story of Fortschritt, and that in and of itself had meaning.

In a society dedicated to the pursuit of the occult, eldritch and arcane, very little can truly be called coincidental. Rite and ritual seeps into every aspect of existence. Initiates and masters alike choose clothing and accessories to accentuate or undermine symbols in the hidden alphabet of the society's arts. They schedule events to coincide with particular alignments of the stars or numerological oddities of the calendar. In Vienna, as in London, a number of such societies were flourishing in the autumn of 1888. Theosophist circles, Rosicrucian orders and Templar revivalist brotherhoods rubbed shoulders in the tawniest circles of Central Europe's tawniest city.

Most of these orders had precious little to show for all their ritual. They had raised no demons and if they had miraculously augmented certain members' fortunes, it was due as much to the presence of aristocratic patrons in the membership as to some great mystic working. For all their pretense at uncovering the secrets of the ages, the vast majority were little more than social clubs dressed up in cultish attire.

The *Hermetica Aedicula ex Tremere*—the Hermetic House of Tremere—was very much more. Unlike the dilettantes of the rose and cross, the Tremere had faced death and damnation and stolen power from them both. They had a continuous history going back to the nights of Charlemagne. Some in their number could make fire dance with a wave of their hand. Others might, by sheer force of will and manipulation of the hidden keys of the firmament, make a man lift from the ground as if he were no heavier than a feather. In certain of the sancta of Fortschritt, demons had been summoned and bound. In others, lead had become gold. Homunculi and scrying pools, warding circles and ritual knives stained brown with blood were all in regular use there.

Added to all this, the Tremere were unliving vampires as well as practiced sorcerers. They called themselves thaumaturges—makers of miracles—but others among the undead used less generous terms: warlocks, witches, blood sorcerers.

Thus, among the Tremere, rites and symbols were

everywhere. Even unplanned happenstance was understood to be part of a grand design to be deciphered, mastered and enslaved. The circumstances behind the construction of Fortschritt itself were a perfect example of this.

In 1857, the Emperor Franz-Josef, then a much younger man, came under attack on the very site where the great chantry would rise. A Hungarian madman, armed with a knife, decided to take the Hapsburg monarch's life and very nearly managed to do so. Imperial blood spilled on the still-forming Ringstrasse and the blow would have been fatal had not a votive token Franz-Josef wore about his neck become wedged between his breast and the knifepoint.

To the Catholic Viennese , this was evidence of saintly intervention on their monarch's behalf and there was talk of building a church on the site. To the Tremere magi it was evidence of a rite unfolding. Imperial blood spilled, sanctifying a binding circle. The image of a saint marred to save a life. Martyrdom symbolized and reenacted. There was power in such things and the order sabotaged the church project and built Fortschritt in its stead. In its very center was a patch of unbroken ground with a brownish stain of Hapsburg blood. Nearby a case held the talisman that saved the emperor's life, the monarch's bloodstained jacket, the knife that had shed the blood, and the perfectly preserved severed hand of the assassin himself. The eldritch architecture of events had been perceived, usurped and made the Tremere's own.

Thus, that four of their number walked down the hall toward the sanctum of a fifth had meaning. Four meant the cardinal points and the classical elements. Two sets of opposites that together formed the whole of space and creation. Unity through diversity.

They passed through the ornate doors of the chantry's central library, a large open room dominated by reading carrels, glass display cases and walls of bound books that ascended to the domed ceiling some four stories above them. Curving mezzanines interrupted the climb of the stacks, with wrought-iron spiral stairs connecting them to the main reading room. Doors to private sitting rooms and special collections dotted the mezzanine walls at precise intervals. The marble floor concealed an intricate pattern of alchemically transmuted base metal that served as a warding circle, protecting the Tremere Order's greatest treasures—its books.

Anton Wellig, one of the four magi, could not resist a quick glance at some of the stacks. There, bound in green leather, were the notebooks of Nicolo Gambetti di Roma, one of the leading members of the order during the Renaissance. Gambetti had unfortunately fed the flames of an inquisitor's pyre, but not before putting his research to paper.

Dr. Claas Drescher, the stout German who was leading the quarto through the chantry, stopped at the bottom of the left-hand stairs up to the first mezzanine. A light iron chain was draped from one banister to the other and he unlatched it, muttering something—an incantation, a prayer, a curse—that Wellig didn't quite catch. He then stood aside and let the only woman in their party proceed first up the stairs.

Wellig felt a chill and bowed his head as the ethereal, raven-haired beauty passed him to begin her ascent. Lady Meerlinda was thin as a reed and with skin so white that it reminded him of lilies. Eight hundred years ago, she had been among the cabal of mortal magi who damned themselves by choosing endless unlife over death. Wellig owed her the very eldritch blood in his veins.

"Herr Wellig," Dresher said, raising his hand to wave him up the stairs, allowing him to follow closely behind Meerlinda. "Dr. Bainbridge," the German then said, addressing the fourth member of their party, "wait for us here in the sitting room, please."

Wellig looked over his shoulder to see Drescher latching the chain behind him, leaving Edward Bainbridge behind. Bainbridge, a portly and all too jovial Englishman, gave Wellig a quick glance, his eyes full of contrition, even pity.

Wellig's blood boiled and he had the sudden urge to rip Bainbridge's head form his meaty shoulders, or better yet to do the same to Claas Drescher and the rest of the lickspittles in the so-called Fatherhouse. The German had planned this precisely, jettisoning Bainbridge as the three ascended the left-hand, or sinister, stairs. The stability of the four elements collapsed and Wellig was suddenly vulnerable, stripped of the man who was his purported ally. Everything was ritual and Wellig felt he just might be the sacrifice. Drescher's hand on the banister made a disconcerting metal-on-metal sound as they rose.

They made a quarter revolution around the mezzanine, stopping at the southern-most point in the whole library. There, a wooden door bore a brass plaque with the somewhat overblown title of TRISMAGESTOS SALON. Drescher opened the door for Meerlinda and Wellig, then entered the salon and closed the door behind them.

The salon was a tasteful reading room, with tall windows on the southern wall giving a nice view of the University of Vienna and the tower of the Town Hall beyond. The eastern wall easily surpassed the southern, however. It bore a large frame displaying under glass six parchment pages of tightly scripted Greek. The writings of Hermes the Thrice-Greatest, who gave the salon his name. The western wall was decidedly mundane, with a single bookcase stacked with leather-bound volumes, a scroll-case, and roll-top desk where one might study and take notes.

Four comfortable chairs were arranged at the cardinal points of the room, and sitting in the eastern one, its back a mere few feet from the medieval parchment said to be the earliest known transcription of the *Tabula Smaragdina*, the "Emerald Tablet" that formed the basis for Hermetic alchemy, was Ardan Lane. He had a pleasant, calm expression on his face. "Please, have a seat."

Wellig could, of course, try to usurp another's seat here, but it hardly seemed worthwhile. Instead he sat in the western seat, facing Lane, while Drescher took the southern seat and Meerlinda the northern. Wellig was here to be judged, again.

"Herr Wellig, perhaps you can explain why you saw fit to allow Frau Blake to leave the confines of the chantry." Ardan Lane used a conciliatory tone. Inquiring rather than attacking. "There seems to be some question about the wisdom of such a course of action."

"She is my childe," Wellig said. "Seeing the city is part of her education." His eyes kept wandering to the Hermetic texts behind his interrogator—although he knew the writings by heart, he could not help but scour such fragments for any hint of additional revelation. It was in the occultist's nature to do so, and he knew very well it was no coincidence his was the only seat facing such a tempting distraction.

"You think us fools, Wellig," Claas Drescher said. "Last month, you called the Englishwoman an experiment in breeding. Now she is your dear childe? I think not."

Wellig noticed Meerlinda raise an ebon brow at Drescher's accusation, but when she said nothing, he chose to respond. "I said she was the end product of experimentation in breeding and eugenics. I have spent several lifetimes refining the blood of the Ducheski family and Emma Blake, or Emiliana Ducheski to use her maiden name, is the end result of that. That does not preclude her visiting the Café Landtmann, I hope."

"She's done more than that," Drescher said. "She and that elderly aunt of hers went on a tour of the woods. They stray far afield."

"That elderly aunt is firmly under my grasp," Wellig answered. "She monitors my childe in my stead." Looking squarely at Drescher allowed Wellig to face away from Lady Meerlinda, which relieved much of the pressure on his soul. The German was a pain, but Wellig had faced many enemies in his existence and he was more than happy to give as good as he got. "Do you shackle your Serbian like a dog, Herr Drescher?"

"Anastasz is a Croat, not a Serb."

"Regardless, the question remains," Wellig pressed on.

"Unlike yours," Drescher said, "my childe is neither prone to wild fits of rage nor subject to some ill-defined blood relationship to an ancient creature like Mithras of London."

"Gentlemen, please," Lane put in. "Petty bickering is pointless. Herr Wellig is right that the traditions of our society make the education of his childe both a paramount concern and principally his own business. However, Herr Drescher's point is a good one. I visited Frau Blake in the warding chamber on the evening of the eighth of this month and found her in the grips of a wild rage. Were that to repeat itself while she was wandering the streets of our fair city, the results would be unfortunate."

Wellig bit back the urge to leap across the room and plant the fangs straining in his gums into Lane's oh-so-pleasant jugular. Where was the Tremere order he had joined all those cold years ago? The order of magi so daring they'd embraced undeath in the name of their own power and enlightenment? The order where each magus pursued his studies in the chantry he mastered, largely free from the interference of faraway superiors? Modernity had brought many strengths with it, but the addition of petty bureaucracy and farcical inquiries were not, he thought, among them.

This whole inquest was, after all, a charade. The opinions of Lane, Drescher and all the others posing questions were of very little import. The only people who truly mattered were the elders of the Tremere's Council of Seven, the archmagi who sat atop the order's supposedly pyramidal scheme. Elders like Lady Meerlinda and Lord Etrius himself, the high regent of the entire order. Etrius was certainly present at Fortschritt, but he'd refused to even answer Wellig's requests to see him. Lane, Drescher and the rest played at authority, but if Etrius or Meerlinda decided Wellig's activities were worthwhile, then he was untouchable. If they decided he was too troublesome, he was as good as ash on the morning wind.

So, although it was pointless and wasteful, he had little choice but to play the game.

"Emiliana was fatigued and underfed from weeks of examination at Herr Drescher's hands when she lost control, Mr. Lane," he said. "Blood-hunger can drive any of us mad. So long as she remains relatively sated, there is no particular risk in having her among the herd."

"What a convenient assertion," Drescher said.

"You are right," Wellig said to the German. "To have a blood-hungry predator loose among the beautiful Viennese is far too dangerous. We must lock up all members of the order lest they lose control. And perhaps hunt down all of our erstwhile kindred in the city as well. Certainly, if we can't risk a closely watched childe on the streets, we can't risk the mass of us in the same condition. I suppose you'll want to be the first to cage himself in the name of your precious kine."

"How dare you—!" Drescher started, but cut himself short.

Wellig followed the German's gaze and saw the hint of smile on Lady Meerlinda's bloodless lips. He'd scored a telling point against these fools.

"No," Lane said, continuing with the pretense that he was somehow in charge, "that won't be necessary. Your point is well made. After all, who of us is free of the beastly urges of our nature?"

***

The first thing Regina was aware of was the hunger. Like a slow-burning fire spreading from her stomach, it intruded on the blissful nothingness of unconsciousness. Victoria's face followed shortly thereafter, much more welcome. Her rust-red locks framed her face so perfectly that for just a moment, Regina thought she might cry.

That single implication of movement brought with it an immediate, horrific sense of her own body. She was prepared—as much as one ever is—for pain, and there was indeed pain. The dull, deep ache in her jaw; the hot needles in her fingers. Far worse, however, was the crawling, itching, burning sensation of *things* moving through her flesh. A certainty suddenly overwhelmed her that thousands upon thousands of beetles were feasting, burrowing and nesting in her hand, her cheeks and her throat. She began to convulse.

"Shh, darling," Victoria said, her voice full of sisterly concern. "All is well. You are healing. Do not fight it."

Regina raised a hand to fend off whatever was consuming her, but some quality in Victoria's soothing tones—the ring of experience, perhaps—worked to quell the wave of panic. Regina looked instead at the hand she had

THE WOUNDED KING

raised and saw its pitiful condition. Two fingernails were completely broken and a third was utterly missing, her ring finger's tip raw and bloody. An angry gash ran down her index finger and the white of bone peeked through its mangled middle joint.

The girl wondered why her hand felt as if it should be crawling with burrowing, feasting insects. Soon enough, the answer came as a sheen of skin and tissue crept across the exposed finger-joint as if by magic. The angry edges of the gash closed like the lips of some obscene mouth, sealing to one another without even a scar. The tip of her ring-finger sprouted a new nail, strong and true.

Acting entirely by instinct, she brought her hand to her chin and pushed slightly down and left. She felt a jolt as her jaw slipped back into its hinge under her skin. The crawling-bug sensation of preternatural healing coursed there—muscles and cartilage knitting, teeth sprouting from empty sockets.

"Very good," Victoria said. "Can you speak?"

"Y… yes…" Regina answered, with only a slight croak. "What, what happened?"

"You lost control, my dear." Victoria voice was almost devoid of reproach. "It has passed, however."

"I tried to kill you." She swallowed. "With my bare hands."

"You might have succeeded, too, had I not been what I am. What we both are."

A flash of emotions—revulsion, dread, anger—boiled up in Regina. "Yes, you—"

"Wait," Victoria interrupted. "You've exhausted yourself. Please, just wait a moment."

Victoria's face vanished from Regina's field of vision and the girl realized her companion must have been kneeling over her prone form. Gathering what little strength she could muster, Regina rose to a seating position. The expected swell of vertigo did not materialize, but in its place came twin shocks. First, the condition of the room—here, a smashed chair and scattered maquillages; there a hole torn in the plaster and paper of the wall itself. Second, the knowledge that she had done all this herself.

Victoria was in the adjoining room, the vestibule of the suites, whispering. "This way, you naughty boy." She emerged, leading a young man dressed in the red uniform of the Hotel Sacher's discreet staff. A black silk scarf was tied around his eyes as a blindfold and he had his arms extended forward as if he expected to find a wall at any minute.

"*Was?*" he asked as Victoria led him past a bewildered Regina and toward the bed.

"Just like on the train," Miss Ash whispered to Regina as they passed her. Then to the boy—whom Regina had to admit seemed quite handsome indeed—"Onto the bed, darling." She pushed the boy over and he fell onto the plush mattress face-first.

The boy let out a small laugh, rolled onto his side and reached for the blindfold. Victoria joined him on the bed quickly enough to arrest that movement. "No, no, my darling." She gathered her skirts in order to straddle him and leaned forward, her left hand holding down his right (with which he'd tried to clear his vision) and her left loosening the buttons of his jacket. "Just relax," she whispered, her lips a bare inch from his ear.

Regina looked at Victoria, who caught her eye and shifted slightly, encouraging the boy to extend his pinned arm off the edge of the bed. The hand hung there, exposing the wrist and the large purple veins there. Regina was moving before the thought even made it to her brain.

The hunger. It was all she could think of. But it wasn't food, drink or mere sustenance she craved, but the hot, tangy stuff of life itself. Even after her explosion of rage and the freakish healing of her terrible wounds, her skin was cool and her heart still. When her hand grasped the boy's, and her lips made it to the taught skin of his wrist, she felt the heat and the pulse there and had to have it. When the twin enamel-covered daggers in her mouth sliced through the skin and past the arterial wall, the hot gush was like nothing she had had ever felt.

She was dimly aware of the boy's own moans of ecstasy, of the orgasmic spasms that wracked him, of Victoria leaning in to add her own predatory pleasure to his abused flesh.

But all that was eclipsed by the rich, coppery flavor of the blood rushing down her throat and suffusing her every cell. Every second brought her pleasure to a new and heretofore unknown plateau. She never wanted it to end.

"Enough," Victoria hissed and pushed Regina away from the boy.

She fell on her behind, swallowing still at the last traces of heady blood on her lips. "I want more," she said.

"Are you ready to dig a grave for this boy?"

Regina looked, really looked at the hotel valet sprawled on the satin bedspread. Victoria had thrown open his crimson high-collared jacket, and Regina could see the frightening pallor of his flesh, and smell the salty sheen of fever-chill sweat rising there. "N– no," he said, unsure if she was lying or not.

"Good." Victoria buttoned his jacket in quick movements. She then got off the bed, slipped her arms under the unconscious valet and lifted him with an ease that belied her slender form. "Wait here." She took the boy out of the suite and returned alone ten minutes later.

"Where did you take him?"

"The other suite on this floor. It's unoccupied and he had the key. I laid him on the bed, where I hope he will either sleep through the day or be found by a maid. We took a great deal from him. He may fall ill."

"My God. Won't he report this?"

"You forget the blindfold, and the confusion. He'll remember a night of intense pleasure, something he himself was complicit in."

Regina swallowed again. "I see."

"You must get dressed quickly," Victoria said. "We are to meet Herr Schiller in less than an hour."

***

"Tell us about these masters of yours," Kohler said. "Tell us about Fortschritt."

James Blake was watching the old Austrian work on Ducheski. He was leaning against the sill of the window and he found himself often turning to get a gulp of fresh air and look at the Carmelite church across the way. The smell of bile and effluvia was overpowering.

Ducheski, for his part, was on the floor, spitting up blood while Kohler made demands of him.

It was now late into the evening. Once Blake's baptism was done, they'd pressed him for more information and he'd told them most of what he knew. He'd explained that his wife Emma's family was somehow in league with the undead. Her relatives could not abide her living a normal life and had dragged her into their dark clutches last Christmas. He neglected to mention that she had had several other brushes with the occult, from the wretched creature who'd caged her in a Southwark workhouse shortly after their marriage, to the Arab sorcerer who'd seduced her in Cairo two years ago. He did allow that he had at first despaired at his wife's fate, hoping against hope that she were truly dead or that if transformed, she could be forgotten. Their daughter Regina had not accepted that coward's answer and so had gone into the night to find her mother. Now, she too was missing.

Kohler had been especially interested in the role of Gareth Ducheski, Blake's prisoner and Emma's less-than-human cousin. And with good reason: Not only had Ducheski attempted to murder both Blake and his daughter, not only had he killed John Claremont (a friend of the Blake family), but he had boasted that Fortschritt was Emma's ultimate destination and the nest of the undead things who had descended on James Blake's family.

They had brought the wretch, half-mad with the pain of his marred face, to the flat on Karmeliterplatz that served as a chapter house of the Society of Leopold in Vienna. Blake's Bible gave the impression of a veritable army of the Lord, but in actuality the erstwhile inquisitors of Vienna met in the sitting room of the apartment where Kohler had lived all his adult life, only a few doors down from the Strauss family house where he'd first caught sight of Blake. And if the chapter house was tawdry, the chapter proper was almost pathetic. The aging Kohler, the reedy priest (whose name was Father Metz), and the burly man Johann were the only "soldiers of God" in the city. They had had only occasional contact with any others who followed their calling in other cities, and had no idea how to call upon their aid. Still, they were the only help Blake could hope for.

Once at the flat, Kohler had insisted that they "put the question" to Ducheski, a process that involved a poker heated in a small hearth and the use of additional blessed items from Father Metz's liturgical repertoire. That had gone on to very little avail for several hours. Blake did not take part. He'd spent several weeks in August interrogating Ducheski while the man hung from a large hook in Blake's cellar, and he'd gotten precious little information. An hour after sunset, however, Kohler had hit on the idea of forcing the man to take the Eucharist. Given the effect of the holy water on the wretch, this had promise and Blake had stepped forward to participate.

Blake had held open Ducheski's mouth with the help of fireplace tongs while Johann and Kohler held him down. Father Metz had whispered a perfunctory "*Corpus Christi*" and placed the wafer in his mouth. Johann shifted then, Blake removed the tongs and they had cooperated to clamp Ducheski's jaw shut and force his chin toward the ceiling. He'd thrashed mightily, but finally swallowed.

When they'd released him, he'd collapsed and vomited up a good quart of blood and bile.

"Tell us!' Kohler demanded again. "What is the purpose of Fortschritt? Where is Emma Blake!"

Ducheski, blood caked on his cracked lips, looked up at the raving Austrian and smiled. "It's too late, you know," he said. "She's one of the masters now."

A wave of nausea blossomed in Blake's stomach. It had nothing to do with the stink in the small apartment.

"Who are these masters?" Kohler continued.

"Sorcerers," Ducheski said at last. "They are sorcerers who have conquered death."

Kohler kicked the man in the gut. "Only Jesus Christ can conquer death," he said, and Ducheski chuckled. He kicked him again.

"Wait," Blake said, stepping forward and putting a hand on the old man's shoulder. In the pregnant pause once he did so, Blake got a good measure of the men he was with: Kohler, succumbing to a terrible rage as he understood the scope of these creatures' infiltration of the world of men, his frail body panting with the effort; Metz, shrinking back from the gory truth of his calling; Johann looking on, excited by the violence.

Kohler stepped back and Blake crouched to look this beastly man in the eyes, or at least the face. "My wife was"— he caught himself—"*is* no witch."

"Are you so sure?"

Blake turned away, fighting to suppress the memory of his wife in May of 1886, naked and reveling in the ritual of a godforsaken Arab fanatic in Cairo. He and his friend and ally Othman al-Masri had found Emma, ritual scars across her flesh and a new incision traced between her bare breasts. Blake had thought she'd been intended as a sacrifice, but could she have been another form of participant. *Was* his wife a witch?

"Fortschritt," Blake. "What is it?"

"A library. A center of learning."

"Don't lie to me!"

Ducheski smiled his bloody-toothed smile. "The masters are sorcerers, scientists of the occult. Fortschritt is their university."

"A church of the damned," Kohler said, "right under our noses."

The elder Austrian must have given some signal because Johann stepped forward and rolled up his sleeves. Blake barely had the chance to step back before the giant Teuton was doing the work for which his fellow inquisitors had obviously chosen him.

Blake went back to the window and ignored the meat-on-meat slapping of Johann's blows.

***

Victoria and Regina made it to the Café Landtmann without a minute to spare. A well-dressed gentleman who smelled of fine cologne and finer apple liqueur held the door open for them to enter. He tipped his satin-brimmed hat in appreciation as they passed and then headed out into the night, suddenly regretting his decision to seek out divertissement in another establishment. Still, he'd told his drinking companions that he was leaving, and he was above all a man of his word.

Herr Schiller was not hard to pick out of the crowd. His diminutive form was propped on a large firm cushion laid on the seat of one of the booths at the back of the café. Regina was astonished to what point his presence was not remarkable, however. In a London club or well-appointed dining hall, an apparently prepubescent boy dressed in the eveningwear of a gentleman and acting the part without irony would have attracted stares, glares, shunning silence and in all likelihood forceful requests to vacate the premises reserved for proper company. Here, the other patrons paid him little or no heed, continuing in a variety of heated discussions. The wait staff—all men wearing white shirts along with black trousers, waistcoats and bowties—moved agilely up and down the aisles, bringing trays of coffees, liqueurs and an amazing assortment of sugary pastries.

One platter of confectioneries passed near Regina as she followed Victoria toward Schiller's table. She noted the aesthetic beauty of the fine little tartlets with shining berry fillings and the chocolate-stuffed puff pastries, and remembered having much loved such delicacies. But the idea of eating such a thing now seemed to her equivalent to bathing in desert sand or dressing in burlap sacks. It was possible, but it hardly seemed desirable or even sensible.

Herr Schiller's table was not empty when they arrived. Sitting with him was a tall, thin blond man with enough flair about him that he merited being called a dandy. His jacket was a perfect black, while his waistcoat and tie were of a vibrant green that matched the emerald hue of his eyes. Regina thought instantly of Miss Ash's own striking irises, but saw very little of her patron's warmth there. The man's full lips parted in a pleasant, if rakish, smile and he rose from his seat to welcome the two ladies. He wore not one, but two rings on his left hand.

"Miss Ash, Lady Regina," Schiller said in his accented English, "may I present Professor Anastasz di Zagreb, currently in residence at the library of Fortschritt."

"A pleasure," Victoria said as she took her seat.

"Professor," Regina added, trying to understand how such a popinjay could qualify for professorship, even among the undead. She was certain that he was no living man—some instinct told her that despite the flash of his smile and the vibrancy of his attire, he had none of the warm, true life she'd so recently tasted in the hotel houseboy. "Thank you for seeing us."

"Not at all, Milady, Miss Ash." His English was almost flawless—the refined tones of a university man, with only a hint of something more oriental to hint that the Queen's tongue was not his first. "Mr. Schiller's appeal to me on your behalf was quite moving."

"Thank you, Herr Schiller," Victoria said and received a polite nod from the centennial boy.

"I hope that you may also indulge me in some news of London. For all Vienna's glories, I find I still miss the energy of Queen Victoria's capital."

"I'm afraid," Victoria said, "that you would find cold welcome there these nights, professor. His Royal Highness has made clear that he holds certain prejudices…" She waved her hand in deference to politeness.

Di Zagreb allowed himself a slight chuckle and idly toyed with the silver spoon that accompanied his untouched coffee. "Against my colleagues and I, yes. That is a shame, but Dr. Bainbridge and a few others do manage to survive the disdain of the most noble of us."

Regina had met Dr. Bainbridge during the summer. A portly Englishman, he had hosted a soirée among the kindred of London and received a carefully worded snub from the undead prince of the capital, whom most referred to simply as His Royal Highness. It had, in fact, been Dr. Bainbridge who had provided her with the information to piece together that a member of the Hermetic House of Tremere had absconded with her mother. Di Zagreb was a member of that self-same occult society.

"Do you know Dr. Bainbridge well, Professor?" she asked.

"I know him professionally rather than personally," he said, casually making the spoon dance through his fingers. Between eye-blinks, it stopped its circuit and simply vanished. "My studies have led me to consult him on a few occasions, but until recently I had not had the pleasure of meeting him face to face."

He flinched his other hand, which Regina was sure had been resting on the white tablecloth all along, turned it over and opened it. The spoon was in its palm. Regina could not quite prevent herself from gaping, this simple act somehow seeming all the more astonishing amid a gathering of the unliving.

"Ha-ha!" Schiller exclaimed.

Di Zagreb smiled. "You must forgive me, Lady Regina. I have a weakness for prestidigitation and legerdemain that I have never been able to outgrow. Much to my betters' chagrin, I'm afraid."

Regina had the odd sensation of expecting herself to blush. She felt the discomfort of having been caught staring and looked down instinctually, but she was very much aware that the flush of blood rose-tinting her cheeks did not follow. Another small sign of her grave condition.

"Quite amusing, Professor," she said to cover her discomfort. "And what do you study beside the translocation of cutlery and the entertainment of foreign visitors?"

Schiller made a happy half-laugh, clearly enjoying the interplay at work here. Victoria simply observed.

"A great many things," di Zagreb said. "Above all, the fundamental properties of our condition and the vital fluid upon which it depends. I also dabble in economics."

Regina knew that it was important to continue this patter. Unless Schiller was deceiving them, di Zagreb could be of critical assistance in their search. It would not do to offend him or scare him off. Still, the topic presented itself and before she could quite tell herself it was not a good idea, she asked, "And is it reversible? Our condition?"

Schiller had been moving his cup on its fine saucer and the sudden shake of his hand resulted in a loud clink and the spillage of dark coffee. Regina caught a peripheral glance of Victoria's eyes, alight with warning, staring at her. None of the four vampires sitting in the back of the Café Landtmann spoke or moved for several minutes.

Then Anastasz di Zagreb's mouth surrendered a

delighted smile. "Brava, Lady Regina. You have the spirit of scholar, cutting directly to the most central point. But I'm afraid that if I knew the answer to that particular question, I would be a scholar of significantly greater standing than you find me tonight."

"By that you mean 'no,' Professor," Regina said rather than asked.

"I suppose I do, in practical terms at least." He raised his porcelain cup of coffee to his lips and put it back down, without taking an actual sip. "Now tell me about your mother."

Chapter Six

"This experiment of Wellig's has a childe? Already?" Claas Drescher, magus pontifex in the Hermetic House of Tremere, was wearing a brown woolen coat over a tweed suit. He appreciated precision in all things and this suit was well tailored to fit his barrel-shaped frame. His gray wooly beard was long enough to cover his collar and much of his cravat, but it was well clipped and his mustache was waxed.

His apprentice, Anastasz di Zagreb, favored fashions more daring. His sand-colored hair was properly coiffed and his own suit fit his reedy frame well, but his taste for jewelry— ring, tie-tacks, gemmed cufflinks and collar pins—made him a contrast to his master. His loyalty, however, was not in question. Herr Drescher had remade him and brought him into the hidden world of thaumaturgy and unlife and for that Anastasz would be eternally grateful. What was mere life compared to the eternity of undeath and the secrets of the blood?

"No, sir," he said. "Lady Blake did not remake this girl. Regina was her mortal daughter, presumably since embraced by the Englishwoman Victoria Ash."

"Ash," Drescher said, stroking his beard. "A red-haired beauty. Eyes the green of emerald?"

"Yes, precisely." *Of course*, Anastasz thought, *he remembers her from his time in London*. Drescher had spent a great deal of time in the English capital in the 1860s—where he had found, among other things, a Croatian immigrant with a penchant for the occult.

"She is no Englishwoman. I believe she is American or perhaps French."

The Croatian nodded. "I see. Regardless, she is Lady Regina's sire."

"She told you this?"

"Not in so many words, of course. She has the English facility with the subtleties of our condition." Anastasz smiled. "Lady Regina is her 'ward,' but she is also among our kindred and it was my impression from Herr Wellig's report that this was not the case last winter. So, unless some unseen other has remade our young Englishwoman and had Miss Ash serve as a surrogate…"

"Unlikely, I agree," Drescher said, then grew silent. His right hand, encased in a white silk glove, clenched with sudden anger. "*Verflucht!* I wish that fool Wellig would have learned some of that same discretion."

"Do you think he intended the daughter to come under Miss Ash's care?"

"No, precisely the opposite. I believe he took his childe carelessly and left a trail for the girl to follow. Damn his bull-headed medievalism!"

"He does seem somewhat oblivious to the dangers of modernity," Anastasz agreed. It was , he'd found, a not uncommon problem among those who had cheated death for centuries. Such conveniences as the telegraph, daguerreotypes and even rapid travel by train were just not part of their experience. They did not understand that word of an "undead horror" could spread faster than ever before. All vampires practiced an elaborate masquerade to hide their existence from the living (who, although weak, far outnumbered the undead), but kindred like Wellig tended to be slipshod in their practice of this tradition. Herr Drescher, despite his own age, thankfully understood the necessity of discretion.

"If this girl found her way this far, surely others could have," Drescher said. "All it will take is one more mistake and this whole business could become utterly disastrous for the order."

"It seems that Don Cerro and his American childe, Mr. Bell, have been in London since April," Anastasz said. He guessed that his sire knew this already—Cerro was an archon among the undead, one of those charged with enforcing the traditions that kept them all safe, and had been in Vienna with his new childe two years previous. There had been some trouble, and Herr Drescher likely kept an interest in the Spaniard's movements. Still, best not to assume. "I imagine he took note of the events there."

"Assuredly," Drescher said. He looked not at all pleased by his own certainty. "And did this Miss Ash and her childe have any demands?"

"No demands, but a request. Herr Schiller introduced us at the Café Landtmann and the Englishwomen petitioned my assistance in gaining access to Lady Blake."

"Why, precisely?"

"I believe Lady Regina—the childe—retains mortal affection for her mother and fears she has been abducted for purposes nefarious." Di Zagreb paused to allow his sire to respond, but filled the silence when he didn't. "Which, as it turns out, is relatively accurate. Had Herr Wellig's plans come to fruition, Lady Blake would be ash already."

"Perhaps, but Lady Blake is Mr. Wellig's childe and our traditions are very clear on this: he can do with her as he wishes. Even more, given that she was born into the Ducheski brood." Drescher said the last with undisguised disgust. "She was his to remake and his to destroy. The bonds of mortal family do not trump his claim. They are not even a factor."

Anastasz had a fleeting thought of his own living family. Father was dead now, buried in a family plot in Slovenia alongside the bone-chips and ashes he had received from the British authorities twenty years ago, along with an apologetic note telling him that his son had died in a tragic theater fire. Mother was still living, but Anastasz imagined she would now be bent double with age, although still able to play the tyrant with the servants in the grand house in Zagreb. He closed his eyes to push back the memories.

"Of course," Anastasz said, hoping his sire hadn't noticed his momentary nostalgia, "but seeing as Lady Blake's daughter has joined the ranks of the British kindred and shown up here in Vienna, it seems doubtful she will be discouraged."

"True."

"And," di Zagreb added, "the fact is that Herr Wellig's plan did not come to the fruition he wished. Lady Blake survives and he has brought her to the Fatherhouse. Her unfortunate episodes seem to have passed, and he now allows her to visit the city, I believe. Given that, it might be said that it behooves us to further her education. For the good of the order, of course."

Drescher did not smile, exactly. "I believe you have a gift for legalistic arguments, Anastasz. A mother-daughter reunion might well be in order."

"Of course, sir."

***

Regina and Victoria's carriage from the Hotel Sacher took a straight route toward their destination. From the front of the hotel, they crossed Albertinaplatz and headed northeast up Augustinerstrasse, along the façade of the Hofburg Palace complex, which was the very epicenter of Hapsburg power. Despite the gravity of the situation, Regina could not prevent herself from craning her neck to take in as much as possible.

"This is a museum of art, I believe," said Victoria, indicating the first wing of the palace-complex. "The Albertina."

The palace museum soon merged with a church, marked mostly by the sudden appearance of a spire. There was little disruption in the continuous façade that spoke of a palace full of rooms and secrets. They passed before a grand square with the equestrian statue of a past emperor at its center, but even that didn't open to heart of the palace complex. The continuous façade of buildings, stables, libraries and palaces simply looped back to make space for the square. Regina gasped slightly as they passed the square stables and came onto Michaelerplatz. This oblong square had as its eastern frame the great curving colonnade of the entrance to the Hofburg. A vast dome overlooked it all and Regina could see the signs of masonry work in progress on either side of the huge doors. She imagined new additions to this magnificent baroque entrance—grand fountains, perhaps—and let out a long, cleansing breath. Just as the last of the air left her lungs she felt a single strong pulse in her chest. She placed her palm flat against her breast as if willing the strange spasm to repeat itself, and although it did not oblige her, it was not long before she realized just what it was. For the first time since her passage into undeath, Regina Blake's heart had beaten.

"Victoria, I—" She stopped short, when she turned to face Miss Ash and realized the other woman had been speaking to her for some time.

"… can you hear me now?" Victoria completed her sentence. "Regina? Do you understand me?"

"Yes, I… Yes."

"I've been trying to get your attention since we passed onto Josefsplatz."

Regina risked a glance back out of the carriage and noted that they were well passed the St. Michael's Gate that had thrilled her. They were heading up the chic Herrengasse, away from the palace and toward their destination. They were, in fact, just entering the edge of Freyung and turning onto Schottengasse.

"I… I was distracted. The gate of the palace. It was…"

Victoria smiled but sorrow was in her emerald eyes. "It is an effect of the blood, my darling."

"What blood?"

"Mine, I'm afraid. Lineage is a powerful force among our kindred, my dear. I inherited a great deal from Maximilien and some of that I have passed on to you."

"I appreciated architecture long before I ever met you, Victoria." Regina wished she could keep the defensive edge out of her voice.

"Of course. It isn't the actual appreciation of beauty that is in the blood, but its intensity. Just as the hunger for blood far outweighs any appetite we might have had in life, this craving outdoes any past sense of the aesthetic. It is the flip side of the rage you felt last night."

"But I… That is, I felt my heart."

"Yes, I know." Victoria's eyes were filled with longing. "That is the worst and the best of it, I'm afraid. In that moment of purest rapture we can, for an instant, remember the pure sensation of life. Of true life."

"Only for a moment?"

"Always. Just one single, intoxicating moment. I myself have felt it as a sudden intake of refreshing air, as if my lungs had become functional once more. Your heart gave a single beat. It never lasts, although it always feels as if it could."

Regina thought of the beautiful façade on St. Michael's Square, of the colonnades and great dome. The perfect symmetry and baroque grandeur. She could feel her blood rushing through her veins and felt as if her heart was about to flutter anew, if she could just get lost in the experience again....

"Yes," she said at last, "I can see that. Everything else seems to fade away."

Victoria smiled again, a confidence between friends. "When I see true beauty, the rest of the world may as well not exist. Anger, danger, fatigue, even our eternal hunger, it all melts away. I love those moments more than anything, but I loathe them as well."

"Because they end," Regina said, completing her companion's thought. "And you... And we are left no closer to life than before."

"But all the more aware of that distance." Victoria placed her gloved hand on Regina's cheek, a sign of tenderness they hadn't shared since the latter's embrace into undeath. "I have done you a grievous wrong, my darling."

Regina leaned her head into Victoria's hand. "No more than was done to you," she said. "No more than I would have done alone had I the power."

Victoria drew Regina in so that the younger vampire's head was resting on the exposed flesh running from her shoulder up her neck. "You can't deceive me so easily, my darling childe," she said, "but thank you for the lie nonetheless."

They sat nuzzled together in silence for a while longer as the carriage turned east along Schottenring and then north on a smaller avenue, to finally return west on Maria-Theresien-Strasse and come to a stop before the small square that fronted Fortschritt, the high chantry of House Tremere.

"Where do you see true beauty, Victoria?" Regina sat up again from the porcelain coolness of her companion's flawless flesh and looked into her emerald eyes. "Since... Well, since the events on the train, I've experienced the sensation you describe with architecture most of all."

"Yes, the gaping I mentioned."

Regina felt the tingle of embarrassment but didn't look away. "Yes. I always loved classically inspired buildings and now, well, I feel it most acutely. But you said it was a sensation I inherited from you. Where do you feel that longing? Where do you see beauty so strong it makes you remember... before?"

Victoria held Regina's gaze for what seemed like an eternity. Those perfect emerald irises framed pupils of basalt-black. Regina felt herself falling into those ebon pools, as if they were drawing her into their depths.

Victoria suddenly turned away. She looked outside the carriage at the coachman dutifully waiting to open her door. She raised a delicate lace kerchief to her face. "We should go," she said, "lest our hosts think us rude."

The coachman opened the door and Victoria descended to the pavement. Regina followed shortly thereafter and when her companion looked her way, she noted that Victoria hadn't quite daubed all of the red from the corner of her eyes. The tears were still fresh and still flowing.

Perhaps reading Regina's gaze, Victoria brought out a second kerchief and finished the job. "This way," she said when all signs of her longing were gone.

The square in front of Fortschritt was roughly triangular. Its broad base was to the west, facing the private institute's façade, while its sides were defined by the streets to the south and north.

A small sign marked it as Erasmusplatz, and standing on its edge, Regina could just see a statue at its center which she took to be an effigy of the famed Dutch scholar of the renaissance. It was he who had brought the study of classics to the fore in Northern Europe, and Regina felt she owed much of her own intellectual curiosity to that fact. She made to enter the square, to examine the statue more closely.

"Carefully," Victoria said, laying a protective hand on her. "Professor di Zagreb said to remain on the gray path."

Regina looked down at the surface of the square itself. It apparently had no gas or electric lighting of its own and the lampposts along the nearby boulevards were not doing a very good job of penetrating the gloom here, but she could make out patterns in the cobblestones of the square. A series of lighter flagstones formed a path leading from the corner where they had alighted from the carriage, toward the very middle of the square's western side, where the stairs leading to Fortschritt's great front door began. Regina could see other patterns, paths set with different stones, leading to other paths through the square. Although she could not grasp the whole pattern for lack of light and distance, she guessed that the whole square formed an intricate puzzle. No two paving stones were quite the same size.

Regina and Victoria walked along the gray stone path and neither spoke. Regina was acutely aware of a discomfiture rising within her. She felt watched and judged, but from where she could not tell. Just as they reached the base of the massive building's front stairs, she felt the hairs on the back of her neck rise with a chill. She spun on her heel, certain she was being watched.

The square was empty, save for the statue of Erasmus, which was now clearly revealed. The great scholar stood on a square pedestal that itself sat on a hemispherical base. He was dressed as a scholar of his age and held a triangular object—a mason's square or a primitive sextant perhaps—straight ahead of him, in a direction Regina somehow knew was directly east. Something about this positioning chilled her already cold heart, but exactly what escaped her.

It was only once they'd ascended the twenty-one broad steps to the intricately carved gothic doors that she remembered why. The squared-circle with a triangular point was a symbol of power for alchemists and sorcerers. The elemental phalec, Dr. Bainbridge had called it back in London—the merging of elements and will to form power. It had been used by the people who abducted her mother and by the Tremere in London. To see it here, encoded in the statue of Erasmus, affirmed to Regina that she was indeed entering the belly of the beast she'd been hunting since last Christmastide.

Just as Victoria reached for the beast-headed knocker, the door opened as if of its own accord. The two women stepped through.

Regina had the distinct impression she was going to leap out of her skin. After months of searching, after trauma upon trauma as she peeled back the layers of secrecy in London and Paris, reunion with her mother was finally at hand. She and Victoria walked at what felt like a snail's pace down a broad, well-lit corridor. A servant, the same broad-browed Slav who had met them at the door, led the way a few paces ahead. He had yet to say a word.

Regina looked back the way they had come and had the disconcerting impression that the hallway was quite literally endless. It was an illusion, of course, caused by its curvature—they were walking a circle within the square structure of the building itself, another reiteration of that unholy geometry, another reminder that this place, despite appearing like a cross between a school and a mansion, was in fact the lair of unliving warlocks.

Victoria placed her arm in Regina's and gave it a squeeze, both comforting and somehow charged with warning. Regina looked ahead again and noted that the footman had stopped at one of many doors along the inside of the main corridor. He knocked gently and it opened an instant later. Bowing and taking a smooth step back and to the side, he extended his hand to indicate that the women should enter.

"Thank you," Regina said as she passed him, but he did not respond. Inside was a well-appointed sitting room, lined with books and featuring a guttering hearth, several plush chairs and divans, and two large curtained windows. Regina was struck with the question of just what those windows might look upon—as the room was on the inside of the peripheral hallway—but upon seeing the figure in the chair closest to the fire all other questions vanished from her mind.

"Mother!"

She drew her hand from Victoria's grasp and ran the dozen steps to the chair where Emma Blake was sitting. Regina threw herself at her mother's feet as a child half her age would have, grabbing her legs and burying her face in the skirts at her lap. Sobs rose up and she did nothing to stop them. "Oh, Mother, Mother, at last."

"Shh, my darling girl." Emma Blake stroked her daughter's hair and spoke in a quiet, even voice. "Regina, I asked you not to follow me. Please…"

Regina lifted her face from her mother's lap, and she felt the cool line of tears slip down her cheek toward her mouth. An instant later, the coppery tang of them was on her lips and she knew they were blood-tinted. Regina looked deep into her mother's eyes, hoping only for the comforting, maternal love she'd been deprived of for these last trauma-filled months.

"Oh, no." Emma cupped her daughter's face. "No, not you."

Regina drank in her mother's emotions, and instead of warm love she read a cold sadness frosting her face like a silver-hued mask. What's worse, that icy sadness was fractured only by hot moments of fear. Because she had nothing else to say, Regina whispered, "I'm sorry, Mother." She hated herself for saying it.

Lady Blake looked up from her once-living child and focused on the third woman in the room. "You."

Victoria Ash inclined her head slightly. "Hello, Emma."

Lady Blake stood up in a flash and Regina felt her mother's anger like a hot red wave. "How dare you?" Lady Blake demanded. "What have you done to my daughter, you monstrous woman!"

Regina felt a wave of vertigo when she stood again, even though no blood rushed through her veins. "Mother, please, Miss Ash—"

"Miss Ash," Emma Blake spat, "has destroyed you!"

"Regina came to me for assistance, Emma. I offered it." Victoria's voice was cold and fragile as ice.

"You monstrous creature," Lady Blake said. "Could none of those I loved escape your perversities? Will you sell her to your whore-mongers too? Will you?"

Victoria remained implacable before this tirade, barely reacting at all to the barrage of questions. She only glanced at Regina, who watched from behind the suddenly enraged Lady Blake.

Regina felt as if she was being battered. Her mother had ever been a placid, even wilting creature. Sickened by fever or fatigued by the vicissitudes of life, she'd been bed-ridden for much of the last few years. To see her behaving so forcefully, to be screeching like a bullying child, was more than a little disconcerting. "Mother, please. There's no call for this."

Emma Blake turned to look at her daughter, fearful affection on her face. "Regina, you mustn't trust this creature. She is heartless, a murderess! She abducted me and had me sold as chattel!"

Regina, already battered by shock and relief-run-cold, struggled to get a hold of herself. "What…" She closed her eyes for an instant and beat back the well of panic she could feel in her chest and behind her eyelids. "What are you talking about, Mother?"

Emma said shrilly, "You have to believe me, Regina—"

Regina cut her off. "Mother, please stop screaming. Miss Ash has, has,"—she stumbled on the words—"has yet to sell me into slavery. Please, let's sit and we can talk about all this."

Emma Blake looked from her daughter to Victoria Ash and nodded. "Very well."

"Thank you, Mother." The three sat in the plush chairs and divans of the sitting room, but that did not dispel the tension and suppressed violence running between them. Her mother, dressed in a cream-colored gown, with a burgundy shawl around her shoulders, practically radiated fury. "Now," Regina said, "please tell me what happened between you."

Victoria drew out a lace kerchief and handed it to Regina. She used it to blot the pink tear-streaks from her face.

Emma Blake closed her eyes before speaking. "This all happened before you were born, Regina. Your father and I had just been wed, but my family wasn't as yet reconciled to the union."

Regina thought back to her interactions with the Ducheski relatives at the time of her mother's "death" last winter. Their disrespect for her father had been palpable. "I thought Father and you had eloped."

"Indeed," Emma said. "We hadn't yet announced the fact when my family brought me to London for the social season of…"

"1869," Victoria completed.

Emma glared at her but restrained any retort. "Yes, 1869. I attended a variety of salons and balls, as was the fashion then. You understand that our family was not aristocratic per se, but that spring I understood that we had many friends among the upper echelons of a whole new society."

"The night society," Regina said. "The undead."

"Yes." Emma looked down at her lap. "I didn't fully understand their nature then, but I found it all intoxicating." She locked her gaze on her daughter. "Regina, you have to understand, I had spent much of my life at Lion's Green among cousins and aunts and uncles, in a family where beauty was an aberration."

Regina and Victoria had both attended Lady Blake's mock funeral on her maternal family's estate at Lion's Green in County Durham. The panoply of hunchbacks, hydrocephalics and other aberrations had been like the cast of some bizarre menagerie.

"When I met your father the year previous," Emma continued, "he appeared to me like a knight from some epic."

"Still, you went to London," Regina said.

"Yes, I did. And there, I found a night society rich with men and women more beautiful, more sophisticated, than I ever thought possible. And at the center of it was the finest rose of them all: Ophelia Merritt." A placid expression crossed Emma's face, like the blue stillness of a lake on a windless day. "She became my protector, my…"

"Your lover," Regina said, feeling a distant echo of shame in her voice—her mother's experience was a precursor of her own with Victoria some twenty years later. "You drank her blood."

"Y– yes. Heaven help me, but yes, I loved that woman more than anything."

"And Father?" Regina asked.

"I loved him as well, I think, but this was different. His

regiment was abroad that summer, and Ophelia was intoxicating. Even after everything happened, after you were born, I still had dreams about her."

"What did this have to do with Miss Ash?"

"She was there too," Emma said with sudden ice in her voice, "one of Ophelia's kindred, looking for position, for pride of place. She was jealous."

Regina glanced at Victoria and although the redheaded woman's face barely reacted, Regina thought she glimpsed a slight twitch of bitter mirth.

"When she had enough of me," Emma Blake continued, looking straight at Victoria, "this creature took me into Southwark and handed me over to, to a *creature* of her acquaintance. He was like a wraith, appearing and disappearing at a whim, but his grip was strong and his skin like scabby leather. He drank my blood and made me… that is I was forced to…" She looked away and when next she spoke her voice was small. "If your father hadn't found me, I surely wouldn't have survived my first week in that thing's clutches."

Regina looked at Victoria. "Is this true?"

Miss Ash looked at Emma Blake. "Did you ever wonder how Lord Blake found you, Emma?"

"James told me he received a confidential correspondence. I think it must have been Lady Merritt herself…"

Regina thought back to the cold, blonde beauty she had met at Merritt House last spring and summer. The thought of her being altruistic seemed like a poorly played comedy. "She would have retrieved you herself, no?"

"Regina sees the truth, Emma," Victoria said, "why can't you? I was Lord Blake's secret correspondent. I arranged for your rescue."

Emma Blake sprang to her feet. "From captivity you arranged! 'I always pay my debts,' you said, and *pushed* me into that thing's clutches! I'll see you dead for that!"

Regina felt her own blood rushing through her, the prospect of violence—especially between these two women—triggering some electric fear in her. She placed herself between her mother and Victoria, staring down the black hate she saw in Emma Blake's eyes. "Mother, no."

Lady Blake's voice was raw and rough. "Regina, step aside."

"No." Regina took a step forward. "I've come too far for this. I will hear Miss Ash out just as I've heard you out, Mother. Now, sit down." Small hairs on the back of Regina's neck stood up in response to an animal instinct and she was momentarily certain that her own mother would strike her. Instead, Emma Blake dropped her gaze and then sat.

Victoria continued. "Lady Merritt is a woman of passion. In the years I spent as her guest, she professed the perfection of one plaything after another. It never lasted. She would become entranced by another debutante or marquis's son and all past passions were forgotten." She looked directly at Emma. "The evening she showed you to me, Emma, was just a week after she had been extolling the incomparability of another protégé of hers, one Sir Michael Grant."

"I never met such a man," Emma said.

"Of course not." Victoria's voice was cold and mechanical. "By the time of your next visit to Merritt House I had seen him buried in a potter's field."

Regina felt a flush of sudden revulsion rising in her throat. Could she even vomit in this half-living condition?

"You see," Emma said. "She is a murderess."

"Yes," Victoria answered with only a slight flicker of emotion in her voice. "It was the price I paid for Lady Merritt's hospitality. I was charged with cleaning up those toys of which she had tired. In May, that was Sir Michael. In June, it was you."

"No…"

"Yes. She decided the Ceylonese woman Horace Holden brought to the Solstice Ball that year was more to her taste. You had, in her words, 'become a bore.'"

"I don't believe you…" Emma's voice was small, like a child's.

"Just as you didn't believe me when I told you your husband was still alive. Or do you not remember that Lady

Merritt told you he died in Africa?"

"My God…"

"So, yes, I gave you to that beast Samuel in Southwark. But I also guided your husband there so that he might rescue you, and take you away from London, from Lady Merritt and all the rest. Even when you returned to Merritt House in later years—"

"Enough," Emma Blake said. "Ophelia never accepted me back. I know that. Have you come here just to throw the perversities of my life at me?"

Regina spoke then. "No, no, Mother. We're here because you were taken from us, from Father and I. I couldn't let you be stolen away from us. I'm here to, to rescue you." The words, which Regina had never before spoken aloud, sounded foolish, even to her.

"It's far too late for that, my darling girl."

Regina took her mother's hand in hers, beseeching her. "Please, Mother. Come to London with us. So much has happened, but please, we can still…"

"What can we do, my darling? My life with James was an aberration. I loved him, and you and your brother, so much, but I was never complete. I longed for Ophelia, or for something more than that. I… I think I've found that."

"What have you found?" Regina asked, her voice becoming shrill. "Undeath?"

"Yes. I was born a Ducheski, my darling. It was always my fate. I was a fool to ever believe I could escape that."

"But, Mother, I've come so far. I've given… my life…"

"I know, my darling girl, and I'm so sorry. But even the rest of the night society isn't my home. My future is in these walls."

"No—"

"Regina, my darling daughter," Emma said shifting her hands so that she was now beseeching the girl in return. "You've ever been so full of life and even now, transformed as you are, I think you are more alive than I ever was. My soul has been half-empty since I was a girl. I've tried to fill it with the fear of my cousins, with love for Ophelia, with your father—God forgive me, even with participation in pagan

acts in the backstreets of Cairo. None of it has ever lasted."
She raised her hands to encompass the room and the building
housing it. "This is why. This is what I have been meant for
all along."

"But Mr. Wellig… at the Crystal Palace… with Prince
Mithras…"

A faraway look passed over Emma's features for just a
second. "I… I know you can't understand, my darling, but
I've tried for so long to fill a space in my heart and I think
that this is what is meant to be there. I'm tired of fighting."

"Don't give up, Mother. If I found you, anything is
possible."

"I'm sorry, Regina. I can't come with you." She laid her
hand on Regina's cheek. "I think you should go, now."

"But…" A rich red tear rolled down the girl's cheek.

"Please, Regina." Emma had blood tears of her own
rising in her eyes. "Please."

Regina closed her eyes and turned away from her
mother. A second later she rose to her feet and walked
haltingly toward the door through which she had entered
the sitting room. Victoria was two steps behind her.

"Miss Ash," Emma said when the redheaded woman
was at the threshold, "if anything you've said is true, then
please protect my daughter."

Neither Regina nor Victoria turned around, and the
manservant who'd waited in the hall closed the door behind
them. He escorted them back to the front gate of Fortschritt,
where they crossed Erasmusplatz and boarded the carriage
still waiting for them. Neither spoke for the entire walk there
or the ride back to the Hotel Sacher.

Regina felt as if the air itself had become a crushing,
leaden weight. Sadness seemed to flow through her like
smoke, and red tears streamed down her face without sound.
She would not allow herself to sob, for that would require
breath and movement and those were beyond her now. She
accepted another kerchief from Victoria when they
disembarked and dabbed away enough of the tears so as not
to shock the hotel's discreet staff.

When they made it upstairs to Baron Grünwald's suites,

Regina collapsed on one of the beds and hoped for nothing except the oblivion of unconsciousness. Her new condition would not let her have it, however. She squeezed her eyes tightly closed so that colored lights danced in the blackness and blood-tinted tears stained the coverlet. Sleep, however, would not come. Instead, she passed into a state of distorted awareness, one in which those things missing from her nocturnal existence were loudest in their absence. She had not even the iota of will left to power those symptoms of life she'd unknowingly kept up in her unliving masquerade. There was no heartbeat or swishing pulse to give rhythm to the dark world that lived under her lids. No breath raised her chest from the bed. She remained immobile and the tactile sensations that had been so acute at other times also fell away. The constant weight of organ on organ, the smooth texture of her dress and petticoats on her skin, the very slight current of air in the room—it all faded into a hazy physical numbness. And yet, she remained utterly and painfully aware. A total stillness filled her mind's eye and carried on for a timeless interval. No thoughts or memories came unbidden. No urges or desires, save for a small wanting that she could not quite place. That smallest of sparks seemed the only thing that existed within her, the only feature of the empty shell Regina Blake had become.

She remained there, staring at the ember of inhuman hunger that kept her out of the grave, until the dawn came and Victoria guided her to the shelter of the boudoir.

***

The servant who had escorted Regina Blake and Victoria Ash to and from the sitting room where Emma Blake had met them was a Ukrainian named Petro. He had had the double misfortune of being born to a destitute mother in Kiev who was willing to sell him to a foreigner in exchange for a few rubles, and that that foreigner had been a German scholar named Claas Drescher. Once the two Englishwomen had left Fortschritt and Lady Blake had returned to her sleeping chambers, Petro reported to Dr. Drescher's private laboratory. There, the magus let Anastasz di Zagreb use steel shears to clip the black catgut that bound Petro's lips together and feed him three drops of a ritual concoction that included blood and bile in equal parts.

Petro then began to speak, repeating word-for-word the entire conversation he'd overhead between the three women. Petro spoke no English and had no natural talent for mimicry, but thanks to the long nights of experimentation by Drescher and di Zagreb, he spoke the words almost perfectly, as if his stomach might contain a wax cylinder. He collapsed onto the tile of the laboratory floor once he was done.

"Lady Blake is in all likelihood lying," di Zagreb said once Petro had stopped thrashing. "She didn't mention her wild episode, for example."

"Perhaps, but she did not leap on the opportunity for escape from our care," Drescher said. "And these questions of pagan rituals in Egypt and of having been bound to Lady Merritt may explain a few things."

"Did you have much reason to interact with Lady Merritt during your time in London, Herr Doctor? I don't recall meeting her before I began my studies here."

"Dr. Bainbridge's predecessor as our order's representative in London was a frequent guest of hers, I believe. It hardly protected him when Prince Mithras returned from his exile, or so I hear."

"Lady Blake's liaison with a prominent member of London's night society does raise further questions about Herr Wellig's discretion," di Zagreb pointed out.

"That it does." Drescher looked down at the Ukrainian on the laboratory floor. "Speaking of discretion, see to it that Petro's lips are resewn before you retire."

Chapter Seven

"My God," James Blake whispered. "It's Emma."

He was sitting in a drafty, half-finished room in the new home of the University of Vienna, Herr Kohler and Father Metz at his side. Johann was still back at the flat on Karmeliterplatz with Ducheski, in all likelihood stretching the wretch's recuperative abilities to their limits.

Their vigil had begun just before dusk, using the cover of the still-incomplete school building across Universitätsstrasse from the domain of the undead sorcerers. Each man had a spyglass with which he scanned the baroque façade of the building, the dreary square facing it (and directly across from their position) and what side entrances they could see.

They had spent the night before in a similar vigil from street level, using a hired carriage parked on Schottenring as their main observation post. The comings and goings of those partaking in the Viennese nightlife, and the concerns of some of the municipal constables, had made their observations impractical, however. Yesterday they had found this room in the school building and hoped that the vantage of height would give them an advantage in spotting the monsters whom they believed resided in Fortschritt.

Thus far, tonight's watch had borne no more fruit, and Blake now assumed that these monsters either never left their shelter or that they had some hidden way to enter and exit the foreboding structure. No one ever came in or out by night, when—according to both what Kohler said now and what his old companion Othman had told him in Egypt—the undead could move about. The idea had come to him of catacombs under the city streets, lined with the graves of these sorcerers' victims, perhaps. Earlier this evening, he'd even half-convinced himself that the granite gargoyles perched at the corners of the roof had moved. Madness.

He'd decided not to search the building proper, but to scan the boulevards that passed near it. The dark, cheerless square separated Fortschritt from Maria-Theresien-Strasse and Schottenring beyond that, but that was surely no impediment to the creatures within. If they were to walk the city streets at night, why not the boulevards facing their home? Thanks to the well-positioned gas lamps along the streets, he could watch the coming and goings there with relative ease. There were a good number of folk about, no doubt moving from nearby theaters, restaurants and cafes, but for several hours no one who seemed any more suspicious than any other Austrian had passed under Blake's eye.

Then, as if as a gift from God Himself, a woman emerged from the shadows of the small square and walked into the light on Maria-Theresien-Strasse. She waited a minute at the corner and then crossed the north-south road and heading for the Ring proper. Another figure emerged from the square and the first woman turned when she reached the far corner to look at the newcomer, her face catching the light of the nearest gas lamp.

Emma.

"Your wife?" asked Metz in his heavily accented English, moving toward the window. "Where?"

"On the corner of the north-south road," Blake said. "In the green, or black, gown. With the scarf." The night washed the colors from the scene, but Blake suspected that his wife's gown was not actually black. He would never admit it, but that she'd shed—or never worn—a widow's weeds while he still favored blacks from head to toe in mourning for her, cut him to the quick.

The newcomer who'd attracted Emma's attention entered the frame of Blake's spyglass and although she was turned away from him, he had no trouble identifying the bent-over frame of the crone whom he blamed most of all for his beloved's vanishing last Christmas. Eleanor Ducheski, Gareth and Emma's great aunt and the matriarch of that damnable family.

"We have to get to them," he said between gritted teeth. He stood and collapsed his spyglass with perhaps too much force for its expensive lenses. "Quickly."

"Wait," Kohler said. "They are being watched by

THE WOUNDED KING

another. By the tram-stop on Schottenring." The old Austrian was gazing out of another window in the room, which they'd chosen because it was at a corner of the unfinished school building, giving them a vantage on Fortschritt and much of the Ring before it.

Blake went there and reopened his spyglass. "Where?" One of the horse-drawn trams that serviced the Ringstrasse was just leaving the stop one block from their position, continuing its long counterclockwise circumference of the inner city. He searched for this watcher.

"*Ja*," Metz said. "In the shadows."

"By the malfunctioning lamppost," Kohler said.

There was indeed a darkened gas lamp a few yards east of the corner on Schottenring that left a gap of shadow in the yellow luminescence of the ring road. As the tram pulled past it, some of the light from across the boulevard filtered into that darkened space and Blake could just see the silhouette of a man standing near the dead lamppost. "I see, but is he really—"

Blake stopped his own question midstride when he saw the man step out of the shadows as Emma and Eleanor crossed the Ringstrasse between their two positions. The man waited a beat and then merged with the other pedestrians crossing to the inner side of the boulevard.

"A spy for the warlocks, perhaps?" Kohler asked rhetorically.

Blake didn't answer. When the man stepped into the light of another lamppost, Blake had noted his long hair and hawkish nose. Though the view was far from perfect, Blake recognized him immediately. He had seen this man twice before. The first time had been in Cairo, in 1886, when he had been present in the same strange ceremony Emma had. The second time had been just a few weeks ago, in London, when the man had rescued Blake from the clutches of Gareth Ducheski and warned him not to pursue his missing wife. He had gutted Ducheski with inhuman talons that had sprouted from his fingers.

"Yes," Blake said. "Perhaps."

***

Emma Blake waited for her great aunt to cross Schottenring and catch up. The possibility of simply fleeing from Eleanor had presented itself several times before this, and then like now, she felt it was an illusion. Eleanor Ducheski's slight waddle as she approached was, if not an intentional deception, then at least a natural camouflage. The crone had her hooks in Emma always, never more so than since her passage into undeath. Emma had tried to run before, when she married James Blake, when she gave herself to Ophelia Merritt, when she whispered the secret words of the doomed Arab madman Anwar al-Beshi, and it had all been for naught. Were she to turn tail now, it would be the same and the scolding, too-small face of her great aunt couldn't help but remind her of the fact.

"Don't just stand there," the crone scolded. "There are only a few hours before we have to get you back."

"Herr Drescher has more questions, I suppose." Emma didn't bother to hide her dislike for the portly Austrian.

"Surely." Eleanor didn't hide it either. "Come."

They headed eastward into the inner city, leaving behind the large boulevards for the medieval streets of Old Vienna. After a few minutes of walking in silence, Emma asked, "What did you mean about the Tremere and our family, Aunt Eleanor?"

"You ask questions instead of thinking for yourself, girl."

They emerged onto a triangular public square which an intricately lettered sign attached to one of the corner buildings identified as Freyung. To their left stood a large church fronted with a broad, five-storied building that had the aspect of nothing so much as a large chest of drawers. Shops occupied the ground floor of what, from its proximity to the church proper, Emma assumed must have been a priory of some sort.

"This is the place some of your ancestors fled to, child." Eleanor was looking up at the baroque bell tower of the church itself, peeking out from behind the priory. "The Schottenkirche."

"The Scottish Church," Emma translated.

"Yes. In those times the missionaries here had the right to shelter foreigners and thieves from the those hunting them."

"Freyung," Emma said. "Freedom square."

"Or so Janos Krevcheski thought. He fled when the family gathered in Vienna to pledge themselves to the Tremere and found his way here. The priest offered him protection."

Emma longed to step toward the large wooden church door, but she knew better. "It didn't work."

Eleanor turned suddenly to face her niece. "Of course not. How could church walls protect him when his family's blood was available to those hunting him? His cousins, sisters and father all cooperated with the warlocks to cast a spell on him."

"What happened?"

"They drove him mad." She looked back up at the clock tower. "He threw himself from that tower on the night before the Feast of Advent"—her gaze followed the imagined arc of the body falling to the pavement at her feet—"but not before slitting the throat of the priest who had offered him sanctuary."

"But escape is possible," Emma said. "That's what you meant."

Eleanor looked at her without saying a word. The shadow of a smile passed over her withered lips, but she kept her own counsel.

"Emma!" The voice came from the edge of the square and sent shivers down Lady Blake's unliving spine.

"James?"

***

James Blake was turning onto Freyung when he saw Emma and the crone Eleanor Ducheski standing and chatting before the church on its northern edge. Herr Kohler and Father Metz were operating according to their hasty plan, but he couldn't wait. He'd let his wife escape once before and could not risk her vanishing into the Viennese night again. He only hoped the two Austrians would be ready when they were needed.

"Emma!" he exclaimed and both women turned to face him. Emma seemed shocked and confused and uttered his name, as if questioning the reality of his presence. Mrs. Ducheski just looked angry.

"James?" Emma said. "You can't be here."

"But I am," he said and took several steps forward. "I won't abandon you again, Emma."

Lady Blake remained where she was, but the aged Ducheski woman took several steps forward, teetering on her cane. "What do you think, Blake? That you can come and *rescue* your woman from her very blood?"

"Yes," he said, not altogether convincingly. "Yes, I do."

"Oh, James," Emma said. "Please, it's too late."

"She was never yours," Eleanor said. "From the moment of her birth she has been a Ducheski and nothing can change that."

He took several steps forward, rage mounting in his heart. "Damn you and your blood, old woman!" He turned to face his wife. "We loved each other once, Emma. Don't turn your back on me, on us."

"James, please," she pleaded. "We tried, but it was no use. I can't change who I am. Certainly not now."

"Why? Why can't you come to me this very instant?"

Emma Blake looked nervously around. Although the square was hardly as populated as it might have been during the day, the commotion was attracting some attention. "I am past saving, my darling man."

"You heard her, Englishman," Eleanor said, her eyes tight with anger. "She rejects you and your salvation. Now *go!*"

Before even thinking about it, he did just that, turning on his heel and taking several steps west back out of Freyung. His heart felt light and he realized just how *glad* he was to turn away from the realm of horror his life had become over the last year. If his estranged wife rejected his open hand, why should he fight for her? Let her continue into the guts of whatever damned world she had entered. He would continue without her and without their daughter Regina.

Regina.

The thought literally stopped him in his tracks. He'd last seen her at Dover in the company of the creature Victoria Ash. How could he let her go too? How could he let Emma go, for that matter. His hand fell to the hard leather Bible in his cot pocket. He turned again.

"No," he said, stepping back into the square. "I will not leave without you, Emma."

She faced him again. In the few moments when he had been walking away, Eleanor had returned to Emma's side and the crone now clutched her arm like a withered serpent. Here eyes pleaded with her husband, but no words escaped from her mouth.

"Do you remember Lady Winthrope?" Blake asked his wife while he continued forward. "Who visited you in Egypt?"

"James," she said, her voice hoarse, "please."

"She was involved with these creatures too, and she is free now." He was within a few steps from Emma now. Eleanor just watched him, her mouth gaping slightly. "She found safety in God, Emma. She's free."

"Your sacrificed god cannot protect you," Eleanor said. "We are older than your petty faith."

"Be quiet!" Blake screamed at the withered woman, raising his walking stick as if to strike her.

Then his eyes caught sight of Father Metz emerging from one of the shops in the white building fronting the church. Had he been inside or just hiding in the recessed doorway? No way for Blake to tell, but either way he'd followed the plan to use side-streets to sneak around and cut off Emma from the other direction.

It was not part of the plan for him to be wielding a sharpened wooden stake.

"No!" Blake's warning was too late, and the priest made contact with his target.

There was an audible crunch of wood, bone and flesh as the stake struck Emma Blake. A shocked expression bloomed on her face just as the front of her gown and cloak tented from the point of the stake protruding from her breast. She collapsed.

Blake had seen battle-fatigued soldiers and the paralyzing effects of first coming under fire before, but had never experienced them. His had always been the cool tactician's head in battle, either acting from behind the front lines, or leading his cavalrymen into the heat of battle. The soldier on horseback brought fear to his enemies, he did not suffer from fear himself. Now, he found his limbs leaden and his senses strangely malfunctioning. The world was a slow, silent pantomime of itself with sounds registering only as faraway echoes: There was an animal-like screech when Eleanor Ducheski's bony hands found Father Metz's throat; a cork-like pop and the smell of gunpowder when Herr Kohler emerged from his own hiding place on the other side of the square, firing a pistol; another scream when one of those bullets hit a passerby, a young artist carrying a canvas covered in brown paper.

Blood spattered the paper and the artist fell against the wall of the church.

The high-pitched trilling of police whistles seemed like distant bells of no particular import. Blake's senses were focused on his wife, lying on her side, paralyzed in a rictus of shock. Metz and the old Ducheski woman rolled on the pavement in a mad grapple.

"Emma," Blake whispered and managed a few steps forward. He was aware of a fog rolling low across the ground of the square, but paid it little attention. The Viennese simply could not compete with the pea soup fogs of London.

People were screaming in German and chaos gripped the square as the first policeman to arrive tackled Kohler from behind. The passerby attracted by the sound ran for cover when the old man squeezed off another round from his pistol. Blake paid it no heed at all.

His attention focused on his wife, whose horrified face was ashen and drawn. She was completely immobile and, he soon noticed, utterly rigid. Indeed, she was lying not quite on her side, but propped up with one arm and one leg, still in the shocked position from when Father Metz had attacked. Her back was still arched, her head thrown back, and her eyes bulged open.

Blake looked into those eyes—their pupils reduced to pinpricks and their whites rimed in clotted blood—and despaired. Leaning over Emma, he spread open her cloak and saw the angry tip of Metz's stake protruding from the front of her shirt and corset. Black blood had welled there but in no great quantity and as if by magic it was already sticky with coagulation.

"Oh, Emma," he whispered and took a half-step back. He himself had pounded a stake through the cold heart of John Claremont to prevent him rising as one of the undead. To see his wife so treated was like a blow to his gut.

A thick patch of fog blew over her body and settled there. The thought that he'd felt no gust of wind was just penetrating Blake's brain when the mist began to billow like the steam from a pot. But it refused to rise, instead folding in upon itself and coagulating into a thick, whitish clot.

Then the clot resolved itself into the shape of a man and Blake remembered that he had lost track of the long-haired stranger who had been following Emma.

"No!" Blake was on the man in a second and it felt very much like he had just tackled a stallion. Tensed, hard muscles bulged under the man's long coat and although he kneeled down when Blake jumped on him, the man never lost his footing. Then, like a spring releasing, he stood upright and threw his arms open, sending Blake sprawling.

Blake hit the pavement with considerable force, but managed to roll with the fall. He'd been thrown by his fair share of horses and knew that a cavalryman who couldn't take a fall wasn't worth the wool in his uniform. He rose onto his hands and knees right out of the tumble and saw the man reaching behind his prone, dead wife.

"One moment," the long-haired man said, his tone calm, even jovial. There was a sickening wet sound and he pulled the bloody stake out of Emma Blake's back. He then got her up to her feet and put one arm around her shoulder.

She's alive. Or undead, Blake thought. And indeed, as the man started leading her out of the square, her legs were moving sluggishly.

"Emma!" he called and she turned her head toward him. Fear was splashed across her features and it fired Blake's will.

And then two Viennese policemen were on top of him, using wooden clubs to pound him into the submission. "Emma," he called once more before a club-blow to the head ended his struggle and sent him into the blackness of unconsciousness.

Chapter Eight

"This is not acceptable, Mr. Wellig," Ardan Lane said indicating the late edition of *Wiener Zeitung*, Vienna's leading daily.

The newspaper was splashed with an inflammatory headline about an exchange of gunfire in Freyung the previous night, with the suspects believed to be anarchists of some stripe. Other newspapers were calling them nationalists, although of what nationality seemed unclear in the reports. The Emperor was said to be safe, but concerned about this outbreak of violence along Schottenring.

"Do I need to remind you that we value subtlety among our kindred?"

"My childe has been abducted, Mr. Lane," Wellig said, letting his pique show. "Do my Viennese kindred and fraternal brothers intend to help me recover her from this interloper or shall we waste time with schoolboy scolding?"

Tension floated through the council chamber. Five of them were arranged around the room. Other than Lane and Wellig, there was the English sorcerer Dr. Bainbridge, Pontifex Drescher, and his childe Anastasz di Zagreb. Lady Meerlinda was absent, although it was a safe bet that she was aware of the goings on despite any wards or precautions they might take.

Drescher began to speak, outrage bubbling up on his features, but a raised hand from Lane cut him short. "I find your attitude disturbing," Lane said, calmly. "As I'm sure you know, one of the men arrested last night was none other than the mortal husband of your childe. This does not speak to your having taken proper precautions when you chose Emiliana for elevation into the blood."

"I'll be happy to end the problem of Lord Blake," Wellig said.

"That remains an option, certainly, but I have my doubts as to whether the Englishman is acting alone. We have obtained reports on the incident from members of the city authorities and the two men with Blake were carrying a goodly amount of religious paraphernalia. One of them is a priest, it seems." Lane drummed his fingers on the heavy oak table. "I would not want to see an ecclesiastical investigation result from any of this."

"You are still cowering from monks and their empty threats?"

"They hardly seemed empty when inquisitors and witch-hunters were combing the night in search of heretics and devils. No small number of our kind walked to the pyre, Mr. Wellig. You are aged enough to remember that, I believe."

He smiled. "Pontifex Drescher has accused me of being unaware of the realities of the modern nights, while you, Mr. Lane, tell me I have forgotten our past. Perhaps you'd be kind enough to coordinate your accusations?"

"Are you familiar with the Santé Prison in Paris?" Drescher asked.

Wellig looked genuinely confused. "What has that to do with anything?"

"There was a riot there on the evening of the fifteenth of this month, which the Parisian press has blamed on anarchists. Our allies in France report, however, that the prison was used as a haven and feeding ground by one of the city's elder kindred."

"And prison riots are suddenly my concern?"

"This was no riot," Drescher said, "but a coordinated attack on the prison. Our kindred report that the supposedly anarchistic attackers also had with them religious paraphernalia."

"Emiliana and I were in Paris for two nights in the middle of August, Herr Drescher, and we had nothing at all to do with elders lurking in prisons. If you care to blame me for every incident in every capital of Europe, that is your right. But in the meantime, I will begin my search for my childe."

"Now, Anton—" Dr. Bainbridge began, trying to calm his compatriot. It was too late, however. Wellig rose and left the chamber.

"Your colleague seems oblivious to the danger in which he is putting the entirety of House Tremere," Lane said to Bainbridge once Wellig had left.

"Mr. Wellig does have point," Bainbridge answered, "about the disappearance of his childe. The order owes him its support in locating her."

"Do not concern yourself on that count," Drescher put in. "We will dedicate the full spectrum of our resources to cleaning up this little fiasco. And with that in mind, might I ask you about Lady Blake's daughter, Lady Regina?"

Bainbridge's gaze traveled up and left, searching his memory. "Ah, yes. I believe she is a plaything of one of the more social kindred of London. Miss Victoria Ash, if I recall."

"A recent plaything?" Anastasz di Zagreb asked.

"I first met her this spring, I believe. How long her association with Miss Ash has been ongoing, I would not dare to guess."

Di Zagreb continued the questioning. "And it didn't strike you as worrisome that the mortal daughter of Mr. Wellig's childe suddenly appeared among London's night society after her mother's embrace?"

Bainbridge shifted slightly in his chair. "Much less than if she had materialized unaccompanied. Since Miss Ash was her guardian, I surmised that she was under the same interdictions as any ghoul."

"Assumptions can be dangerous, Dr. Bainbridge."

"I do not assume, sir," the Englishman said, "but I do make cautious deductions. I concluded that Miss Ash or one of her confederates had some interest in our affairs, but I did not assume that the wrath of a new holy inquisition was descending upon our heads."

"I suggest," Ardan Lane put in, "that we see what Miss Ash and Lady Regina have to say on the matter."

"The affairs in Vienna are yours to manage, Mr. Lane, but I would be derelict in my duties were I to begin questioning the kindred of London at length about our activities. Our order's position in England is somewhat precarious, as I'm sure you know."

"Even so," Lane said, "given that these two English roses have seen fit to appear in Vienna itself, I would like to know why."

Bainbridge opened his mouth, but didn't allow any words to escape.

***

Emma Blake was still not fully recovered from the events of the previous night. She was fairly certain they were somewhere outside of Vienna proper now—she had a vague memory of a ride in a cart or carriage—but every time she tried to reconstruct the precise sequence events, the trauma of the attack at Freyung returned to her.

She had thought herself beyond any new brand of fear. Putting aside the horror of her own embrace and her past associations with the undead, the last few months should have exposed her, she felt, to the full range of possible degradation. Over the last six weeks, she had been questioned extensively by the blood sorcerers of House Tremere—of her house, she reminded herself—and they had employed very unpleasant methods indeed. Her blood had been drained and processed. Savage fits of rage had gripped her and filled her mind with visions of fog-clouded alleys and disemboweled women.

Nevertheless, the shock of seeing James again, followed immediately by the sensation of a shaft of wood piercing her back and heart, had been too much to bear. Both Mr. Wellig and Aunt Eleanor had provided some instruction in the realities of undeath, including stories of the paralysis that would result from wood driven into her unbeating heart. Wellig had spoken of it in the clinical tones of a doctor addressing a recalcitrant patient.

"Even more than the living," he had said, "the sanguine humor drives us. Blood sustains us and empowers us. It is through its consumption that we defy death. Our hearts may not beat, but they remain the center of the sanguinary system. Inside that key organ rests the very essence of existence, what cassocked priests call the soul. I have seen that dark heart's blood, the very stuff of the spirit. It is merely a trickle, but without it we are mere rotted dead flesh. Less than an ounce it weighs, but it is the most potent of all substances. With mastery of the heart's blood, nothing is out of reach. A simple shaft of roughhewn wood inserted into the heart, even a sliver of lowly pine or willow, causes utter paralysis. The heart's blood is cut off from the body, leaving it rigid and frozen."

Mr. Wellig's warning had seemed highly theoretical on that cold winter night in London. Who would try to plunge a wooden shaft into her heart? And how difficult would that be to accomplish?

All too easy, it seemed. The priest at Freyung had done it with one strong thrust into her back, and none of her sire's words had been of any help at all. The paralysis had indeed been complete, but the worst of it had been what remained: all her senses. Lying on the pavement of the old city, she could feel with perfect precision the wooden shaft within her. It was wedged near her spine, between two ribs. It wasn't even squarely into her heart—her left lung had in fact taken the worst of the blow. One sliver of wood, however, had lodged in her heart, and that was enough. The pain was intense, but blissful unconsciousness refused to take her.

Vision and hearing were fickle, hateful things during that eternal time. Words and screams and whistles and shots all came to her as if from far away or even under water. Her eyes, unmoving, remained locked on the wall of the Scottish Church before which she had fallen. Her mind filled in the image of James that had been her last before the attack. Time stretched and compressed, so that she was equally certain she had remained unmoving for endless years and mere seconds.

Now, the next night, the physical pain was long gone. The blood in her veins, free to move and heal again, had repaired all the damage to her unliving tissue. But still, every time she closed her eyes, she was back there—feeling the wood in her chest, hearing the faraway screams of her husband, and seeing the gray patch of pavement upon which she'd fallen.

"It will become easier to handle with time, you know," the stranger said.

These were the first words the long-haired man in red-tinted glasses had said to her all night. They were in what appeared to be a barn of some sort and she had awoken from her daylight slumber with the flesh of a farmhand pressed against her. She'd drunk the boy's blood—not as much as she had wanted, more than enough to weaken him—and that had helped clear her head. The stranger had carried the unconscious lad to who knew where and returned. Now, he was speaking to her at last. In English.

"I suppose it must," she said.

He smiled just slightly and it was the wolfish grin one might imagine on a privateer from a past age. "Are you ready to speak with me then, Lady Blake?"

"Do you always feel the need to abduct your conversation partners, sir? If all you wanted from me was talk, surely there would have been an easier way than arranging for that attack."

"I think you are confused, Lady Blake. I was not responsible for that ambush." He brushed his unruly mane back from his face. "Some people might even say that I rescued you."

"Where is Lord Blake, then?"

"Not here."

"That, sir, is plain. Can you be more specific? Or do you intend to 'rescue' me from such petty concerns altogether?"

"Forgive me. In all likelihood your husband is in the custody of the Viennese authorities."

"Thank you, Mr....?"

"Beckett," he said, with just a hint of nod. "At your service."

"I very much doubt that."

He smiled again and Emma wished he wouldn't, "Tell me about Anwar al-Beshi," he said. "And Kemintiri."

***

The messenger from Professor di Zagreb arrived in the lobby at the Hotel Sacher precisely three minutes after midnight. A short man of Turkish descent, he had darker skin than most Austrians and wore a heavy mustache. He presented a card to the concierge, who invited him to wait in the ground-floor café. Fifteen minutes later, Victoria Ash and Regina Blake found him and accompanied the man outside to the carriage awaiting them on Philharmonikerstrasse. The man never spoke and it was only as they were disembarking in front of Fortschritt itself that Regina noted the thin strands of catgut that bound the man's lips together. She remembered the other silent manservant.

By a quarter to one, Victoria and Regina were in a well-appointed receiving room, face to face with an assemblage of members of House Tremere. Anastasz di Zagreb, reed-thin and straw-haired, and the Englishman Dr. Edward Bainbridge, spectacled and portly, were known to them. Along with them was a bearded and rather severe German who introduced himself as Dr. Claas Drescher.

Di Zagreb did much of the talking. "I presume you have read of the incident in the Freyung last night?"

Regina had paid little attention to the hubbub, so consumed was she with her own melancholy, but Victoria had said something about recognizing the signs of her kindred's presence in between the lines of the press reports. Both Englishwomen nodded.

"I regret to inform you," di Zagreb continued, directing his attention to Regina, "that Lady Blake was abducted by unknown interlopers during those events."

Regina let a slight gasp escape her lips, before mastering herself. "What, precisely occurred?"

"That, perhaps, is a question for us to ask you, Lady Regina," di Zagreb said.

"The reports I read," Victoria said, "indicated that some of these interlopers were detained by the police. Surely, given your house's associations here, you are privy to some of the interrogations. How do these people remain unknown?"

Di Zagreb's smile was a curved slice between bloodless lips. The pleasant dandy with a taste for legerdemain, the man whom they'd first met only a few nights ago, seemed to have been replaced by a cruel doppelganger. "Yes, we have access to the prisoners. But it seems that they deny association with the actual kidnapper, a long-haired man whom we believe to be a kindred of yours."

"This is the first we are hearing of this, I assure you," Regina said.

"Indeed," Victoria added when she noted the eyes of the German Drescher on her.

"It is difficult to credit such assurances, Lady Regina," di Zagreb said, "when your relations continue to appear at inconvenient times."

"I thought, Professor, that it was my mother's *disappearance* that concerned you?"

"Forgive me, I referred instead to your father, Lord Blake." Di Zagreb smiled thinly. "He was one of the attackers and currently sits under the watch of the municipal authorities."

Regina felt a rush of warning flash through her and she recognized it as a sign of the strange bond she shared with Victoria. This had suddenly become a much more dangerous situation. Despite that unspoken caution, and years of social gatherings that had taught the value of emotional restraint, Regina could not wholly mask her dismay. Her mouth opened to loose some exclamation but it caught in her throat. She felt a burning in her guts, like the angry cousin to indigestion. She swallowed it down.

"You fear that Lord Blake followed us to Austria," she said, once composed. "I can assure you that is not the case."

"Miss Ash has explained our traditions, *ja?*" Drescher spoke with the directness of a butcher, but he addressed Victoria, not Regina.

"Indeed I have," said the redheaded woman. "My ward is fully cognizant of the importance we place on discretion and the severe penalties for infractions."

"I last saw my father at the beginning of August in England," Regina said. "I did all in my power to discourage any interest he might have in the affairs of your, of our kindred." That was the truth, but stretched to an onion-skin thinness, and Regina felt tension in her spine.

"And yet Lord Blake is here," di Zagreb said. "The problem remains."

Victoria shifted slightly and the light of the room seemed to shift to accent her. "It seems evident that Lord Blake followed some of the same traces we did in following Lady Blake. Your inquiries are thus better directed at your own clansmen, I think." She looked directly at Dr. Bainbridge.

The attention obviously discomfited the portly Englishman. "See here, Miss Ash. You are a long way from Lady Merritt's salons—"

"And yet," she said, taking advantage of a brief pause in the doctor's protestations, "my ward and I have found ourselves here, and if we are to believe Professor di Zagreb, so has Lord Blake and other irritable kine. This hardly speaks of the traditional subtlety Dr. Drescher mentioned."

Regina had a sudden sense of the rage building in Bainbridge. She saw him draped in pale crimson light, like a flickering ghostly fire. The impression vanished before she was even fully aware of it, but she was certain that his coldly logical words masked a seething pool of anger.

"It behooves us then," he said, "to remove any lingering traces of Lady Blake's passage into our night society." His beady eyes held Victoria's gaze for an instant then shifted to indicate Regina.

She saw murder there and her blood ran cold. She refused to cower, however. "If you summoned us here simply to arrange my murder, sir, I do wish you had been civilized enough to get to it rather than playing at being a decent man."

Victoria laid a hand on Regina's knee. "The killing of kindred is as much against our traditions as the casual revelation of our natures, my dear. Dr. Bainbridge seems to have forgotten that."

Bainbridge bristled. "The traditions are less than strict when it comes to the fate of illegitimates, Miss Ash. Perhaps upon my return to London I can inquire whether Lady Anne or any of the prince's representatives authorized Lady Regina's becoming. She seems quite changed from when last we three met."

Regina's hand found Victoria's and squeezed, then she spoke in her own defense. "If I recall, Dr. Bainbridge, you have not had a terrible amount of success in gaining audience with His Royal Highness or Lady Anne. I wonder if you truly believe they will forgo their distaste in this instance, and not instead see you as usurping their authority."

There was a long moment of silence, as Regina stared directly at Bainbridge. She imagined his red aura running to bilious yellow as anger gave way to hate, and to fearful orange. She felt tension in herself as well. She was extrapolating from her experience that the Tremere were unwelcome and barely tolerated in London. Bainbridge might well have more sway than she thought in English circles. He might be able to explain away her murder with a hand wave. Still she steeled herself—she had come this far and would not back down to the threats of a doughy, self-righteous warlock.

"Perhaps," di Zagreb put in, "I can offer a mutually agreeable solution. If you ladies can ensure Lord Blake's silence on this issue, many of our fears about the spread of troublesome speculation would be assuaged. In that case, I'm sure Dr. Bainbridge would have no reason to raise any issue with those of London's host who have the ear of the prince and his seneschal."

Regina felt a cold wave of dread wash over her. "This is monstrous," she said, fighting to keep the sudden shaking in her hand from showing. "You can't expect me to harm my own father." *To murder him*, she added to herself.

Claas Drescher answered, his voice entirely devoid of sympathy. "Our laws are entirely clear on his matter, Fraulein Blake. Either you silence him or we shall."

Regina glanced at Victoria and then back at Drescher, and a scorching heat ran up her arms and down her back. "No! I refuse!" She leapt to her feet and it was as if red-hot filaments were strung through her veins. She wanted to run, to escape, or to strike. She stared at the bearded monster Drescher, suddenly ready to eviscerate him with her own hands.

"Stop," he said.

She felt as if she'd suddenly been swallowed under a numbing wave of icy water. Drescher's eyes were two black voids that held her in an unholy bond. The fire of a mere instant ago was doused and her limbs felt leaden. She could neither look away, nor speak, nor move. She could barely think.

"You will do as we say, Fraulein Blake," Drescher said, "because you understand that it is necessary."

And, God help her, she did. What choice was there but to send her own father to his grave? The man whom she had loved unreservedly these past eighteen years had to die. It was obvious. *What? No!* Deep inside, some reddish spark of outrage yelled out against the freezing tide of Drescher's will, but it was fading quickly.

"Wait."

To Regina's ears, Victoria's voice was a distorted whisper, like a voice carried over the surface of a lake on a summer's night.

"We will be free to leave Vienna unmolested?" the whisper asked.

"Of course," answered Drescher and his voice was like a cannon-shot. His eyes never wavered from Regina's.

"Then I agree," Victoria's faraway voice said.

The ember inside Regina screamed anew. *No! No! No!* But soon she was unsure even what she was denying. All she could see were the twin black pools of Herr Drescher's eyes, like wells open to some infinite void that was pulling her in.

Regina's world went entirely black.

***

The horses were visibly uncomfortable, shifting from hoof to hoof as if they were improperly shod. They were both black mares, bridled in a team to pull a fine carriage that was as dark as they were. The coachman sat stock-still in his seat, keeping a touch of tension on the reins to hold the beasts in place. The clip-clop of their hooves on the paving stones echoed off the façade of the old Carmelite Church in Leopoldstadt.

When the carriage-door opened, the left-hand horse turned her broad neck and snorted. Hot breath condensed in the cool September night. The passenger, a short man wearing a stiff cloak and a tall hat, and carrying a oaken walking stick, gazed hatefully at the offending horse.

"Filthy beast," he whispered to the night, his voice like a blade on a whetstone. The horse fell silent. Claas Drescher, magus pontifex of House Tremere, allowed himself a smile. At least one creature knew its place.

Drescher proceeded to the green-painted door at No. 8

Karmeliterplatz. He ignored the lion-head knocker and used the cold-iron head of his walking stick to rap four times on the door. He did not do so lightly and the intricate pattern in the metal left a series of triangular and circular indentations in the wood.

He noted that there was a crucifix attached to the doorframe, a small brass-and-wood effigy of a deluded carpenter hung to stave off the evils of the night. Drescher paid it no heed and rapped a fifth and final time. A few seconds later the metallic clicking of turned locks and the scratching of removed bars came through the wood and the door opened.

The man who opened the door was two heads taller than Drescher and outweighed him by a hundred pounds of muscle. "*Mein Herr*," the man said and lowered his eyes like a cowed puppy.

"Let me in, Johann," Drescher said. "The time has come."

"But—"

"I know all about your guest, Johann. And Herr Kohler is being seen to."

"He says God is with him, Mein Herr." The giant's voice cracked as if her were revisiting puberty. "The priest says so too."

"And is God with you, Johann?" Drescher asked. "Is He in your heart? Did He heal your shattered bones and mend your torn flesh when you returned from the factory? Was it Him who gave you the foreman's wife?"

Johann stepped back, assaulted by his visitor's words. "N— No…"

Drescher stepped inside and the night seemed to follow him in. "Who gave you those things, Johann?"

"Y— You did, *Mein Herr*…"

The blow was sudden and terrible. Drescher swung his heavy walking-stick with a might fired by the cold blood in his dead veins. The iron head cracked against Johann's jaw, toppling him like a rotted gate hit with a battering ram. The giant sprawled awkwardly on the black and white tile of the small landing between the front door of No. 8 and the tight staircase leading to the apartments upstairs.

Outside, the team of horses shifted and snorted, and the coachman pulled the reins taut.

Drescher stepped fully into the tiny vestibule and swung the door closed behind him. "Who gave you all that, Johann? Who was it?" The knife of his voice grated across the stone anew.

The fallen man looked up from the floor, blood trickling from between his lips. A large welt was rising on the side of his face. "Y— You did, my lord. You did!"

Drescher kicked the man and threw his walking stick aside. "And to whom did you swear yourself, boy? Who?!"

"To you, master. To you!"

"That's right. And if you've been playing at being a witch-hunter, it is at *my* leisure." Drescher unfastened his cloak and let it fall to the ground. "That game is now over." He took off his fine gloves, revealing liver-spotted hands. The nails of his thumbs had long ago been replaced with filed pieces of iron.

"Yes, master." Johann sobbed, snot, blood and tears streaming down his face.

Drescher slipped off the braces holding up his trousers and reached his right hand down his waistband. "Who is your god, boy?"

Johann, bleary-eyed, stinking of fear and awe, stared as his unliving master unfastened his trouser-front and pulled out the swollen root of his dark power. It was like a thick, veined serpent, its dry, hard head pushing out of its sheath of skin like an opening maw.

"You are, master." Johann's words were heavy with the twin burdens of longing and despair, like a forlorn lover's or opium addict's. "You are my god."

Drescher pushed his sharpened iron thumbnail into the dead flesh of his engorged glans. The dark blood came out in a stream, like crimson urine pissed against a wall. It hit Johann in the face, splashing onto his cheek until the large man positioned his mouth to drink up the devilish effluvia.

"Yes," Drescher said. "I am."

Chapter Nine

The man Johann—really more of a boy, Victoria thought, despite his size—displayed the characteristics of the worst type of ghoul. Mortals fed on the blood of vampires were not a novelty to her. Indeed, it was one of the dirty realities of unlife that trustworthy servants to protect one during the day and to deal with mundane matters were hard to do without. Feeding mortals undead blood made them loyal, could also extend their lives and often even granted them a useful fragment of the vampire's powers. It also turned them into blood-addicted slaves.

Victoria had had many ghouls and had few illusions about the bondage imposed upon them. She herself had been one for a normal lifetime before her departed sire Maximilien decided to bring her fully into undeath. That she had imposed the same fate on Regina Blake was largely because she did not wish to enslave the girl with her blood.

Still, there were degrees of bondage. By administering the blood during intimacies or as part of compacts, one could affect the tone of the relationship. The bond of blood might feel like love (although desperate love) or steadfast loyalty (although always the loyalty of inferior to superior). Dear Cedric—once her lover, and more recently her coachman and guardian of several decades—had been so bound. And despite the claims of the socialists and anarchists so vociferous in certain circles, Victoria felt that most chattel did prefer their cages gilded.

Johann, the large man who led her down the hall of the municipal jail, clearly had benefited from none of those kindnesses. Herr Drescher, who had confided him to Victoria's company, had shattered the man's will like delicate bones under the wheel of a medieval executioner. His eyes were dull things, stripped of the spark of independent thought. His mouth was never fully closed, and Victoria had the distinct impression that his ears were permanently cocked to catch his master's call.

This treatment spoke of a master with little appreciation for the beauties and pleasures of society and the human heart. It spoke of a taskmaster who treated his ghouls as tools and little else. Still, she was not here on any business that could be considered humanistic, so perhaps Johann was indeed best suited to guide her.

Better him than Regina, she thought.

"This way," he said, using a long key to unlock one of the steel-reinforced doors leading into the courtyard of the police jail. A bare corridor revealed itself beyond the door.

Victoria had last felt an actual chill several lifetimes ago. Her undead flesh just did not respond to cold as a living woman's might. Still, walking down this dank corridor, she felt her skin pucker into gooseflesh as fingers of dread coiled up her spine.

There's nothing to be afraid of, she told herself, and she was right. Herr Drescher had arranged for her access to prisoners with ease and there was a conspicuous absence of any of the municipal policemen who normally staffed the jail. Nevertheless, her mind conjured memories from her recent time in Paris and the mad, animal thing that was her damned soul screamed for her to run. She showed not a whit of her worry.

She and Regina had gone to Paris last month for very much the same reason they were in Vienna now, to find Lady Emma Blake. Victoria expected enemies from her past to be awaiting her there, but instead she and Regina had ended up in the demesne of a vampire with a God complex. Father Anatole—as the lunatic called himself—laired in Paris's Santé Prison, where he transformed the prisoners into a congregation of zealots. In a few weeks, he had peeled back centuries of unlife and convinced Victoria that she could be redeemed. She had drunk his blood in an unholy sacrament and the chains around her had been gilded with the promise of heaven. If not for Regina, Victoria would still be in the Santé, eternally pledged to the mad priest, eternally hoping for the holy absolution she knew could never come.

Even now, it just took a moment of distraction for Anatole's long blond locks and icy-blue stare to return to her mind's eye. He was, she guessed, as much her elder as she was Regina's, which made him ancient indeed. Was he watching her still? There was no way for her to know for sure—for all she knew, his ancient gaze could see across an ocean as easily as it could across a room.

And what was worst of all, of course, was that a goodly part of her *wanted* him to be watching her. The cynicism she'd worn as an armor against the vicissitudes of existence for so long was back, but it fit poorly and felt eggshell-thin. Were Anatole to reappear and offer her communion again, could she say no?

"The men are in here," Johann said, tripping the latch on one of the cell doors. "The old woman is down the hall."

The cells were cramped rooms with stone walls and no windows, so that when Johann pulled open the heavy door, the pitch darkness within was pushed back. The smell of unwashed men, urine and feces crawled out of the gloom and Victoria ceased breathing altogether in a vain effort to ignore the pungency of incarcerated life.

"Johann!" An older man, his hair wild and mustache broad, stumbled out of the shadows, a look of relief lightening his dirt-caked features. At some point he had received several heavy blows to the face, which had left purple and green bruising there. "Praise God!"

"Hello, Herr Kohler," Johann said.

The old man moved out into the dim light of the hallway. His eyes, one swollen almost shut, fluttered. After who knew how long in the dark, even the pale light must have burned like acid.

"Father Metz is still unconscious," he said. "I think the police are in league…" His voice trailed off when he saw Victoria standing a few yards away.

She allowed herself a smile, sensing the subtle mix of emotions coming off the man like a mist. Relief. Fear. Caution. And the distinct blend of lust and shame so particular to those who considered themselves Christians elevated above their fellows.

"Where is Lord Blake?" Victoria's German was accented and just slightly awkward, but her voice still had the charm of a singer's. She crossed the few steps to the door of the cell and moved past Kohler.

He glanced at Johann, confusedly.

The gloom of the cell did not bother Victoria's night-made eyes. Lying along one wall was the man whom she assumed to be Father Metz. His bare chest was patterned with scars and bruises that spoke of tortures dating from years ago. Lively welts clustered around his neck where Victoria could well imagine an attacker crushing the life from him. He was breathing, but barely.

"You!" Blake exclaimed and advanced from the far wall of the cell. "What are you doing here?"

He was in better shape than the prostrate priest, but not by a great degree. Blake had used some cloth to fashion a makeshift bandage, which now covered his left eye. Had Drescher's men among the police plucked it from its socket? No, she decided, there would be more blood were that the case. Probably just a cut on the lid. He took a few more steps until he was facing her.

"Kohler, Johann," he said in English. "She's one of them. She took my daughter."

Victoria didn't turn around, but she didn't have to, the scenario was so predictable. Kohler, shocked by the revelation, turned to face her with an exclamation— "*Was?*"—and then Johann revealed his true colors to his witch-hunting confederates. The wet smack of his fist on Kohler's head was surprisingly loud in the empty jail.

Victoria read the shock on Blake's face as Kohler fell under a barrage of blows from the giant ghoul. Bones broke and the heady smell of blood filled her nostrils, exciting the hungry thing at the core of her.

"That's right, Lord Blake. Your little pursuit is over."

"Where is my daughter?" he barked. "What have you done with her?"

He raised an arm to strike her, but she was much faster and grabbed his wrist in her hand. "I've done nothing but help her," she said, stretching the truth until it broke. "She is well."

"What do you want?"

"For you to leave," she said. "To forget everything and return to your pedestrian life."

Kohler groaned and Johann kicked him once more, sending a splash of spit, blood and teeth near Victoria's foot. It was vile and disgusting. She wanted more.

"That's impossible," Blake said. "I can't forget!"

"I know," she said, long dagger-pointed canines peaking from behind her ruby lips. She pulled him to her.

"No," he gasped and pushed her away. "No!"

Lord Blake's strength, despite his size and sex, was no match for Victoria's, whose undead physiognomy granted her predatory might. Still, that he resisted, that he pushed her away at all, brought her up short. She fixed her gaze on him and whispered, "Yes."

He swallowed. She watched the blood pump along his ceratoid artery. His fear and his desire—sensations far less discordant than most believed—wafted from him like the hues of impure gas burning. The beating of his strong heart filled her ears and she felt the erotic charge of hunger building further. "Yes," she repeated, her voice a husky murmur of want.

He wobbled slightly, drunk in the heady aura of the unliving beauty before him. "You've bewitched me. As you did my daughter."

Victoria's tongue licked moisture onto her lips. "Regina came to me, Lord Blake."

"And Lady Winthrope," he said, "did she come to you as well?"

An icy chill ran through Victoria's dead veins. "I—"

Lord Blake cut her off, anger overtaking his fear. "Don't deny it, witch. I talked to her in the nunnery where she sought shelter. She told me how you plucked her from the edge of womanhood for your amusement. Just like you did Regina."

A barrage of sensations overtook Victoria as Lord Blake spoke. The sharp tang of anger and defiance from him, along with the bitter sting of shame coming from her own unbeating heart. With the shame came memories, of a young and beautiful girl named Mary-Elizabeth Sterling whom Victoria had met in her early years in London. She had been an amusement and a distraction, an innocent to feed from in an existence full of lies and sins. And when, besotted, she had wanted more, Victoria hadn't had the will to refuse her. Games of blood and of sex had made Mary-Elizabeth her lover, her servant and her slave.

Victoria silently damned herself and her superior attitude. Was it only minutes ago that she was priding herself on being better than Drescher and the rest? That she was lauding the relative morality of servitude based on pleasure rather than fear?

"She damns you to hell for what you did to her," Blake exclaimed, "and I do as well!"

A red hot memory of five years ago bubbled up from Victoria's mind: Mary-Elizabeth, recently widowed when the Baron Alfred Winthrope had finally died, lying across Victoria's bed on the third floor of her house on Charlotte Place. *The same bed in which I took Regina*, she thought, but even that recrimination couldn't chase away the memory. Mary-Elizabeth had been lovely as ever, now a woman rather than a girl, though the blood she'd sipped from Victoria's veins held back the full truth of her age. She looked twenty when she was actually thirty.

Out of respect for her dead husband, Mary-Elizabeth's corset had been black. It contrasted sharply with the pale cream of her naked flesh and the red trickle of blood running down the inside of her bare thigh. She'd placed a pillow under her bare buttocks and parted her legs, so the blood flowing from the incisions she'd made just above her knee would trickle toward her sex.

"Harold tried to mount me the night of his death, you know," she'd said in a drunken lilt. "I like to think it's what finally did in his old withered heart."

Victoria had watched the woman's blood flow and felt disgust and ennui knot in her guts. It had only been a matter of time before Mary-Elizabeth murdered her husband. Where was the young thing excited and scared of the dark delights Victoria could show her? Who had replaced her with this blood-addled harlot craving only the next degradation? Victoria had known the answer then and she knew it still now—she had remade the intriguing virgin into a predictable whore. Victoria had only herself to blame.

Mary-Elizabeth's delicate fingers had traced the folds of moist flesh where she wanted Victoria's bite, smearing them with blood. "Now we can be together forever," she'd said, as Victoria knew she would.

The vampire had tossed her ghoul a coverlet with which to hid her nakedness. A bead of red stained through the white cotton blend. "I think not."

The past receded with Lord Blake's accusing tone. "She warned me and I won't be made into your slave. And neither will my daughter." His finger, fat and slightly crooked, pointed in her face.

"Regina is not my slave," Victoria said, her voice small. She could feel pressure building behind her eyes, as if she were a dam submitted to a sudden and overwhelming flood surge. "I... I saw to that."

"How? By giving her to another of your kind? Like my wife?"

"I had nothing to do with... that is..." The dam of her soul was cracking under the pressure. She tried to step away.

He grabbed her. "And my daughter? Did you have nothing to do with her? You've damned her to hell!"

She lifted him bodily off the dusty ground of the cell. "Your daughter's only crime was not abandoning the wife you let slip away! Your daughter will be killed because of the damnable priests you've brought here! Do you understand?"

"Lies," he said. "You're trying to trick me..."

She dropped him. "Believe that if you must. I don't have the luxury of your illusions."

He looked at her and for just a moment, she saw a wave of sadness and regret wash over him, followed immediately by hot rage so strong it eclipsed sanity. "No! You and your kind are parasites on the face of God's green earth. I won't rest until I've scourged you from it! Do you hear me! I'll never stop! Never!"

Victoria had the sensation of falling, of the dam of her mind breaking. Then, there was nothing but black anger, white rage, and red, red blood.

"Try to remain calm," Beckett said, holding the pewter cup of goat's blood to Emma Blake's mouth. Her lips were drawn back and her teeth gnashed like a beast. "The night is half over."

The small cellar was just north of the main road of the walled Jewish ghetto in the town of Eisenstadt just over the intra-imperial border between Austria and Hungary. The town was only forty miles from Vienna and they'd taken a quick train trip from there this very evening. The trip had been uneventful, even easy.

That was before Emma Blake's fits had started.

The first came as they walked up Rusterstrasse toward the oldest part of the town, built around the impressive Esterházy Fortress. The Englishwoman had suddenly fallen to her knees and Beckett had had to shake her to rouse her. By the time they were crossing into the Jewish ghetto just northwest of the fortress, she was trembling and speaking in word fragments.

Abraham Mazel had been less than thrilled to see his old acquaintance Mr. Beckett return to his house with a shivering, muttering madwoman in his hands. He'd gladly locked them both in the cellar under his house, and gone to lie with his wife Ruth two stories above. He hadn't answered her questions about the strangers directly. "Suppliers," he called them. Herr Mazel was a dealer in antiquities and occasionally sheltered men who made their livings acquiring such things in ways the authorities might not find acceptable. Ruth Mazel decided not to ask about the female voice she'd heard.

"Drink," Beckett said, tipping the cup so the dark blood ran in a heavy stream into Emma's lips. She sputtered and swallowed, blood running down her cheek and spattering her cloak. She was tied with a rough rope to a chair.

"I know it tastes bitter," he said, "but it's the only thing available." He'd sneaked back out into the streets of Eisenstadt once Herr Mazel retired and returned with the goat now cooling in the corner. "I won't risk Mazel's position by being responsible for a disappearance that might be traced to his home."

With sudden force, Emma Blake spat out the animal blood and spouted a long string of syllables in a language that was most assuredly neither her native English or any German she might have picked up in Vienna. Anger and outrage flared in her expression and she strained against the ropes that bound her.

Beckett fell back. He strained to understand what she was saying. "I don't…"

"*Adamithra!*" she yelled, "*Sayabiyasayabiyanam.*"

"Wait," he said and tried an experimental world, "*xsáyabiya?*"

She stopped yelling and looked at him for a second.

"Lady Blake? How did you learn Persian cuneiform?" Beckett was dumbfounded. Fifty years ago, he'd traveled to Persia after hearing the reports of English explorer Henry Rawlinson, and thrilled to the stories of the man's deciphering of the region's ancient alphabet. But to hear those words spoken was another matter altogether.

"*Adam Mithra!*" she exclaimed.

Now that she spoke a little more slowly and that he had guessed her language, he managed to translate: *I am Mithras*, she was saying.

"What do you mean, Lady Blake?"

"I'll take your liver," she suddenly said in English, "and eat it fried!"

"What?" Beckett was at a loss. He approached her again. "Does this have to do with Kemintiri?"

"Oh," she said, staring intently over Beckett's shoulder, "have to go." She passed out.

Beckett turned around, looking for whatever it was she was looking at. There was nothing on the stone wall of the cellar save an old clock without hands. Beckett removed his pocket watch and checked the time, curious if that might provide some clue of Lady Blake's behavior. It was just past 2:00 a.m. on Sunday, September 30th, 1888.

He sat in the corner of the room and tried to make sense of it all. She'd called herself Mithras, which was the name of an ancient Persian deity but also the reigning vampiric prince of London. Beckett had heard that the prince fostered the impression that he had been that same deity in hoary nights past, but those stories almost always ended up being half-truths in Beckett's experience. Far more likely, this unliving potentate had appropriated the name of a deity from his mortal life to give himself additional authority.

But what did Lady Blake have to do with any of that and what was this whole matter of eating a liver? The unliving fed off blood, but usually could not consume flesh.

And how did Kemintiri, the Thousand-Faced Daughter of Set, fit into any of this?

Beckett looked down at the dead goat on the floor beside him. He'd have to dispose of that before dawn. Herr Mazel did not approve of slaughtering animals under his roof.

***

Regina became aware of herself again while riding a freight train westward out of Vienna. It was dark, but her vision was sharp enough to make out a crowd of heavy crates, and the rocking of rail travel was unmistakable. Victoria was sitting next to her, dressed in a farm-girl's simple shift and head-scarf.

"We'll be in Wels before dawn," she said. "We will take the Grand Express for Paris there tomorrow evening."

It took Regina several minutes to make any sense of that statement. She expected to fall back into the oblivion of Drescher's eyes at any second, and before she could even let herself listen to Victoria, she had to assure herself that the German sorcerer was not in the train car with them.

"What happened?" she asked.

"I'm sorry, Regina," Victoria said, voice quiet. "I truly am."

What is she sorry about? Regina wondered. Then she remembered, and she screamed into the night. Her voice was swallowed by the rhythmic knocking of the rails under the train.

Interlude:
The Calais-Dover Ferry,
Late September, 1888

*In which loyalties are tested and
despair eclipses hope.*

Crossing the Channel in the autumn was not an activity for those fearful of the sea. A strong, cold wind was blowing that afternoon, creating angry swells in the choppy water and sending salty spray across the bow with every dip of the ship. The skies were overcast, threatening to add rain to the stomach-churning conditions.

Lt. Malcolm Seward leaned once again over the wooden bucket clutched between his legs and felt his guts clench in a vain attempt to expel their non-existent contents. He spat a sour wad of bile and mucous into the bucket's swill. The stinking froth there was tinted pink.

He groaned and leaned back against the cold wall of the small cabin he and his companion had claimed in Calais. The wood was varnished and beads of cold moisture hung on it, echoing the fever-sweats on Seward's skin.

"Take deep breaths, my friend," said Othman al-Masri, Seward's traveling companion. An aged Arab wearing the *galabiyya* robe so typical of his Egyptian home, al-Masri spoke in a rich, throaty English. "This will pass."

Seward closed his eyes and tried to believe it. A cavalryman who had fought in Egypt and the Sudan, he'd certainly traveled by ship across rough seas before. Never had it had such a disastrous effect. Perhaps it was the result of weeks of French food on his English bowels, or simply an effect of the time of year.

"We must have strength," al-Masri went on, "if we are to face what is coming."

That was it, of course. The Channel's surface could be as calm as a limpid pool and Seward's innards would still be in knots. The rise and fall of a rough passage was just the excuse his torn soul needed to impose a physical toll for the horrors of the last months.

Remembered sensations pierced the veil of nausea to assail him: the swell of pride when he was brought into the Taurus Club for Gentlemen, a venue where his military career could advance by leaps and bounds; the intoxicating thrill of learning the secret rites of the club and the select brotherhood at its core. Above all, he could feel the heady power of the initiation ceremony—the coppery taste of the sacrificial blood on his lips, the weight of the dagger in his hand, the slick sensuality of the bull-woman wrapped around his manhood, and the climactic release of slashing her throat.

Each pleasurable animal memory, however, triggered a spasm in his stomach as the horror of his own acts became clear to him. In his memory he could clearly see the face of his beloved Regina behind the bull-mask and recognized the intimate curves of the body he'd savaged. He had chased her to Paris to free her from the clutches of an undead creature, only to have her confront him with his own perfidy. Every remembered word was like a blow to his midsection:

"It was me," she'd said when he finally found her in the bowels of Paris's Santé prison. "I was the bull-woman. You took me and then drove a knife across my throat." He'd tried to protest, but her accusations were too true, too strong. "My heart is dead, Malcolm, and you've killed it."

He'd raged at her. She was in the company of the harlot Victoria Ash, whom he had reason to believe was something less than human. She'd had truck with the undead, not he. To that she had almost laughed. "Have you ever seen your darling Captain Ellijay under the light of day?" she'd accused. "Ask yourself why not. Do you even know who you've become?"

The thought of that final question bent him over double again and sent more bile into the bucket.

Once he'd finished heaving, Seward sat back again and let Othman take the bucket from him. The Arab stood and headed for the deck, swaying with rocking of the boat. His left arm was in a sling, a plaster-of-Paris cast encasing it from above the elbow to below the wrist, and with the bucket in his right hand, it was only his natural balance that kept him from collapsing. Guilt assailed Seward again as al-Masri headed above decks to dispose of the refuse. This aging man had had his arm broken by a Parisian policeman while helping Seward and others break into the Santé prison. He too wished to save Regina from the clutches of the dark powers that had drawn her in. Didn't Seward owe him the truth, at least?

Lieutenant Seward wondered to whom he *did* owe the truth. He had owed it to Regina, certainly, before he unwittingly made of his beloved fiancée his victim. Did he owe it to her father, Lord Blake? Another one trying to save Regina, it was at his behest that Seward had gone to Paris. The man had been his commanding officer and his patron in Egypt, and he'd hoped he would become his father-in-law.

And Captain Ellijay, then? Ellijay was the man who'd brought him into the Taurus Club, who'd made him a member of Her Majesty's Own Horse Guards—a regiment whose prestige should have been out of reach for a yeoman's son. Ellijay had become the patron Lord Blake had once been, preaching the value of soldiery, loyalty and empire. Seward could still see the man's hard gray eyes as he agreed to let him go to Paris and ordered that he find Victoria Ash and report back. Did he deserve the truth?

Seward reached into his jacket and drew out the copy of the telegram he'd sent the captain just two days ago from the French capital.

```
SIR—MISS ASH & LADY REGINA HAVE
VANISHED—AM CONTINUING MY SEARCH—
WITH RESPECT—LT. M. SEWARD
```

The proof of the lie to his sponsor and commanding officer, to the man Regina Blake accused of being more monstrous than those she kept company with, sent another spasm through Seward's gut. He stuffed the message into his pocket and tried to fight down the dry heave. A minute or two later, he felt the bucket being slipped between his knees again.

"Tell me," al-Masri said, taking his seat once more, "do you think your regimental brothers, or your commander perhaps, can be of any assistance to us?"

Seward clenched his eyes shut. The pressure caused sparks of color to dance in the blackness of his field of vision. In them he could not help but see the slate gray of Captain Ellijay's eyes. "No," he whispered.

He wasn't sure just to whom he was speaking.

Part Two:
London, October, 1888

*In which a final elevation occurs and the
streets of the East End run red with blood.*

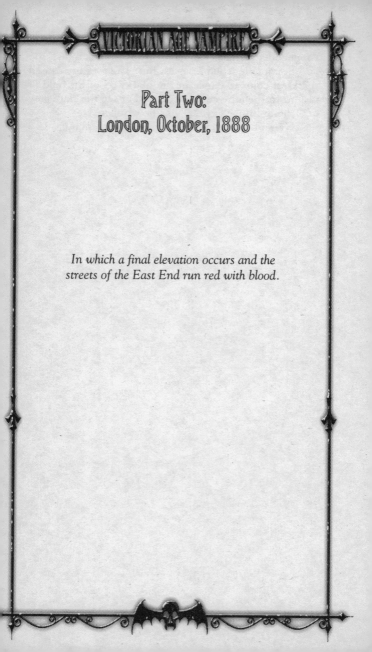

Chapter Ten

"This is becoming tiresome, Miss Parr." Lady Anne Bowesley, widely thought to be the second-most prominent creature among the undead host of London (and hence, to some ways of thinking, the world), paced slowly along the third-floor hall of the Highgate Asylum. "You had assured us that His Royal Highness would be safe here."

"He is, Your Grace." Juliet Parr, dressed in the height of evening fashion for one not of her sex—a suit of fine black wool with a starched white high-collared linen shirt and matching gloves and tie—forced herself to maintain a leisurely gait. She was used to decisive, precise movement and her instinct was to walk briskly down the hall to their mutual destination. One did not outpace Lady Anne, however. "It is the other guests of the asylum for whom Doctor Thomas might be concerned."

Anne turned to look the younger woman in the eyes. "I have little concern for the worries of your current pet, Miss Parr."

"These are not Tom O'Bedlams and other disposable folk, Your Grace. The asylum exists to discreetly care for the afflicted from the best families. Deaths are noticed here, especially ones so overwrought."

"Do you feel it necessary to remind me of my duties, Miss Parr? Perhaps I should instead be reminding you of yours."

"Not at all," Miss Parr said, omitting the honorific due Lady Anne. "Protecting us all from intrusive inquiries is always my primary concern. That is precisely why I thought to—"

"Enough," Lady Anne snapped, without raising her voice but still endowing it with more than enough strength. "You proposed this asylum as a safe shelter for His Royal Highness during the current troubles. I will not accept seeing him moved again so soon. If Dr. Thomas is so concerned about his patients, perhaps he should see to them elsewhere for the time being."

"Yes, Your Grace." Parr tried to bury the indignation rising in her. She almost succeeded. "Here we are."

Juliet Parr threw open the latch on the large cell door at the end of the hall. A buzzing of flies greeted her and Lady Anne as they entered. Although the carnage was fresh, it seemed the first generation of insects had already hatched—or were laying their eggs in great number.

If she expected Lady Anne to be impressed or shocked by the display in the cell, Parr was sorely disappointed. The undead seneschal looked at the body of the half-mad son of a Welsh marquis and took in the mess the fool had made. The boy, only fourteen years of age, had apparently gotten hold of a blade and used it to open the veins of his arms. He'd also taken the opportunity to slit his own belly open and liberate his looping viscera. He'd done all this, it seemed, while strolling around the cell, leaving a strange spiral pattern of blood and intestines behind him. He'd collapsed near the only window.

The staff had found the boy—who'd uttered not a single yelp during his baroque suicide—at three minutes to midnight, not quite two hours ago. The plentiful blood had cooled and dried into a sticky, brownish mess that was less than useless for the purposes of any refined predator. Lady Anne crinkled her nose slightly and gave the impression of disapproving of the waste of so much sustenance. This was the fourth patient to have drained his own blood in a self-destructive fit.

"Yes," she said before turning to leave, "do see that this is cleaned up."

"The boy's name was John Albert Paul," Miss Parr said, "but he was universally known as Jack."

Lady Anne's attention returned to Miss Parr, communicating with a raised eyebrow and a steeled gaze just how unwelcome this news was. They had both woken that evening to the mania surrounding the murders of two more prostitutes in the Whitechapel district. More sensational still had been the printing of not one, but two letters supposedly sent to the press by the killer himself. The *Daily News* had one in the morning edition and the *Star* another in the evening edition. In each, the killer gave himself a frighteningly gothic appellation: "Jack the Ripper" in the *News*, "Saucy Jack" in the *Star*.

"Coroner Baxter has begun an inquest into the death of the Stride woman," Parr said, "and according to my sources he places her murder in the first hours after midnight. The Eddowes woman shortly thereafter."

"These are the two latest bawdy women."

"Yes."

"Mutilated, as I understand it. By night, like the previous prostitutes."

"Exactly so."

"One of our kindred then, or a foreigner." Anne said this with the tone of a ruler who, in the midst of directing a military campaign against an implacable enemy, receives news of a revolt at home.

"I have my doubts," said Miss Parr. It was her duty to enforce the laws of the undead north of the Thames and if one of London's unliving host was hunting so carelessly in Whitechapel it was her responsibility to stop the offender. "My understanding is that the killer has an appetite for violence, and perhaps for organ-meat, but not for blood. None of the bodies were drained."

"A mundane killer then, with a flair for publicity."

"Perhaps, but the timing of the deaths—"

"Thank you, Miss Parr," Lady Anne interrupted, "Make sure our kindred are not involved and guard against discovery by the overzealous."

"And His Royal Highness?"

"Will remain within these walls." Anne stepped back into the hall and headed for the main stairway, leaving her sheriff to clean up the Jack messes, big and small.

***

Lady Anne only wished she could dismiss Miss Parr's concerns as easily as she could the boyish woman herself. General Halesworth, who was Miss Parr's superior and one of Anne's close advisors, had been right to recommend her: Despite her choice of attire, she was determined and perceptive, to a fault it seemed. The timing of the Whitechapel deaths was worrisome indeed.

Anne descended the stairs to the asylum's second floor and then glided along the empty hall. She passed by empty wards and cells and her boots made a light clicking sound on the wooden floors. She turned the corner and nodded to the man standing stock-still by the double doors at the end of the hall. He removed a long iron key from the pocket of his green-hued regimental uniform and inserted it in the heavy lock, giving it two turns. He then held the door to the floor's eastern wing open for her and she walked in.

The rooms there were in a much improved state, she was relieved to see. In the last twenty-four hours, all the furniture had been replaced and the mess tidied. She inhaled through her nose, something she avoided whenever possible, seeing that inhalation was only necessary to have the breath with which to speak and that

London was not, generally speaking, a sweet-smelling metropolis. There was the faint smell of lye and even of some perfume used to cover the worst of last night's mess.

Another man stood by the door to the bedchamber. He stood at attention, and the bonds of blood kept him loyal and deferential. He was a living man enslaved by the blood of one who'd left behind that condition, what the more sensational of Lady Anne's kindred dubbed a ghoul for their consumption of undead vitae. Nevertheless, she sensed some trepidation in the man. The creature who slumbered in the next room had, after all, spread the viscera of two of this man's companions across the floral-print wallpaper in a fit of apoplectic rage. Still, the man stood his ground and Anne respected that.

"Open it, please."

He undid the largely ceremonial latch on the French doors leading into the bedchamber and pulled them open. He then stepped back to allow his better to pass. "Your Grace."

"Thank you, sir," she said.

Prince Mithras, who presided over London's unliving as Victoria did over the living, was a surprisingly small creature in his slumber. "Man" was not a term Anne thought to apply to one who had last seen the sun sometime before three wise kings came to mark the birth of the Son of God. When he moved and walked, Mithras seemed a giant, his chiseled perfection almost painful to gaze upon, even for one like her. He had been the very essence of might until that fateful evening in Sydenham. Could less than two months have passed? That was hardly a time worth noting for Anne, less than an eyeblink for Mithras, yet those fifty or so nights had stretched themselves into an eternity. The capital, the Empire itself, seemed gripped by dread.

Perhaps, Anne reflected, the dread was only hers. With His Royal Highness incapacitated, the weight of rule fell on her shoulders but not squarely so. She was a woman in a man's place, and despite centuries of practice overcoming the male resistance to direction from another gender, she felt the eyes of her various kindred upon her. Even allies she thought secure were in doubt, much less those whom she knew would welcome her fall along with the prince's.

And then there were His Royal Highness's occasional fits. His slumber had never been peaceful. Creatures such as they slept, quite literally the sleep of the dead during the daylit hours, but his nights had been much less peaceful. Although he rarely rose to even a semblance of consciousness, he whispered fragments of language, made sudden outbursts, and called for sustenance. These symptoms, which in a living man might be considered evidence of troubling dreams, reached their apex in fits of increasing violence. Last night, he'd apparently risen from slumber after midnight and set about destroying anything and anyone in his immediate vicinity. Anne, long attuned to her prince, had felt his rage from the City, several miles away. By the time she arrived at the asylum with the only thing that could calm him, he'd brutally killed two ghouls and torn his chambers to splinters. At roughly the same time, Elizabeth Stride and Catherine Eddowes had met their own gruesome ends in Whitechapel.

Sheriff Parr had noted that fact, which raised many a question. For Anne two were primary: Would anyone else note the coincidence in timing? And could Miss Parr be trusted to keep her mouth sealed firmly shut?

She pondered those questions for a good hour, during which time Prince Mithras only murmured a few words in a language she did not recognize. Greek, perhaps? Finally, she turned and left, leaving the two ghouls alone to guard her stricken monarch.

Captain Ellijay was waiting for her in the front courtyard of the asylum when she emerged. He stood by the door of her carriage, dressed in the smart blue uniform of Her Majesty's Own Horse Guards, and had, it seemed, every hope of riding back to Mayfair or Whitehall with her. She nodded to him, and he helped her up. He sat across from her as the driver pulled out for the brief journey back into the heart of the West End.

Neither spoke until the carriage stopped in front of the Taurus Club for Gentlemen on Pall Mall. Ellijay had reintroduced the same request several times in the last seven weeks, often subtly and a few times quite blatantly. It was a nuisance, but one that might serve a purpose.

Lady Anne, who had scarcely moved during the journey, looked at the military officer just as his hand reached for the door to disembark. "You may proceed, Captain," she said.

**

Lieutenant Anthony Pool never made it to his appointment on the evening of October 2nd. A certain Mister Evans, solicitor for Dr. Harold Claremont, had insisted they meet for a late drink after the theater let out and they'd agreed to find one another at the Boar & Lion, on the Strand near the Law Courts. Dr. Claremont was the brother-in-law of Joanna Claremont, sister to Pool's friend Lieutenant Malcolm Seward. It seemed there was some question in the doctor's mind about the circumstances of his brother John's death this past August. John had been Joanna Claremont's husband, and as Seward had put it before his trip for the Continent, there was foul play involved. Pool was to act as a go-between for Seward in the matter.

Pool was not a great fan of the comic operettas that had become the rage at the Savoy Theatre and elsewhere, although he did enjoy overhearing the worried talk of his social betters about the loathsome effects of such base entertainment. Thus, he had instead enjoyed a leisurely supper at the humble St. George Inn within sight of Lambeth Palace. He felt the warmth of the mutton and boiled potatoes that now filled his stomach and was enjoying his walk across Waterloo Bridge when he became aware that he was being followed.

There were two of them, as far as he could tell. Both in the wool suits and bowler hats of the classes to which Pool was most accustomed. No top hats, tails and weak spines in these two. One would be well described as a man crossed with a bear, while the other seemed fully ursine. They were hard to miss, even in a crowd—and there was no crowd, this late. They were perhaps twenty yards back, keeping pace with Pool across the bridge. He realized that he'd seen them as he left the St. George but hadn't then suspected they were after him. Their appearance on the bridge left no doubt. Pool was still deciding whether to run or confront them when he spotted their partners coming up the bridge from the northern end.

The two bears stayed back a few yards while the other two—similarly dressed but somewhat less gargantuan—approached. There were, of course, any number of reasons these men could be here. Tony Pool had left perhaps more than his fair share of young ladies in a state of less-than-virginal perfection and these might be cousins and brothers come to exact vengeance. They had a more coordinated look about them, though—like men who'd had ample opportunities to perfect the art of trapping wayward souls. Pool's mind excitedly tripped to the possibility of the Whitechapel murderer—whom yesterday's *Daily News* had called Jack the Ripper. He was supposedly butchering people left and right. Could these four collectively be the monster that was so confounding the constabulary? But no—those murders were committed on women and in Whitechapel, across the river and further east. The Bag's Alley Gang, then. Pool had left London without fully recompensing some of the tarts who worked their turf last year. Perhaps it had been foolish to think they'd have forgotten by now.

The shortest of the thugs was the one who spoke. "You'll be coming with us, then."

"I'm sorry, but—"

Pool's plan had been to rabbit-punch the larger of the two in the throat and then run. Few men had any great tolerance for a blow to the Adam's apple, he'd found, or much expectation of one. It was a decent plan and it might have worked had he not taken his attention off the shorter speaker. As it was, that shorter man's blow to Pool's gut caught the lieutenant off guard and stole all the wind from him.

After that there was a rain of other blows as the bears joined in. And then darkness.

***

"Right, ya Spanish glock. Time to wake up."

The voice, which pierced the veil of Pool's unconsciousness, was soon joined by a chilling blast of dirty water to the face. His eyes opened as he spat and gasped to clear his throat. There was a substantial amount of pain and he tasted blood along with the excrement that had been mixed with the water.

Pool's primary concern, however, was the fact that he was tied to a post of some sort and surrounded by men who, very evidently, did not wish him well. His vision was blurred by the water, the pain and the after-effects of blessed unconsciousness, so he could not make out more than the vague shapes of most of his captors. The pig-like face of the short man who had punched him the gut was all too clear, however. The man was putting down the bucket he'd just used and smiling evilly. He had stripped to his undershirt, like a laborer ready for heavy work. It was damp and cold, but the man seemed unconcerned with the chill.

"Here we are," he said, "awake at last."

"Lieutenant," came a voice from one of the blurs. Precise and well-bred, that voice, nothing like the East End mish-mash of Undershirt. This blur had a top hat. "We represent here the interests of Her Majesty's government and we hope you will be willing to provide us with some answers to rather vexing questions."

Pool's instinct was to answer with some sort of stinging retort about the man's lineage and the presence of sheep therein, but instead he waited for him to continue.

"I wonder," Top Hat said at last, "if you might tell us just how you became involved with the Taurus Club for Gentlemen, located on Pall Mall?"

Pool had barely had time to process the question and take a breath when Undershirt stepped forward and fired another blow to the soft flesh on Pool's left side, just under his ribcage. Stars of pain exploded in his blurred sightscape and bile rose up his gullet.

"It would be much easier if you cooperated, Lieutenant," said Top Hat. "For all of us."

"I don't mind a little work," said Undershirt, coming close enough for Pool to smell the pickled oysters on his breath. "Not at all."

The man was smiling a gap-toothed smile when Pool shot his head forward, breaking the thug's nose with his forehead. He followed with a swift kick into the man's knee, which resulted in the satisfying snap of breaking kindling.

Pool lunged to his right, or did the best he could with his arms tied to the post. There was some give in the ropes, but they tightened quickly, and his shoulders screamed as his arms were pulled back by his own weight. There was, however, some shifting in the post itself, which gave Pool the hope of freedom.

Several of the shadowy figures stepped forward. The most alarming was neither of the bearish brutes from Waterloo Bridge, although they were there. No, it was the tall man in the deep blue coat of the Metropolitan Police. He had removed his tall rounded cap, but the man was undoubtedly a Peeler and he had the standard issue club to show for it. That club swiftly and repeatedly found Pool's skull.

***

"Hello? Lieutenant? Time to wake up again."

Darkness gave way first to vertigo, then to pain, then to a cloudy image. There was light coming from a lantern, held aloft by one of the Bear Brothers. It illuminated a writhing shape that resolved itself into Undershirt, moaning and clutching at his (hopefully) broken leg. That joyous thought brought a touch more awareness to Pool and he took note of Top Hat, who was standing at the edge of the lantern's glow, and of the other Bear Brother, who was holding a very large knife.

"You have done service in India, have you not, Lieutenant?" Top Hat's voice had lost none of its poise.

Pool grunted through swelling lips.

"My companion here chose to deal with Indians of another type, traveling to the American frontier. The Wild West Mr. Cody and the rest have made such a spectacle of in recent years."

The brother with the knife got close and held the blade aloft. It was broad and oblong, something like a knife one would use to clean a fish. It caught the yellow lamplight quite clearly.

Pool tried to lash out again, but he found that he'd been tied much more securely this time—trussed up like witch on the pyre.

"The savages in Oklahoma," Top Hat continued in the tone of a lecturing don, "have a gruesome practice of collecting the scalps of their foes as war trophies. Those of white men—and women—are the most prized, apparently. This is certainly barbarous, but it has led to the development of a type of wide blade well-suited to the cutting of man-flesh. This is just such a knife."

The Bear Brother moved with surprising finesse, sticking the sharp tip of the blade into the skin of Pool's right arm. With a few quick jerks of his wrist, he'd filleted into the biceps. Already numb and abused, Pool felt the pain like a distant echo.

"Now, Lieutenant, the Taurus Club for Gentlemen on Pall Mall," Top Hat said.

When Pool didn't answer, the knife-wielder smiled. Pool spent the next two hours rediscovering the pain he thought he'd forgotten, repeatedly blacking out only to have some new outrage draw him back into consciousness.

Finally, when much of Pool's blood was soaked into the muddy soil of the unfinished basement, Top Hat leaned close and said, "This is your last chance, Lieutenant. We stand here as representatives of the Crown, which you have sworn to defend. Denying us can only lead to your execution as a traitor. Are you sure you choose that seditious club over your country and your Queen?"

"I think," Pool said, in a wreck of a voice that broke up into a wet cough, "that's obvious. You can fuck the Queen on my behalf."

Top Hat's face stiffened with something like shock or dismay and stood up. "Well," he said, "I suppose that settles matters." Then he turned and walked away.

Pool braced himself as best he could for the killing blow. Instead, a familiar voice pierced the gloom that was settling across his vision. "Well done."

He opened his eyes to see Captain Ellijay, dressed in the dashing blue of the Horse Guards, standing not three yards away. Top Hat was standing near him, speaking quietly. "Exemplary resiliency, sir," the well-dressed torturer said.

Pool croaked, "Captain?" His mind ravaged by pain, fatigue and blood-loss, he struggled to make sense of this. What was Captain Ellijay—the very man who had brought him into the Taurus Club and its secret nocturnal world—doing so casually speaking to these men. Unless…

"Your final elevation is at hand, Lieutenant," Ellijay said. He took a few steps forward and loomed over Pool. "You have taken the first two steps already, joining the Taurus Club and becoming an initiate into the Taurine Brotherhood itself. For months, you have been a squire among knights, a cadet among soldiers. You have seen the great general who guides us. Name him."

The answer bubbled into Pool's mind. The eternal general had guided soldiers through countless kingdoms and cultures. He was Mars, Arthur Pendragon, St. Michael, and St. George, but he had one name above all. "M– Mithras."

"Praise be," Ellijay answered, reverentially. "A select few of us have surrendered the day altogether to serve at his side through eternity, to build an Empire that has existed since time immemorial. We have abandoned lesser gods and lambs for him." As he spoke, Ellijay loosened Pool's bindings and lowered him to the slick, wet ground. "Are you ready to join our ranks?"

"Yes," Pool whispered. "Yes."

Captain Ellijay leaned in and Pool caught a glimpse of sharp teeth before the ecstasy of elevation overwhelmed him at last.

Chapter Eleven

Halim Bey's discreet shop on the Borough High Street in Southwark, fronted only by an equally discreet sign introducing it as KARNAK IMPORT AND EXPORT CO., had been the site of many a transaction that would raise the eyebrows of the well-heeled (both living and dead) who lived further north, across the Thames. Halim Bey was a member of the less-than-well-seen bloodline known variously as Setites, desert vipers, sand serpents, and perhaps most colorfully, kaffir snakes. He was especially fond of the ironies of the last term. Used among the undead who had colonial experience as a derogatory term for a "bastard line" of vampires claiming heritage among the dusky-skinned people of the Egyptian and Sudanese deserts, and among Caucasian mortals for any dark-skinned man they wished to belittle, the word *kaffir* was actually the Arabic *kafre*, or infidel. And Halim Bey, who maintained a discreet crypt beneath his shop in which he prayed to an effigy of the Dark God Set, was quite happy to be called infidel by Christian and Muslim alike. He was a Follower of Set and happy to peddle the sins that addled and confused the weaklings who called this Empire theirs.

This particular night early in October, the sin Halim was helping to indulge was an erotic mixture of slavery and homosexuality. Halim himself did not consider either of these things inherently sinful, of course. Set led the way toward freedom from the falsehood of law, and compared to the bondage of society, a few chains were hardly worth mentioning. And the extraction of sexual pleasure from one gender or another was hardly more than a matter of personal taste. All in all, it would be quite petty of anyone to think what was happening in the private room in the upstairs of the Karnak Import and Export Co. was in any way scandalous.

But the English, living and dead, were an extremely petty people and that was why Halim Bey loved them so.

"Yes, he is perfect, Bey."

The speaker was a mortal dealer in antiquities named Wim Hendriksen. Originally from Antwerp, he'd settled in London years ago and become a force to be reckoned with in the discreet market in antiquities and *objets d'arts* that made their way into the imperial capital. He and Halim Bey were, technically speaking, competitors, and Halim had made it a priority to render the man indebted to him. Mr. Hendriksen was at the very least peripherally aware of the night society of London's undead. Halim felt, in fact, that the city's vampiric authorities would feel the Dutchman knew too much for a breathing man not bound into perpetual slavery to one of the undead, and if Hendriksen was someone's slave, Halim had not been able to find out whose. All this made him even more interesting, and made exploiting his peccadilloes even more valuable.

Hendriksen passed his hand, still in a light-gray silk glove, across the bare thigh of the nameless young man who was bound on what might be mistaken for a medical examining table. The man—and just barely that—whimpered beneath his gag as Hendriksen's fingers brushed through the blond curls around the prisoner's exposed sex.

"Beautiful," Hendriksen said. "Where do you find them, Bey?"

"Revealing a supplier is the first step toward being cut out of commerce, sir." In fact, the young man (like those who'd come before him) had been easy enough to obtain through the use of an especially potent soporific in the hands of a prostitute in the bordello he'd been visiting. Halim Bey had several agents among the bawdy houses, both popular and refined.

Of course, Hendriksen could surely find young men anxious to be sodomized by a wealthy Dutchman on his own. Despite the moral pretensions of Queen Victoria, her capital was far from free of those who preferred the carnality of their own gender. But Wim Hendriksen did not, it turned out, want willing partners. He wanted men secure in their masculinity. He wanted to drink up their fear as well as fill them with his semen. He'd once let on that he had simply become bored with women, who were no challenge, so engrained was their inferiority. Men would fight and feel true despair as they became nothing but the objects of his perversions.

"What a strong young man you are," Hendriksen said, removing one glove and then the next. "I'm sure your heart will fight a long time." He smiled and reached into the small case he had previously laid on a nearby chair. From it he retrieved a pair of very thin and very long shears. (Halim Bey had yet to find out who had made them and why, but he was sure the truth would only add to the Dutchman's cheap and tawdry history.)

Halim caught the jingle of the bells he hung at the shop's front door and made a small motion to politely excuse himself. Hendriksen acknowledge him with a slight nod and returned to his work. Halim paused at the doorway to admire the scene one last time: the Dutchman dressed as if ready to attend an opera at the Royal Albert Hall, the unfortunate young man splayed naked and bound on the table before him. Tears and phlegm were running down the man's face and whimpers were coming from behind his heavy gag as Hendriksen used the shears to open the cluster of nerves located just behind the man's scrotum. Halim knew the man's terror was being eclipsed by self-loathing as he realized just how acutely his erect member was reacting to the ministration.

Pain, pleasure, submission, and shame. So very English.

Halim made his way downstairs, making sure to lock each door as he passed through it. It would not do for an idle customer to find these chambers. When he entered the back storeroom that led directly into the storefront, he nodded to his ghoul Daran, a wizened and rail-thin Kurd he'd made his in Mosul some thirty years ago. The man moved from his position at the peephole into the shop. He looked aged, but had a keen eye and was very adept with a knife. He'd saved Halim's existence twice already.

"Two," Daran said in Kurdish. "Both English, I think. The man was here last month, with Ruhadze. The woman I do not know. Neither has taken a breath since they arrived."

Halim nodded again, opened the wooden door to his left and turned into the darkened corridor beyond. A right-hand turn and a clatter of hanging beads later he was emerging into the storefront, near his counter. "As-salaam alaykum, Mr. Beckett. Welcome back to my humble shop."

Beckett wore a long wool coat with a wide collar, the type of vestment one might wear against the bitter cold of an October night, and so he did not look out of place. His long hair, tied back in a loose braid, might raise some eyebrows in the West End, but here he seemed like nothing so much as colonial traveler who might have gone native to some degree. Either that or an American.

He had his arm draped around a woman Halim had never seen, although he could make an educated guess. She was in a distinct disarray, covered in a rough tarp as a shawl of sorts. It, like the shift that peeked out from under it, was stained black with soot. Her face, which might have been beautiful, was similarly marred by black steaks.

Her hair was matted and damp. Her eyes, though, were strong.

"*Wa alaykum as-salaam*, Halim Bey. This is—"

"Lady Blake, I presume," Halim said with a slight bow. "It was my pleasure to attempt to locate you when Mr. Beckett and Mr. Ruhadze were here last. I'm glad they have found you, although I hadn't expected it would be in quite so much disarray."

Lady Blake seemed past shame. "Mr. Beckett though it best we enter the city aboard a coal train. How he emerged clean, he refuses to say."

"And best you did," Halim said, turning his gaze to Beckett. "I doubt General Halesworth has quite forgotten your altercation last February. I'd suggest keeping a low profile."

In February, before much of this whole business had occurred, Halim had secured a speedy departure from the city for Beckett. The Englishman was a collector of texts and items of import to the history of his kindred and a certain manuscript had come onto the London market. Of course, Beckett hadn't been the only interested party, and arguments, fisticuffs and outright hostilities had ensued. Two of London's unliving host had gone on that long-delayed trip to meet their maker, and General Halesworth—who enforced kindred law south of the Thames—had declared Beckett persona non grata in the city. All of which made it unhealthy for him to be standing in Halim Bey's shop with a soot-covered woman at his side.

"Is Ruhadze here?" Beckett asked. "It's him we need to see."

Halim did his best to mask dismay as simple regret. "I'm afraid I have not had news of our mutual friend for several weeks now. I had hoped he might be with you, in fact."

Beckett didn't speak and barely even moved, but Halim felt a tingle of alarm run up his cold spine. The near-silence of Daran drawing his weapon in the backroom came to him then, and he noted that Lady Blake tried to subtly shift out of the arm Beckett had at her back. The air itself felt the threat emanating from the long-haired vampire, whose frustration, fatigue and other emotions had riled his inner demons.

"Shh," Lady Blake said, placing her dirty hand on Beckett's pale cheek.

Halim's disused bowels clenched in anticipation of the frenzied rage about to explode out of the English vampire. Instead, Beckett placed his own hand over Lady Blake's and the coiled anger seemed to bleed from him.

"We need," he began, then started anew. "Might you shelter us for a few nights, Halim Bey?"

The dark-skinned vampire thought of the peccadilloes being explored upstairs. "Not here, but I have a small storehouse a few minutes from here that will suit your needs. It is, I think, unknown to the local authorities and you may come and go as you please."

"Thank you," Beckett said.

"Yes," Lady Blake added. "You are most kind, Halim Bey."

Her politeness brought a slight smile to Halim's face, as genuine as any could be in one in his position. Her tone indicated that she understood that "Bey" was not his name but a Turkish title, and her usage was thus correct. The number of Englishmen—or even that Dutch maggot Hendriksen upstairs—who proved their foolishness by calling him "Mr. Bey" always astonished Halim.

"Halim," Beckett asked, "when I was here in February you showed me a hieroglyph that caught my interest…"

The Turk's memory for such things was flawless and he made to finish Beckett's thought. "Yes, the Thou—" He stopped short when he saw the look of caution and anger in Beckett's eyes. "Yes, I know the one."

"Could you bring it to me once we are squared away?"

"Of course, of course." Halim then led them into the imperfectly lit High Street and through several downright dank and shadow-clogged alleys. A cold, misting rain was falling, making Southwark even less likely to surrender its secrets. When they reached the nondescript building Halim used as a secondary storehouse, he handed two large iron keys to Beckett.

"Thank you," the Englishman said.

Halim only smiled and nodded, excusing himself. Sparing the couple one backward glance, he confirmed his impression that Beckett continued to keep a hand on Lady Blake's shoulder or side, protecting and claiming her, as he might a sister. Or a lover.

***

Lady Anne Bowesley was hardly a woman known for her light, happy attitude. A vampire of long standing and preeminent position, she had spent several lifetimes battling against the expectations of her sex and excelling nonetheless. Not a suffragette by any means, she nevertheless refused to let the accident of her gender get in the way of her natural superiority. If she occasionally had to use male figureheads, she did not mind. She refused, however, to play at being silly or empty-headed. Despite the accusations of some of her detractors, she was not a man in woman's flesh—that would be Miss Parr if anyone. No, inasmuch as centuries of undeath allowed it, she was quite fond of her own femininity. She wore gowns of the finest styles, if a shade severe, and she had a long series of suitors among the mortal parliamentarians and lords from whom she fed. But at no point would she act the fool. This grated on many male egos, earning her a reputation as a harsh flower, full of thorns guarding any petals. It had also earned her the respect of undead older than she and made her seneschal of London.

Nevertheless, on this particular cold and rainy night, General Sir Arthur Halesworth found Lady Anne in an especially foul mood. He wished he could blame her.

"This is not acceptable, General," she said, dropping the Sunday edition of *The East London Advertiser* on his lap. "I will not have this type of madness in my city!"

Halesworth noted the slip of pronouns but made no mention of it. Rather, he looked down at the creased and dirty newsprint, although he'd already read through it, along with *The Times*, *The Pall Mall Gazette*, and most other papers covering the mania surrounding the murder of prostitutes in the East End. Several headlines competed for his attention, including "A Thirst for Blood" and "The Supernatural Element."

"The editors of this rag," Halesworth said, "have a flair for phrases that will sell more copies, Mary-Anne, but—"

She ripped the paper from his hands, and her voice rose in volume. "Do not make petty excuses, General! Have you even read these reports?" She scanned the page, frustrated that the desired passage wouldn't give itself up immediately. "Ah yes, here: 'It is so impossible to account, on any ordinary hypothesis, for these revolting acts of blood that the mind turns as it were instinctively to some theory of occult force,'—listen carefully—'and the myths of the Dark Ages rise before the imagination. Ghouls, vampires, bloodsuckers, and all the ghastly array of fables which have been accumulated throughout the course of centuries take form, and seize hold of the excited fancy.' They are practically calling our kindred to task,

General!"

Halesworth felt the words like a seaside cliff being buffeted by the gale. Lady Anne was a creature of granite will and her anger was palpable, even if he remained stoic before it. He noted her fingernails ripping the thin paper and the ivory glint of sharp canines behind her drawn lips. The General knew all too well that all undead were subject beastly, destructive instincts. He had never seen Lady Anne give in to that frenzied rage, and he had little desire to be trapped with her in an office on Piccadilly when she did.

"I will point out, milady, that that same article goes on to discuss the murderer as a mortal man. The rest I believe to be hyperbole."

"You and your second are betting everything we have built on that belief, General. I recommended you to His Royal Highness for your thoroughness, not your passivity."

Halesworth ignored the implicit threat—she was responsible for his position as the sheriff of London's undead, and she could see those duties confided to another. "Miss Parr and I are perhaps less inactive on this matter than it seems to you, milady," he said, keeping his tone even. "Even as we speak she is investigating the authors of those very reports to ensure that no one has been indiscreet. There also continues to be no solid evidence that this 'Ripper' fellow is anything more than a kine with a more-than-average sense of the macabre."

"That will hardly matter if every petty newspaperman and vigilance committee member gets the impression that hell-spawned devils are responsible. They will look for those devils, General, and they will find us."

Halesworth's grip on the arm of the chair he'd chosen tightened enough for the wood to issue a moan. "I am well aware of my duties, Mary-Anne. I would be attending to them right now if you had not—"

"You dare!" Anne interrupted, leaning forward across the polished oak table she'd been using as a desk. Her hands curled around the edge as if she were preparing to toss the offending furniture aside—a feat her undead blood made altogether possible.

Then she stopped. It was very much like a curtain falling on a stage, her iron will sealing up the rage and bloodlust boiling within her. Her muscles relaxed with enforced calm and her expression lost its hard edge. She was transformed, from one moment to the next, back into the proper noblewoman she had been in life and remained in undeath.

"This is pointless, General. Keep this matter as your top priority. I realize Whitechapel is technically Miss Parr's responsibility, but she is your second and this matter demands your personal attention."

"Yes, milady."

"Excellent. Now, I'm sure we both have busy nights ahead of…" Her voice trailed off as her eyes focused on something behind, or beyond, Halesworth. He read surprise and concern on her face before those too were covered by the hard shell of propriety.

General Halesworth's own senses were not, he knew, the equal of Lady Anne's. His eyes could, it was true, push back the veil of night almost entirely in the manner of a wolf or other predator, but Anne's perceptions operated on levels known only to those with long centuries' experience in unlife. Thus he did not sense what had caught her attention until the very moment before the French doors separating the sitting room from the upstairs hall of Trenton House opened. The hard, bristly hairs that ran up the back of his neck under his collar stood on end and, just as the door latch clicked, the general had the distinct impression of being submerged in the warm summer sun he had not known in over forty years. There was only one creature whose presence had evoked that comfort in him since his rise from the grave.

"Milord," he said, rising from his chair and turning on his heels just in time to see Mithras, prince and potentate of London's unliving host, enter.

The prince's appearance registered as disturbing with Halesworth, at least in some part of his mind capable of distancing himself from the volcanic rise of awe in his own heart. Indeed, the general had last seen his lord up and about in August, at the grand celebration of His Royal Highness's third year back in London. There, Mithras had seemed like a chiseled statue of masculine perfection, with not a hair out of place. It had been very much like being in the presence of Grecian or Italian statuary of the gods. Tonight, Mithras was disheveled, as if he had traveled through a driving rain. The dampness of the exterior clung to his hair that framed his face in long slick locks. His eyes were deep-set under lids that showed the purpling of immense fatigue. His mouth was set in a scowl and seemed marred by the age that had not touched the Prince of London for thousands of years.

The general's awareness of these symptoms and the concern that accompanied them, however, were soon drowned in the sheer relief of seeing his lord and liege before him. Months of worry as the prince was kept in seclusion to fight off the effects of some strange affliction lifted from Halesworth's heart and the conviction that all was well and right returned to him. His master was here before him and he could not help but fall to one knee, his head bowed. "Praise be."

"Your Highness," Lady Anne said from behind him, her voice markedly less sure.

Halesworth dared a quick glance behind him and noted that Lady Anne's curtsey was far less deep than his bow.

Chapter Twelve

Liverpool Street Station was, in the dark of early morning, the home of stevedores loading and unloading various goods trains feeding the belly of the capital. Workmen effected minor repairs on some of the passenger trains, loaded the coal chutes and made things ready fro the crush of passenger traffic that would arrive in the morning. Trains would go out to Southern England from here, and others would arrive bringing their daily cargo of the hopeful, the enterprising and the desperate.

By this time, Regina Blake was not overly worried that her exit from the third car of the supply train would attract too much attention. Victoria's beguiling ways—which she seemed able to focus at will—had enraptured the stevedore who opened the car doors before the man even realized it. Regina felt the reflected awe ripple off Miss Ash like the tingle of lightning in a stormy sky, before it strikes.

The befuddled man smiled and made an awkward bow. He mumbled some gracious amazement and helped Victoria down with a sooty hand. He then did the same with Regina, but kept his attention on the statuesque redhead who had first caught his eye. Regina suspected that some days from now, when he told this story to his companions, the man would berate himself for not questioning the appearance of a beauty in the freight train in the middle of the night. At the moment, however, he could barely put together a few words and was simply content that this apparition had chosen his shift to manifest.

"Could you show us to the exit, please?" Victoria's voice was a polite whisper.

"Of course, ma'am," the man said more loudly in a heavy accent that spoke of proletarian roots going back many generations.

Regina glanced up and down the quay. A few of the others working in the station had noticed them and glanced their way, half-confused and half-delighted. They all had work to attend to, however, and none approached.

It had been like this since Wels, the Upper Austrian town where they had boarded the Grand Express for Paris, with the twilight still fading in the evening sky. Regina now appreciated, at least in pragmatic terms, why the undead seemed to surround themselves with those living men and women they had enslaved with their blood. Traveling across Europe and to England without such aid and fearing the rise of the sun had been less than amusing. To ensure they remained undisturbed, Victoria had used every iota of her seductive charisma, convincing various porters and passengers that they didn't dare approach this particular compartment, even as they traveled across Germany and France. That the border crossing had taken place after dawn was a source of especial concern and Victoria had spent much of their first night aboard securing the cooperation of the car porter.

Making it from Paris to London had been even harder. Putting aside the danger inherent in retracing their steps through places where they had made enemies, Victoria and Regina faced the simpler challenge of finding shelter from the day, travel at night, and the sustenance of healthy folk who would not question weakness of blood and the passions of traveling Englishwomen.

Every move had to be planned carefully and every hiding place secured. In the five nights since they had left Vienna, they had sheltered in a coal cellar in Wels, the compartment of the Grand Express, the basement of a boarding house outside Paris, the basement of an abandoned farmhouse in the French countryside, and in a fetid sewer in Dover.

Regina was very much looking forward to any sort of secure shelter—although she wondered where that might exist.

They hired a hansom cab outside Waterloo Station and headed across the bridge and toward the West End. Victoria spent the first part of the journey looking intently outside and Regina was that much happier not to have to look at the woman who had brought her into this dark world of death and unlife.

"There's something happening here," Victoria said.

"'Something'?," Regina said without looking up. "What do you mean?"

"I'm not wholly sure. You will find, Regina, that your senses will take on many added dimensions over the years. You've learned to see at night as well as you did during the day, but there are countless other facets yet to reveal themselves. Emotions, wants, needs, even the marks left by traumas and other events, can be seen, smelled or touched."

"And you smell something now?"

Victoria gave Regina a look that fell somewhere between scorn and disappointment. "Are we reduced to petty jibes now, darling?"

Regina had the urge to throttle Victoria, but despite the vivid imagery that came to her, the raw desire to draw blood from that porcelain flesh, she didn't move. The hunger within her that had exploded in Vienna was quiescent now, still numbed by the events of their departure from the Austrian capital. All her feelings, even the most savage, were muted and dead. "No," she said, "what do you feel is happening?"

"I cannot put a name to it yet, but the air feels unsettled." Victoria cocked her head as if actually catching a scent. "Violent."

"You would know, I suppose," Regina said, without even thinking about it.

Victoria's gaze grew harder and Regina could see red-hot anger boiling under her cool ecru flesh and behind her emerald eyes. But Victoria just looked away.

They didn't say another word until the cab had gone all the way up past Oxford Street, along Tottenham Court Road and Good Street, and was turning onto Charlotte Place itself. "No," Victoria said in a whisper.

Regina detected a slight acrid smell and put a name to it just before the cab's movement brought Number 49 into view: burnt wood. Indeed, the fine home Victoria Ash had kept at this address had been reduced to a crumbled pile of blackened timbers and a few skeletal remains of the exterior walls.

The cab stopped and both women alighted, Victoria with a haste that almost—but not quite—superceded her inhuman poise. Several of the other homes on Charlotte Place had suffered in the fire, as well. What had been Numbers 51 and 51-A was a blackened ruin and the façade of Number 47, with shattered windows and long black soot-trails up the brick, spoke of devastation within. The fire brigade had apparently stopped the blaze from spreading further, but that was surely of little consolation to Victoria. Her home was utterly gone.

The stone wall that had blocked off her tiny garden from the surrounding city still stood, although one part of it had come apart from the crumbled brick of the house proper. Only the rear-right corner of the structure still stood to its full height of three stories, a lone sentinel over the ruin, small fragments of beams and platforms of floors suspended awkwardly in midair.

It was there, Regina thought, imagining a second story bedroom that was now empty space. *It was there that I lost my soul.* Memories arose of that terrible night, when she had sneaked into the Taurus Club and found her fiancé in the midst of an arcane ritual, of his rough treatment of her, his hands on her bare breasts, him between and within her legs, of the knife he'd drawn across her throat. Then, being carried here, drinking the dark black blood from Victoria's pale arms— how she had loved that sickly, cold opiate!—and spending the night in the throes of passion with her. The bite of Victoria's pointed teeth on Regina's skin came back to her and she could feel now-unnatural heat rising in her blood. She had taken her first step into undeath then—and still what she remembered most was the forbidden pleasure of it all.

Her lips flush with stolen blood, she looked over at Victoria.

"Whoever did this will pay dearly for it," Victoria said, cold steel in her voice. To Regina's eyes, although Victoria stood stock still, it was as if she were a smoldering fire. Lapping flames of red rage leapt up from her, testament to the passions that had kept her moving centuries after her death.

Regina, who had felt so cold, so numb, for the last five nights, realized she wanted nothing more than to share in that passion. To *steal* it if need be. To make it her own. She approached Victoria and put a hand on her arm. It felt like she was touching a drum, vibrating with energy.

Victoria turned to face her. Hatred, black and stinging, mixed with the flames of anger. "Do you hear me, Regina? I will see them ash for the morning."

Some distant, quiet, still rational part of Regina's mind heard that last comment and made a connection. Victoria's face, her pearly skin and blood-red lips, was bathed with reflected light. Regina looked up and saw the low cloud banks over the city were pale.

Something cold and fearful ran through her dead veins.

"Driver," she said to the cabby still sitting atop the hansom waiting for payment or directions. "What time is it?"

The man pulled out a pocket watch and consulted it. "Just past 5:30, ma'am."

"Victoria," Regina said, turning to her. "The dawn."

Cold realization played itself out over Victoria's features. They had counted on shelter at Charlotte Place, but now they were homeless again. "Quickly, where can we go?"

"I don't—" Regina began, but then she did know. The thought was a cold and evil thing, but there was no getting around it. "Come."

As they leapt back into the cab, Regina gave their destination. "Monroe House, on Arlington Street, St. James. And do hurry. It's urgent."

With her mother vanished and her father dead, Regina Blake was going back to her family's London home.

***

"How do you deal with it?"

Emma Blake and Beckett sat across from each other in the concealed loft of Halim Bey's Southwark storehouse. The ground floor was a mess of crates, boxes and various stacked bric-a-brac. Shipping indications and other notes had been burned into the wood of the crates in various languages—Beckett had already spotted English, French, Arabic, Turkish, Farsi, Cantonese and Hindi, and there were probably more. The loft was more orderly. It was accessible through a cleverly concealed trap door in the main storeroom's ceiling. A few pieces were arranged on the shelves, and Halim had left a small lantern and wash basin for their use. Stacked tarps and blankets (relatively free of insects) served as a bed-down for the two vampires.

The room was utterly lightproof—pitch sealed every seam—and with the lantern extinguished, Emma and Beckett found that even to their inhumanly keen senses, they appeared only as dim, ghostly silhouettes floating in a black void.

"I'm not sure what you mean, Lady Blake."

"With… That is," she answered, her voice louder than his. "All of it. This unnatural condition of ours. Existing in a world of monsters who prey on the living. *Being* one of those monsters. How do you tolerate it?"

Beckett didn't speak for several minutes. "Because I have to, I suppose. I exist and I wish to carry on existing, so I must accept my condition."

"But the hunger, the anger, all the rage that boils up… There are moments when I can imagine sundering the living flesh of everyone I've ever loved. Moments when I long for that release. Aren't you afraid you will give in to that?"

"I don't fear it in the way you mean, Lady Blake. I *know* I will indulge those urges sooner or later. I have before and I will again. It's inevitable."

"But…" she stammered. "Then it's all hopeless. We're but monsters and devils, then. Undead and damned."

Beckett advanced through the darkness, his boots making a single whisper-like scuff on the pine floorboards. He put his hand on his companion's arm. "I don't believe in hopelessness, Emma. There are monstrous urges within us both, to be sure. To survive, we feed on the living, and sooner or later, the hunger drives us to kill. The anger will boil over, but it will also recede. To survive, we must bear that price."

She did not seem to note his use of her Christian name. When she spoke again, her voice was a whisper. "Why not just give in, then? If we can't resist then why not surrender?"

"Because we can resist. We can offset the evils forced upon us, delay them, curb them, and put our existence to some purpose."

"What purpose?"

Beckett shifted his weight and sat at Emma's feet. "I've spent more than a lifetime trying to answer that question." He allowed himself a mirthless chuckle. "I suppose that the search itself is my purpose. Piecing together the puzzle of our origins, of why the undead exist at all, keeps the beast within me at bay."

"But surely not all of us seek those answers."

"You might be surprised just how many of the undead are interested in their origins. Still, you're right. I suppose most others find different matters to occupy themselves—the pursuit of power and influence, the destruction of an ancient enemy, the mysteries of the truly dead. I've seen them all and more. All never-ending passions that keep the soul-killing hunger at bay."

"Like Sisyphus and his stone, my daughter would say." Emma's voice was soft, far away.

"Perhaps, but I don't choose to look at it as so hopeless. If the struggle were easy, there's be very little point, after all."

"I wish I could believe you, Mr. Beckett. You may find joy in the enigma of our condition, but it seems to me to be but a bleak end to a bleak life. Hope has not, in my experience, stood the test of reality."

"I know the last few months have been difficult," he began, before she cut him off.

"Months? This has been going since the night I was born. Before it, even."

Beckett tried to settle himself into a sitting position, but a familiar tingle was building in his spine. He'd felt this same shiver when he opened the lost tomb of the vampire Nahum ben Enosh in the Sinai Desert: the heady mixture of excitement and dread that presaged any great discovery.

"You've had a connection to the undead for quite some time," he said. "Halim Bey knew about your relationship with Lady Merritt."

"That's a very diplomatic way to put it," she said. "Twenty years ago, I was her…" She stopped for a moment and Beckett felt her shiver beside him. The words, when they finally came, were full of bitterness. "I was hers, I suppose. Her plaything, her slave. I lapped up her blood under the pretense of it being the finest claret, or some exotic opiate. I loved her as I'd never loved another. She was my world."

"And she threw you away." Beckett had seen this melodrama repeated countless times in his unlife. Kindred with a passing fancy for a breathing man or woman destroying lives and then tossing them aside for the next plaything. Socialites like Lady Merritt were especially infamous for it.

"Yes," Lady Blake said, her voice small, stripped of the rage of a moment ago. "I blamed another for it, but yes, Ophelia tired of me. I suppose I always knew that —" Her voice broke off in a slight sob. Though two decades old, these memories evidently resided close to the surface.

Too close for Beckett's liking. "What do you think of Lady Merritt, Lady Blake?"

She stiffened slightly. "What? I don't—"

"Please," he said, facing her and laying a hand on each shoulder. "Indulge me. All that history being said, how do you feel about this woman?"

"I hate her! She took… She told me James was dead! She was *everything*…" Further sobs, each growing stronger, made her stutter and pause. The coppery scent of her bloody tears filled the air. "I love… I *loved* her… Why did…"

The question went unasked as the sobs overwhelmed Emma Blake. Without thinking about it, Beckett pulled her to him and she came willingly, curling into his chest as if it might shelter her from the monstrosity of her existence. In a faint, tear-soaked whisper, she said, "I miss her. God help me, I still miss milady."

Beckett bit back the rage that was welling up in him, the urge to simply rip asunder those who had used and abused this woman. "It's the blood, Emma," he said. "Her blood is still within you, twisting your heart." Was there ever a more potent example of the temptation of undeath? The blood of a vampire could enslave and enrapture another—living or undead—to the point where even decades of neglect couldn't fully erase the thrall's twisted love. It seemed to Beckett tailor-made to leave discarded thralls and lovers as the detritus of unlife.

He squeezed Emma Blake tightly. There were still mysteries to uncover here and, he suspected, further layers of abuse at the hands of his purported kindred.

A semblance of clam returned to Emma after a few minutes and Beckett felt her sobs ease within his arms. "Tell me about Anwar al-Beshi," he said. "In Cairo."

"How do you..." She drew away from him. "You were the one, the one who interrupted the ceremony that night. I thought it was James..."

"Your husband was there, but I arrived first." Indeed, Beckett had been in Cairo in May of 1886 at the behest of Halim Bey when he had interrupted what appeared to be some form of blood sorcery. The sorcerer, a vampire named Anwar al-Beshi, had perished. His two ghouls had survived. Emma had been one of those ghouls. "Tell me about al-Beshi."

"I met him at the bazaar, in Cairo, at a coffeehouse near there, and..."

"Lone Englishwomen don't just wander into Cairene coffeehouses, Lady Blake. Especially not at night."

Her faces was streaked with the remnants red tears, but she still managed a slight start of surprise. "No, I suppose they don't. I must have been sleepwalking, or something like it. I'd had difficulty sleeping ever since we arrived in Egypt, you see. James blamed it on the climate, and so did I at first, but nothing I did could keep the dreams at bay."

"What dreams?"

"Terrible nightmares," she said, and Beckett felt her shiver again. "A jumble of everything I feared, I suppose, of my husband betraying me, of... of Lady Merritt, of the desert and the savage tribes that lived there. I was lost in the dreams, wandering from place to place, looking for something or someone." She swallowed. "I remember one place in the dreams, walking through a huge room with its roof held up by dozens of pillars. There was a man there…"

"What sort of man?"

"A soldier… or a general… James? I think sometimes it was James, but sometimes not. I loved him, I think. I wanted to find him…"

"How did this lead you to al-Beshi?"

"I'm, I don't know. I must have wandered out of the compound or taken a carriage or…" Panic mounted in her voice. "I don't know, I just remember entering the coffeehouse at night and finding it almost empty. Except for Anwar, who smiled. I think he was expecting me."

Beckett had only passing knowledge of the mesmerism some of the undead were capable of. He knew some vampires could twist the memories, urges and passions of others, but many of the finer details escaped him. Could they call to a mortal through her dreams like this? In the case of an Egyptian blood sorcerer like al-Beshi, Beckett was unwilling to dismiss the possibility.

"Was he the man from your dreams?" he asked.

"No, no… I thought so at first, I think, but no. He said I had called to him. That my blood had called to him. He called me *Binti.*"

"Little cousin," Beckett translated.

"Yes, of course you speak Arabic as well," she said. "He, he said we should exchange blood. God help me, we did."

Beckett frowned in the dark. Most of it sounded like the typical trappings of a vampiric seduction, making the prize feel special and saying the she had called to him rather than vice versa. But what if it were more than just hyperbole in this instance? Could her blood— or the blood still within her—have called to the sorcerer?

Instinct told Beckett that dawn was approaching. Even in this lightless room, he could feel his blood slowing and his limbs growing heavy. Emma Blake slouched against him as the slumber rose within her as well. Beckett was convinced that they should call on Lady Ophelia Merritt, but that would have to wait until the following night. Just as he was surrendering to sleep, a thought occurred to him: Lady Blake had said she'd been the plaything of the undead since even before her birth. What had she meant by that?

Chapter Thirteen

Waking to the familiar was, in some ineffable way, even stranger to Regina. The room that had been hers in Monroe House during her every visit to London, and during much of the last two social seasons, was both a reminder of things lost and a lingering accusation . The south-facing windows, which Victoria and she had draped with layers of curtain and sheet that morning—fighting the terribly heavy fatigue of dawn. The three porcelain dolls that had been gifts from her mother, surrogates for children of her own—children now forever beyond her reach. The dressing screen, there to preserve a propriety to which she no longer had any claim. And worst of all, put there by the maid and against Regina's wishes, the simple mourning card announcing her mother's ersatz death last December. A terrible sadness rose as if from earth itself and threatened to swallow her.

Beside her, Victoria lay immobile and insensate in the bed. In Vienna, Regina had usually woken to find Victoria already up and dressed. Since their departure from that city, however, she'd woken ahead of the woman who had remade her. During the journey westward this had been a terrifying experience, waking alone in dark and unfamiliar places, unsure of what to do. Thankfully, Victoria stirred only a few minutes later—although during their night day in Paris, she had slumbered for a half-hour longer, to the point that Regina had feared she might have slipped into some torpor or even found the eternal rest she had so long been denied.

This night, gaining some tiny measure of reassurance from having successfully made it to London and found shelter, Regina dismissed the notion that Victoria might not wake and simply observed. They'd shared the bed as they had since August, and Victoria lay wearing naught but what God had given her and the Devil preserved. The sheets had remained perfectly in place— Victoria's red-auburn locks and pale face were visible at all only because Regina herself had pushed the covers off her own face upon waking. Now, she drew them back more fully.

Regina understood something of Victoria's uncanny magnetism. Part of it at least was willful and in her slumber she withdrew much, or even all, of that aura of awe. Nevertheless, she remained a beauty of the highest order. During her sleep she returned to the aspect of a true corpse in many ways: much of the color had drained from her lips and the delicate network of bluish veins that was sometimes visible under her alabaster flesh had faded save for a few now-black lines. And yet, she was still a masterpiece—like a marble effigy of Venus herself.

Regina delicately stroked her cold flesh, starting from the silk-straw of her hair, moving along a fine jaw-line and touching thin, bloodless lips with her thumb. She found them to have taken on a strange plasticity, so that they deformed slightly with her touch. The girl then descended Victoria's long neck toward a fine clavicle. Her fingers feathered the cold but not at all clammy skin—flesh that might have been chilled and powdered—finding the curve of a full breast. Her palm found the hard nub of Victoria's nipple, which refused to react but sent a tingle of desire through Regina's own nerves. She looked down at her own bosom, slighter, more girlish than womanly, and saw her own nipples contract with her want.

She shifted on the bed, drawing her legs under her so she might use both hands for her task. She continued their journey down Victoria's body, following the curve of her waist and the slight roundness of her belly. Her fingers touched with their whole lengths now, unsatisfied with the soft marble on the tips alone. Her wrists pushed the sheets down further, revealing the small nest of russet curls there. She continued down Victoria's long legs—longer than her own by several inches. Over thighs, knees, shins, ankles and delicate feet she traveled, the sheets slipping to the floor with the whisper of cotton on cotton.

Regina shifted to straddle Victoria. She rose back along that motionless form, slithering her torso to bring herself into the slightest contact. Her nipples stroked Victoria's legs and her lips passed a hair's-breadth over the skin, descending to plant gentle, lingering kisses on thigh, pubic thatch, stomach, breast, sternum, and the notch at the base of Victoria's throat. Regina lowered herself fully onto her unliving lover, sliding her right knee up and feeling blood flow into the delicate folds of flesh between her legs. She shifted to press that engorged skin against Victoria. At the same time, Regina felt the erotic motion of long, sharp canines slipping from their sheaths in her gums, like the release of a tight corset by a lover's strong hands. Her tongue, moist with anticipation, tasted the slight coppery echoes of the skin in the crook of Victoria's throat. Her fangs' tips slid to the surface of that alabaster skin—

"No…"

Barely a whisper. Regina dismissed the voice as a phantasm.

"No!"

Regina's world, reduced to the points of contact between her flesh and that of the suddenly mobile form under her, swirled and tipped as Victoria pushed with inhuman might. Regina was flipped over onto her back and Victoria followed, pinning the girl under her. Victoria held a hand over Regina's chin, keeping her securely away from her. It all happened in less than an instant.

Regina felt a wave of pique and rage wash over her. *How dare Victoria deny her? Her, of all people!* But Victoria kept her gaze, her emerald eyes remaining calm and fixed. And she had Regina securely pinned, her thighs securing the girl's body and one arm, her hands holding the other arm at the wrist and Regina's head at the chin. It was enraging and frustrating and Regina wanted her all the more for it.

After a few moments, Regina realized that Victoria was speaking to her.

"Darling… come back… that's it. You can't feed from me, Regina. It would undo everything."

Thought returned to Regina's mind. She'd been enslaved to Victoria once by drinking her blood. But that was as a living woman. She attempted to speak and Victoria released some of the pressure on her chin so she could. "Still? Even after everything?"

"Yes, I'm afraid so. The bonds are not as harsh, perhaps, but they are real. I doubt anything could undo them this time." Victoria sat back, still straddling her childe, but no longer imprisoning her. "Drink from me again and I fear you would be bound for eternity, Regina. I cannot allow that. Not after all I've already subjected you to."

"But," Regina said, and raised a hand to stroke Victoria's side, which responded with a slight but true flush. "But I want—"

A sudden knocking at the door cut her short. "Hello? Lady Regina?"

Victoria looked at her and whispered, "Who?"

"Mister Goosehound," Regina answered just as quietly. "Father's agent in town."

"Hello?" Goosehound said. There was the sound of a key being inserted into the lock.

"A moment, Mister Goosehound!" Regina called. "I will see you in the parlor momentarily."

The key slipped out. "Very well, Milady."

***

"Thank you for understanding, Mr. Goosehound," Regina said. "Our travels were quite taxing and the day's rest has done us a world of good."

"Of course, milady," Goosehound said. He was a tall man and quite bald. Dressed in the heavy woolen suit of a man of his station, he still affected the black mourning dress he'd ordered for the entire staff to mark the death of Lady Emma.

Victoria had not spoken as yet. The three of them were seated in Monroe House's downstairs parlor and she had allowed Regina to manage things. As the lady of the house, it was her place to do so. While Regina and Goosehound conversed, Victoria watched and grew worried.

Who set that fire? Even asking the question stoked rage in her long-dead heart. She dismissed the possibility that the fire had been accidental. Although such fires were all too common in London, the coincidence that only her home and its closest neighbors had burned was too much in which to put much stock. The haven of a vampire was, if not sacrosanct, then at least protected by a serious taboo. It was much too easy for such attacks to escalate and none of the kindred wished to be caught without a safe place to spend the day. *Whoever did this…*

And what of Theresa, Victoria's maid and last ghoul? Had she perished in the blaze or was she sheltering with some relative? Victoria had found the girl in the East End, but her family hailed from Hampshire. *She is not irreplaceable,* Victoria thought, *but still…* It took several minutes spent planning contingencies and reviewing the few hidden havens she'd been able to establish in London, for Victoria to realize she was quite sure the girl was dead and that the knowledge should, on some level, bother her more than it did. The death of her coachman Cedric had cut her to the quick, but Theresa—

well, Theresa had been with her for only a decade and she had grown tiresomely possessive. When sorrow wouldn't come, Victoria filled the void it left with more anger. *Something else they'll pay for.*

"Miss Ash?" Regina's voice broke into her reverie. Victoria realized there'd been a question, but she couldn't recall it.

"Pardon me, Lady Regina, Mr. Goosehound," she said. "I believe the fatigue of travel is still getting the best of me."

"Mr. Goosehound was inquiring whether you were quite all right, Victoria," Regina said.

Victoria looked at the agent and saw concern and a touch of fear there. Like a slight red-orange haze caught behind the façade of his professional demeanor, it lurked. The man sensed something, she knew, like a child or a housecat might. He could not understand what he sensed—that the two women before him were trapped between life and death—but it made him uncomfortable. Such men were not common, but hardly unheard of. They were also dangerous to spend much time around.

"Yes," Victoria said. "Thank you for your concern, sir. We had a rough crossing from the Continent and its effects are lingering."

"Of course, ma'am," he said and turned back to Regina. "I can have Dr. Finney come by in the morning if you'd like, Lady Regina."

"Thank you, but that's quite all right," Regina answered. "I'm sure Miss Ash's constitution will recover soon enough, and if we have any need of medical attention, I'm sure we can call on Dr. Harold Claremont, the brother-in-law of my friend Joanna Claremont. I shall make a point to see her and her husband John, in fact."

Regina's facility with the dissimulations that were so critical to masquerading as a living woman was impressive to Victoria. No small number of kindred had to be kept from mortal company for years before they learned the fine art of discretion. She was about to confirm Regina's assessment of her health when she saw the pained look on Goosehound's jowly face.

"Oh, Lady Regina, I had assumed you knew…"

"What is it, Goosehound?"

"John Claremont was the victim of foul play this August last, milady. An intruder broke into his home on Sydney Mews." He coughed lightly into one hand. "You had already left on your travels, I believe."

"Poor Joanna," Regina said. "She must be devastated."

Joanna Claremont was Regina's oldest friend and confidante, Victoria remembered. She was also the younger sister of Malcolm Seward, to whom Regina had been engaged to be wed—the same Malcolm Seward who had fallen under the sway of the Taurus Club and its kindred backers. Before leaving for the Continent last August, Victoria had made sure she knew to whom Regina might send any tearful confessions—such were not unusual in those new to the night-world—and had tasked Theresa with diverting any such mail. The girl had a very useful contact in the Royal Post. If she was gone, however, had that diversion continued? Was there an incriminating letter out there, still to be discovered?

Goosehound coughed again, more forcefully this time, and looked away from Regina. "That is," he said, stammering slightly. "I…"

Regina laid a hand on his arm, returning his attention to her. "She *is* well, is she not, Mister Goosehound?"

"Not, not exactly, milady," he managed at last. "It's my understanding that Mrs. Claremont actually witnessed her husband's murder. His lordship your father saw to it that she was taken into Highgate Asylum."

It was, it seemed, Regina's turn to be lost in thought. Victoria filled the silence. "Lady Regina, I think it may be time for us to depart. We have an appointment to keep."

Goosehound raised an eyebrow. "Should I have Gerald come around with the carriage?" Victoria suspected the man, who as an agent oversaw the city properties of his aristocratic employers, had hoped to use the Blakes' carriage and coachman for his own purposes—at the very least to get to his home later in the evening—but he could not see his client's daughter go without.

"Yes," Regina said. "Please do."

Soon enough they were traveling up Bond Street, along Oxford Street and returning to Charlotte Place. It was Sunday evening, so the shops were closed tight and the streets less congested than they might be. Nevertheless, the source of the instability Victoria had sensed the previous evening quickly became apparent from the headlines on the previous evening's editions of newspapers, still posted at newsstands along Bond and Oxford Streets. Murders in the East End had apparently caught the collective ear of the jaded metropolis and the newspapers were full of gruesome details.

It had rained during the day and so the ash heap that had been Victoria's home in London was now wet with a blackish slurry in places. Other than that, it looked much the same as it had the previous night, and the sight still sparked hot anger in her. She'd spent no small amount of time arranging things just so, in just such a way that whenever she chose to she could find an object of profound beauty. All that was gone now. Twenty-five years before, the fine colonial house she'd kept in Savannah had fallen victim to the victorious Union forces of General Sherman. She'd escaped to England and managed to rebuild her existence, although at a price in status and position. Now even that was gone.

She would rebuild again—once she'd extracted a bit of vengeance.

"What are you searching for?" Regina asked as she followed Victoria into the ruins. They both had to hike their skirts to navigate the bramble of half-burnt boards and debris, and Victoria noted how well Regina managed. The ethereal grace of undeath was coming upon the girl already.

"Anything of note," Victoria said, scanning the pile-upon-pile. She had an instinct that this was not a terribly recent fire. It had been a month, she thought. Perhaps a little less, perhaps a little more. More than enough time for the desperate and the opportunistic to loot whatever valuables had survived the blaze. The house's legal owner was a man who'd had the misfortune to catch Lady Merritt's eye in 1870. He had departed suddenly for India that summer—India being a euphemism for a shallow grave near Greenwich—but not before granting Miss Ash unlimited access to this property while he was abroad. The constabulary or others might have tried to wire him in Bombay, but nothing had been done to secure the site and much of the furnishings and fixtures had probably been taken for salvage. Another slight to avenge.

After no more than fifteen minutes, Regina gave up the search for unidentified things of note. Victoria could sense the annoyance in her. The news about Joanna Claremont had obviously shaken her again and neither of them had fed since arriving in England. But Victoria needed to do this. She continued her search.

She found one of the posts from the bed where she had usually slumbered—the same bed where she had made Regina her ghoul. *No*, she thought. Finally, she returned to the front of the ruined house and found the remains of the front door. *Yes,* she thought, *that will do.* She picked up the largest fragment, which included part of the knocker.

"What are you doing?" Regina asked in a whisper.

Victoria hadn't noticed her approach and chided herself for her distraction. "As I mentioned last night, the past leaves traces for those who have the eyes to see them."

Victoria had that eye, but rarely chose to open it, for it was a risky and imprecise sense. That actions, people and sentiments left ephemeral traces on objects was not something she found hard to believe. One only had to see the care with which a lover kept the mementoes of her paramour, and destroyed those same when he betrayed her. Letters and daguerreotypes might be preserved for their literal content of words and images, but many other objects could spark a memory or a forgotten sensation. How many men had touched the lace of a lady's kerchief to remember the softness of her flesh or the musicality of her voice? The spirit left its mark on everything. But just as a lover's token might spark both remembered joy and sorrow, Victoria could not control just what her magnified senses would bring to her. In the past, first her senses and then her reason had been overwhelmed by these vicarious sensations.

So, with a long pause during which a living woman would have taken a deep breath, Victoria Ash readied to immerse herself in the scorched remains of what had been the front door of her home. Symbols were important in such matters and the door, as the guardian of the whole house, could stand for it. She closed her eyes and then reopened them, focusing just slightly beyond the surface of the door fragment in her hands.

…the smell of a greased fry pan burning… the sight of paint on the door cracking and bubbling… flames… raging fire consuming everything…

Victoria felt the terrible urge to run rising in her like a geyser. First her hands and then her whole body shook, but she refused to give in. Deeper, she had to look deeper. To before the fire.

…the smell of a jasmine perfume she hadn't worn in several

years... the sound of shears through fabric... a voice, the maid Theresa's... 'I hate her'... 'she should be mine'... a knock at the door... the bitter taste of jealousy... a report like a gunshot...

She strained to make sense of the images, to organize them into some order.

...Theresa opening the door in response to the knock ...it's a young man, his features indistinct... pale daylight behind him... 'Miss Ash is away'... sudden movement... the man pushing past Theresa and into the house... she pushes back and the man falls... she must close the door lest the neighbors see... pain!... a blow, two, three, four...

...figures moving through the house... two men looking through all her things... Theresa bound and gagged and bleeding... she wants her mistress... the men are in the maid's room looking at letters... anger and hatred... she will kill them for Miss Victoria... the two men turn and their features snap to clarity... the younger of the two points... fire, pain and noise explode from his hand... a gun... the older one lights a fire... Theresa sees him step over her... the fire...

Victoria came to on a wave of rage. Her fingers ground into the wood with nails stronger and sharper than any woman's had a right to be. They'd invaded her house, killed her maid, and burned the place to the ground! She knew those men!

***

Regina Blake became aware of a low, animalistic growling at the edge of her hearing and turned to face Victoria again. She'd wandered a few steps away from Miss Ash, who seemed to have slipped into some trance-like state, but now her attention was refocused on the redheaded woman.

Victoria had adopted a slightly bent-over posture, her muscles tense and her elbows gauchely separated from her torso. The low keening was coming from her throat.

"Victoria..." Regina said, unsure just what to ask. She struggled to remember her violent outburst in Vienna. Had this been how she appeared to Victoria?

Victoria dropped the fragment of the front door back into the ash-strewn rubble. "Your men did this," she said.

"What? What do you mean?"

Regina was aware of Victoria turning toward her but not of the woman covering the few steps between them. She was just suddenly right there, her lips drawn to expose prominent fangs and her eyes in slits.

"Your father. And Seward, your fiancé," Victoria said. "They destroyed my home. They killed Theresa."

Regina felt a tickle of shame in the pit of her stomach. "Oh, Victoria, I'm so sorry." She placed a hand on the other woman's arm.

Victoria knocked it away. "I'm glad he's dead," she spat.

The shame in Regina's gut vanished, swallowed by something else. "Excuse me?"

"I'm glad your father is dead. I drank his blood until his heart stopped and I'm glad for it. He deserved it."

The animalistic thing slithering inside Regina, the beast that had lain numbed and dormant since their departure from Vienna, rose like a hooded cobra ready to strike. Her nails dug into her own palm. "What did you say?"

"I wish I could kill him again," Victoria hissed.

Regina lunged, heedless of anything but the anger inside her. Her hands closed on nothing but ash and soot.

Then Victoria was on top of her, first pushing her into the muck, then flipping her onto her back. She leaned in close to Regina, her mouth full of tooth and menace. "Don't provoke me, childe!"

The rage in Regina's heart died like a fire doused in water. In its wake, shame and a terrible sadness at all that had passed rose, backed by not a small amount of fear. Her eyes stung with bloody tears.

Victoria released her and stepped away with a huff, like a cat bored with a mouse. Regina, not taking time to think about it, scurried to her feet and made for the carriage.

"Home, Gerald," she called to the coachman as she jumped in. "Quickly!"

They left Victoria there, stewing in her own rage.

***

It was past two in the morning when Regina Blake called for Gerald again. Covered in soot and dirt, she'd had to bathe and dress all over again. Mr. Goosehound had had a young Irish girl named

Catherine brought in to serve as Regina's makeshift lady's maid—apart from Gerald, the coachman who remained to tend the horses and guard the house, Goosehound had largely shut down Monroe House with Lord Blake's departure in September. Regina allowed the girl to draw the bath but then barred her from the rooms and insisted on dressing herself. This was, to say the least, a laborious process, with most clothing designed explicitly to be donned with the handy assistance of a servant. Regina opted for some of her simpler clothing and a bonnet to cover the hair she simply couldn't get to behave quite right. Evaluating herself in the mirror, she admitted the effect was imperfect but passable.

Leaving her rooms, she pushed past Catherine. The girl had remained awake waiting for her employer to call for her despite the late hour. As she waved away the maid's question, Regina was uncomfortably aware of the warmth radiating from the Irish girl's flesh. "You may retire, Catherine," she said, then quickened her pace and called for Gerald to bring the coach around.

The coachman of Monroe House had been Regina's accomplice in her ill-fated investigations last spring, taking her to a variety of strange locales without informing her father or asking very many questions. She hoped he would continue to exercise that discretion.

He helped her into the compartment and asked, "Are you not cold, Lady Regina?"

She could feel the pulse of his circulation even through his woolen gloves. She'd donned a lighter dress and shawl and she realized that she *should* be feeling the cold of an October night in London. But compared to the coldness of her unliving flesh, the air had no bite. She pulled the shawl more tightly around her shoulders in a show of false need. "I shall survive, Gerald."

"There's a blanket in there, I believe, milady." He closed the door and waited for his instructions.

"Thank you," she said. "Highgate Asylum, please."

"Yes, milady."

The journey out of St. James and toward Hampstead Heath and Highgate took the better part of an hour, time Regina spent with a variety of unpleasant thoughts. She'd half-expected—and half-desired—that Victoria would appear at Monroe House while she was still dressing. In a city of hansoms and omnibuses, leaving Victoria behind at Charlotte Place was hardly a limit on her mobility.

But the elder vampire had not appeared, and so Regina realized that she was in all likelihood truly alone.

She hated herself for the fear that prospect brought with it. She despised Victoria Ash, didn't she? The woman had killed her father and gloated about it! The urge to rip apart the tartan blanket now draped needlessly across her lap rose up in Regina, testifying that her anger at the redheaded vampire was real enough. But still, she longed for her, for the caress of her lips, the feel of her skin.

The blood, she thought. *It must be the blood.* How many times had she drunk the black vitae in Victoria's veins before her own transformation into one of the undead? The traumatic events of the Santé prison might have knocked loose some of the chains on her heart, but she well knew she wasn't entirely free. Still, the longings that called to her felt anything but unnatural—they seemed the very fiber of her being.

Hunger. Hunger was a whole different problem. It had now been two nights—or was it three?—since she and Victoria had fed lightly from a man on the ferry from Calais. And how many nights between that and the porter on the Express? Or the bellman at the Hotel Sacher? Or Baron Grünwald? The hunger was like a constant itch that might be easily scratched if she only knew how. That was the rub. She had never fed alone—Victoria had always brought her to a man willing to surrender himself to two mysterious beauties. Now, sooner or later, she would have to do it herself. But she could not so easily entrance others, could she? And even if she could, or if she could find a man or woman willing not to ask too many questions, she had no idea whether she could go through with it alone. To drain blood from another, to take enough but not too much, to lick the wounds closed as Victoria had showed her—it was all so monstrous. But if she did not do it, the hunger would only continue to grow. And how long then before she rose disoriented and wild and drained the very life from Gerald, Catherine or some other unfortunate?

"Oh, Mother," she whispered, "what have I become?"

***

Gerald pulled the horses up the small drive of Highgate Asylum with the disc of the moon still high in the night sky. It was almost full and even with the cover of some clouds, its silvery light was enough to see by. Regina wondered if that was true for Gerald, or just a benefit of her unliving and night-made eyes. She alighted from the carriage once he opened the door. "Wait here for me, please."

"Please, do be careful, Lady Regina."

"Do as I say please, Gerald," she said, her tone sharp and stinging. A pang of regret followed that initial anger, but it was too late for words. He'd already turned to resume his post on the driver's seat. Regina tried to calm her nerves with a few unnecessary breaths and then mounted the stairs before the front door and pressed twice on the door-ringer.

It took several minutes, and another few rings, but the bolts of the heavy door finally tripped and a tall man in a slightly rumpled suit opened the door. "May I help you, ma'am?" He adjusted his spectacles while asking the question.

Regina tried to behave as Victoria had, acting as if the late hour of her visit was hardly noteworthy. She smiled and said softly, "I would like to visit with a patient here."

The man, although not especially aggressive, clearly did not take on the doe-eyed look of lust and admiration Regina had seen on Victoria's social partners. "I'm sorry, ma'am, but the hour is late and…" He let his voice trail off, as if the rest were obvious.

"I'm terribly sorry for the intrusion, sir—or is it doctor?"

He smiled slightly. "Yes, Doctor Gerald Watson Scott at your service."

"A pleasure, Doctor Scott. Lady Regina Blake." She smiled her brightest smile. "As I was saying…" She stopped, because she noted that his gaze was wandering. "Doctor?"

"Oh, please forgive me, Lady Regina. And forgive my rudeness, please come in." He opened the door wider.

"Thank you, Doctor."

Once inside, Scott led Regina from the rather formal front hall to a converted sitting room at the back of the main wing of the asylum. The windows were closed but the drapes drawn back, and Regina could just make out the bulk of Hampstead Heath overlooking the blackness that must be the facility's private gardens. Doctor Scott held a seat for her, then took one of his own near a small desk.

"I understand that my father, Lord Blake, saw to it that my dear friend Mrs. Claremont was brought here for care last August. I have only just returned from the Continent to hear the terrible news about

Joanna and I rushed here as soon as I could, hoping against hope that I might see her."

Doctor Scott adjusted his spectacles again. "Ah yes, Mrs. Claremont is indeed a patient of ours. Her case is quite severe, I'm afraid."

Regina leaned forward slightly. "How so?"

"Your father explained the circumstances of her entry to my care, I assume. The murder of her husband? Well, without entering into overly technical fields of study which would only baffle you, I'm sure, Mrs. Claremont has suffered a terrible shock and has become wholly alienated from her existence."

"Alienated?" Regina hated herself for confirming the doctor's opinion of her facility with the terminology of madness.

"She is in a sort of coma, or paralysis. She eats when fed and so forth, but has neither spoken nor taken any independent action since her arrival here."

"Oh, no. Poor Joanna…"

"I can assure you and your father, Lady Regina, that she is receiving the best care possible. But in a case such as this, progress is slow and painstaking."

"Thank you, Doctor. May I see her, please?"

Scott removed his spectacles and manipulated them with a series of frantic finger movements. He then returned them to his face. "It is quite irregular, but I imagine that it would be acceptable." He rose. "Please follow me, Lady Regina."

"Thank you, doctor."

He led her toward a stairway and up two stories. The gaslights were lit in several halls, but the doctor carried an oil lamp to light the way nonetheless.

"I hope I did not wake you, doctor," Regina said as they made their way down a long, door-lined hallway. Each door had a small slot next to it, which held a note-board of the sort used by doctors in hospital.

He turned and gave her a strange sort of smile. "Oh no, not at all. I'm afraid my work makes me quite the night-dweller."

He fished a master key from the ring in his vest pocket and fumbled it nervously into the lock of a door like all the others. Regina noted that the slot next to this one, however, held no notebook. The door opened with a slight squeak.

"Here we are."

Joanna Claremont, née Joanna Seward and widow to John Claremont, sat in a wicker-backed chaise furnished with large wheels and handles for a nurse to push her about. She was facing the room's only window, which looked toward the Heath as the sitting room downstairs had. A wood-framed bed was made and unused against one wall, beside a low cabinet with wash basin and pitcher atop it.

"I will leave you, Lady Regina," Scott said. "I will be nearby if you need me."

"Yes," she said, barely paying attention. "Thank you." She walked over to the stricken woman who had been her dearest friend since childhood. "Joanna?"

Regina knelt by the wheelchair and positioned so she could look into Joanna's face and was shocked to find her friend's eyes open and shockingly blue. "Oh, my darling Jo!"

But the eyes didn't respond, they simply moved slightly to fix on some other faraway point. Joanna was dressed in a nightgown and her chest moved slightly with each hollow breath. Her lips parted slightly, and Regina saw they were dry from lack of wetting.

"Oh, what have they done to you?" Regina practically fell into her friend's immobile lap, clasping to her the shockingly warm frame under the cotton nightgown. She had no doubt that John Claremont's death and Joanna's catatonia were the doing of some member of the monstrous society she had wandered into. *How many more will suffer for me?*

Regina felt tears of frustration and pangs of rage rising simultaneously within her. Guilt and anger seemed like the twin serpents of a caduceus, mounting her spine in unison, each as poisonous as the other. She buried her face in the soft cloth and sought shelter there, as she had done as a babe with her mother.

Just this, she told herself, *there's nothing more than this feeling right now.*

She turned her tear-streaked face and let out a silent gasp at the friction of her skin on the cloth. She moved her hand to clasp Joanna's and she found it warm and silky smooth. She pressed the palm to her face and kissed the tender flesh there. The slow but regular beat of Joanna's pulse echoed through Regina's whole being.

"Jo…" Regina lifted herself up the insensate woman's body, propping herself on the arms of the wheelchair and leaning forward to maintain contact between her face and the texture of Joanna's gown. The slight swell of her belly and breast brought the reality of Joanna's relatively recent motherhood to Regina's mind. *Poor Millicent*, she thought, but then pushed that and any other thought away. *Just this…*

Regina's lips passed over the neckline of the gown and found the alabaster skin—so much warmer than her own—above it. She planted kisses there, tasting first the slight salt of skin and sweat and then the coppery tang of blood as her needle-sharp canines left a series of tiny cuts. She planted a stronger, blood-stained kiss on Joanna's lips and the chair shifted slightly, causing a substantial gash on the living woman's lower lip.

Regina deftly moved to the side and slipped one arm under Joanna's legs and another under her right arm. Her body was light and Regina moved her easily to the bed, leaving only a few drops of blood on the room's wooden floor. The wounds were flowing more freely when Regina laid her down and Joanna's neck and chin were red with rich blood. Regina leaned in, the succulent odor filling her senses, and ran her lips and tongue along the marred skin. The blood was tangy and still somewhat thin, and Regina could feel the explosive effect it had as it went down her throat, even these few drops—like a fuse lit by the tiniest of sparks.

Regina kissed Joanna again, greedily sucking on her torn lip and then slipping her tongue along the cut. When she'd first fed as a vampire, she had been amazed how her lick could heal the wounds left by her teeth with ease. Now it was simple instinct.

Hiking up her own skirts so as to straddle Joanna, Regina grabbed at the slight V collar of Joanna's nightgown. The fabric tore with a high screech but little resistance. Looking at Joanna's large breasts, her slack expression, her mad eyes, her sallow skin, Regina was momentarily chilled by the banality of it all. But not for long— she could sense the intoxication of what awaited just under Joanna's skin.

She brought her mouth back to Joanna's neck repeating the tiny nibbles until she found that place where the pulse beat the strongest. Then, riding a wave of animal hunger and red-hot desire, she bit. Her sharp canines sliced through skin and arterial wall like the keenest of blades and a hot stream of blood suddenly washed into Regina's mouth and down her throat. There was a split second of revulsion, a slight gag that allowed a dram of blood to splash beyond her lips and run down the side of Joanna's throat and into the sheets.

Then the pure pleasure of it all eclipsed everything else.

The hot, rich red blood sent silent shrieks of ecstasy through her. Echoes of past pleasures arose in her mind only to be swallowed up in the immediacy of this experience. Private thoughts of exotic lovers and dashing soldiers that had warmed her as a budding girl…. Forbidden stroking late at night as she awaited the arrival… Passionate stolen embraces… Secret moments in Cairo when she and Joanna had shared unsisterly thoughts… Dreams of Malcolm, of Victoria, of Joanna too… They were all like single voices in the soaring chorus of the blood rushing in spurts into her. Her legs clenched and her pelvis thrust slightly, first in memory of the lust she'd once had for Malcolm, but soon she was more keenly thinking of squeezing every drop of blood as a thirsty sailor might from a wineskin.

"That's quite enough, I think."

Regina raised her head and her torso in a single, quick motion. Her senses screamed of a threat, like a cat who becomes suddenly aware of another in her den. And indeed, standing only a few steps from the bed was a slight woman with loose chestnut hair. She was wearing men's eveningwear and had the most striking hazel eyes rimmed with gold. Blood dribbled from Regina's chin and flowed from the terrible gashes on Joanna's throat.

"Lick those wounds closed, Lady Regina," the girl in man's dress said.

Without a second thought, Regina did so.

"Now, come with me." Those eyes remained fixed on Regina for what seemed like an eternity. Then the slight woman turned on her mannish heels and walked to the room's door, which swung open.

Regina was aware that she didn't especially want to follow this woman. Nevertheless she did, barely acknowledging Doctor Scott, who held the door open for her.

Chapter Fourteen

Steam blew from the locomotive's whistle and whooshed from its pistons, signaling that the special train north from Liverpool Street Station was soon to depart. The porters had just finished moving the last heavy crate of archeological artifacts into the private goods car that had been hitched adjacent to a passenger car for the wealthy—and well-connected—scholar heading toward Northern England. The scholar, dressed in a severe woolen cloak with a high collar and wearing a top hat, had watched the proceedings for the past hour, three times barking quick commands. He had never introduced himself, and neither had the shorter, more portly man who had come to see him off.

"This still seems reckless to me, Anton," the shorter man said.

The taller man turned to stare at his fellow blood sorcerer. "Now is not the time to quake in your boots, Bainbridge."

Edward Bainbridge let out something of an exasperated sigh. "Please, Anton, we are far from Vienna and I do not wish to engage in yet more verbal parrying and quips. I've had quite enough of all that."

"It's foolish libertines like you who will be the undoing of this age, Bainbridge."

The shorter man closed his eyes behind small spectacles and attempted to squeeze down his anger and frustration. "Be that as it may, Mr. Wellig, I simply point out that if we are to deal with the situation here, then it might be best to remain in London."

"I care very little for this city."

Another sigh. "You are being intentionally contrary, Wellig. Our fellows in Vienna have *requested* that we see to the matter of His Royal Highness and that compels us to remain in the capital, I think."

"You can chase after Mithras' coattails if you wish. I will make him come to me."

"You have no doubt he will come north?"

"Ha!" Wellig reached under his cloak and drew out one of the local dailies, filled with continued coverage of the Whitechapel murders. "It already begins, Bainbridge. He will have no choice once I complete the ritual."

"And Lady Blake, your errant childe?"

Wellig turned away and pronounced, "They will all come to me." With that he strode up the few steps of his passenger car, quickly followed by his ghoul, Eleanor Ducheski. Her scabrous and half-mad relative Gareth, whom they had recovered in Vienna, was already aboard.

The train pulled out, headed for County Durham and Wellig's Lion's Green Chantry. Bainbridge, although he thought the departure a strategic mistake, could not help but feel relieved to be out of the presence of the other blood sorcerer.

Now, all that was left for him to do was repair the damage Wellig had done in London. "All the king's horses and all the king's men," he mumbled to himself as he headed for the exit.

***

Despite Beckett's urge for immediate action, he and Emma Blake agreed to Halim Bey's request that they lie low in the warehouse all through the night following their arrival in London. Their conversation was limited that long night by another spell of Emma's—although not gripped by the same violent dementia as in the Hungarian basement, she was nonetheless fatigued and distracted. She complained of gnawing hunger pangs, which the rats and other street animals Beckett was able to coax to them did not sate. Animal blood, although not useless, was a thin and bitter substitute for that of men.

Eventually, in one of her more lucid times, Emma discussed her family. "I think the Ducheskis have been playthings of the Tremere order for centuries. Regent Wellig talked to me as if we were all some grand experiment in eugenics, although given the number of deformities and defects among my relatives, I can't imagine them to be successful."

"You are not what any man would call deformed, Emma," Beckett pointed out. By this time, he had slipped into the habit of using her given name, and she had yet to object.

She smiled slightly. "Not in the common way of a clubfoot or some such, no. But my aunt always accused me of having thin blood. I've never had any of the gifts of my cousins."

"Gifts?"

"My aunt would say that our line is descended from the mating of man and pagan god, and that the gifts are the proof that our heritage still runs in our blood. 'We are the daughters of Shaagra and sons of Byelobog,'" she said, adopting a croaking imitation of a an old woman's voice. "Regent Wellig felt they were the result of his own experimentations."

Beckett felt a flood of questions roiling within him and tried his best to organize his thoughts. "What is the nature of these gifts?"

"I'm not wholly sure because I never experienced them myself, you understand. But I had cousins who could smell as well as any hunting hound and others who could summon cold greenish fire with a few passes of their hands. I've seen terrible wounds heal in mere minutes as well."

"Did these gifts come from partaking in any ritual with Wellig or the other Tremere? From drinking any form of potion, for example?"

"For some," she said, curious now, "but my cousins were all born with at least some mark of their blood. All except me."

"Your family originated in the East, yes? What's now Hungarian or Turkish land."

"Yes, although I couldn't tell you the exact region. Why?"

Beckett paced as best he could in the cramped space. It wasn't much, but he felt the need to move, to allow the scenarios he was piecing together to arrange themselves. "You understand that mortals who drink our blood can gain a measure of our strengths, correct?"

"Yes. Ghouls," Emma said.

"There are stories of families descended from ghouls who develop some of these strengths without drinking undead blood. They are born to it. I've never been able to find a great amount of detail, but all the sources I've found associate them with an especially fiendish clan of vampires called the Tzimisce. And both Shaagra and Byelobog are names that I've also come across associated with those fiends." Beckett paused and when he resumed, he seemed to be talking more to himself than to Emma. "Now I suppose Wellig could have replicated whatever the Tzimisce do to create these ghoul families, but with those stories and your family's origin…"

Emma sat forward. "Ehovar Krevcheski."

Beckett turned, genuine confusion on his face. "Excuse me."

"Ehovar Krevcheski betrayed the gods of the land, forcing his decedents to find shelter with the masters. With the Tremere." Emma recounted what she remembered of the story her Aunt Eleanor had told her in Josefsdorf the previous month.

When she was finished, Beckett sat down again, more

determined than ever to make for Merritt House. When, near the end of the night, Halim Bey arrived with the documents Beckett had requested, he took them anxiously but decided not to unwrap them or show them to Emma.

***

"Right here," Emma told the driver as he pulled the hansom cab up to the drive of the grand house on Park Lane, at the edge of Hyde Park. She and Beckett descended immediately. They had left the warehouse mere minutes after waking for the night and taken a cab straight there.

"She certainly has a taste for the finer things," Beckett said, looking up at the grand house. Most of the impressive dwellings his life led him to were tombs.

"Her private garden is the grandest in London," Emma said with more than a hint of pride.

Beckett let that comment go and they ascended the steps to the front door. He rang the bell. The door opened almost immediately.

"Good evening," said a butler dressed in clothing that seemed culled from a less morose era. He was visibly suppressing a sneer directed at the couple's attire. Beckett wore his standard choice of canvas pants and simple jacket, which someone had once told him made him look like a pauper's version of Buffalo Bill Cody, one who couldn't afford real buckskin. Emma was no better, her well-made dress and jacket stained with coal dust—despite an abortive effort at cleaning.

"We're here to see Lady Merritt," Beckett said.

"Milady is not here, sir." The disdain dripped from the man's lips.

Beckett felt a snarl rising in his throat and swallowed it down with difficulty. This dandified domestic was almost certainly a ghoul, enslaved to his mistress and obsessed with nothing more than pleasing her. Beckett had no doubt that the lady of the house was here, simply not for them.

"Tell here we're here about the thousand-faced daughter," Beckett said, and he felt Emma stiffen beside him. He was using one of the appellations of the ancient vampire Kemintiri, and jumping somewhat blindly to conclusions.

The butler's mask of flat disdain didn't waver. "I'm sure I have no idea of what you mean, sir. If you would care to leave a—"

The servant stopped short as another cut across him from inside. "It's alright, Mr. Wilson," came the rich male voice, spiced with the accents of the East. "I know this couple."

With just a hint of consternation on his face, the butler stepped back and opened the door wide to reveal the hidden speaker. "As you say, Mr. Ruhadze."

Hesha Ruhadze, with whom Beckett had made common cause earlier in the year in his quest for Emma Blake and Kemintiri. With skin a shade browner than ebony and a completely hairless pate, Ruhadze might appear to the Victorian eye as a colonial savage were it not for the fine evening wear and gold-rimmed monocle he affected tonight. The suit fit him perfectly and the tie's stripe had a slight green tinge that added to his sophistication. He smelled, Beckett thought, of cardamom or cumin. Ruhadze was from the same line as Halim Bey, an undead worshipper of the god Set.

"Our paths cross again, Mr. Beckett," he said, then turned to face Emma. He bowed slightly to her. "Lady Blake. Please, do come in, both of you."

Hesha led them into Merritt House, down the main corridor and past rooms luxuriant in their appointments. Framed artwork and sculpture from various cultures meshed with floral arrangements and fine teak and mahogany furniture. Like all Victorian houses, Merritt House was crowded with accoutrements, but they seemed positioned with exquisite care, riding the knife-edge between good taste and excessive ornamentation.

"Ruhadze," Beckett said. "Have you been here since I left for Vienna?"

Hesha ignored the question. He paused in front of the French doors that led onto the terrace and turned to face Beckett and Emma. He looked them up and down and a shadow of the butler's distaste speckled his features. He pocketed his monocle. "Ah, yes. You will want to change before joining Lady Merritt and her guest. I'm sure Lucy and Harold can help you find proper attire." He signaled with a nod. A footman and a maid entered the room from a side door.

"Ruhadze," Beckett asked, "what the devil is going on here?"

"Come now, Mr. Beckett," the African man said. "This is not a dusty Mesopotamian tomb. There will be plenty of time for questions once we are all gathered in a civilized manner."

Beckett gave Ruhadze a blank stare and finally shrugged. The undead made an existence out of masquerades of various sorts and if another was in order, then so be it. He turned to the footman. "Lead the way, Harold."

While Beckett and Emma climbed one of the large staircases to the upstairs rooms, the servants just behind them, she asked "What was that about the thousand-faced daughter? Anwar al-Beshi used that term."

Beckett didn't answer.

***

Spending time in the East End of London at night was not, Edward Bainbridge thought, the wisest thing for one of London's kindred to be doing. With the murders in Whitechapel and the subsequent hue and cry, any lone man was suspect. Feeding here seemed even more dangerous, fraught with the risks of being mistaken for the madman and perhaps even rending the precious veil of secrecy that protected the undead form mortal attention.

The streets were both emptier and more crowded than normal. There were fewer prostitutes and other street dwellers, but they were hardly absent. Bainbridge did his best to avoid contact with this sort of mortal, but it wasn't hard to understand that many of them had little choice but to walk the night streets if they wanted a shilling to eat with. And there were no small number of people actually attracted by the prospect of a madman with a knife. Vigilance committees had swollen in membership and several times Bainbridge avoided the attention of groups of men out looking for any suspect to beat into the ground. Other lone Ripper-hunters were about as well: reporters, thrill seekers and perhaps even a few policemen. All in all, not a healthy time or place to be undead.

Still, it could not be helped. The walk from Liverpool Street Station was easy and it took only a few minutes to cut through Spitalfields. From there, it was not a far walk to the aging manufacture just beyond Mile End that he knew to be the haven of Valerius, once prince-regent of London's undead, now fallen from grace.

Bainbridge used his cane to announce his presence, knocking on the building's stout front door with its cold iron head. A few moments later, he heard a shuffling coming from the long dark space off to his left, the grandly named St. Michael Lane, which was little more than a yard-wide gap between structures. "This way," said the beggar who appeared at the lane's mouth.

The ousted regent was apparently affecting misery to employ such a servant. Bainbridge followed him into the cramped space, strewn with various detritus. Rats scurried underfoot, uninterested in the taste of unliving flesh. A steep stair descended into Valerius' current residence and the beggar, who had all of two teeth left in his head, waved Bainbridge down.

The cellar smelled of mold and was utterly dark. When the heavy door closed behind Bainbridge he did not move at all. He was the guest here and he would wait for the host to show himself.

A minute later there was the sound of a striking match and Valerius appeared, lighting a sooty oil lamp. It cast a meager orb of yellow pallor, barely enough to sketch out the prince-regent's features and the shape of the wooden chair near Bainbridge.

"Sit," Valerius said. Tonight he had apparently forgone the elaborate toilette in which he was said to indulge. His beard was unshaven and full, merging with the red mass of hair that tumbled to his shoulders. Only the top of his skull was bare, having surrendered to baldness before his Embrace. He wore breeches but no shirt. His chest and stomach were hairy save for a brutal scar that slashed from his left to his right side. Another memory of a life long ago left behind. His right hand was covered in drying blood.

"Where is Wellig?" he asked.

Bainbridge took a seat. The chair creaked. He could smell no great amount of blood or viscera in the damp basement air, so he assumed Valerius had left whatever occupied him upstairs. "Regent Wellig has boarded a train for his chantry in County Durham. He sends his regrets."

"I care not one whit for his regrets, doctor," Valerius said, and stepped closer. "The prince yet lives, the city is gripped by madness, and I want answers, not regrets!"

Looking into Valerius's eyes, Bainbridge felt it was not the city's madness he had to worry about. "Yes, of course. Regent Wellig tells me matters are still proceeding. I believe there was a slight delay, but—"

"Delay!" Valerius grabbed Bainbridge's shirtfront with his bloody hand and hefted the man up off the chair. The Tremere's head impacted noisily with the low ceiling. "I handed over to you a vial of Mithras' blood, sorcerer! In seven centuries of service to that deluded whore's son I obtained one such vial and one only! It was irreplaceable!"

Valerius punctuated each point with another slam into the ceiling. None of the damage done would last—blood could heal almost all for the undead—but that did not offset the pain any great deal. Bainbridge tried to speak, to explain, even to apologize, but it was no use.

"I wish to build a pyre out of the bitch Anne and her lickspittles, Bainbridge! I was to be prince!"

The chair shattered as Bainbridge fell back into it. "You still may be," he said, trying to calm the madman.

Valerius was suddenly interested. "How so?"

"If Regent Wellig's ritual—"

"Lies!" Valerius exclaimed. He drove one of the chair's wooden legs through Bainbridge's breastbone and into his heart. The Tremere magus never saw him move.

***

Beckett had the distinct urge to rip the jacket into shreds and the footman holding it into bloody pulp. The domestic insisted that the deep brown three-quarter-length jacket Beckett had chosen from the wardrobe was not quite appropriate, and wore the same trademark sneer as the butler had. This was jacket number five and they had been at it for over an hour. He'd already run a comb through his unfashionably long hair and tied it back with a black silk ribbon. The footman had even tried to take away Beckett's tinted glasses, which had actually caused him to snarl.

There's something in the air, Beckett thought. *Something dangerous.* He snatched the jacket from the servant's hands and pulled it on over the white shirt and vest. He grabbed a cravat and roughly tied it about his neck.

The footman looked aghast and made to adjust the neckwear himself. This course of action might well have cost Lady Merritt a loyal manservant, but he stopped short when a distraught voice came from across the way.

"I can't! I can't!" It was Emma.

Beckett pushed past the footman and into the hall. The servant exclaimed something, but Beckett ignored him. Emma's voice continued to plead and Beckett turned the knob to the room she and the maid had entered earlier. It was locked. A frustrated growl escaped from his clenched jaw, and he felt the hot charge of blood rushing to his muscles, engorging and fortifying them. He pushed and the doorjamb surrendered with a crack.

Inside, the maid who was assisting Emma stood seemingly petrified by the bed. She was clutching a deep-red evening gown and looking directly at Beckett. She dropped the gown, which slipped to the floor in a flutter of skirts, and began to shake.

"Go," Beckett barked, and pointed a thumb toward the door through which he'd just entered. The girl practically ran past him.

Emma was also shaking. She stood by an elaborate dressing table, the chair of which had been knocked on its side. A variety of powders, soaps and creams adorned the table surface, under a large mirror. She was protecting her modesty by clutching a white sheet to herself. The red tracks of blood tears marked her face. "I can't," she repeated hoarsely.

Beckett felt the tension in him not lift so much as lose its focus. He'd charged in expecting danger, an opponent to combat. Instead he found this neonate, vulnerable and seemingly traumatized. And unclothed. He approached and saw a bath sitting in the center of a smaller room accessible through double doors behind Emma. All the soot from the coal-train had been scrubbed away, apparently.

"What is it?" He tried to keep his voice as even-keeled as he could. His sensitive nose picked up the scent of jasmine coming from Emma, an echo of the soaps and oils she'd used in bathing. He noticed the new luster in her dark hair, which hung unpinned past her shoulders.

Her eyes, limpid and hazel, darted to her left, toward the dress that now lay by the bed.

"This thing?" Beckett picked it up and stepped back toward Emma. He held it up.

Emma gave a weak nod. "I wore it for her… before. Twenty years ago. When I was hers."

She paused, and Beckett stood stock still, feeling the blood in his veins run hot and the rage in his unbeating heart grow hotter.

"But now," she said, "I can't. I was a girl then. Now, I'm… I'm an old woman. It won't fit. I'll never be what she wants again…"

Beckett yanked and the dressed ripped apart. He threw down the two halves of the ruined garment. "Good," he said. "Never be hers again. Do you hear me: never!"

She trembled, seemingly unable to speak.

He grabbed her and shook her, the anger roiling in him. "Do you hear me, Emma? You left that behind! I've seen dozens of men destroyed by going through what you did. They didn't last a year without the blood of the bastard who enslaved them. You've lasted twenty." His voice softened slightly. "You have eternity ahead of you, Emma. Go though it on your terms, not hers."

"Eternally old," she said. "Ugly."

He put a hand on the side of her face and she leaned into it. "Don't be a fool, Emma. You're beautiful."

The word slipped from Beckett's lips and he only then realized how true it was. He'd already spent more than a lifetime among the undead, who with certain exceptions, had the alluring air of predators. Among the well-heeled vampires of London, Paris and Vienna there were men and women so physically perfect, so ideal, that one would think Olympus had surrendered its gods. But none of them had Emma Blake's beauty.

Parts of him he'd almost forgotten hungered for her physicality. That satiny hair with just a few strands of gray. The pale but not quite white flesh. The swell of her pear-like breasts and the curve of her hips. The hazel pools of her eyes. The thickness of her lower lip and the slightness of her ears. But her true beauty, he understood, lay in the life that miraculously remained in her. Undead and damned like all their kind, she kept the longings of a living woman alive in her. She'd spoken of her concern for her daughter, her husband. Despite her seemingly lifelong association with the margins of undead existence, she took not at all to the predator's ways and for that—as much as he could—he loved her.

"Let me see your eyes," she said, and reached with one hand for his spectacles. The sheet clutched in her other hand shifted, revealing the curve of one breast and the blue vein there.

Beckett felt frozen and frantic, hot and cold, terrified and exhilarated. Unlike most of the vampires in civilized London, Beckett came from a line of undead much closer to their bestial natures. He'd learned many benefits of this lineage over the decades, from quickly slipping into the earth to avoid the day's sun, to taking on the aspect of night-creatures like a bat or wolf. But his lineage had its price, too: clear physical marks of his own savage heart. They were not things he was especially proud of.

Still when Emma Blake removed his tinted glasses, he did not close his eyes to hide their feline pupil slits or amber irises. Instead he looked into her very human eyes and saw there a hint of sympathy floating in twin lakes of understanding.

He reached for the sheet and pulled it away from her. She resisted for a split second, then let it fall, revealing her nakedness. Beckett's gloved hand descended her neck, to her collarbone. Her body was marked in a pattern of scars he realized must have been left there by her time with the sorcerer Anwar al-Beshi. White puckers of scar tissue, like a series of witch's teats, ran in a V-shape from below her breasts toward her sex. His hand followed them, lingering on each one and passing his fingers through the coarse hair of her pubis. His other hand followed the thin linear scar that ran down her sternum.

He had first seen her in al-Beshi's thrall, when during the ritual that ultimately destroyed the Arab sorcerer, she had used a knife to slice open her own body. She'd been nude and bloody then, but now she was so much more. His hand circled her left breast.

Her hands moved to that hand, leaving the other where it was below her stomach. He could feel her touching the digits under his thin leather glove and he let her pull off that sheath, exposing another sign of his blood's taint. Dark hair, slick like sable, covered the back of his hand, fading to more human-seeming growth on his forearms. His fingers were longer than a man's should be, and the nails were hard and thick like a dog's.

She brought the hand to her mouth and kissed its tough palm.

Beckett removed his other glove, elucidating a sigh from Emma. She undid his cravat and the buttons of his shirt, at first slowly but then with increasing speed. His hands moved down her back and found the soft flesh of her posterior. She leaned in and passed her tongue along his chest and he clenched his hands in response, clawing welts into the white flesh of her rear and causing her to gasp.

The scent of the jasmine soaps, the copper tinge of blood tears and musk of his own animal nature filled his nostrils. Still clenching her tightly, he pulled her to him and up, forcing her to grab onto his back for purchase. He took a few steps, pivoted and threw her bodily onto the large bed.

She let out a wild gasp and bounced when she hit the mattress, ending up on her stomach. Her rear bore ten distinct and deep gouges from his tough nails. Her blood was clearly coursing through her system, as a wine-colored bead of it seeped from the deepest of the cuts. Beckett stood there a second, and already he could see the shallower cuts closing in response to Emma's unliving instincts.

He jumped onto the bed and rode his tongue over that now-black bead of blood, feeling its electric tingle as it slipped down his throat. His nose filled with the coppery imitation of sex scent that Emma's unliving body sent forth. Slipping a hand under her hip to raise her rear slightly, he moved tongue, mouth and face down to the source of that aroma. She unfolded for his tongue, welcoming him. His fangs slipped from his gums like twin blades and sunk into the most delicate of her flesh. She trilled in pleasure as her rich, cool blood slipped into his mouth.

He lifted his head from her after an endless moment—one that could have been a second or an hour for all he knew or cared. Savage instincts for pleasure and predation roiled within him and he roughly flipped her onto her back. She looked up at him from beyond the delicious expanse of her scarred torso and sharp fangs like daggers appeared between her lips. She pounced up toward him, pushing him back and off the end of the bed.

He hit the floor with a loud thud and she was atop him, pulling at the remainder of his clothing. He shrugged off coat and jacket while she worked his belt. Together they disposed of what remained to cover him and she looked over his nakedness. Her hungry hands found what had once been the root of his manhood and stroked it.

How long since he had felt anything there? Distant memories of living passion bubbled slightly and he knew she wanted him as a living and a dead man. Smiling wickedly, he let his blood rush to that unused organ and what had been semi-flaccid in Emma's hand became powerfully erect. This in turn awoke a distant memory—a girl in a field under the sun, the salty taste of her kiss and the slick warmth of her womanhood. Beckett rose from under Emma, carrying her across the room and pressing her against one of the walls.

She squirmed and fought wildly, raking his flesh with her fingernails and pulling at his hair. Acting on instincts he'd thought long erased from his undead soul, he thrust into her, feeling the cool earthy wetness of her folds and hearing the squeals of pleasure she gasped into his ear. His teeth throbbed in his mouth and her legs clamped around him like serpents, drawing him into her again and again. On the fifth thrust he plunged his fangs into her shoulder and she did into his.

The pleasure was like nothing Beckett had ever felt before. He hoped it could last forever. It lasted until dawn.

Chapter Fifteen

The room in which Regina awoke was not especially uncomfortable. It was even pleasant in its own way. Once she opened the shutters, she could see the moon low in the eastern sky, and she guessed she was on the opposite side of the Highgate Asylum from Joanna's room. The window was small, but the furnishings were fine and if not for the reinforced door with a viewing hatch at eye level enclosed (on the inside) by a small iron cage, it could be a guest's room at a country estate.

The door itself wasn't the problem, because it was unlocked. Upon waking Regina had quickly tested it and found that the latch came loose with one good tug and the door pulled open with ease. The corridor, lit by dim but sufficient gas lighting, beckoned.

But Regina had absolutely no idea how she should go about crossing that threshold. Common sense—*a faculty I may have lacked recently*, she thought—told her that it was possible to cross that thin strip of wood. She'd surely done it to enter and knew well she'd crossed countless other such barriers in her eighteen years—now almost nineteen—on this Earth. And yet, crossing this particular threshold seemed inconceivable, as different from leaving another room as throwing a scoop of coal into an oven was from throwing an innocent babe into it. This barrier was sacrosanct, inviolate, taboo.

And no matter how hard she wracked her brain, Regina Blake could not remember why it was so.

"Quite a conundrum, isn't it?"

Regina started because the voice was coming from inside the room. She spun on her heels and looked around, stepping away from the doorway to search out her interlocutor. She spun again when a light squeal announced the door closing. As it swung back into place, it revealed a slight, chestnut-haired woman dressed in the navy blue wool uniform of the Metropolitan Police. She smiled slightly and said, "An unlocked-room mystery."

"Miss Parr," Regina said. "The constabulary of the undead."

"Ah, I suppose it would be poor sport of me to begrudge you using such a dramatic appellation given the circumstances. I do generally use the title of sheriff, however."

"Sheriff Parr, then." Regina had met Juliet Parr several times over the spring and into the summer, when she was first peeling back the layers of London's night society. Her very first night doing so, in fact, Miss Parr had intervened when she fell under the spell of a Spaniard named Don Cerro. "In retrospect, it appears I owe you a certain amount of thanks for stepping in last April."

"Yes. Don Cerro had overstepped his bounds, but then I suppose you know a great deal about overstepping bounds." Miss Parr stepped forward, coming uncomfortably close to Regina. The sheriff was an inch shorter than Regina, and looked to be several years younger. That, Regina guessed, was an illusion of undeath.

"The asylum is your lair, then," Regina said, "and Joanna is what, your feeding stock?"

Parr smiled. "I was not the one who drained her of most of her lifeblood last night, Lady Regina. But to be entirely up front with you, Mrs. Claremont is here under Dr. Scott's care quite legitimately. The death of her husband was a terrible shock, as was your arrival fresh from Miss Ash's bed late last July."

"How did you—?" Regina had fled to Joanna's home after waking beside Victoria's cold, dead form. After the first night she had drunk freely from the redheaded creature's blood—blood that had healed a terrible wound. She had been confused and half-mad at the time. "How?"

"I am not in the business of revealing all my methods, Lady Regina. I would rather we discussed the last few months, and how they relate to the current state of mind of His Royal Highness Prince Mithras. And to your own rather grave condition." She looked Regina in the eye. "And I'm sure you understand that it would not be sensible to lie to me, or even to withhold anything."

And that, suddenly and naturally, Regina did. Some distant whisper told her that this boyish girl wished her no good at all and that it would be wise to perhaps not tell her the whole sordid tale of the last year. But it was only a whisper and lying to Miss Parr was as inconceivable as leaving the room. And so she told the tale form its beginnings, as she understood it. Her mother's ersatz death, her own entry in the night society, Anton Wellig's use of her mother to affect Prince Mithras, her misadventures in Paris, her transformation on the Grand Express and the entirety of her time in Vienna. Even her falling out with Miss Ash and her misgivings both about being angry with the woman who had remade her, and not being angry enough.

It took several hours to tell. Miss Parr largely let her speak at her own pace, only asking a few questions here and there for clarification. At the end of it Miss Parr smiled and said, "You certainly have had a busy year, Lady Regina."

With that she stood, crossed the room, opened the door and stepped out. She turned around and said, "There is someone you will have to meet, I'm afraid. Oh, you may follow me out of the room, Lady Regina."

And she could. So she did.

***

Lady Anne Bowesley had very little desire to meet with anyone on the night of October 9th. The tension that had been lurking behind her eyes since His Royal Highness had fallen ill in August had now bloomed into a sharp pain. It throbbed as if tied to a beating heart, something Anne knew very well was not possible. It put her on edge and threatened to crack the veneer of control she'd spent two hundred years constructing, and upon which her position as seneschal to Prince Mithras depended. This night, she felt it would be best to be alone and focus her energies on taming the beast within her, which seemed determined to throw itself, again and again, against its cage.

The city refused to let her be, however. Mithras, now awake but hardly well, was prone to wandering the city streets and the various haunts of undead. Anne had a personal agent of hers following the prince and reporting back. This agent, a kindred of recent blood named Mary, was discreet and of commendable subtlety, despite her unfortunately horrific mien. She had in only two nights of work already tracked Mithras to any number of hidden corners of the city. "It's as if he is searching for something," Mary had reported just before dawn on the previous night. "But I have no idea what, Your Grace."

It would be a shame to lose Mary, Anne thought as her lady's maid finished dressing her, *but that may be unavoidable.* The serving girl straightened the last detail of her attire, and Anne shooed her away with barely a motion. The girl had been in her service for near on a decade and was well tuned to her mistress's will.

Anne then headed to the receiving room downstairs, footmen appearing only long enough to open doors for her. They never looked at her and she did not acknowledge them any more than she did the furnishings and carpets.

The large sitting room featured a half-dozen chairs and two divans, along with several cabinets and other fine furnishings. The walls sported a large oil painting of the Warwickshire countryside where Anne had grown to womanhood, and several portraits of monarchs she felt deserved a place of status. Queen Victoria was most prominent, but William of Orange and the deceased Prince Consort Albert were also given places of honor. Sitting in the room were four of Anne's kindred, although the use of the term felt especially loose in the case of some of them.

Sitting were the dilettante Victoria Ash and her newly made childe Lady Regina Blake. Standing were General Halesworth—the duly appointed sheriff of the city's night society—and his aide, Miss Juliet Parr. The latter was dressed in the blue wool uniform of a Peeler.

The beast within Anne reared again, and this time her hand slipped off the leash somewhat. "Miss Parr," she snapped. "I have had quite enough of your foolishness. This is a proper house and I will not have you treating it as a fancy dress ball."

"Your Grace—" the boyish girl started, but Anne cut her off.

"Leave and do not return until you are properly attired, Miss Parr. Immediately." Her voice was an icy stab and the slight girl visibly flinched. That greatly pleased Anne, as did seeing Parr incongruously curtsey in her trousers and then scurry away.

"Now, General," Anne said, turning to the only man in the room and ignoring the two seated women. "Would you kindly explain to me why I should not make an example of Miss Ash and her unauthorized and unpresented whelp?" She sat down.

"Now see here—" Regina said.

"Silence, girl," Anne said, drilling her gaze into the young thing and stealing her voice. "General?"

"I'm honestly not sure, Your Grace," he said, his voice gruff. "Miss Parr has already obtained the childe's report, which corroborates our suspicions that His Royal Highness is the victim of a sorcerous scheme. Lady Regina witnessed the poisoning in Sydenham with her own eyes."

"Very well then," Anne said. "Set them out for the sun and be done with it."

***

Regina felt the thrill of fear running through her. Lady Anne and General Halesworth were stone façades of iron will, calmly discussing her and Victoria's destruction as they might the decision to purchase a trinket or host a party. Regina knew she had to defend herself, but could not conceive of what to do to remedy the situation.

"May we speak in our own defense, Your Grace?"

Victoria's question was polite and her tone even, but it sent a charge through Regina. *Yes*, she thought, *speaking! Please let us speak!*

Anne looked at Victoria and then at Regina, who felt she was ready to explode out of her cold skin. "You may," she said.

Regina clamped down on her own tongue to suppress the urge to blurt out the stream of pleading, arguments and invectives that wanted release. Just because she could suddenly speak again, didn't mean she should. She glanced at Victoria.

"Thank you, Your Grace," said the redheaded vampire. "I accept that I have violated tradition by not presenting my childe to His Royal Highness, but it has only been a scant few nights since we returned from the Continent. The current situation seemed to preclude my seeking out the prince and so I chose to await the next public gathering to present Regina."

"As I understand it, Miss Ash," Anne said, "Miss Parr found your childe in Highgate with your guiding hand nowhere to be seen."

Regina spoke now, fighting to still the trembling in her voice. "I'm afraid that was my fault, Your Grace. I disregarded Miss Ash's sound advice upon hearing of the poor condition of my friend Mrs. Claremont."

"All the more reason to be done with her," Anne said, to Victoria. "London has no need of another disobedient childe."

"Of course not, Your Grace," Victoria said. "Regina is a woman of breeding and refinement and understands the importance of our laws. Our separation was a byproduct of the fact that, during our absence from London, parties unknown burned my home to the ground. The pressure of finding shelter for the day superceded caution."

Anne turned to face her sheriff. "General? Is this true?"

"A fire on Charlotte Place, Your Grace. It happened last month and was set, I believe, during the daylight hours."

"Churchmen?" Anne said.

"Possibly."

"Your Grace," Regina said, "the same sorcerer who poisoned His Royal Highness took my mother as his childe and left traces for others to follow. I was fortunate enough to cross paths with Miss Ash in my quests, but I believe others have become party to religious zealots."

Anne did not interrupt, but neither did she deign to address Regina. To Victoria, she said, "Supposing matters are as your childe says, Miss Ash. How does this relate to the more serious violation of tradition, namely your unsanctioned Embrace of her?"

Victoria did not answer immediately and Regina could feel her weighing the answer. Finally she settled for what Regina thought might just be the truth. "During our time in Paris," Victoria said, "Lady Regina was able to free us both from the clutches of an elder who had enslaved us for his own mad purposes. Even before then, I found that I had come to admire her keen judgment and intelligence, elements that tend to be eroded by the bond our blood may impose on a mortal. Thus, knowing it was critical that I protect our grand masquerade, I was faced with the options of either further enslaving the woman who had freed me and thus destroying all her best qualities, killing her outright, or making the secret of our existence her own."

"There are other options," Lady Anne said. "The mind can be made to forget many things."

Regina thought of Miss Parr, who peeled back her will, and of Lady Anne herself, who stole her voice. She shuddered slightly.

"I'm afraid that such things are beyond me, Your Grace, and beyond any I would trust with such a matter," Victoria said. "I had to choose among the things possible to me."

"That was not your choice to make, Miss Ash," Anne said. "You had no authorization to bring another into our night society."

"I remade Regina while between Paris and Vienna, Your Grace. There was no local prince to sanction such a choice."

Anne let a scowl cross her features. "Do you take me for a drunken judge who will wave away crimes based on such technicalities, Miss Ash? If you expected to return to London, then it was into this city that you were bringing your childe."

"In retrospect, I understand that, Your Grace," Victoria said. "Embracing Regina seemed the best choice among poor options."

"I am not without compassion," Lady Anne said, but Regina

found she didn't believe that. "You and your childe will be spared, but you are no longer welcome in this city or its associated domains. You are exiled."

Regina glanced at Victoria and saw a cold glare of hatred pass over her features dragging a large amount of fear in its wake. Victoria had been exiled before and it was not, Regina knew, something she wished to repeat.

"Your Grace," Regina said, "what about His Royal Highness's condition?"

Anne said nothing, but did finally look Regina in the eye.

"It was clear when the poisoning occurred that Mr. Wellig, the sorcerer in question, expected the prince to succumb. He seemed to believe that using the avenue of my mother to deliver his poison made it irresistible."

"He was obviously wrong," Anne said.

"Only because Miss Ash intervened," Regina said. "I doubt he will be satisfied until the prince is destroyed. He must be found and stopped."

"That would be our concern," Halesworth said, "not yours."

"I respectfully disagree, sir," Regina said. "It certainly is your purview to protect the city, but this sorcerer uses my mother's family as his shield and cat's-paws. He remade my mother in his image and then was to throw her away as nothing but a glorified dart for his poison. I wish to find him and I think that given our common history I am uniquely suited to do so."

"You can search from somewhere else, girl," Halesworth said.

"But he has spent time in London," Regina said. "He must have co-conspirators and other aides I could uncover."

"I'm also confident we can find Regina's mother, Mr. Wellig's own errant childe, here," Victoria said. "I doubt anyone but Regina can guarantee her cooperation."

Halesworth made to speak, but Anne raised her hand just slightly and he kept quiet. "Very well," she said. "Your exile is delayed until the end of this month, to allow you time to continue to search. Should you uncover material elements that help in bringing justice to those who would bring low the prince, His Royal Highness may see fit to reevaluate your status."

"Thank you, Your Grace," both women said.

"There are, however, conditions to your remaining in London.

Firstly, Miss Ash, your childe's conduct is entirely your responsibility and I will not tolerate her proceeding unaccompanied. Keep her on a short leash, please."

"Yes, Your Grace," Victoria said.

"Secondly, this entire affair has only reinforced my feeling that it is beneficial for His Royal Highness to have allies in Vienna, if only to keep an eye on the activities of these scheming sorcerers. One such friend of ours is a certain Mr. Schiller, whom I am given to understand you and your childe know."

Regina felt a chill of dread run through her at the thought of the centennial Viennese vampire in the body of a boy.

"Mr. Schiller has communicated to me that he has asked of your childe a service. I would expect that she fulfill her agreement post haste. I would be most displeased if a mere childe were to sour what could be a valuable relationship."

Victoria looked at Regina, who fought the lump in her throat and said, "Of course, Your Grace."

Lady Anne stood then and said, "Then good evening to you both." She left and Halesworth with her.

Regina followed Victoria out to the grand house's drive, their way indicated by silent servants. As they strolled to the waiting carriage, she asked in a whisper, "How can we find Mother? She was abducted in Vienna to Lord only knows where."

Victoria paused a few steps from the fine carriage. "That is actually the least of our concerns." She turned to face the driver. "To Merritt House, on Park Lane, please."

Chapter Sixteen

Othman Ibn Saleh al-Masri faced southeast, toward the Isle of Dogs, the Victoria Docks and, far beyond that, the holy city of Mecca. The sun was rising from that same direction, as it had every morning since his and Lieutenant Seward's arrival in this small boarding room in London's East End two weeks ago. Seward had yet to leave the room, and Othman had only done so to purchase provisions and carry out waste—always in the daylight. They were in the very midst of the ghastly Ripper madness. He understood without being told that an Arab man of Muslim faith, living in a terrified and uneducated neighborhood, was as likely a suspect as any. He had no desire to be the victim of an overzealous vigilance committee.

His forehead touched the woven prayer rug a second time, and in his memory, he could hear the imam's voice guiding him in his supplication to God. This very rug he had obtained from a friend in Najaf during his sole pilgrimage to the tomb of Ali, Blessed Be His Name, and had carried with him ever since. His morning supplications complete, he did not stand but instead laid his other most precious possessions on the rug before him. These objects might appear mundane, banal even, to another's eyes—but to Othman they were the testaments to his life of faith.

First, and most precious, a small clay phial stoppered with cork. Inside was a small quantity of sand, gathered in a single hand-scoop from the courtyard of Mecca's Great Mosque, the space surrounding the holy Kaba, which he had circled seven times during his hajj. Next, a rock fragment on whose flat façade could be seen the delicate pigmentation of flowing, richly designed Arabic script. Othman had found this architectural reminder of the faithful deep in the Western Desert when he had become separated from the caravan that would eventually take him to Timbuktu and the mullah, who would set him on his current path. Finally, a piece of parchment on which Othman himself had transcribed a passage from the Holy Koran the tomb of Ali eighteen years ago. It had been whispered to him by a dervish and spoke to his place in the world and the devilish enemies he faced. From the third sura, Al-Imran, it read:

If good comes your way, they are vexed; but if evil befalls you they are pleased and rejoice; yet if you are patient and guard yourself against evil, their cunning will not harm you in the least, for whatsoever they do is well within the reach of God.

Othman looped a thin cord around the neck of the clay phial, turning it into a pendant. He rose from his position of supplication and walked to the bed against the northern wall of the small room, where Lieutenant Seward was securely tied down with thick leather straps.

"How are you feeling, Lieutenant?"

The young man didn't speak, but gave a single firm nod. The first few nights had been the worst, full of thrashing and screaming and foul invectives. Last night had been Seward's first calm sleep.

"I believe you are as free from their spell as you ever will be, my friend," Othman said, and unbuckled the first strap. "Have you confronted the evil in your own heart?"

"Yes," Seward said in a parched half-voice.

"Then it is time to face the evil without." Othman undid the final strap and then placed the hanging phial over Seward's neck, where it replaced the bull's head pendant that had marked his slavery—the very one they had tossed into the brackish waters under the Dover cliffs.

"Yes," Seward said and looked down at himself. He'd sweated through these clothes time and time again. His hand ran over the scraggly beard that had sprouted on his face. "I will need to clean myself up first, I think."

Othman smiled slightly. "Of course. But before that, we must pray again. You have heard the words of my faith these last weeks, Lieutenant. Perhaps we should address God in those of your religion this time."

Seward nodded. He closed his eyes and said, "Make me a clean heart, O God: and renew a right spirit within me. Cast me not away from thy presence: and take not thy Holy Spirit from me."

"Amen," added Othman.

***

It was quarter to three in the afternoon when Seward, dressed in the uniform of Her Majesty's Own Horse Guards, exited a hansom cab on Pall Mall to face down the site of his own damnation. The Taurus Club for Gentlemen was one of many private clubs housed on this most well-heeled of streets. Its particular inclination was the cause of the Empire, and of the soldiers and sailors who defended and promoted it. Through connections made here, an ambitious and talented man could see himself rise up the ranks of even the most prestigious regiment. Seward's uniform was a testament to that.

The Taurus Club also shared the proclivity of several such societies for a heady mixture of secrecy and occultism. Indeed, the club itself had been presented to Seward as the public façade of the Taurine Brotherhood, a secret society that honored the soldierly ideal with religious fervor. True advancement required dedication and sacrifice, and Seward had been willing. In his final initiation into full brotherhood, he had partaken in a grand ritual that had cost nothing but his own damnation. The bull-woman. Regina. If she were to be believed, then the Taurine Brotherhood was the domain of the undead, and Seward had enslaved himself to them.

He swallowed, pushing down the nausea roiling in his guts, and headed up the stairs from the street. He rapped firmly on the oak door using the bull's head knocker and was admitted.

One of the club's footmen took Seward's overcoat, and another led him through to the main reading room. Daylight streamed through the windows. The room was not crowded. A few men in uniform sat scattered about, each engrossed in his own newspaper or other text, each with a drink by his side.

Seward turned to the servant who'd escorted him in. "Please tell Captain Ellijay that I am here to see him."

"I'm afraid Captain Ellijay will not arrive until this evening, Lieutenant." The footman spoke evenly and without hesitation, and Seward was reminded of Regina's words to him in Paris: *Have you ever seen your precious Captain Ellijay in daylight?*

"I shall wait with the *Times*, then."

"Of course, Lieutenant."

***

Those nights in the middle of October at Merritt House were, Regina felt, perhaps the strangest she had yet spent in the night society. Her ordeal in Paris had certainly been more extreme, but after months of searching and danger, after barely escaping a death sentence from Lady Anne, to find herself reunited with both her mother and Victoria in the pleasant circumstances of a fine house seemed profoundly odd.

A relaxed atmosphere had reigned since Regina's arrival. She'd delighted to hear her mother and herself laugh for the first time since this whole affair had begun. Lady Merritt hosted five of them and together they fell into the roles of three couples who have escaped the hardships of the outside world.

Regina and Victoria rapidly resumed the bond they had had in Vienna, now untainted by the resentment Regina had suffered at her transformation. In Merritt House, there never seemed a reason to be upset at the demands of undeath. Indeed, the lady of the house provided an entire panoply of young men and girls willing to give up their blood in exchange for the pleasures of the feeding. Victoria and Regina slipped into slumber each day in the luxurious suite provided for them on the house's second floor, their bare flesh comfortably enmeshed with each other and the warmth of at least one of Lady Merritt's retainers. Regina found that the joys of feeding together, of feeling the flush of pleasure in a boy's skin as Victoria took the first bite, almost completely replaced the urge to take blood directly from her sire's alabaster flesh.

The second couple in their troika of lotus eaters brought a combination of apprehension and joy to Regina's heart. Her mother Emma had visibly bonded herself to the longhaired and bespectacled man who had abducted her in Vienna. That kidnapping seemed more like a rescue now as Emma Blake and Mr. Beckett were visibly enraptured by one another, in a way that Emma had never been to her husband James. This jealousy in her father's stead was real and gave a bitter aftertaste to happy evenings spent relaxing in the amazing hedge maze Lady Merritt kept in her garden. What was worse was Regina's understanding of the erotic charge that bound all those in Merritt House together. On her third night there, Regina wandered through the maze and came upon a scene that sent trills of sensation through her every fiber. Mr. Beckett, his hair loose and his chest bare, had Emma Blake pressed up against the thicket of a hedge. Without a word, he grabbed the plunging collar of her gown in both his gloved hands and yanked, tearing apart corset and all as if it were mere tissue. Emma did not flinch as her breast and scars were exposed to this wild man. He then reached down and tore off her petticoats, rendering her stunningly nude save for silk stockings, the lace garters that held them up, and a choker fit with a disc of black opal. Beckett went down on one knee slowly, passing his face just over her collarbone, bosom, stomach, pubic thatch and thigh. He hovered there for a second and then bit fiercely, lapping and sucking at the rich vitae. Emma's legs buckled after a minute and she fell on him, returning his bites with her own in a wild, erotic abandonment to desire. Regina watched for as long as she could before slipping away, overwhelmed by the heady rush of shame and desire. She fed liberally from Benjamin, one of Lady Merritt's serving boys, all the while imagining herself in her mother's place and in Beckett's.

The final, and oddest, couple in the house consisted of Lady Merritt herself and her consort, an African man named Ruhadze. Ophelia Merritt was a fine and English beauty, all blond hair, pale blue eyes and milky flesh. Her lover was a darkly black-skinned man with a bald pate and a taste for finely tailored suits, accented with golden jewelry. The thought that he might be properly called a savage barely ever passed through Regina's mind. Not only had her years in Cairo given her an unusual appreciation for the cultures of those born in more southern latitudes, but Hesha Ruhadze was a consummate sophisticate, speaking in a careful accent that added to an upper-class tone only the most delicious spices of the Dark Continent. His rich brown eyes reflected a slight amber in the proper light, making them twin jewels to accompany the golden loops in his ears. In a house of grace and propriety, he and his lady seemed to be engaged in a constant and elaborate dance.

The evenings were cool but the rain miraculously held itself at bay those nights, as if responding to the desires of their hostess that only pleasure greet them. The susceptibility to rapturous sensations Regina had found in Vienna, the undying amplification of her admiration for architecture, did not leave her those nights. In fact, with every passing night she found herself drawn more and more often to the gardens and the amazingly complex hedge maze. She gazed out at it from an upstairs balcony on a few occasions, but it was not the view of it—built in a series of concentric circles and radial passages—that excited her. No it was the experience of strolling through the tall green walls and letting the beauty of its structure guide her. It was the sensation of motion and orchestration, of a clockwork so delicate that a single trimmed leaf could make the difference between masterwork and disaster.

She found the fountain of Narcissus, where the Spaniard Don Cerro had come so close to draining her of her living blood in April. The maze held much more, every turn revealing a new image or identity. She came to think of it as a symbol of the masquerade all the undead seemed to practice, each new view a new mask, each layer another dissimulation, but somehow closer to the dark truth that must lie at the core of each of them. Victoria took to following Regina through the maze, staying a few steps behind, unhidden but also utterly silent. Regina guessed the redheaded creature did so to lap up the emotion that Regina experienced in her perambulations. That was the element that brought rapture to Victoria—the sight of others surrendering to pleasure. It all served as a potent preamble to their feeding, a foreplay to acts of eroticism that would occupy the two women until the next dawn.

On their fifth night there, Regina and Victoria walked into the circular clearing at the center of Lady Merritt's maze. Compared to the various smaller clearings, with their mythological statuary and other flourishes, this space was utterly simple. A bare space perhaps four yards in diameter with black slate flagstones forming a dark disk under the two women's feet. The hedges surrounding them were easily nine feet tall, broken only in two places: the gap through which they had just entered and another directly opposite. It was utterly still in that place. None of the sounds of a large city at night reached even their preternaturally acute ears. The air itself was without motion or even apparent temperature. Regina looked up at the expanse of sky she could see above her and surrendered a slight gasp. Through some trick of the weather she did not understand, the night sky was utterly black and starless. The nearly perfect half-moon she'd seen in the northern sky upon waking was gone, as were the twinkling stars and the wisps of cloud. Instead was a perfect empty disc that echoed the slate circle at her feet.

No, she thought, *it is the stone disc that is the echo. This perfect empty firmament is the original.* She reached for the pendant that now hung at her sternum, just below the divot of her clavicle and above the swell of her breasts: an opal disc gifted to her by their hostess. She thought of the similar disc on her mother's choker. The black-disc cufflinks Mr. Beckett always seemed to wear and the similar tie tack favored by Mr. Ruhadze. The cameo Victoria wore, an obsidian disk floating in mother of pearl, shone from her neck when Regina turned to face her.

"We're all her pets," Regina said.

"Yes," Victoria said, stepping closer, her skin ghostly pale in the darkness between slate and sky. "Well kept and safe in our gilded cage."

Regina took a step of her own toward Victoria. She was now standing in the precise center of the slate disk, at the very axis of the web of silken pleasure that was Merritt House. Moving unhurriedly as suited the perfect calm of this place, she kissed Victoria's ruby lips. She was careful not to bite or nip, not to exchange blood, but the embrace was lingering and passionate—and answered in kind. Victoria's hands grasped Regina's waist, and her own found Victoria's face. After a minute or a year, their lips parted.

"I've searched for this for three hundred years, darling," Victoria said.

"I know," Regina answered. Gently as she could, she unfastened the cameo from Victoria's neck. She felt the other woman's trembling hands doing the same to the pendant hanging around her own.

First one, then the other jewel slipped from their hands and fell to the slate paving of the clearing. The clattering of their contact with the stone was muted, but final. Regina turned and with Victoria's hand in her own, she walked out the other opening in the hedge maze's heart.

A few minutes later, they emerged through a hidden gate in the high western wall of Merritt House's grounds, stepping into Hyde Park under the light of the half-moon high in the sky.

Neither spoke, but Regina could smell the coppery scent of Victoria's tears.

***

"Seward!"

Malcolm looked up from his paper at the welcome tone of his friend Tony Pool's voice. Pool, who had stood by Seward's side in his hardest times—the battles in the Sudan, their foray into Lions Green last Christmastide, his initiation into the brotherhood, all save that terrible confrontation with Regina in Paris. It was an hour past dusk and Seward was glad to have a true friend at his side again.

"Tony," he said, rising to his feet and foregoing propriety to grasp the man in a brotherly embrace.

"Oh," Pool said. "Well, I'm pleased to see you as well, old man…." He finally surrendered and gave a hearty squeeze back. "There, there, man."

Seward released his friend, feeling a flush of embarrassment at his display of affection, and sat back in the chair he'd occupied for several hours now. Pool took the seat facing his, and picked up the *Times*.

"Dreadful business," Pool said, referring to the ample coverage of the Whitechapel murders. "Bloody mess, this is." He looked up then. "But Captain Ellijay told me you were still on the Continent. When did you return?"

"I need to discuss that, Tony. Do you know where the captain is?"

"We entered the club together, as it happens. I believe he has business with Admiral Bartow, but he should be around momentarily. What happened?"

An awareness was tickling at the edge of Seward's perception, but he could not identify just what it was. He shrugged slightly and dismissed it as a symptom of the tension in his own heart. Seward could feel his own rapid pulse and shallow breathing, and surely that accounted for any twisted perceptions.

"I have certain doubts," Seward whispered, "about the captain. About the club. Certain things have come to light and—" He stopped short, when he saw Captain Ellijay himself walking into the clubroom and heading their way.

"Ah," the senior officer said, "our errant brother returns at last! I must say that you chose a fine time to come back to us, Lieutenant."

"How—" His voice caught. "How so, Captain?"

"Well, I've just received word that Lieutenant Pool has been called to appear before our supreme commander, the General himself. In two nights' time." He placed a hand on Pool's shoulder. Pool looked up at Ellijay with undisguised pride.

"Praise be," Pool said gently.

"Praise be," Ellijay answered.

Seward felt swirls of confusion. As far as he knew, the General, who was the head of the Taurine Brotherhood, was a mythical figure, the soldierly ideal of Mars, Mithras and Arthur. Was there an actual flesh-and-blood person who filled that role?

"And you will join him, Lieutenant Seward, I think," Ellijay said, looking directly at him. "As second and witness. And you will remain at the club until then, of course."

Seward felt the clay phial scratch slightly against his chest under his uniform. Heat flushed through him and he wanted more than anything to flee, but all he said was, "Of course, sir."

Ellijay had not taken a breath other than to speak, Seward realized. He then remembered the coolness of Pool's flesh in their embrace and it dawned on him the same could be said of his friend. Seward was the only living man of the three, he knew with sudden certainty, and he despaired.

Chapter Seventeen

"Karnak Imports," Regina said to Gerald Albin, her coachman. "On the Southwark High Street."

Upon Regina and Victoria's return to Monroe House, they'd quickly communicated to Mr. Goosehound that they could not answer any questions about Lord Blake's whereabouts. The agent had other business to attend to and left the maid Catherine and the coachman Gerald in the care of the ladies of the house. Regina made clear that neither butler, housekeeper nor even cook would be necessary for the time being. They would be barely present in the house, she said. After that, they obtained solemn oaths from the two servants not to disturb them during the day under any condition, but be available in the hours after dusk. The well-trained inclination of domestic servants not to question their masters' whims (at least not to their faces) did a wonderful job of smoothing over this unusual request, as did Victoria's preternatural charm.

Taking a full night to recover from the aura of Merritt House, Regina and Victoria then set out to undertake those tasks necessary to assure their position in London. Thus, Karnak Imports, which both Mr. Beckett and Mr. Ruhadze had mentioned in casual conversation as the haunt of a certain Halim Bey, kindred of theirs and dealer in antiquities. It seemed a good place to start.

The shop, a simple storefront with a few Egyptian pieces displayed in a window, was not what one would dare call a 'lair.' Even in her brief experience among her fellow undead, Regina had come to expect grandeur from their residences. Beyond Merritt House, she'd met the unliving in the halls of the British Museum and the Louvre in Paris, not to mention the Botanical Gardens and Opera House in Vienna. Humble shops seemed less than typical. "Hardly the Belvedere Palace," she said to Victoria as they alighted from the carriage.

Victoria smiled. "No, not at all. That is most likely the point. Mr. Bey's ilk have a knack for moving through the shadows less traveled."

"And so know things that others do not?"

"Exactly."

Regina pushed open the door, provoking a tinkle of bells. The front room was crowded with a variety of bric-a-brac and reminded her very much of the bazaar shops of Cairo. Every possible space was filled with clay amphora, bits of hieroglyph and funerary arts, scimitars and sabers. Several Persian carpets—most rolled, some hung—and a full-fledged sarcophagus completed the scene. A portly man of dusky complexion, and wearing a red fez, stood behind the counter.

"Good evening, ladies," he said. "How may I be of service this evening?"

"Halim Bey?" Regina asked.

"At your service, Miss."

Regina felt more than heard the slight brush of leather sole on pine board floor coming from beyond the door behind the shopkeeper. There was someone else here, tense and ready. "I am Lady Regina Blake," she said. "My companion, Miss Victoria Ash."

"A pleasure." He gave a slight nod and Regina caught a slight wisp of surprise about him. He buried it almost immediately, so quickly she was unsure she'd seen it at all.

"We are here upon the recommendation of Mr. Beckett," she said.

He nodded, but gave no other indication of his state of mind.

"He led us to believe that you might be able to help us in a certain matter. He and Mr. Ruhadze spoke well of you, Halim Bey."

The tell was much clearer this time. The shopkeeper's mouth moved to speak, but he swallowed back his comment. A second later, his mask of calm was almost fully replaced. He turned his head to the left and barked a quick order in a language Regina did not recognize—Farsi or Turkish, perhaps. Emerging from behind the rear divider, the hidden figure, a tall man dressed in the loose clothing of the Turks or Persians, moved to the shop's front door, which he latched closed. He was carrying an impressive dagger, but kept it low.

"Forgive me for Daran," Halim Bey said. "These are strange times and I must exercise caution."

"Of course," Regina said. She felt a slight tingle running up her back, something she had come to recognize as an echo of tension mounting in Victoria. She did not risk looking back at her sire, who as agreed, was standing slightly back and letting Regina do the talking. She hoped Victoria was simply, and subtly, tensing in case violence erupted. Regina knew the other woman, when she willed it, could move at a speed that was difficult to describe. "My mother explained to me the cautions you took on her behalf, and I am thankful for your wariness, Halim Bey."

He nodded to acknowledge the compliment. "Lady Blake and Mr. Beckett were most kind guests, and I am relieved to hear that they are well."

"Tell me, Halim Bey," Regina asked, after a nod of her own, "what do you know of a Mr. Wim Hendriksen of Exeter Street?"

"Hendriksen? An antiquarian. Our paths have crossed on occasion. He is not one of your kindred, I believe."

"Do you consider him an asset or a hindrance to your own position?"

"I'm unsure of what you mean, Lady Regina."

Regina was altogether certain that Halim Bey knew exactly what she was asking, but she indulged him, up to a point. "It has come to my attention, Halim Bey, that Mr. Hendriksen may be forced to leave London on short notice. He may never return, in fact. Given the kindness you have extended to my mother and her companion, I would be disheartened to learn that this turn of events were to cause you any inconvenience."

He smiled, apparently willing to play the game. "I do have certain business in progress with Mr. Hendriksen. His departure could be costly to me."

"I wonder if our assistance in locating Mr. Ruhadze might offset that cost."

"Perhaps it would," he said, "along with another small favor. Mr. Hendriksen has a strong room at the back of his shop."

"I am not a thief, sir," Regina said. *A murderess but not a thief.*

"You misunderstand me, Lady Regina. I would not have you take from Mr. Hendriksen. Rather, I'd ask that you place something within the safe. A letter, which I will retrieve momentarily." He signaled to the door through which Daran had entered. "I have a small sitting room, if you would care to wait."

"Thank you."

Regina and Victoria waited in silence for less than fifteen minutes in the crowded office the undead shopkeeper had called a sitting room. It was crowded with various smaller pieces of artwork and pieces of Egyptian lore. A series of lithographs showed frescoes and murals, presumably taken from far-off temples and tombs. One of these caught the women's attention—a black disc atop the shoulders of a female figure, linked by dark rays to various animal heads.

"What is this, Halim Bey?" Regina asked him when he returned with the letter, sealed in an envelope marked with the name of a prominent solicitor.

"An obscure goddess of the early dynasties, I believe," he said. "Kemintiri the Thousand Faced."

"And these?" Regina asked, pointing to the series of slight mounds on the goddess's bare chest. They formed a vague V-shape from her breasts to her lap.

"A fertility aspect, I believe. The teats to feed her many children."

Regina looked at him and smiled slightly. "You will find Mr. Ruhadze at Merritt House, in the company of Lady Merritt herself."

***

Malcolm Seward spent the two days before Tony Pool and he were to meet the Great General of the Taurine Brotherhood in much the same way he had the week after his return to London: locked in a room, unable to trust anything he felt. Whereas Othman al-Masri had been there in that first week, using prayer and other means to help Seward fight through the dark urges that had been imposed upon him, this time those dark urges were his only company. Captain Ellijay ordered him to wait and so he did, spending the daylight hours under lock and key, daydreaming about freedom. The nighttime he spent with Ellijay and Pool, unable to even challenge his superiors in this order of the damned. Malcolm Seward knew despair during his time back at the Taurus Club.

When the night finally came—after forty-eight hours, which felt like forty-eight years—Seward found a dark thrill running through him. Ellijay, who'd always been the picture of propriety, was clearly excited by the event to come. Pool had an easy smile at any time and was now laughing happily at the least provocation.

"Come, Seward," Tony Pool said, still chuckling at an inane joke he had made, "laugh with me at least. This is the night we've been working for."

Seward swallowed the automatic agreement that leaped up his

throat and tried to push out his true feelings. "I'm no longer sure I want any part in this initiation, Tony."

Ellijay appeared as if summoned by Seward's small defiance. "We're all well past initiation, Lieutenant," he said. "Pool went through the ceremony of the Bull Woman a full year before you did. What's more, he has now been elevated—he only awaits confirmation of his hallowed position."

Seward felt a wave of nausea at the thought of his friend Tony Pool's new and supposedly hallowed position. He remembered that cold hug two nights ago, when Tony's body had been cool as the grave. He thought of how his friend had yet to take a breath other than to speak in the last few nights. Elevation was undeath, Seward knew and could do nothing to stop.

"Don't look like a sour puss, Seward," Pool said. "Perhaps the General will choose you for elevation tonight."

Seward tasted bile in his throat.

***

Exeter Street was a small block between the Strand and Covent Garden, just another series of shops, apartments and taverns. Hendriksen Antiquities occupied a discreet second-story space atop a haberdashery. It displayed only a small brass sign next to the door that led to the stairs up. Those who came to see Wim Hendriksen already knew his business, Regina guessed.

She glanced sideways at Victoria, who remained seated in the carriage. Regina hesitated, hoping not for the first time that she could somehow wind back the clock and undo what she had done.

"I will—" Victoria started to say, but Regina cut her off.

"No. Thank you, but no. I made the promise to Herr Schiller and I will fulfill it." The boyish vampire had seemed terribly insistent that it be Regina who carry out this task—who knew what ways he had to discover whether she had or not? "It's my weight to bear, Victoria."

Victoria seemed as if she was going to say something else, but did not. She simply placed a gloved hand on Regina's skirted knee and gave a light squeeze. Regina opened the carriage door and exited.

"Drive down the Strand, Gerald. Return in a half-hour's time." *Would that be enough*, she wondered. *It will have to be.*

The coachman flicked his reins and the horses pulled him and Victoria away, while Regina walked toward the discreet door next to the haberdashery. It was unlocked and opened easily, despite the leaden weight Regina felt spreading from her stomach. A slight tinkling sound came from upstairs before the door was all the way open. She doubted a living man would have noted the mild ringing. Regina looked around and up and saw that a cord ran from the door's top corner back to the front wall and then, through a series of eyelets, upstairs. A bell to warn Mr. Hendriksen of visitors.

She headed upstairs and, after a moment to compose herself, rapped on the upstairs door. A smaller version of the brass sign outside told her this was indeed the Dutchman's enterprise.

Hendriksen opened the door almost immediately, presumably forewarned by the bell. He stood a foot taller than Regina and perhaps ninety pounds heavier. A large, bearish man dressed in eveningwear half discarded. His pants were well pressed, but his jacket was missing and his collar was loose. One shirtsleeve was pulled out. He simply glared.

Regina swallowed needlessly, momentarily paralyzed by the sight of the man. She could feel the tension and excitement in the man, like a wound spring or a bomb with a short fuse. She saw surprise, curiosity, even anger behind his brown-black eyes and wondered what was there.

"Halim Bey recommended you, Mr. Hendriksen," she finally said.

He cocked his head in curiosity. "I'm sure he did. Whose acquaintance do I have the pleasure of making, then?"

"Forgive me," Regina said, regaining some of her composure. "Regina, the daughter of James, Lord Blake." That almost caught in her throat.

"A pleasure, Miss Blake." He stepped back. "Please come in."

The room she entered was a mix of office, receiving room and museum. Every square inch seemed to be covered by a stack of paper or a piece of art imported from the colonies or even further afield. There wasn't a chair or divan that wasn't stacked with papers or half-opened wooden crates overflowing with straw stuffing.

"You'll forgive me, Miss Blake," he said, "I have just received a very large shipment that must be checked piece by piece." He waved to the desk, which had several other boxes on it, a crowbar laid across one.

"I understand," Regina said, half mumbling. The leaden feeling in her stomach had spread to her limbs and she felt a chill. Her tongue felt like a bloated piece of leather caught in her throat. She felt that her heart should be racing but of course it was not, and that realization made her swoon ever so slightly.

"Are you alright, Miss Blake?" The Dutchman asked, his accent mild but rich, like the scent of the tulips his nation was so famous for. He stepped closer to her.

She turned to face him and ran her deadened tongue across her teeth, hoping for once to feel the pointed canines that made of her an unliving predator. Her fangs stubbornly refused to make their presence known. She looked into the man's eyes and spoke with what she hoped was the tone of command she'd felt in Miss Parr's voice at Highgate Asylum. "Tell me that you are a monster, Mr. Hendriksen."

Nothing but puzzlement. "Pardon? I'm not sure I understand—"

Regina suddenly screamed, as much at herself as at this man. "A monster! Tell me you are a monster!"

"I think perhaps you should leave, Miss Blake."

Hendriksen put a strong hand on her forearm and began to pull her firmly but slowly toward the door. He dragged her a single step and she felt something loosen from under that heavy dread within her. She pulled her arm away and a low snarl escaped her throat.

The Dutchman looked directly at her and for a second, she saw fear in those eyes. That fear made her strong. "Herr Schiller sends his greetings," she said.

Without any further hesitation, Hendriksen delivered a left cross to Regina's head. It felt as if she had been hit by a cannonball, not so much snapping her face aside as battering her skull into the wall behind her. Black bursts filled her vision and she slumped. The fear she tasted was her own.

She pushed away from the wall, trying to shake away the shock of the blow and noticed too late that Hendriksen had had time to lay his hands on the crowbar that had been on his desk. She raised her right arm in some defensive instinct, and the bar came down upon it with a terrible snapping noise. The pain shot through her just a second after she noticed that her arm was now bent in a way—and in a place—that normal physiognomy did not allow. The second blow with the crowbar came the instant after that across her back.

Pain, fear and rage shot through Regina in equal measure and she launched herself at Hendriksen like a feral thing. Her lunge was not at all graceful, but the small, cluttered space worked to her advantage and she was able to grab onto the man's legs. She was not thinking at all when her mouth—fangs now fully extended—clamped onto his left thigh and sank through trousers and flesh alike.

Some part of her heard the man scream as she gouged out a chunk of the large muscle there. Salty blood gushed from the wound, and they both toppled to the ground in a mass. She bit and gnawed at the wound, tearing flesh to lap up the red fluid.

He thrashed and wailed, but she could feel the blood strengthening her. A blow from his fist knocked her loose but she launched herself back, this time digging her mouth into the flabby flesh near his kidneys. She tore and ripped like a wild dog, and blood soon ran freely from a half-dozen wounds. The ground became slick with the charnel mess and the smell and taste were all she could perceive.

When the red haze parted, Regina was straddling the ruined form of Wim Hendriksen. He was lying on his back, shallow breaths escaping between teeth clenched in pain. A pool of his own blood was spreading under him and a goodly amount of the stuff was also spattered about the room. Regina felt that even more of it was in her belly. Several ragged wounds gaped from his body, holes torn into him by the wild animal she had become.

Regina didn't say anything and didn't move. She wanted to flee, to return to Merritt House and the painless existence that had been there, but she didn't. Instead, she looked at Wim Hendriksen and watched the life leave his eyes and heard the rattle escape his throat.

She remained there, staring at the Dutchman's cooling corpse as his blood dried to a sticky mess on her, for almost an hour. She was dimly aware of Victoria finally arriving and carrying her back to the carriage, but the sight of Hendriksen's eyes and the echo of his death rattle never quite faded.

Chapter Eighteen

Seward followed Pool and Ellijay into the basement of the Taurus Club. He'd walked this path before, upon his initiation into the brotherhood. He knew there was something akin to an operating theater deep below the club, a ritual chamber with a gallery for brothers to watch the progression of their fellows. The last time he'd come there, he'd been charged by the thrill of the moment and the great step he was to take, little knowing or caring that he was entering into a compact with the undead.

This night, he was hyperaware of every detail and felt nothing but dread. There was no blindfold this time, so he followed their progress around the gallery—empty of spectators—and toward the staircase that led into one of two anterooms for the ritual chamber itself. He hazarded a glance down into the chamber and found it changed from his last visit. Before there had been an altar of sorts, with a short roman sword and a bowl of bull's blood as ritual accoutrements. It was on that altar that he had taken the Bull Woman, the ritual lover, idol and sacrifice. He ravished her and sliced open her throat to seal his initiation in blood. The Bull Woman. Regina. She said it had been her and Seward, damning himself, believed her.

The altar was now gone, however, replaced by a dais upon which sat a basalt throne of sorts. It was stark in its simplicity. Spartan, as befit the holy of holies of a brotherhood of soldiers. What blood rites, he wondered, would be committed in the name of that perverted ideal?

The antechamber seemed more lavish than the ritual chamber itself. Here, ritual dress was waiting on special clotheshorses, giving the impression of an ancient temple. Captain Ellijay removed the Oxford blue uniform of the regiment and both Pool and Seward followed suit, almost by rote. Ellijay donned the first, and grandest of the ritual costumes. It was, Seward thought, roughly derived from the dress of a Roman centurion: heavy sandals, a skirt made of overlapping tongues of boiled leather (each studded with a golden bull's head), and a tunic of white linen. Ellijay then donned a breastplate made entirely of a single gilded bronze front piece that bore the bull's head symbol of the brotherhood in the flaring solar disc. Two shoulder guards bore similar symbols. He next girded himself with a sword-belt and scabbard, which held a stout Roman sword with further bull and sun motifs. Last came a held grand helm, which bore a full facemask and the horns of a large bull.

Seward's own ritual uniform was in line with the Captain's. He was to be a legionnaire in the Bull God's army, it seemed. He wore a simpler version of the same skirt and tunic and a plain breastplate. He held a javelin and large tower shield, which was emblazoned with a bronzed bull and sun motif. He wore no helm and the small clay phial Othman al-Masri had confided to him remained around his neck, tucked under his tunic.

Pool's dress was starkly different from the others. He wore the sandals and tunic, but little else. Only bracers and a silver diadem—with a bull's head at its front—added any flair to his costume.

"You will have your arms soon," Ellijay said to Pool and then opened the door into the ritual chamber itself.

It reminded Seward, suddenly and acutely, of his time in Egypt and the Sudan. Stepping into that room was like leaving a thick-walled house into the oppressive noonday desert sun. Then, the heat and light had been physical blows, trying to slam Seward and his men into the dusty ground like the stomping foot of some mythical beast. Now, he felt the same force, although the source was neither heat nor light, but the mere presence of the Great Soldier King.

Indeed, sitting on that simple basalt throne was a god. The divine perfection of his form, including the chiseled beauty of his flesh and the radiant power of his gaze, forced Ellijay, Pool and Seward to their knees. In unison, they bowed and Seward felt the words of their greeting flow out from him without conscious effort. "Praise be to Mithras," they proclaimed. "Greatest of all Soldier Kings!"

"Praise be," said a voice slightly to the left of the holy center of the room. "Lieutenant Pool, rise."

Seward caught the slight hesitation in Pool's movement and glanced up. He could not bear to look directly upon the Great King, but he did make out the figure standing beside him. This man wore the grandest of ritual costume—a great golden Centurion's armor and a great bull-helm that put Ellijay's to shame. This was the General, the Great King's sword-bearer. He had given Pool leave to rise.

"Approach your king, Lieutenant Pool," the General said.

Pool took three steps, stopping at the very edge of the dais.

Seward saw that he was trembling slightly.

"Lieutenant," the General asked, "how do you come here?"

"As a faithful soldier ready to serve his King and the Empire."

"Praise be," Seward and Ellijay said in unison.

"And why do you come here?"

"I come seeking elevation," Pool answered.

"Come forward." The voice was like quiet thunder, emanating not so much from the Great King's mouth as from his chest. Pool stepped onto the dais and then knelt before the king, and the monarch spoke again. "Come forward, Captain."

Ellijay moved to the edge of the dais, but Seward stayed where he was and watched. Perhaps because he was not the center of attention, he managed to pick up on signs that all was not as it should be. The General and Ellijay both seemed slightly nervous, even hesitant. *This was not expected*, Seward thought. *The King is not following ritual.*

Such was the privilege of a divine monarch, Seward realized, but he still chanced another glance at this mysterious figure. It was still very much like looking directly into the sun, so powerful was the effect of the divine, but Seward nevertheless caught a few glimpses. Whereas everyone else in the room was wearing some variation of ritual garb, he realized the Great King was dressed in a rumpled suit, with a bull-and-sun medallion hanging loosely around his neck. His hair was disheveled, even matted. And yet, overriding these flickering and tawdry images, an aura of greatness overlaid Mithras. Seward felt a pain bloom behind his eyes as he tried to reconcile the two images.

"You are ready to make sacrifice," the king said, his voice rolling like a thunderhead.

"Yes," said Pool and Ellijay in unison. Seward felt the same answer slip nearly silently from between his own lips.

"Lieutenant," the monarch said to Pool, "what is the greatest sacrifice a soldier can make?"

"His life." Pool answered without hesitation, but Seward caught a glance between the General and Captain Ellijay.

"And Captain," Mithras said, "what is the greatest sacrifice a father can make?"

Ellijay's hesitation was brief, but very clear. "His— his son," he said.

"Your king is pleased," Mithras said.

There was a long, pregnant moment filled with tension and rapturous anticipation. Then the Great King stood and accepted his sacrifice. Pool was standing directly in front of Mithras, so he did not have far to go. Still, Seward caught a terrible glimpse of that perfect face opening its mouth to reveal long and animalistic fangs. They clamped into Tony Pool's neck with an audible crunch and Seward took in a shocked breath.

Pool seemed caught between pain and pleasure, varying between falling into the blood-draining kiss and trying to fight free. Even had he decided to fight with all his might, Seward knew, Pool stood no chance. A terrible slurping sound filled the chamber as Mithras drained the soldier who lived to serve him.

Ellijay seemed frozen on the step, but shook with what Seward guessed must be rage. He saw the captain's fists clench fiercely.

The feeding took only a few minutes, but they were long and terrible. Pool seemed quite literally to shrivel as his very essence was drawn from him in hungry gulps. At one point, Mithras shifted his bite and Pool's head lolled back so that he locked gazes with Seward. Malcolm saw the pain of betrayal there, the crushing realization that all he had fought for was being stolen to feed an unquenchable thirst. Seward felt he saw his greatest friend's soul die then and there.

A moment later, Mithras was done and he simply released the now desiccated corpse. Pool fell backwards off the dais, hitting the ground like a sack of potatoes right in front of Seward. Pool's skin was chalky, dry and flaking. His eyes, open in final pain, were like dried marbles, the left one already dissolving into ashy dust. His lips were drawn back in a rictus, exposing the long fangs of a brief undeath. *Where can such a hunger come from*, Seward wondered, *to eat the very soul?*

"From Hell," Mithras answered in a raspy voice that sounded small and dangerous. Seward locked gazes with him, and the king was suddenly nothing but the tawdry monster, terrible in his vileness, but no more glorious than a bloated corpse on a battlefield.

"It was very nice," Mithras said, and turned to Ellijay. "The other."

Seward looked to the Captain, who seemed as shocked as anyone. At some point he'd removed his helm and the rage was clear on his face. "No," he said.

The General, still helmeted, stepped forward. "Obey your king, Captain," he barked. "Immediately." He pointed to Seward.

Seward didn't have time to realize what was about to occur before Ellijay was on him and knocking him to the ground. Ellijay's long canines flashed in the half-light of the chamber. "Captain! No!"

"Quiet, you treasonous wretch," the General barked. "You will feed your king once your blood is readied."

There was an infinite moment before Ellijay plunged his maw into Seward's neck. Long enough for the Lieutenant to despair at the thought that he was about to be doubly damned, to be remade into one of the unliving only to be fed to their unholy king. Then Captain Ellijay buried his teeth in Seward's neck, and he felt a wave of perverse pleasure.

Followed almost instantly by a hot jolt of pain and the sound of Ellijay's scream.

Seward opened his eyes to see the captain gnashing his bloodied teeth and spitting in rage. "What is this!" he barked. "It burns." Ellijay ripped at Seward's chest. He yanked at the pendant around the Lieutenant's neck—the clay phial placed there by Othman al-Masri. Ellijay yanked at it but couldn't get it free, so clenched his fist.

Seward clearly heard the phial crack, quickly followed by Ellijay's scream. The captain opened his hand, releasing a shower of sand and clay. Where they fell on Seward, he felt a golden warmth that reminded him of the beauty of the desert.

The effect on Ellijay was wholly different. The Captain rose to his feet again and stumbled back, gripping his right wrist with his left hand. His right palm was lanced with clay shards and spread with sand, and the effect was like embers on paper. Wisps of black smoke rose from the cuts and Seward saw a piece of clay burn its way through the hand. It fell onto his own chest and was perfectly cool.

Still prostate on the floor, Seward saw Mithras appear behind the panicked Ellijay. The king reached to the captain's side and drew out the man's ritual sword, which glinted with very real sharpness. Mithras made a single thrust, cutting through the exposed flesh on Ellijay's side, right through his kidney. Pain and hate registered on the wounded man's face. Seward wondered if a sword thrust could truly kill an undead thing like Ellijay.

"I may send you the knife," the king said in that same raspy, vile voice, still seeming to read Seward's mind, "if you only wait a while longer." With that, Mithras plunged his maw into Ellijay's neck and began to drain him as he had Pool.

Seward—covered in sand, his neck still bleeding, but his heart still beating—fled back out the way he'd come, onto Pall Mall, and into the London night.

Chapter Nineteen

Regina woke on the evening of Friday, October 19th feeling little better than she had the night before. It had now been several nights since she visited—*no*, a voice inside her insisted, *the term is "murdered"*—Wim Hendriksen. She had fed once since then, when Victoria brought a fine-clothed gentleman by the house, but it had been a hard effort not to fly into a fit. She'd insisted that Victoria sleep in her own quarters since then. She wondered if Lady Anne's agents would come to stake her for the sun at the end of the month before she built up the courage to leave Monroe House again.

A gentle knocking announced Catherine, the maid. Regina mumbled a quick, "Come."

The Irish girl slipped into the room. "Ma'am," she said, her voiced laced with nervousness. "There's a man here to see you. An Arab, I think. He's been waiting since early afternoon."

That eliminated Halim Bey or Hesha Ruhadze as candidates—both of whom an Irish girl might think Arab. Could it be one of their agents? But why come by day, then? "Wake Miss Ash and then show the gentleman to the front sitting room, Catherine. I will be down presently."

When she entered the sitting room a quarter-hour later, Regina was quite sure her legs were going to give out from under her. There, standing as she entered, was the scholar who had tutored her in French, Latin, and Greek. The man who, during her years in Cairo, had shown her the wonders of history and architecture. "Ibn Saleh," she said, more loudly than she was expecting or was entirely proper.

His well-weathered face—its beard grayer than when last she had seen him, but its eyes just as lively—split into a broad smile that woke memories of long afternoon lessons. "Lady Regina," he said with a slight bow. Regina noticed that he had a newspaper folded under once arm.

"My goodness, sir," she said after they'd both taken a seat, "what brings you to London?" She laid a hand affectionately across his.

"I'm afraid that you do, Lady Regina, and your good mother and father." His voice was serious and it sent a spark of alarm through Regina's already-chill blood.

"Excuse me, Ibn Saleh? What do you mean?"

He closed his eyes as if he were straining under a great weight, and then suddenly grabbed one of Regina's hands. He ran his fingers under her wrist and held them there for a moment. Then, while Regina remained dumbfounded, he shook his head again. "I am afraid I have failed you all, however."

"That's enough, sir," Regina snapped. "Please explain." She withdrew her hands and was uncomfortably aware of the ache in her gums from where her fangs wanted to slip from their fleshy sheaths.

"I am Othman ibn Saleh al-Masri," he said with great formality, "and for the last thirty-two years I have been a *sayyad al-ghulan*.

Regina struggled with her Arabic, far less extensive than the other languages Ibn Saleh had taught her. "A hunter…"

"Yes, a hunter of monsters." He looked at her with a terrible sadness. "Monsters like that which has plagued your lady mother for so long."

"Monsters like me," Regina said, her voice tiny. "Othman," she said. "It was to you that Father sent a telegram…."

"Yes," he said. "James called me for help in the spring, fearing the worst for Emma. I had first come to your house in Cairo to help protect her from the creatures I felt around her. I weep that I ultimately failed you and yours," he said. "But I come to you tonight hoping that there is still something of the beautiful soul I knew in Cairo. For the sake of a good man who may still be saved."

A black vein of rage rose in Regina's soul. "You come here to call me an unclean monster, to tell me that you lied to me all those years in Cairo, and now ask for my help? Why should I help you?"

"If not for the memory of sunny days with mother and father," he said, "then for the love you once had for poor Malcolm Seward."

The words were like dagger-thrusts into Regina's heart. "Malcolm? Where is he?"

"I met him in Paris in September," Othman said, "where he was searching for you."

"He found me," Regina said bitterly.

"Indeed, he said you woke him to the truth that creatures in London were blackening his soul. Shocked and strengthened by the realization, he and I returned to this city where I tried to prepare him for a confrontation with the dead. With this thing calling itself Ellijay."

Regina felt the rage in her soul dying, replaced by sadness and regret. "Oh, Malcolm. His sister Joanna, does he know?"

"Yes, he buried her husband before traveling to Paris, I think." He fixed Regina with his gaze. "I thought I had lost him as well, for he was gone three long days and nights. But then on Tuesday, he returned to the flat we had taken with a terrible story. He was nearly incoherent and it took several days to piece it together, but it seemed that he confirmed that both this Ellijay and his companion Tony Pool were… as you are."

Regina was hardly surprised. Although Pool's transformation must have been as recent as her own, she had seen him in the company of Captain Ellijay and other kindred last summer. "Go on," she said.

"They forced him into a terrible ritual with a great, mad creature he called by the name 'Mithras King,' a name stolen from Zoroaster. This creature consumed both Pool and Ellijay and would have done the same of Malcolm had he not escaped."

Ellijay and Pool are dead? Consumed by Prince Mithras?

"I hoped that he might recover, but I realize now that the whole city is in the grip of this madness."

Regina didn't disagree with that assessment, but still felt compelled to ask, "How so?"

"Malcolm was close to recovery this morning, until he read this newspaper." Othman took out a copy of *The Times*, covered with more coverage of the Whitechapel murders. "Here," he said, pointing to part of the main story on the case. "They reproduce a letter received from the killer along with a poor woman's kidney."

Regina read it. The letter was reproduced in the poor orthography in which it was originally written, but as she spoke it aloud, she found herself correcting it without thinking. "From Hell: I send you half the kidney I took from one woman and preserved it for you, the other piece I fried and ate it was very nice. I may send you the bloody knife that took it out if you only wait a while longer—"

Othman interrupted her. "Malcolm says that this monstrous king spoke those very words during that ceremony. That he pronounced them like a ritual incantation."

"Are you saying…"

"This creature must be the murderer of Whitechapel," Othman said. "This Ripper."

Regina tried to make sense of this. How could this relate to the poisoning Lady Anne had mentioned. "What do you wish me to do?"

"I have come to realize," Othman said, "that there is a society of creatures as you are. I will do my very best to guard Malcolm's soul, but I fear that he will be dragged further into the darkness, just as your lady mother and you have been. I am here to appeal to you, as one who once loved this man truly, to secure his safety."

**

Halim Bey had made quick work of moving into the offices of Wim Hendriksen, Victoria found when she visited him on Exeter Street. An address off the Strand was a step up from the Southward High Street, certainly, but she suspected there was more behind his aid in the murder of the Dutch antiquarian than the acquisition of real estate. That, however, was a matter for some later date. Tonight, they had more pressing issues to discuss.

"They've headed north, you say?"

"Two nights ago, Miss Ash, by train," Halim Bey said, sitting behind the large desk he'd already installed in the main office. There were no signs of the bloodletting that had taken place here four nights ago. Victoria's kindred were very effective at covering their tracks.

"All of Lady Merritt's entourage? Mr. Beckett and Lady Blake as well?"

"And Hesha Ruhadze, along with a few ghouls to facilitate daylight affairs. The agent I interviewed told me they were heading for Edinburgh, but who knows what their ultimate destination might be."

"Indeed," Victoria said. Scotland would not be unfriendly territory for Lady Merritt, who had some acquaintance with the prince there, and of course access to a port on the North Sea could bring them to the Continent almost as easily as heading to Dover could. "And did you make contact with Mr. Ruhadze, Mr. Bey?"

"I thought it best not to, for the time being."

Victoria caught a blend of excitement and fear in the tones of Halim Bey's voice and in his posture. "Perhaps," she said, "if you would like our further assistance in this matter, you should explain matters more fully."

**

St. James Palace, until the ascension of the Queen and her

move to nearby Buckingham Palace, had been the home of British monarchs from the time of Henry VIII and his many wives. Regina was no longer surprised to find that it also served, at least on this night, as the site of the undead court that existed parasite-like in the shadows of England. The ride from Monroe House was short enough that it was done exclusively for appearances. It did give Regina time to ponder just how much of the dark realities of her new existence had taken place within a mere few hundred yards of here. Indeed, Merritt House in Mayfair was only opposite Green Park from St. James, and the Taurus Club and its secret brotherhood stood on Pall Mall just east of the palace, near St. James Square. The last year had brought her as far as Hapsburg Vienna, but somehow London's West End seemed to contain a major portion of the damnation that had swallowed her.

"Maudlin airs do not suit you, Regina," Victoria said as the carriage passed through the palace gates at the head of St. James Street.

"I have very little with which to be overjoyed," she said, not bothering to hide either her fatigue or her creeping despair.

Victoria's tone turned cold. "You will have less still if you enter court like this. Lady Anne could very well just decide that we are no longer worth her trouble and reinstate our sentence. Mask yourself with confidence, for goodness sake, lest you damn us both, girl."

"I—" Regina's angry retort caught in her throat. How could Victoria be so passionate one moment and heartless the next? Was that what it took, ultimately, to survive among the undead? So be it, then. "Very well, Miss Ash."

Regina caught just a hint of pain in Victoria's expression at her use of a formal address, and she was glad for it. Then, barely acknowledged, the pain was gone and Victoria's porcelain façade of unassailable beauty was back in place.

Footmen dressed in formal attire styled during the Regency greeted them when Gerald stopped the carriage in the grand courtyard of the palace. Regina allowed herself the opportunity to look up at the structure itself. They'd passed through a red-brick guard tower, which hinted at its Tudor origins, but the interior façade of the palace itself was still impressive. Stone arcades supporting a red-brick structure topped with faux crenellations, the palace seemed to Regina to be a successful compromise between the function of a social palace and the history of a true castle. It was not the neoclassical glory of Vienna, but it had an English beauty all its own. After what she hoped was only a few moments of gazing at the architecture, Regina allowed the footman to take her arm and guide her through an arcade into the palace proper.

The gathering had every appearance of being a formal ball thrown by one of the Queen's more exuberant relatives, which of course, was the intention. Everyone was dressed in their finest, with a distinctive lean toward the formal court fashions of the era before the Queen's sense of propriety—and endless mourning for Prince Albert—had cast a pall on English fashion. Regina and Victoria both wore tightly corseted gowns—Regina's in ecru and Victoria's in a pale green that brought out the color of her eyes—whose low-cut bodices did more than hint at the swell of their bosoms. This was the first truly formal occasion Regina had attended since her transformation. She found that, in this one circumstance, no longer needing to breathe was a distinct advantage.

When they had been readying for this event just after waking, Regina had questioned the gowns Victoria had had prepared for them. They were beautiful, certainly, but they also seemed just on this side of scandalous. Victoria and Lady Merritt both seemed enamored with such styles, but Regina wondered if it was truly appropriate for such an event. "It is expected," Victoria had explained, "and it is often best to appear to be what others think you are."

The rest of the guests seemed to agree, for they were all gaily dressed as well. Men wore white or pale breeches and three-quarter coats of blues, greens and reds. Women of all sorts wore open necks and colorful gowns. Only a few others—whom Regina recognized from events the previous summer—were quite as exposed as she and Victoria, but none batted an eyelash at their choice. More than a few, in fact, made a point to come and greet the two women. Victoria invariably introduced Regina as, "My ward, Lady Regina Blake," and even those whom Regina had met during the summer made a point of saying how pleased they were to meet her.

"This is my coming out, I take it," she said when she and Victoria were afforded a moment to themselves. "I do wish you had forewarned me, Miss Ash." When Victoria answered only with a slight smile, she said, "Unless you were not forewarned either."

"Lady Anne has let it be known that you are kindred to her

court," Victoria said. "This is a good sign."

"It means she wants something new from us, I think," Regina said, eliciting another smile from Victoria.

The evening continued as any ball might. A chamber orchestra played several dances and Regina found herself drawn into more than she would have liked. A self-consciously dashing man by the name of Eric Barring-Gould managed to be her partner through several waltzes, passing her only reluctantly to other men during quadrilles.

Only halfway through the evening did Regina realize how easy it now was for her to tell living from dead. Whereas last spring and summer, before she even understood the true difference, she had dedicated much energy to parsing out the underlying social codes at these affairs, the distinctions now stood out. The depth of color in the flesh of the living and its absence among Regina's kindred was so obvious to her now that she marveled that everyone did not notice it so clearly. She supposed that this was a result of the new acuity of her senses. She wondered if she too appeared pallid and lifeless, despite the hours spent dressing and primping.

Lady Anne made her appearance only once the evening was well underway. She wore a pale yellow gown with a properly high neck and her hair tightly wound. She was, in appearance at least, the serious reflection of Victoria and Regina. Although she participated in one dance, waltzing with a goateed man in military uniform whom Victoria identified as General Halesworth, her sheriff and closest advisor, Anne spent much of the evening in private discussions with various of her kindred. His Royal Highness Prince Mithras was very obviously absent, and Lady Anne seemingly had much court business to attend to in his stead. A few minutes after the clock struck three, it was Victoria and Regina's turn to see the seneschal.

"Miss Ash, Lady Regina, if you will follow me, please."

The speaker was a fine-boned young woman in a beautiful deep cream gown with paler lace. The girl's chestnut hair was expertly curled and hung maiden-like to her shoulders. It took Regina a moment to recognize her as Juliet Parr, Lady Anne's second sheriff. Apparently, dressing as a man would not be tolerated this evening. Miss Parr led them up the stairs from the main ballroom, past several living men in military dress uniforms, and into a large salon where Lady Anne awaited them, General Halesworth standing behind her.

"Thank you, Miss Parr," Lady Anne said. "You may enter, Miss Ash, Lady Regina."

Victoria and Regina both curtseyed deeply. "Your Grace."

"Please be seated."

One of the two soldiers who had been standing outside the door, reached in and closed it, leaving Regina and Victoria alone in the salon with Lady Anne and her two sheriffs. Regina sat on one of the two seats set before Lady Anne and Victoria took the other. Halesworth and Miss Parr remained standing.

"Mr. Schiller sends his regards, Lady Regina," Lady Anne said.

Regina nodded slightly but thought it best not to speak, as she tasted bitter bile in her throat.

"Thank you for your kind words on my ward's behalf, Your Grace," Victoria said. "Your guests have been very gracious."

Anne nodded slightly. "London welcomes its loyal subjects, Miss Ash."

No one spoke for several long moments, and Regina realized that Victoria and Lady Anne were engaged in some sort of contest of wills. A contest to see who would break first. Regina knew she was, by virtue of her nocturnal pedigree, to be an extension of Victoria in this, and that felt like a thorn in her flesh. She'd had quite enough of being a piece in games of posture and position. She decided to break the impasse.

"Prince Mithras is missing." Regina kept her focus on Anne, despite her awareness of both Halesworth and Parr shifting slightly.

Anne kept an even tone. "Indeed. Two weeks ago, you assured me that you would uncover the coconspirators in this whole affair, but as of yet I've received no reports of your progress. There has been no sign of this sorcerer Mr. Wellig and even Dr. Bainbridge, the Tremere order's local representative, has gone missing."

"My mother, Lady Blake, has been in the care of Lady Merritt for much of that time," Regina said. "They too have headed north toward County Durham."

"To Lion's Green," Anne said, naming the Tremere chantry outside Durham maintained by Anton Wellig.

"Most likely," Regina said. "Miss Ash and I are to meet with Mother, as soon as we can arrange proper transport."

"Transport will not be a problem," Anne said, "so long as you are acting in His Royal Highness's best interests."

"That goes without saying, Your Grace," Victoria said.

"These are times when very little does, Miss Ash," Anne answered. "The prince has explicitly asked that his officers and their aides not pursue him. Given our past history with the Tremere of County Durham I have reason to believe that our road north would be a difficult one."

"Assuredly," Regina said. "We will, of course, act on your behalf."

"I'm sure I need not emphasize that this city is suffering a surfeit of trials this autumn. Festivities such as this evening's will only distract the prince's subjects for so long."

"We will act with whatever haste is possible, Your Grace," Regina said.

"I wish I could believe you based on your simple words, Lady Regina, but these are difficult times. I have seen to your proper introduction to London's host as a sign of good faith. I would ask such a sign in return."

Victoria leaned forward slightly. "I would be remiss in my duties as protector," she said, "if I failed to point to my ward's actions in your behalf on Exeter Street. I feel good faith has been established."

"Nevertheless, Miss Ash," Anne said, "I must still ask your ward to tell me the whereabouts of Lieutenant Malcolm Seward."

Regina felt gooseflesh on her neck and back. Anne and Halesworth were both looking at and into her. Othman ibn Saleh had mentioned an armored general in the ritual Malcolm had escaped from, and she guessed that Halesworth fit the bill. She thought a quick prayer and hoped God had not abandoned her.

"Your Grace," Regina said, "I know you to be a woman of your word. I will thus surrender Lieutenant Seward's whereabouts so long as I might have a promise on your part regarding his treatment."

Halesworth bristled visibly, but Anne remained perfectly composed. "Go on."

***

"Please enter, Lieutenant Seward."

Malcolm swallowed and pushed open the front door of the dilapidated flat he shared with Othman al-Masri. It was well past midnight, but the gas lamps were still lit. They suffused the single room with a pale yellow light. Malcolm could see two figures awaiting him, one man standing and a woman seated.

"Close the door behind you, Lieutenant," the man said. He

was older than Seward, dressed as a civilian but with some of the aura of a military man. His voice was used to command. "Sit down, please."

An animal instinct, what the Darwinists might call a memory of jungle monkeys they claimed all men had descended from, crawled its way up Seward's spine. The urge to turn tail and run was strong, but so was the chilling certainty that flight was futile. Seward was, he felt certain, the only living soul in the apartments.

He sat.

"Thank you, General," the woman said. "If you would leave us, please." Her voice, though distinctly feminine, wore an aura of command that eclipsed the older man's. Malcolm had some sense of what it must be to listen to the Queen. The instinct of obeisance almost eclipsed the monkey-fear still residing in his spine.

Seward was vaguely aware of the older man bowing slightly as his boots scuffed against the room's threadbare rug. He had a fleeting urge to turn to see just where this general went next—into the hall or into one of the suites—but Seward's attention remained fixed on the brunette before him. He would have guessed her age at just over his own twenty-eight years, but he knew such things had little meaning among those risen from the grave.

"General Halesworth worries about my safety in these times, but I do not think you wish me harm. Do you, Lieutenant?"

He swallowed audibly. "I doubt that I would be able to even if I tried, madam."

"You would be surprised, Lieutenant. You pose a significant danger to us by dint of even knowing the details of our night society. Like the club that first brought you to our attention, we value secrecy."

"I think you overestimate my knowledge. I do not even know your name, madam."

"I am Anne, Lady Bowesley," she said.

The name meant nothing to Seward, but he could feel the woman's commanding aura grow stronger. He had the urge to bow. "Thank you, Lady Bowesley."

"As to the rest, I suggest you restrain your urge to be coy, Lieutenant. No matter how piecemeal your understanding of us may be, you have still managed to leave a path of disruption and outright destruction in your wake. I believe we owe the fire on Charlotte Place to you, no? And if I understand correctly, you and Lord Blake made quite the impression upon our Parisian and Viennese counterparts."

"I have never been to Vienna, Lady Bowesley."

"Be that as it may, Lieutenant, I think you must guess at the severity of your situation." When he said nothing, she continued. "Under normal circumstances, I would be inclined to allow the general to take care of the matter."

Seward was unclear as to just what might constitute normal circumstances for creatures such as Lady Bowesley. He was certain he did not wish to know.

"These are hardly normal times," she continued, "and so I find myself having to make agreements for the good of us all. I've reached one such agreement with your erstwhile fiancée."

"Lady Regina? Is she well?"

"That, Lieutenant, is not for me to say. I will say that your own welfare seems to be a major concern of hers. One for which she is willing to risk a great deal. I hope you appreciate that."

"I… That is…"

"Yes," Lady Bowesley continued unabated, "that is neither here nor there. More important is that she has asked of me that I preserve your life and freedom despite the difficulties that entails."

"I… I see."

She smiled slightly and the expression seemed unnatural on her stern face. "Now, Lieutenant, if you would tell me how this whole affair started, going back to your journey to County Durham last Christmastide."

That same instinct that wanted him to flee wanted Seward to be quiet, but it too bowed before the greater urge to fulfill the requests of this unliving matriarch. He told the tale.

On the few occasions he would have to look back on that conversation—usually in the half-conscious moments before sleep—he'd assume he had misjudged the time upon entering the flat. Indeed, by the time he left the first blush of predawn twilight was announcing itself on the eastern horizon, and surely even those tragic events could not have taken six or seven hours to recount.

He told the woman—whose name he would never quite

remember, surely a distant Blake relative—of arriving at Bernan House in County Durham during the winter of 1887, intent on asking for Lady Regina's hand. He found instead that Lady Blake, Regina's mother, had succumbed to her long bout of fever. He had tried to comfort Regina and Colonel Blake in their dark times, but familial squabbles led to his leaving on poor terms with the colonel.

He explained how grief—and perhaps matters of material inheritance—had plunged Lord Blake into alternating bouts of melancholy and rage. The following summer, he had failed to guard Regina (herself distraught) from the lure of certain unsavory types in the capital and she had disappeared that August. In retrospect, it appeared all too possible that she was the victim of some lunatic, like the mysterious Whitechapel Ripper or the madman who had that same summer murdered John Claremont, husband to Malcolm's own sister Joanna.

Lord Blake, he explained, had proven himself still a man of good standing, attending John Claremont's funeral with Lieutenant Seward. He had also helped place Joanna Claremont in the care of a doctor specializing in the traumas of grief. Seward regretted not having seen that Colonel Blake had need of the doctor's services as well. Indeed, when Seward was called on to travel to Paris on a duty for his regiment, Colonel Blake apparently took upon himself to travel to Vienna and get himself killed in a municipal prison.

Adding in the riot of Parisian prisoners Seward had the misfortune of seeing breakout of the Santé penitentiary firsthand, it had been a terrible year and recounting it was not markedly more pleasant than experiencing it. Thus, when he left the East End flat that cool morning, he was all too happy to forget the conversation entirely and report to his regiment.

He would never quite forget the icy blue of that nameless woman's eyes, however.

***

"I still don't trust him, Mary-Anne," General Halesworth said, once he'd reentered from the hall. "This is how secrets slip."

"You've made your feelings clear, General. I value your opinion and respect all you have done for me, but my decision is made. Lieutenant Seward lives, for the time being."

"I'll have to have a man keep watch over him, though." He refused to sit, seemingly full of energy.

"That would seem cautious," Lady Bowesley said. "Certainly, if Lady Regina and Miss Ash fail in their efforts in County Durham then it will be prudent to remove even the slight chance that the lieutenant might recall what I've asked him to forget."

"'Asked him'? I'll never get used to that mental witchery, Mary-Anne."

"Be that as it may, I'll note that it was thanks to that witchery that he paid no heed to you upon leaving these tawdry apartments, General. Do sit down, please."

Halesworth stopped pacing, looked once more over his shoulder, and sat. He seemed very uncomfortable remaining in place.

"Also, the lieutenant was kind enough to surrender the source of at least some of his information. It seems that Colonel Blake and he uncovered a loose end left by Miss Ash. A former companion of hers by the name of Mary-Elizabeth Winthrope seems to have found repentance and religion amidst the Catholic sisters of St. Cecilia's in Sussex. They have not, it seems, imposed a vow of silence upon her."

"Miss Ash has been more trouble than she's worth," he grumbled.

"I would tend to agree, but I will tolerate her for the time being. Her indiscreet handmaiden, however, I could do without. See to it, please."

A predatory grin flitted across Halesworth's serious visage. "With pleasure."

"With discretion," she said. "We've had more than enough sensationalistic murders this season. Do not add fuel to that fire, General."

He rose from his chair and bowed slightly, "Yes, Your Grace." Halesworth then turned and left the apartments, the chance to actually act against a prey he could identify obviously filling him with urgency.

Mary-Anne Bowesley remained sitting, alone for the first time this night. Her hopes were now with the ragtag kindred heading to County Durham. The fate of her prince and his rule in the hands of foreigners, rogues and an untrained neonate.

She barely noticed the arm of the chair crack under her grip.

Part Three:
County Durham, November, 1888

*In which our story reaches its climax
and undead love bears bitter fruit.*

Chapter Twenty

Regina and Victoria returned to the Blake country home, Bernan House in the countryside of County Durham, during the night following Guy Fawkes Day, which this year also happened to fall on the first Monday of November and thus usher in the opening of fox season. They rode from Durham through the night and caught glimpses of men walking the grounds of several large country estates, plugging the holes of the wily beasts who would be the next day's game, so they could not find shelter from the hounds.

Bernan House, unlike those other estates, hosted no hunts this year—at least not for foxes. Regina's family had been scoured away over the last year—her mother and herself among the undead, her father in an unmarked grave in Vienna. Without masters to spend the country season there, Bernan House would be locked up tight, with at most a warden to watch the grounds for poachers. Regina had a terrible certainty that it was the warden who had become the prey when the house's mistress—and her new entourage—returned. She hated herself for having no memory of the poor man's name.

"Your guess was right," Victoria said as the carriage turned up the long private lane leading to the house. Candlelight flickered in windows on two floors.

On the way in, they passed the darkened coach house where Regina and Victoria had first met. The memory was like a fragment from an especially vivid dream, both extremely charged and somehow distant. She remembered the beating of her own heart when Malcolm had touched her, the wet heat of his kisses, the swell of his desire. And, most striking of all, the memory of Victoria—a siren-like apparition hinting at pleasures as exotic as they were damning. Victoria had fulfilled those promises, more than Regina could ever have imagined.

Regina drew her gaze away from the coach house and saw that Victoria was gazing that way too. The redheaded woman's chest rose and fell with a long breath that had nothing to do with respiration.

"Are you ready for this, Victoria?" Regina asked, laying a

hand on her companion's knee. "Seeing her again?"

"I could ask you the same question," Victoria said, and reached for the carriage door.

By the time Regina followed her out, the coachman was bringing down their few bags. Victoria favored him with a peck on the cheek. "Thank you for your kindness, Herbert," she said, causing the man to shake with nervousness and delight. "If you could simply leave the bags by the door, we will send word to you if we need your services again."

Herbert scurried to obey. Victoria took Regina's arm in her own and they headed toward the front door of Bernan House. Hesha Ruhadze opened it from the inside just as they got within reach of the heavy knocker.

"Welcome back, Miss Ash, Lady Regina," he said. "Lady Merritt has been awaiting your arrival."

***

Anton Wellig walked, for the sixth time, around the periphery of the great ritual chamber at the root of the high tower of the Lion's Green chantry. The tower had been the first structure built here and remained the axis upon which the whole eldritch community rotated. All the other structures had come later: the church house and cloister—so named by the ignorant Englishmen who thought of Lion's Green as having once been an abbey—had been built in the reign of Edward II, some of whose advisors had been more than happy to receive less-than-Christian forms of support against the Scotsman Robert the Bruce and the ambitious Thomas of Lancaster. The king had granted a permanent charter to the false friars used as a blind by Lady Meerlinda when she dwelled here. The chantry's lands had expanded exponentially, acquiring vast swaths of rolling countryside expropriated from noble families ruined by conveniently arranged charges of treason and heresy.

The chantry had weathered, in the five-and-a-half centuries since then, wars of religion and succession. Kings had fallen, risen and fallen anew. Henry had broken with Rome to marry and divorce (and behead) at his whim, and the rise of the Church of England had further driven away those troublesome priests and bishops who could actually question the validity of the Lion's Green Abbey. Although the dissolution of all monasteries could have been disastrous, in the end the estate was simply secularized and remained in the same hands. Tudor Kings were willing to accept unorthodox support at times, as well. A century later, during the civil wars, Lady Meerlinda had seen fit to withdraw to Vienna and then set her sights to affairs in the New World. Her old home in County Durham she confided to her childe, Magus Anton Wellig. To secure his own position, the newly minted regent had—in the midst of Cromwell's protectorate—purged the three other thaumaturges of any consequence left at Lion's Green. He then secured his final agreement with the matriarch of the Ducheski clan and imported them wholesale to Northern England. By the time the folly of those years was passed, Anton Wellig had a major chantry filled with an entire brood of acolytes who saw in him their savior. What's more, and here Wellig had to nod in acknowledgement of the blood-crafting arts of the hated eastern fiends who had spawned the Ducheski line, the regent's acolytes were all gifted with an inherent inclination toward blood sorcery. From that point on his position was unassailable. When, shortly thereafter, he discovered that the Ducheski blood could be purified still further through careful breeding, he knew it was only a matter of time before his ascension would be complete.

Wellig completed the sixth perambulation and began the seventh and final. He drew the long knife up the vein that ran from wrist to elbow of his left arm, calling forth still more of his undead blood. A wave of lightheadedness passed through him as his body gave up more heavy red-black gobs of vitae to form this final and most important ring in the grand diagram. His steps remained true despite the bout of dizziness—to misstep at this point would be fatal. He continued, whispering the nineteen names of Vedartha and calling on the elemental aspects of Ahura Mazda and Ahriman. These names were not the most comfortable in Wellig's mouth—when evoking higher forces in words, he most often used a combination of Gnostic, Christian and Celtic symbols—but in this case he called on those symbols which would resonate most assuredly with the subject of the rite.

The seventh and final circle finished, the last Zoroastrian personification uttered, the last drop of blood having fallen to form a perfect sigil, Wellig turned a three-quarter circle widdershins and looked at the precise center of the elaborate binding circle he had spent the last three nights creating. Sitting stock still in the middle of the first and smallest circle was a shaggy haired slumbering male figure. Stripped of all the trappings of his might, Mithras of London seemed like just another wretch.

Anton Wellig smiled, knowing His oh-so-Royal Highness would not even be that in another forty-eight hours.

***

"This is suicide, Mother." Regina and Emma Blake were walking along the path that wound its way in a broad arc around the east wing of Bernan House. It was four hours past dusk and the air was cool and the sky only partially overcast. To the west, over the bulk of the grand house itself, a rich star field rose like a jeweled curtain. "You should flee. Let us face these devils."

"Flight has never been a successful strategy for me, Regina." Emma Blake stopped and took her daughter's hand. "I tried for years to escape and I have always been drawn back. I cannot run again. I must face Wellig once and for all."

"But the danger—"

Emma smiled. "My darling girl, one would think you were the mother and I the child by your words. Had circumstances been different, you would have made a fine mother yourself."

Regina felt a stab of melancholy and knew from her mother's abortive speech and sudden look of concern that her pain was splashed across her face.

"Oh, Regina," Emma Blake said, "I'm sorry. Damn me for a fool! I, of all people, should know the price you've paid to be here."

"It's alright, Mother." Regina looked away for a second, trying to compose herself and chase away the fleeting fancy of motherhood. Hoping her composure would not crack again, she turned back toward Emma. "I do not want to lose you again, Mother. The danger of facing that warlock—it's foolish to go."

"No more than fleeing. Distance hasn't stopped me from suffering, because of the bond Mr. Wellig established between Mithras and myself. The Whitechapel business is proof enough of that."

"So do not return to London."

"I didn't understand it at the time, but I've felt every paroxysm of madness that's gripped Mithras. I read a summary of the Whitechapel murders and I've been struck by rage and fits at every turn." Emma placed a hand on Regina's arm. "I can see those women's torn bodies, Regina. I was in Vienna when those murders occurred and yet I feel as if I was right there. I cannot run away."

"Then, at least you will not face Wellig alone," Regina said.

***

The six undead residents of Bernan House left, headed for Lion's Green, an hour after dusk on November 8th. The coachman Herbert had arrived the night before, following he said, "An instinct that you would be needing me, ma'am." Others had arrived as well, none of whom objected one whit when the beautiful ladies and gentlemen of the house took blood from their veins. As she had in London, Lady Merritt saw to it that all her kindred were well fed and sated.

The nights spent at Bernan House had been quite different than those at Merritt House, however. There was a heavy sense of foreboding hanging over the assemblage now. If Regina and Victoria had been as Odysseus among the lotus-eaters a month before, now Regina felt more like that ancient hero returning to his beloved Ithaca. Many dangers had passed, but there remained one last task ahead and it hung heavy in the future, promising either destruction or a measure of justice at last. There was a reckoning on the horizon.

The carriage carried the four women, Lady Merritt and Emma Blake sharing one side, Regina and Victoria the other. Hesha Ruhadze rode on the driver's bench atop, next to Herbert. Beckett for his part had appropriated one of the house's team of horses and rode alongside. During the two-hour ride, he occasionally spurred the beast into galloping ahead, but he never strayed far.

None of the passengers spoke much. Lady Merritt and Victoria, who were sitting across from one another, could have been mistaken for fine ladies out to meet their gentlemen for some pre-dawn social event. Their expressions were totally calm and Lady Merritt even allowed herself a few casual smiles. Regina doubted that she wore such an innocent mien. Her mother was very obviously suffering under some strain, and Regina found herself fidgeting in unison with her.

They passed through the iron gates in the low wall that marked the limit of the Lion's Green estate. Regina looked out at the rolling hills to the right of the main drive, marked with a tangle of gravestones and other, even less portentous, monuments. She remembered that day, ten months ago, when she, Malcolm Seward, and his two regimental mates Pool and Easton, had undertaken to sneak into Emma Blake's tomb. Bloodshed had ensued, including the death of Thomas Ducheski. Regina had had little idea of the extent of the evil at hand then, nor just how completely it would swallow her and hers. Heading down the drive now, she felt herself haunted by her past innocence.

Beckett drew his horse up alongside the carriage and leaned down, so that his head was level with the windows by Regina and Emma's side. "We have a reception committee," he said.

Indeed, once Herbert had drawn the carriage to a stop in front of the cloister of the chantry, Regina could see a small group waiting for them at the top of the long stairs leading from drive to door. There were three of them, all living and all displaying telltale signs of the inbreeding so prevalent in the Ducheski family. Emma had been a fluke, it seemed, free of the hooked noses, crossed eyes, snaggleteeth, vestigial limbs, albinism and other distinctions of her cousins. Regina had inherited her mother's beauty and despite the feeling that it was far too late for petty vanity, she was very thankful for that.

Regina recognized her great aunt Eleanor among the group waiting for them. A shriveled little hag, she had been the first face Regina associated with the diabolical forces of her maternal family. Although Anton Wellig, the French Madman Brother Anatole, and even Victoria Ash herself were now more deserving of Regina's dislike, the old woman still sparked a red-hot hate in her. The two men with Eleanor Ducheski towered over her and were frankly freakish. The first clearly suffered from extreme gigantism: over seven feet tall, he seemed almost to be patched together from a variety of ill-fitting parts. His hands were oversized doughy mitts and one arm was clearly longer than the other. His head was undersized for his frame, a small melon sitting on the wide shelf of his shoulders. The other man wore a long cloak that failed to hide the hump of his back. His face was glossy, the flesh stretched and scabbed in the manner of those who had suffered the worst of wounds and burns. One hand, which he held close to his chest, was ungloved and the fingers were crooked and bent at impossible angles.

It was only when Regina had reached the top of the staircase, Victoria at her side, that the scabrous man inhaled through his ruined nose, and Regina recognized him as Gareth Ducheski. He had been tall and serpentine last winter, his aunt's constant companion and always seeking out Regina. He had, during that ill-fated foray into this very chantry, murdered Thomas Ducheski, the one member of the family who had been sympathetic to their cause. Regina thought Gareth had died then too, but he had clearly survived, although at great cost.

"You look well, Cousin Gareth," Regina said.

Eleanor gave a light scoff. "This way," she said, and turned to walk into the cloister.

***

From the cloister, Eleanor led them down a tight stone staircase into the base of the chantry's large tower. They proceeded in single file, with Eleanor and Emma leading the group. Regina found herself near the back. She was still negotiating the last few steps when she heard Anton Wellig's booming voice.

"Darling Emma," he said from somewhere past the stairway's bottom landing. "There you are. And you've brought guests! How wonderful of you."

Wellig's incongruously polite, even charming, words were rendered moot when Regina finally emerged into the great chamber beyond the landing. The room took up what she guessed to be the entirety of this level of the tower, most probably its base. A dozen braziers were scattered about the room, each guttering a pale green flame that cast a sickly light on the entire scene. The floor, made of ancient flagstones, was covered in intricately intersecting lines and marked with a variety of glyphs. The overall pattern was circular, with the straight lines of triangles and squares intersecting at numerous points. The glyphs, small characters composed of straight lines and chops, ran along the same pattern. Regina looked at the nearest group of glyphs, glowing slightly not ten feet from the base of the stairs.

"Cuneiform," Beckett whispered from his position beside Regina. "Persian."

A large altar sat at the very center of the chamber, within the tightest of the circles. Wellig, dressed in nothing but a loincloth, stood beside it, while another man lay on it, like a lamb for the slaughter. Four of the green-burning braziers stood at the corners of that tightest of the squared circles, casting enough light for Regina to make out the complex scars and inks that marked much of Anton Wellig's flesh. Long, open and bloodless gashes marred the insides of both forearms and a wide, maniacal grin cracked his face.

"Emma," he said, extending his hand toward them, "would you care to join me?"

Regina and Beckett both moved to intercept Lady Blake. "Mother," Regina said, "no—"

But it was no use. Regina saw that a faraway look had come across her mother's eyes. Emma Blake stepped away from her daughter toward the outermost ritual circle.

Regina briefly clasped her mother's hands, knowing she couldn't stop her but wanting this last bit of contact. With her back to Wellig, she took the opportunity to slip a folded piece of parchment into the pocket of her mother's jacket. She then stepped away.

When Emma reached the outer periphery of the circle, it was as if a delicate clockwork orrery had suddenly been activated. First the cuneiform right at her feet began to move, to flow like text across the thin tape of the telegraph machine, and then the whole pattern of squared circles and intersecting triangles came into motion. The black ink or pigment with which the whole pattern had been inscribed, which had seemed to stain the flagstones, now flowed across the uneven surface like oil across water. Whatever property made the substance phosphoresce seemed augmented by the motion and Regina could see the whole elaborate pattern rotating and shifting across the great room, which she now understood to be at least fifty yards across. The effect was dizzying, even nauseating, to Regina—looking at whatever glyph or line was passing nearest her, she could clearly see that its shape was blurred as the ichor crawled across the textured stone; but gazing across the room she had the impression of a firm structure in motion.

When Emma reached the second major circle, Regina made a concerted effort to watch her mother's steps. She hadn't noted whether she'd simply walked across the first circle, which she felt must be in some way inviolate. *Isn't that the way of such things?* She get her answer when Emma's left foot swept through a tiny gap in the moving circle—maybe four inches wide, just large enough for a lady's foot to pass through. Her other foot found another such gap waiting for it when she stepped again.

"There's a way through," Regina said, mostly to herself. But as the two small gaps continued their clockwise rotation about the chamber, she saw them close. She struggled to understand how this was and became aware of a pattern of noises accompanying the rotation of the great arcane diagram: dripping. Like a terribly slow rain shower or a series of leaky taps, she could hear the *pat-pat-pat* of heavy drops hitting the flagstones. These fat gobs of liquid were fueling the motion, she guessed, allowing the gaps to open and close in a pattern to grant Emma Blake access. Frustrated by this revelation she inhaled deeply by instinct—and the smell of the pattern hit her full force. Blood. The entire elaborate structure was scripted in blood and it was heavy drops of blood that were raining down to support it.

Regina felt a hungry growl forming in her belly and looked up, already guessing what she would see in the shadowy reaches of the great room's rafters. She was unprepared for the scale, however. Indeed, the heavy shadows that had hung above their heads when they first entered had been pushed back by the increased luminescence of the moving pattern and—Regina realized—increased flames from the braziers. There was no ceiling above them, simply the great open structure of the tower, running some two hundred feet up to be capped only by the roof. Wooden beams and rafters cut across the empty space at many levels and at many different angles, and from them hung what must have been the cream of the Ducheski family.

The entire tower was a gallows, and at least three dozen corpses and near-corpses hung above her. Each bled the last of their wretched lives in heavy drops that merged with the great pattern below. Regina looked away from the charnel scene and found herself staring into the eyes of Eleanor Ducheski, matriarch to the massacred victims above. Regina saw just a hint of sadness in those beady eyes, but then it was gone.

When Regina looked away, her mother had reached the center of the chamber. Wellig took her hand and led her toward the altar. "Now, if you would be so kind as to join His Royal Highness." His tone was conversational, but Regina had no trouble picking up the words, even from a distance. *That is the prince*, she realized. The only other time she had seen Mithras, she'd been swept away by the sheer, godlike perfection of him—now, from what she could see, he seemed a man like any other.

"Thank you. Now, shall we begin?" Wellig looked out at Regina and the others. "I do actually appreciate that you have come so far in a vain attempt to stop the inevitable, ladies and gentlemen. Especially you, Little Regina. You have a commendable determination, and I'm gratified to have you as a witness."

"A pleasure to be of service," Regina said. "I'll see you in Hell."

"Tut-tut, Lady Regina," Wellig scolded. "This is no time for puritanical fears of an afterlife neither of us have any reason to ever visit. This is a moment of celebration, of triumph. Of ascension."

"You're mad."

Wellig shook his head. "More invectives. Come now. Tell me, Lady Regina, do you know the history of the order to which your mother and I belong? Of the Hermetic House of Tremere?"

Beckett spat out, "Warlocks who damned themselves. Power-hungry to the last. What's your point?"

Wellig shook his head. "This ruffian speaks without understanding. They were seven of them, magi of the highest order who saw in the blood of the undead a way to steal from the Reaper his due. Every law of man and beast told them it was unwise, impossible and damnable. That did not stop them.

They willed it, and it was so."

"Why are you telling me this?" Regina asked.

"Only because I'd hate for you to have been an instrument of glory and not realize it. You see, the unfortunate truth is that most of the members of my order have forgotten what it is that made us great. Having achieved immortality, they've become fearful of losing it and concerned with petty things like position among the lesser undead."

"Thank you for your kind regard, sir," Victoria said.

Wellig ignored her. "I do not choose to cower. I choose to take the next step on the path—with death defeated, the Godhead is finally within reach."

"You want to become God?"

"Simplistically put, yes. More precisely, I wish to ascend to another level in the chain of existence. Creation is very much like this binding circle," he said, indicating the pattern of lines and cuneiform, "a series of concentric circles, full of many different pathways. At its core is the Godhead, the universal truth that is, in the end, the only thing that matters, because it is everything."

Regina remembered the hedge maze in Merritt House.

"Death is the most powerful guardian between us and the Godhead," Wellig said. "With its defeat, I have worked to take further steps toward the center. So yes, to those such as you, I will become a god."

"And that required the murder of the Ducheski family? The damnation of my mother? The murder of prostitutes in the East End?"

Wellig seemed genuinely confused for a second. "Oh. Why, yes. The Ducheskis above us, and Emma herself, are all fulfilling the purpose for which I have bred them—to power and channel a grand rite."

"And Whitechapel?" Regina asked. "Why the murder of prostitutes?"

"Oh my," Wellig said, "you're confusing symptoms and results, Lady Regina. That business is not part of the ritual, it is just a side-effect, like the luminescence of the blood on the stone."

"But the prince killed those three women," Regina said.

Wellig laughed. "No more than your mother did. No, no, you fail to understand how a being above you operates. This creature," he said, pointing to Mithras, "is beyond you as you are beyond a mortal infant. He has laired in England, in London, for millennia, imprinting the very structure of the city with his essence. Thus when I began this ritual last August, when I fractured his will—"

"Madness in London," Regina completed. "As above, so below."

Wellig smiled. "Yes, yes. Bravo. I neither know nor do I care who has acted on that particular mad impulse for disemboweling prostitutes. It is but a reflection of this ritual. I would guess that tonight will see quite a number of deaths in the East End, however, as we reach the end of the process.

"The mistake most of our kind make," Wellig continued, "at this point is to attempt direct consumption of more elevated blood. It is true that by consuming the heart's blood of one of our erstwhile kindred one can usurp the power of one's victim, but Mithras is no simple kindred. His blood is so potent, it would overwhelm my own in its natural state. Thankfully, I have developed a way to ritually prepare his blood so that I may consume it more easily. I need only have him drink from dear Emma."

Without hesitating, Wellig drew his sharp fingernails across Emma Blake's wrist, drawing out black blood. He then moved her wrist so that it touched Mithras' lips. The prince began lapping greedily.

"Yes," Wellig said, "once he has drained her dry, his blood will be much easier for the taking. To think, it only took a few centuries of breeding to get the right receptacle."

"No!" Regina, seeing her mother grow paler by the second, ran headlong toward her, heedless of the swirling patterns— until she crossed them. When she passed the first circle, it felt as if fire had suddenly lit along her nerves and veins. Stumbling, feeling bloody sweat rise on her brow, Regina made it to the second warding circle, but no further. When her foot come within an inch of the line sliding across the stones, her legs fell out from under her and she collapsed. She had the feeling that red-hot spikes were being driven into her every joint.

"Very brave," Wellig said, "but I am going to have to ask you to remain there for now. At least until I have ascended to godhood."

"And in godhood, what will you become?" Lady Merritt had yet to speak since their arrival at Lion's Green. Now, her voice filled the ritual chamber, resonating with a power that belied her feminine frame. "Once you have ascended in Mithras' place, will you be a truer god than he?"

Wellig looked up from the altar, still pressing Emma's wrist into the prince's hungry mouth. "Gods are neither true nor false, my dear lady, they just are."

"I beg to differ," she said and stepped forward, toward the first circle.

"I think you'll find you'll have even less success than poor Lady Regina," Wellig said. "At least she was born of Emma's womb, so the circle had some attunement to her. You are no Ducheski, milady, so I fear taking another step will only lead you to a great deal of pain."

Ophelia Merritt didn't answer per se. Instead, she whispered a series of words in a language that Regina did not know. The words somehow felt ancient, however, as if they had not been spoken in many, many lifetimes.

"What?" Wellig looked up, a sudden bloom of panic clear on his face. "That is the *Love Canticle to Mithras the Great*! How do you know those words?"

"She wrote them," Beckett said.

The first binding circle seemed to pose no barrier whatsoever to Lady Merritt. The cuneiform and blood-scripted lines simply smudged under her feet. The overall motion of the mystical diagram faltered but continued. Regina glancing back from Lady Merritt to the center of the room, saw Mithras look up and drop Emma Blake's wrist from his mouth.

"What do you mean!" Wellig screamed. "That text goes back over two thousand years."

"Exactly," Beckett said.

Lady Merritt reached the second circle and stood beside Regina, who still felt unable to rise from where the warding had struck her down. Lady Merritt however, barely even paused. She still sung the ancient love poem and stepped through the second circle, which flared with power and then smudged and tore.

Regina could see other smaller wards fraying as Lady Merritt progressed toward the center. High above, there was a hollow *whoosh* and one of the unlucky Ducheski sacrificial victims burst into yellow and orange flames. One of the braziers across the chamber spontaneously tipped over, spewing green-burning coals across the floor.

Lady Merritt's form shimmered like a heat mirage as she shattered the third circle, the blond English beauty in fine gowns fading away to be replaced by a brown-skinned woman with long locks of black hair and eyes the color of sapphires. She wore no clothes at all in this form, and seemed somehow all the more regal for it.

"Kemintiri," said Mithras, his voice a terrible thunderclap in the chamber.

"Who?" Wellig said, looking back and forth, desperate. "Who is she?"

"An ancient," Beckett called out. "The Thousand-Faced Daughter of Set."

Wellig stood and stared directly at the naked beauty who had replaced Lady Merritt. "You cannot enter, my dear. These wardings are made with the blood of Mithras and the Ducheski. You've broken the outer rings but the inner will hold."

Kemintiri stopped at the fourth ring and indeed did not cross it. She reached out her hand and seemed to touch an invisible barrier extending up from the crawling row of cuneiform at her feet. "This blood is of my blood," she said, in a voice that was rich and foreign, nothing at all like that she had used in the guise of Ophelia Merritt. She cocked her head slightly and resumed the form Regina had known her in.

"Milady?" Emma said from the altar, her voice weak.

The ancient creature shed that form again and assumed another, again of a striking beauty but this time with long white hair, milky flesh and eyes like ice.

Wellig started at the sight. "The harlot…"

She resumed her dark-skinned aspect. "All this blood carries my own. All of them have tasted my blood and thought themselves gods. All of them were wrong." She looked toward Mithras, and completed the ancient love poem she had begun.

Wellig turned around, but it was too late for him. Mithras rose from the altar and grabbed the warlock by the throat. The sound of Wellig's larynx collapsing was like that of a horse chewing on an apple, crisp and wet. Mithras then pulled the warlock toward him and buried his fangs in the man's shoulder.

Anton Wellig, drained of blood, spirit and will in one fell swoop, crumbled into dust less than a minute later. His overdue payment to the Reaper was collected at long last.

The elaborate binding diagram collapsed with its maker, lines of phosphorescent blood and ancient cuneiform blurring and cracking like a strange, sabotaged clockwork. Two more braziers spouted greenish fireballs and collapsed on twisted metal legs. The body of one of the Ducheski cousins, having snapped the cord that bound it, hit the flagstones with a wet slap.

Regina, the pain in her veins subsiding, rose to her feet. Kemintiri had already reached the central point of the chamber where Mithras awaited her. Regina moved to get to her mother, who was weak with lost blood but still conscious.

"You've returned," Mithras said.

It took Regina a moment to realize that the actual words she'd heard were in some ancient language, the same that Kemintiri had used for her love poem. Still, she found she understood the conversation between the two ancients regardless of the linguistic barrier. So powerful were these millennial wills that their speech seemed to broadcast directly into Regina and the others' minds.

"Yes, my love," Kemintiri said.

"Noushad," he said, and the word carried a wave of sadness in it. "You turned him against me. You used our son to betray me."

"We are not gods," she said simply, "no matter what we tell ourselves. It is a lesson we can only learn in pain."

Kemintiri touched Mithras' face and Regina felt an echo of the pleasure in that touch, delayed for countless centuries. The Prince of London had looked almost mundane lying on the altar behind the binding circles, but now both he and the ancient woman before him were returning to their inhuman aspects. Regina found it difficult to look upon them, so overwhelming was their combined beauty. She wanted to bow down before them, so unworthy did she feel—and that thought sickened her.

"There is no Godhead," Kemintiri said. "The heart of the universe is empty. Will you walk through it with me?"

Mithras looked deep into those sapphire eyes and Regina felt the longing of the undead prince. If she and Victoria had loved the pleasure of Ophelia Merritt's world, how much stronger must Mithras' desire for Kemintiri be? Would she lift the burdens of an eternity spent as general, soldier, prince and monster?

Then, with the suddenness of a thunderclap, physical pain lanced outward from the ancient couple. Regina flinched as she felt the echo of a blade slipping through her ribs. When she opened her eyes again, she saw what had happened: Eleanor Ducheski was standing over Kemintiri, having plunged a long ivory blade into the Thousand-Faced Daughter of Set's back.

"I curse you!" Eleanor exclaimed. "I am the last daughter of Shaagra and Byelobog, priestess of the Krevcheski clan, and I curse you. You are the seductress of Ehovar Krevcheski, destroyer of my line. I will have vengeance!"

Kemintiri rolled over onto her back and as she did, she took on the pale shape Wellig and Eleanor had recognized. "I am she, priestess of false gods."

"This blade, forged of your lover's very bone by Orik the Shaper, proves you wrong!"

Regina saw, as Eleanor raised her blade to strike that it was made of some form of ivory and carved with elaborate pagan images. She also saw a true bloom of fear on Kemintiri's now-pale face. Regina felt certain that if Eleanor could strike with that bone knife, empowered by some eldritch force from the Old Country, she would have her vengeance.

It was not to be. Indeed, with binding circles down and the hypnotic effect of the exchange between Mithras and Kemintiri passed, those in attendance were all rushing to act. Regina herself was making a line for her mother, but it was Victoria who reached the center of the room first. Exhibiting the same preternatural swiftness she'd displayed in Vienna and

London, Victoria moved like a blur across the chamber and stopped behind Eleanor Ducheski. She grabbed the old woman's raised wrist to stop the knife blow, and used her other arm to restrain Eleanor more fully.

The Ducheski crone struggled but it was no use. "No! She destroyed my people and killed my gods! She will do it again! She must be stopped!" Regina reached her mother's side, and so she could see clearly the sincere terror on Eleanor's face. She could also see the cold hatred on Victoria's.

"No," Regina said, her voice dry and cold. "Don't."

"This is the last killing I perform for you, Lady Merritt," Victoria said to Kemintiri. "Consider my debt to you paid in full." The last word was more growled than said as Victoria opened her mouth wide and, fangs extended to monstrous lengths, bit deeply into the old woman's neck.

Eleanor thrashed twice, released the ritual dagger, and died. Sated, Victoria dropped her corpse to the ground like an unwanted rind. From somewhere behind her, Regina could hear the pathetic wail of Gareth Ducheski. She paid it no mind.

Kemintiri got up, and at some point between beginning and ending that motion, returned to the nude, dark-skinned aspect that most suited her. She placed one delicate foot on the bone knife and with a casual twist of her ankle, shattered it into dust. Regina saw the terrible wound on the ancient's back close as if it had never been there. Only the black, tacky blood she'd left on the ground remained to say that the wound had been real at all.

"Come, husband," she said in that same, ancient tongue. "We shall leave these lands."

Mithras walked to her side. "Yes, we shall."

Regina reached into the pocket of her mother's jacket and retrieved the folded paper she had placed there. She'd hoped to gird her mother against Anton Wellig at the time, now she prayed it would benefit her. She turned to face the ancient couple and said simply, "No you will not."

Regina's voice was like a small drop against a booming tide, and neither Kemintiri nor Mithras seemed to react. "The prince has obligations in London," she said. "He must return."

Kemintiri looked at her, almost saddened. "You delude

yourself, childe. My husband is returned to me and we will not be separated."

"Be that as it may," Regina said. "I swore to return him to his people."

"Oaths are as false as the gods upon which they are sworn, girl."

"Not all gods are false," Regina said and handed Kemintiri the folded paper.

The ancient vampire unfolded it and out slipped three distinct things: first, twelve grains of sand from the Great Mosque at Mecca, recovered by Othman al-Masri from the clothing of Malcolm Seward; second, a distinctly older parchment holding a carefully calligraphed excerpt from the Koran; and third the small crucifix Regina had worn as a young girl. "What?" Kemintiri asked, but as the sand and other items touched her skin, she felt the echoes there.

"I have been told," Regina said, "that events leave imprints on objects. That sand has been trod upon by thousands, even millions of Mohammedans come to avow their submission to God. That text was written by a holy man gripped by a vision of God. And that cross was worn around my neck as I prayed to the Lord for the health of my mother, poisoned by your own blood. In those items, I see God's hand. Do you?"

There was the faintest smell of smoke as the sand smoldered against Kemintiri's unliving flesh. The ancient did not flinch, however.

Regina closed her eyes and whispered her father's favorite psalm: "Make me a clean heart, O God: and renew a right spirit within me. Cast me not away from thy presence: and take not thy Holy Spirit from me."

When she opened them anew, Kemintiri, the Thousand-Faced Daughter of Set, the Killer of False Gods, was gone.

His Royal Highness, Prince Mithras of London, remained, a single red tear streaking his perfect face.

Chapter Twenty-One

The train station in Durham was unusually busy for a mid-November evening. It was still early, barely quarter past five, but the sun was well below the horizon and the night was full. The air was chill and porters, conductors and travelers all breathed puffs of mist—all, save for the two fetching women standing near the end of the main quay. Regina Blake now breathed only by habit, and her cold lungs failed to heat her breath enough to cause any clouding in the wintry air. Victoria Ash, for her part, had given up breathing altogether.

"I won't be here to greet Lady Anne's man," Victoria said.

Regina closed her eyes briefly to ward off the tense ache that was growing behind them. "I thought as much. Where are you headed, then Miss Ash?"

"Glasgow, for the time being." Victoria spared a glance down the long tracks. "I've some acquaintances there, whom I expect will tolerate me for the winter."

"I'm surprised you'd endure anything so dreary as a Scottish winter." Regina did nothing to warm the tone of her voice. "It doesn't seem to suit."

Victoria smiled slightly, but the expression never made it past the level of mere politeness. "Be that as it may, that remains my intention."

"And in the spring? A triumphant return for the London season?" Regina hated herself for the hint of hopefulness she allowed to creep into the question. "Or are you done with the capital?"

"I think the capital is rather done with me, Regina." Victoria grasped Regina's hand. "Lady Merritt was my sponsor in the city and with her nature exposed, I doubt very much Lady Anne will look kindly upon me. Your existence will be easier without me, I think."

Regina felt a shiver run across her skin and removed her hand from Victoria's grasp. "You leave me behind as a treat for the hounds, then. How considerate of you, Miss Ash."

Victoria held her gaze. "Lady Anne has recognized your

right to exist, and the agreement you and she reached concerning the affairs of the prince will hold."

"Because our kindred have always proven themselves to be creatures of honor and square-dealing." Regina turned her back to Victoria and looked along the tracks. The train was making the turn toward the station, the gray smoke just visible against the star-filled night sky. "I'm sure Lady Anne will feel herself obligated to honor secret agreements made with me."

"If I survive to spread the truth should she violate that promise," Victoria said.

Regina whipped back around. "So my existence is to be protected by your skill at rumormongering, then? My entire existence remains hostage to Lady Anne's estimation that angering you outweighs the benefits of silencing me." She fought to suppress the shrieks she felt rising within her. "Or less reliable still, to your own estimation that my survival is more valuable than whatever advantage you can get from embarrassing the prince and seneschal of London. Forgive me if I am not reassured, Miss Ash."

"We are all hostages of a sort, Regina."

"Save your platitudes for one whose life you have not stolen! Whose father you have not murdered!" The sound of the approaching train did not entirely swallow her outburst.

"I will write you in the spring," Victoria said, her calm as shocking to Regina as a slap across the face might have been. "If you need to reach me before then, ask our kindred Ms. Lorna Dingwall. She can get a message to me in Scotland."

"I will be very glad," Regina said, trying—and failing—to match Victoria's cool demeanor, "if I never see or hear from you again."

Regina turned around again and walked up the quay, the screech of the train's brakes and the high note of its whistle drowning out all awareness. When the train came to a stop, a largish group of travelers from London and other points south disembarked. Others, bound for Newcastle-upon-Tyne, Edinburgh or Glasgow, boarded.

Regina saw Juliet Parr getting off and did her very best not to notice the redheaded beauty boarding.

***

Emma Blake leaned heavily on Beckett's left arm as they walked through the heath that extended beyond Bernan House proper. She stumbled every few steps, her long gown catching on rocks and shrubs. They'd left the hunter's path and were headed up one of the hills, where Emma had said the view of the eastern sky and the rolling, boggy heath would be best.

Beckett felt the give of the wet soil under his heavy boots and the stirring of an ancient fear within him. He clamped it down mercilessly, and tensed his whole body in the effort. Emma noticed.

"Thank you," she said. "For everything."

He stopped and turned to face her. They were still on the west side of the hillock. "Emma, please. You do not have to do this. At least wait until you've recovered some, when your head is clear…" His voice trailed off when he saw the sadness in her face.

"I can't, my darling Beckett. If I wait, I will lose my courage."

"Would that be such a bad thing, Emma?" His vClaremont, the brother-in-law of my friend Joanna Claremont. I shall make a point to see her and her husband John, in factice was soft and small, even to his own ears.

She closed her eyes for a second before speaking. "I wish it weren't so, but it is. This is my decision, my darling, but I do need your help."

"But who is to say that Kemintiri will return? Or that Mithras will even care about the bond of blood between you?" He glanced behind his shoulder and saw that the sky was notably paler above the hillock. "We could go far away from either of them—America, perhaps."

She raised a hand and touched a finger to his lips. It felt shockingly soft to him.

"You told me not so long ago that it was your hunt that kept you sane, that kept your darker urges in check. I admire that in you, but it isn't my fate. Even were I free of Kemintiri, Mithras, and whichever sorcerer will want to benefit from my blood's unique properties, that wouldn't change the dark path that stands before me."

"But you aren't alone, Emma."

"You are saying things you wish to believe, my darling," she said, not unkindly. "You know better than I that we are each alone with the beast within us. And I know what shape mine will take, Beckett."

"Lady Merritt's."

"Yes," Emma said. "Ophelia Merritt may have been just another mask for the creature Mr. Ruhadze calls Kemintiri, but it was one that embodied every one of my own dark urges. I've never been able to resist her and even now, I know how easy it would be to remake myself in the image of that empty shell. Pleasure for pleasure's sake, regardless of who suffers. Games of bliss and power made to empty out the souls of any who have a spark of human decency left within them. It would be so easy to damn myself."

Beckett knew she was right. One of the reasons he eschewed long relationships with most kindred was that he could never tell when one would slip from simply ghoulish to utterly monstrous. The prospect of seeing Emma do the same filled him with dread. And yet, he wasn't ready to give up just yet. Not when he had one more card to play.

"And what about Regina?"

Emma's face grew a shade sadder. "Regina has the same strength you do. She inherited much of that from her father, but she's made of even stronger metal, I think."

"But she did all this for you, Emma. She will be crushed."

"I know." A wine-red tear slipped down her cheek. "I've already dragged her into the night, I won't condemn her to follow me into damnation as well. Look in on her when you can, won't you, my darling?"

"I... I love you, Emma."

A slight smile spread across Emma's face, joined by another tear. "I know." She leaned forward and kissed him gently, and he felt a shiver run down his spine. "I know," she said again.

She turned and headed up the hillock. Beckett followed and reached the peak only a steep or two behind her. She stood facing east where the night stars had been swallowed by the purple-red forewarning of dawn. Gray mist hung across the heath, draped between the small, rolling hills like a low tide across a delta. There was little evidence of man or beast save the far-off sound of a few birds.

"Hold me, darling," Emma said.

Beckett did, standing behind her and wrapping his arms around her waist. He felt her trembling, shivers coming in waves as the horizon slowly pinked. She laid her hands on his, and he removed his gloves to expose the coarse hairs and elongated fingers. She clenched them tightly.

"Please," she said, "don't ask me to come back with you, my darling."

"I won't," he said. He wondered if he would always curse himself for that.

"Go when you have to," she said, "but not before."

A low wisp of cloud on the eastern horizon turned a bright orange in warning of the sun just behind the horizon. Emma's shivering became outright shaking, and a gasp escaped her lips just as the first ray of sunlight cut across the heath.

For a moment, the sensation of meeting the dawn—anathema to all his kindred—overwhelmed all of Beckett's other feelings. He could only feel the light strike his skin, feel the painful blisters, then the boils that burst with ashy smoke. His own undead flesh was hardened by long years in the night and the hereditary fortitude of his line. Still, he could stand this only a few moments more.

He became aware of the thrashing between his arms—Emma had neither of Beckett's benefits and her skin cracked and burned in only a few seconds. She held him tight and stifled what must have been a last scream. Red-blue flames bloomed as her exposed flesh ignited, starting on her neck and face and a moment later running up from her fingers.

She turned away from the sun to look at Beckett one last time. He caught only a blurred image of her—he was almost blind by now—but he saw the right side of her face was already black and charred. She mouthed some last words that he could not make out and then fell into him. Her body lost solidity as it was consumed, burning into ash within his arms.

The pain across Beckett's skin was as bad as anything he had ever felt, but still he stood there for a moment longer, the burning gown clutched in his blistered and cracked hands. His vision was gone, now reduced to the fiery white of industrially forged iron. Finally he let go of the ashy fabric and stopped resisting.

The earth fell away under him, opening to accept him in its cool darkness. He neither dug, nor forced his way down—packed soil of the heath simply swallowed him whole like a desert sinkhole covered in quicksand. Beckett had long thought of this trick—rare among those undead who spent their times in salons and along city streets—as a supreme advantage. He needed no shelter or mortal attendants because any loose earth could protect him for the day.

Now, as he felt the ashes of the woman he had loved slip from his fingers and the wet dark earth lull him into insensate slumber, he felt for the first time as if this patch of dirt welcomed him only because his very presence made of it a grave.

***

The steamship *Elizabeth Rose* left the port of Newcastle-upon-Tyne early in the morning of November 10th, 1888. It was bound first for the Hague, then Le Havre, Lisbon, Cyprus and Alexandria. Although principally a freight ship, the *Rose* did some business transporting passengers. On this trip, it would have only two, both Africans retuning to their native continent. The first was a dealer in antiquities named Hesha Ruhadze. The second was a mute woman of very notable beauty. Mr. Ruhadze introduced her to the captain as his cousin, Ophelia.

Epilogue:
London & Essex
July, 1916

In which final goodbyes are said,
between the living and the dead.

Ethan had the evening's correspondence waiting for Regina when she woke that night. She left her bedchamber in the cellar at precisely a half-hour past sunset, when the purple of twilight was still staining the western sky visible through the French doors between the hall and gardens of Merritt House, on Park Lane. Regina's keen eyes could pick out the curls of ivy and laurel that now wholly covered the wall she'd had installed ten years ago. Beyond it had once stretched Lady Merritt's extravagance of a hedge maze, now reunited with the rest of Hyde Park stretching westward from Mayfair. Mr. Abernathy, the architect Regina's proxy had employed, had done his job very well and few people even remembered that the house had once claimed a garden unrivaled in the West End (outside royal grounds, of course).

The great hall had a suitably dour look to it these nights. Much of the furniture had been moved into storage and the great dining table now stood alone with only four chairs. Had it really only been two years since this Balkan imbroglio had led to what was supposed to be a quick, painless war? How foolish those displays of jingoistic patriotism now seemed to Regina, with the numbers of English boys dead in Flanders and France growing with every mad sortie against Hunnish machine guns and bayonets. Could all the intrigues and scandals of the undead amount to anything compared to the Great War's wholesale swallowing of life?

The letters, cards and newspapers Ethan had prepared lay on a silver platter placed on the table beside a three-branched candelabra. Regina tucked her cotton skirts under her legs when she sat, and Ethan appeared at her side to light the paraffin. The sulfur spark of the match made her flinch just slightly, but she appreciated the light. As she made a first inventory of the mail, the valet silently went to the kitchen to fetch his mistress's tea. The man had lost his left arm at Ypres, but he remained terribly competent at service. He soon returned with the steeping pot and china cup balanced on a tray. Regina wouldn't drink the Darjeeling, of course, but she made a habit of having it by her side. The aroma triggered memories of her days as a girl, of her father, and of happy times. The show of mortal habits was also a wise investment in the façade of normalcy her kind cultivated all the more in this century of photographs, telephones and war on a new and terrible scale.

There were several visiting cards sent from kindred newly returned to the capital. Mr. Barring-Gould was among them, she noted. The undead barrister (that concept still brought a smile to Regina's lips) had spent the years since the outbreak of war searching for General Halesworth, the erstwhile sheriff of London's kindred. Had he found the missing man? Regina doubted it—if the general wished to be found, he would surely reappear of his own accord. There were also cards for the Tremere magus Lucien de Maupassant and his childe, Aisling Sturbridge. The thought of the warlocks still raised Regina's hackles, but that Irish lass had impressed her at a gathering of the undead held in this very house three years ago. It might be worth arranging another encounter.

There was also a letter from Victoria. Regina picked up the unopened envelope and noted the return address on the back: Maryland, in the United States. Hadn't Ms. Dingwall regaled a gathering of the undead last year with a story that the prince of Baltimore was besotted with a newly arrived beauty? Victoria was playing her old games, still. Regina tossed the letter aside for Ethan to place alongside all the other unanswered notes from her sire.

Regina turned to the grim business of reading the evening edition *The Times* with its ceaseless reports of imminent victory and mounting casualties. It took her a half-hour to wade through the lies and the blood, by which time her tea was as cold as her flesh.

"Ethan," she said at last, "I am going to Coggeshall tonight."

***

Wartime rationing had made nocturnal transport even harder than usual for London's kindred. The number of night trains was severely limited and petrol for private cars was hard to come by. The fifty-mile journey from Mayfair to Coggeshall, Essex thus took much longer than Regina would have liked. Ethan had little choice but to book passage on a morning train to Stamford. He made proper arrangements for his large amount of luggage, including a heavy iron-banded trunk, which he insisted on keeping an eye upon for the whole journey. The conductor was less than thrilled that Ethan made a sudden decision to stop in Coggeshall, turning a one minute whistle-stop into a longer production as said luggage was unloaded.

Ethan hired aid to transport his belongings to a local inn, where he rented a room and informed the keeper that he expected his sister's arrival. The hosteller accepted the one-armed man's story and sterling with a wink and never noticed that the fetching young lady with whom he left his rooms that night had in fact never entered. Regina spent most of the trip from Coggeshall Station Inn to the Claremont home trying to forget the feeling of waking in the coffin-like chest. They hired a buggy, petrol being even rarer outside the capital.

The home of the Claremont family was a three-story Tudor affair situated on the edge of Coggeshall proper. Harold Claremont had once had his medical practice on the ground floor, in the years after he retired from working in Kent but still tended to local patients. His own ill health had stopped that practice sometime in the last few years, it seemed, and the house was cold and quiet in the night, save for some lights on the first floor. Joanna was still awake.

Ethan rang the doorbell and they waited in silence. Regina noted the small black wreath already hanging on the front door. The house had either already received the news, or death—in such a plentiful supply among the men of England—had visited the house for another's name.

Soon the scuff of shoe leather on tile heralded someone coming down the cold front hall and the door opened after the click of a lock. Millicent Hale opened the door to the home where she'd been raised and Regina felt a chill travel up her already cold-spine. "Lady Regina," the woman said. "Mother has been asking about you."

"Hello, Mrs. Hale," Regina said, fighting the urge to call the girl Millie as she had when the girl was nothing but a babe. Now, she looked a mature woman approaching her thirtieth year, eight years married and with four children of her own at last count. Here was the daughter of Regina's once best friend, the niece of her once best love. In her was the closest thing to the child that might have been, had Regina's betrothal to Malcolm Seward not fallen victim to the undead machinations of that terrible year. Might her own daughter have grown as a best friend for Cousin Millie?

"Tell me, Lady Regina," Millicent said, "I remain unclear on your relationship with Mother precisely. She speaks, that is, when she is lucid, she speaks as if you have been friends since childhood."

The simplicity of the truth was made patently ridiculous to this woman by the fact that her mother was an aged woman, worn even beyond her forty-seven years by the decades she had spent in and out of sanitariums since the murder of John Claremont left her a shattered widow and Millicent an orphan. Indeed, from the ambiguous tones and other subtle emotional cues that came off Millicent when she used the word "mother," Regina felt it likely that the spinster aunt who had cared for her as a child was more deserving of the term than the woman from whose womb she'd emerged. What was that aunt's name? Elizabeth, Regina thought.

It was thus reasonable for Millicent to suspect the arrival of this visitor, who was obviously much younger than even she—a girlish thing in fact—and yet who seemed to be dear to Joanna Claremont's heart.

"My own aunt," Regina said, "for whom I was named, was indeed a friend of the Seward family and your mother most especially. They met in Cairo, I believe. My aunt died when I was but a young girl, and your mother was very kind to me. I'm afraid that in her fragile state, she may confuse memories of myself and of my namesake." The lie was practiced, delivered with slight embarrassment, and not so far from the truth to have lost its ring.

"I see," Millicent said. "I do hope your presence will be a comfort to her, then. You see—"

"I know," Regina interrupted. "I came as soon as I received the terrible news. You have all my condolences as well, Mrs. Hale. The loss of an uncle can be a very serious blow."

"Thank you." She turned to lead Regina up the front stairs. Ethan followed discreetly behind. They headed along the upstairs hall toward the bedroom facing the street. Millicent stopped at the door and knocked very gently. "Mother? You have a visitor."

They walked in without waiting for a response. Joanna Claremont, née Seward, was lying in a large, four-poster bed oriented so that the morning light would bathe the sleeper. Several pillows supported her back, raising her to a semi-seated position beneath a heavy cover and a black blanket. Mourning colors seemed to have invaded the bedroom, with black garments draped over chairs and hanging in armoires. The wan light from a single bedside oil lamp washed out any bright colors that might be hiding in the room. Joanna was asleep, her head lolled sideways on one pillow and her hand still holding one of the many letters she'd obviously been reviewing and sorting on her bed.

"Oh," Millicent said, "we should let her sleep. Perhaps you could return in the morning?"

Regina cocked her head slightly, aping polite submission. "If I could just stay here, Mrs. Hale. Sit quietly in that chair, perhaps, and wait for her to wake naturally? Just being in her presence is a comfort, I think."

She saw Millicent's heart soften. *Yes*, Regina said silently but clearly, *you can, after all, bend the rules of propriety in this one case. What harm could that do?*

"Yes," Millicent Hale said, "I think that would be fine."

"Thank you, Mrs. Hale."

"Millicent, please."

"Millicent, then."

Regina spared a moment to wonder whether Millicent would ever even question why she had suddenly felt it appropriate—important, even—to give Lady Regina license to use her given name.

***

"Ginny?"

Regina had been sitting in the chair by Joanna's bed, entirely motionless, for nearly two hours. When her old friend's wrinkled and hooded eyes struggled to open, she allowed herself a thin, melancholy smile.

"Is that you, Ginny?"

"Yes, Darling Jo. I am here."

"Come sit by me, Ginny, so I can see you."

Regina rose from her chair and sat on the bed itself. The thing was huge for the waif-thin old woman who now occupied it. Joanna's hair, once a long black, was now streaked through with white. When Regina sat, one of the letters strewn nearby shifted and crinkled. She idly picked up the nearest few to make herself some space.

"Yes," Joanna said, "it is you. Just as I remember you always, Ginny." She raised her hand, thin and covered by skin drawn by age into waxy folds, and placed it on her unliving friend's cheek. "Still so cold."

Regina raised her own gloved hand to touch her friend's and brought the two down to a more proper position on the coverlet. "I'm happy to see you, Joanna. It has been far too long."

Some would say not long enough, she realized. Maintaining long-term contact with the living, with those who aged when one did not, went against kindred custom in the most scandalous way. It threatened the great masquerade that was undeath hidden among the mortal masses. The cover of being her own niece and the obscuring effects of Joanna's long battle with dementia could only go so far. For this one night, Regina Blake felt the need to drop the façade of her existence and grieve.

"I read the news in *The Times*," she said, "about Malcolm."

Joanna turned her head, fighting back tears. Her hand moved to the mass of papers, hitting on the edition of a local newspaper buried under the letters. Regina picked it up and scanned the page, full of reports from the terrible battle for the River Somme in Belgium.

"'Among those who fell before the Hun's artillery,'" she read, "'was Major Malcolm Seward, V.C., whose trench and encampment were hit by heavy cannon fire in the pre-dawn hours. Survivors report that the Major charged enemy positions, taking several of the Kaiser's men and saving many of our boys. Unfortunately, it cost us one of our greatest soldiers.'"

"It sounds typical of Malcolm," Joanna said, and Regina found herself suppressing a laugh.

"Yes, yes it does. Never one to run away from danger, he was." Lady Anne's ministrations years ago had accentuated that effect, Regina believed. Over the last almost thirty years, Malcolm Seward had been in the thick of every military adventure he could get himself attached to. It was as if, having had memories of certain horrors plucked from his brain, he was determined to replace them with other ghastly sights.

"I suppose if he didn't like danger," Joanna said, "he never would have pursued you, Ginny."

The cheap newsprint in Regina's hand crumpled as she clenched her fist. That was it, wasn't it? She was as dangerous as any battlefield. If, thirty years ago, she hadn't thrown good sense aside and pursued her mother into the abyss of the night society, how different things would have been. Millicent wouldn't have lost a father or Joanna a husband. She and Malcolm would have been wed, eventually. And even Mother, would she truly have been any worse off had her daughter not chased headlong to free her from a prison with only one, final answer?

Regina closed her eyes, but that didn't block the memories or the shame they caused before this aged friend. Joanna's mind, body and life had all been abused because of her involvement with Regina and the undead parasites about her. For all Regina knew, Juliet Parr still picked facts out of Joanna's mind and replaced them with manias and compulsions. And Regina's own father… How could she forget the price he had paid for her own curiosity?

She turned from Joanna's side, fighting the rising well of rage that always came with despair. She had survived for several decades now, supping with care on the blood of the living, but the hunger was never fully in check. To surrender to it now would more than ease guilt and shame. It would erase them entirely.

"Along with my soul," she whispered to the pregnant air, "what little of it there is left."

Looking for anything to focus upon except the aging woman who would make for a delicious meal, Regina saw one of the letters that had fallen from the bed to the wood floor. She leaned over and raised it, and thrilled to recognize Malcolm's fine hand. Thoughts of him, of his death in some muddy Belgian trench, quelled the immediacy of her beastly urges. She scanned the letter, which dated from that fateful spring of 1888. As he had throughout much of his life, he used letters to his sister to indulge his frustrations—in this case, at being kept from his beloved Regina Blake, and at the stalling of his military career.

"This was that year," Regina said.

"Yes," Joanna said. "I've been rereading all his letters—I've kept them all, you know—but I keep returning to that terrible year. When John died, when you…" She let the silence stand for an acknowledgement. "And when you saved him."

Regina turned to look directly into the astonishingly alert eyes of her oldest friend.

"He had nightmares for years," Joanna continued. "About bulls and Tony Pool, and military officers, and the drinking of blood." She swallowed and it was like sandpaper on wood. "You saved him from all that, didn't you?"

"I… I had a hand in it…."

A thin tear rolled down a crease in Joanna cheek and Regina, her senses sharpened by death, could smell the salty tinge of it. "Thank you," the living woman said.

"I did what I could for him. And for you."

Joanna extended her hand again, laying it on Regina's arm.

She smiled slightly and her eyes closed slowly, sleep retaking a woman weighed down by the years. Regina waited several minutes and then extricated herself from her friend's paper-like embrace. She raised a hand to her own eye and daubed the pink tear that had collected there.

Just as Regina reached the door out of the bedroom, Joanna spoke again, her voice heavy with sleep. "Will I see you again, Ginny?"

Regina looked at the thin figure of her once vigorous friend, having spent twenty-five years in asylums, her body little but skin and bone, her hair streaked white and gray. How much longer could Joanna live, and the answer came from a dark, hungry place within her: *Forever, if you want.*

Disgust at her own selfish urges felt like nausea to Regina. This dear woman, who'd suffered in no small measure through Regina's fault, had just thanked her for the one half-measure of kindness she'd managed. To recompense her with the damnation of undeath or blood-slavery just to assuage her own loneliness? She wanted to vomit, to scream, to run. Instead she said, "No, I don't think so, Jo."

"Oh. Good night, then."

"Good-bye, darling," Regina said, but Joanna was already asleep.

***

The return journey from Coggeshall was undertaken in much the same condition as that from London. Regina spent much of it slumbering in the confines of a lightproof chest. Her day was unusually fitful—as if she truly were sleeping rather than surrendering temporarily to the death that had been delayed twenty-eight years before. Images of Joanna, Malcolm and others danced just beyond her awareness, and she woke with the rare and bitter taste of bile-laced blood on her lips.

Back at Merritt House, she left her valet Ethan to deal with reestablishing residence and making sure nothing untoward had occurred in their absence. He reminded her she was to host a small soiree two nights hence for St. Swithun's Eve, at Lady Anne's request. She approved of his suggestion to prepare the now small garden for that night and retired to a private office upstairs.

There she found a pen and a stack of ecru letter paper. She placed a few sheets on her blotter and began to write.

My Dear Victoria,

How insidious that angry words seems to outlive the emotions that spawned them. For too long I have held onto my spite and indignation because it was easier than admitting just how much I miss you. These nights, with the world seemingly intent on sending all the living to their graves, I find that the purported evils of the past pale in comparison. I wish nothing more than to know that somewhere in the endless night in which we exist there is another creature who understands me.

In that heady, terrible year of my entry into the night, you were that person for me. Despite all the things I have said and heard said about you over the intervening years, I know you have only done your best to negotiate the same trap-filled field upon which we all stride. You have done so better than most, I think. Better than me, I fear.

And so, you read here what passes for apology among our kind. I only hope that you can forgive my decades of silence. The nature of our existence seems to destroy such terms, but you are my mother in the night and I hope you can consider me your loving daughter again. I am always,

Your childe,
Lady Regina Blake

About the Author

Philippe Boulle is the managing editor of White Wolf Fiction, and thus spends far too much time thinking about vampires and other things that go bump in the night. He is the author of a variety of roleplaying games, **Tribe Novel: Red Talons**, and the science fiction novellas *Heavy Gear: Crisis of Faith* and *Heavy Gear: Blood on the Wind*. He lives in Atlanta, Georgia.

Acknowledgments

For their stalwart work on this volume, despite the author's constant delays, my thanks to copyeditors Diane Piron-Gelman and Jonathan Laden. For assistance with things Viennese, special thanks to Oliver Hofmann and Astrid Mosler; for matters Arabic, thanks to Colin Suleiman.

At the end of the long, oft-times *Odyssey*-like journey this trilogy has been, my thanks to the readers who have been so kind with their praise and patience. To all the fellow writers I've had the joy of editing (in my day job) while I wrote this trilogy, thanks for setting an example I strove to follow. Special mention to Greg Stolze, Sarah Roark, Myranda Kalis and Janet Trautvetter for showing me how it should be done.

I'd be remiss if I didn't share a few of my sources. Although my shelves now groan with books and printouts about the Victorian period, I'd like to acknowledge the debt I owe to Stephen P. Ryder's excellent *Casebook: Jack the Ripper* website <http://www.casebook.org> and to Daniel Pool's fabulously readable and useful (a rare combination indeed) book, *What Jane Austen Ate and Charles Dickens Knew* (Simon & Schuster).

And last, as always, for Sara. You're the best, plain and simple.

Dark ages™
Clan Novel Series

City of Blood

Years of strife—from the arrival of doomsaying prophets to the battles of the Inquisition—have left Paris teetering on the edge of chaos. For Veronique d'Orleans, Brujah diplomat, the arrival of an ambassador from the Courts of Love—rivals to Paris's Prince Alexander—could be an opportunity to heal old wounds or to extract long-delayed justice. Can she manipulate the various hatreds and rivalries that swirl around the prince and his new guest? Or will she be destroyed by them, as so many others have been?

BOOK EIGHT
BRUJAH™
BY MYRANDA KALIS

ISBN 1-58846-832-1 WW11212

Available in November!